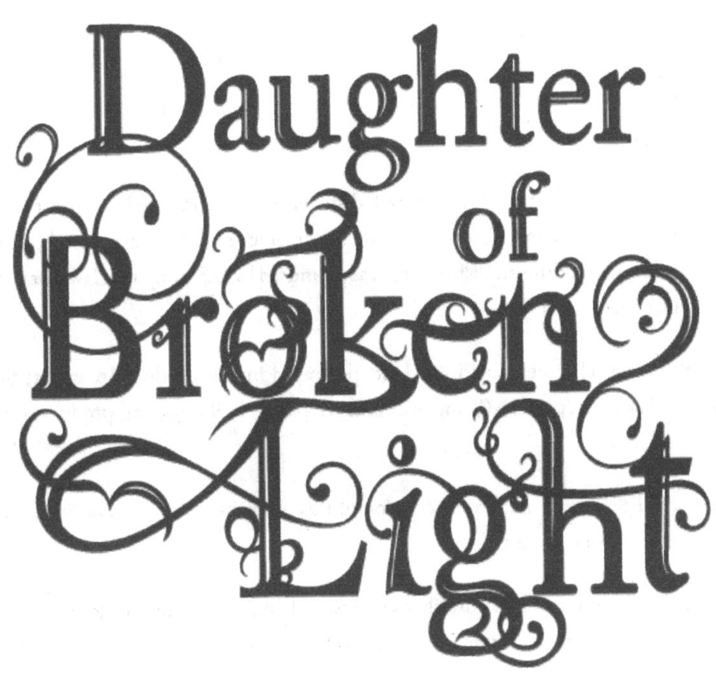

Daughter of Broken Light

Trisha Otis

Book Cover by OddDuckDesign

Illustrations by Trisha & Landon Otis

ISBN: 978-1-969561-00-9 (eBook)

ISBN: 978-1-969561-01-6 (Paperback)

ISBN: 978-1-969561-02-3 (Hardcover)

1st edition 2025

This book contains scenes that may depict, discuss, and/or mention:

- Sexual Content

- Racial Discrimination

- Depiction of Racism

- Death

- Violence

- Depression

- Grief

The dog will never die.

For everyone who has walked through darkness

and still held onto their own light.

TERRATHIS
MORELIA MOUN
NYXARA
GALENRA
RATHGAR'S MIRE
BRIARHOLLOW
DRAEKHAR'S MAW
ARK OUTPOST
PIPWICK
VINTAR RIVER
ARKANTHYS DESERT

PALDOR PASS
VORHI MOUNTAINS
EVERCREST
FALLS
CAIRNFALL
CALENOR
ERYNDOR RIVER
ALIRIEN
REDWAKE
VESPARA

This book could never have come to life without a community standing behind me. Writing may begin as a solitary act, but bringing a story into the world is anything but solitary.

To my **family and friends**, especially my **husband and my best friend**—thank you for holding space for me through long writing days, for listening when I needed to talk through plot twists, and for reminding me to keep going when the words came slowly. Your belief in me carried me more than you know. And thank you for letting me use your personalities as characters in this story.

To the **KC Book Beat community**—you are the heartbeat of this journey. Every workshop, event, and conversation reminded me why stories matter and why they're worth fighting for. The encouragement, wisdom, and generosity of local authors and book lovers inspired me to keep creating. It's an honor to be part of such a passionate, welcoming group, and I am endlessly grateful for the way you champion not only my work, but the voices of so many others.

To my **critique partners and beta readers**, thank you for your sharp insights, your honesty, and your patience in reading draft after draft. This book is stronger, deeper, and truer because of you, especially to **Christy Skidmore**! My book also would not be what it is now without the guidance of author **Jordan Dugdale**. You showed me how to really level up my writing and it changed everything for me.

To **Madison Chase**—thank you for shaping this story with such care and helping me bring it into the world. I cannot thank you enough for designing such a beautiful cover and helping me format and publish it. A huge thanks to **The Wild Marigold,** who allowed me to dream big and hyped me up! To **Staci**, I thank you for showing me what I am capable of. You push me to never stop and showed me how to believe in myself.

And to every **bookseller, librarian, and reader** who makes room for new stories, you are the bridge between writers and the world.

Finally, to **you, dear reader**—thank you for picking up this book and giving it your time and imagination. My deepest hope is that these pages meet you where you are and leave you with something to carry forward.

-Trisha Otis

Chapter One

The soft waves lapped against my skin as I laid along the shoreline. The sunbeams warmed my face, my hands reaching above my head. A contented sigh escaped my lips while my hands gently stroked the soft, golden fur of my friend who lay sprawled on the hot sand. My eyes slowly closed, feeling the sand cooling from the waves brushing the shoreline once again. My furry companion let out a sigh as well, knowing the blissful moment would soon end.

I rolled over and stretched my body, my stomach pressing against the sand. Pushing myself up on my elbows, I wiggled my toes in the wet sand. My sunburst blue eyes glanced up at the palace that I called home. It was constructed entirely from sandstone that radiated a warm, golden hue under the sun's light. The surface was smooth, with intricate carvings of sun motifs etched into the stone, showcasing swirling patterns. These carvings stretched across the walls, creating a sense of grandeur and storytelling in the stone itself. My eyes drifted over to watch the gryphons soaring above the large, ivory dome of the Grand Library. They were helping the Mages prepare the wards for the Sun Stone.

Today was the Stone Summit. Every time I remembered it was on the horizon, my stomach churned. Six years had passed since the last rite, a year delayed. My mind raced with all the lessons my instructors had tried to pass onto me. They weren't the Sun Trials I needed to perform, but it was all that could be done. I felt I would never be prepared.

My mind was mid-spiral when a cold snout eagerly sniffed at my face, tickling my cheek. I laughed and opened my eyes again, meeting my happy dog's chocolate eyes.

"I know, Raiku. We can stay for a minute longer." I nuzzled my cheek against the top of his head.

I had found Raiku when he was a small puppy some ten years prior. I wasn't technically allowed to have a dog and so I kept him hidden in my room, feeding him extra scraps from the kitchen. Eventually, mother found out and let me keep him, so long as I taught him to retrieve birds. And so I did. He eagerly would hunt down seagulls and any other large flying thing in the woods nearby. He knew if he brought them to the kitchen, he would get a large piece of meat as a reward. He was never far from my side.

My body screamed from the intense training from the day before and movement was a struggle. I slowly pushed my body weight back so I was sitting on my knees. My muscular thighs were damp from the water, causing my white linen dress to stick to my skin. The sun's rays sparkled and danced across the ocean as I allowed my gaze to focus over the vast water. It was one of my favorite views and always seemed to help me forget that any darkness exists.

I raised my arms above my head and stretched my back before fully standing up. Dusting the sand off my legs, I clicked my tongue, prompting Raiku to walk with me. He bounded ahead towards a path that was lined with over-sized golden sunflowers on either side. I smiled, watching as tiny, delicate beings played in the giant flowers' centers, throwing pollen at each other. The Luminets, as we called them, were the size of butterflies and had translucent wings in hues of gold and amber. They were helpful in the garden, but a bit mischievous.

The sandy path eventually turned into solid brown cobblestone. Raiku ran ahead a bit, bounding excitedly. He loved going into the town as our people loved spoiling him. He disappeared beyond a large sandstone archway. It was magnificent and welcoming, with intricate carvings of lions on either side. Above the lions, our sun symbols were etched, the rays reaching out to symbolize warmth and vitality. It curved at the top, framed by decorative columns. Beautifully etched in the center were the words *Calenor*, my home.

I walked through it, dusting off the dried sand from my legs. Fortunately, the townspeople were used to seeing their leader so informal. My mother and father always scolded me for lacking decorum. My eyes gazed around the bustling grand town square.

It was paved with smooth sandstone tiles that shimmered in the sunlight. All around the square were intricate carvings of lions and sunflowers. The shops and various buildings were constructed from warm, golden sandstone. Raiku ran over to the bakery and let out a bark, sending small birds flying from the colorful awnings above. It was a busy morning and all of the market stalls were set up, offering fragrant spices and handmade jewelry. The vendors were happily chattering with patrons, only to pause to give Raiku pats on the head. He had acquired a small piece of bread and was happily trotting around my favorite part of the town square.

The fountain was carved entirely of sandstone, with a round basin adorned with lions in regal poses. Water gently flowed from their mouth, echoing the soothing sound of the distant ocean. Rising from the center was a beautiful statue of our beloved Sun Goddess, Eledrinna, The First Light. I always loved how the sculptor captured her grace and warmth. She stood tall, her arms slightly raised as though she were embracing the sunlight. Her flowing robes were so carefully detailed, they almost looked like fabric. A radiant crown of rays encircled her head. The fountain's pedestal was carved with depictions of her journey across the sky. I used to sit and trace the different celestial patterns when I was younger.

My eyes glanced around and smiled as they landed on a nearby story-teller, who had a dozen or so children seated at his feet. A large group of people had gathered around to hear his tale. His face was worn with age and his eyes were a faded grey. He waved his arms around in an animated fashion as he recited the original story of Terrathis.

"The first drop of light to touch this mass of land took the form of a beautiful maiden, cloaked in golden sunlight. Her name was, of course, Eledrinna. She looked around to see the beautiful rivers and the tallest trees and the most incredible mountains, and she knew it would be her home." His arms gestured in a large circle above him, as though to form the shape of the sun.

"But Eledrinna was lonely and became tired, and so she curled up in the fields where Briarhollow now sits. The world dimmed and the first moonbeam touched the earth. His name was Nyxar the God of the Moon." A theatrical pause lingered in the air as the children's eyes grew wide. "The two walked the earth, tending to the land and the magical beings that existed here before. After some time, Nyxar reached into the tides and pulled Nalthera from its foamy mouth. And one after another, they found Tharandur in the mountains, Sylvorith deep in the trees, and they found Solira tucked in a red poppy flower in the meadow."

"Eledrinna and Nyxar gifted their new friends stones from each of their homes and together, they would all take care of Terrathis and its people. Every five years, they would gather and take the Sun Stone and the moon stone, and perform the Stone Summit ritual to keep the lands happy and healthy."

The crowd clapped and the children quickly rose to their feet. In a rather chaotic fashion, they began to run around and began a sudden game of tag. It appeared their attention spans had been used up during the story.

I chuckled softly and nodded to the various passersby, giving brief hellos. I never got used to being easily identified, but my mother had told me it brought people comfort to see their leaders in their midst. I honestly just loved seeing Raiku interact with his people. This *was* his kingdom, afterall. I sat on a bench near the fountain and watched him race around the square. He ran up to a group of small children and licked their cheeks. They dissolved into laughter as he bounced around excitedly. I closed my eyes and breathed in deeply, savoring the smell of the spices, the baked goods, and the distant ocean. This was the smell of home.

"Idrial?" A familiar voice broke my reverie.

My eyes burst open to see a young Mage standing before me. Her dark brown hair was tied up at the back of her head and left to loosely fall down her back. Her violet eyes were bright with curiosity.

Bronwyn was a mage apprentice at The Institute of the Celestial Order and was an assistant caretaker of the library. My sister, Allisara, and her became great friends as children when they went through schooling, and their affections for each other increased as they aged. Because Bronwyn was not of noble blood, it was a bit unusual for the pairing. Our parents made an exception as Allisara was not in line for the throne and at least Bronwyn came from an honorable family.

I rose to my feet. "It is lovely to see you outside of the library stacks!" I pulled her in for a gentle embrace. "Are you all prepared to set the wards for the Sun Stone?"

She nodded, lowering her eyes to the ground. She absently rubbed the sleeves of her indigo robe. "I am. I hope they are enough." Her voice wavered.

I took her hands in mine. "You do a great service to our kingdom by protecting them."

She smiled softly. "Ah, Eldrin told me as such."

I glanced around, looking for any other mages. "Have you come here alone?"

She coughed lightly. "Oh, yes, I just needed some tea." She gestured to the local apothecary. "For nerves."

I watched her movements for a moment. Mage apprentices typically didn't come to town alone. It was highly unusual, and I knew Bronwyn was rather popular in her circle.

"Ah, no one else needed anything?" I raised an eyebrow at her. Something felt off.

She shook her head. "No, after the wards, most wanted to go back to get some rest before the ball tonight."

I slowly lifted my chin in a hesitant nod. "Yes, I should also get back to clean up." I gestured to the sand clinging to my skin and clothes.

She chuckled, breaking the tension between the two of us. "Yes! I am sure you are also a bundle of nerves. Do you feel prepared? You never finished your Sun Trials."

I formed a thin smile with my lips. "I know my instructors did the best they could. I still could never quite master swords."

She laughed. "I don't understand why you need to know combat in order to do a ritual? You aren't fighting anything in Eledrinna's temple!"

I shrugged. "Eldrin said everything was a test of the mind and the heart. Something about connecting all parts of you."

"That sounds like him." She raised an eyebrow. "Do you feel you can successfully complete it? I know all of the realm's leaders will be there."

I coughed, caught off guard by her question. "I suppose I won't know until I attempt it."

The young mage's cheeks flushed. "I didn't mean to doubt you." She paused for a moment. "There's no one from the House of the Moon, I noticed."

My heart skipped a beat. "No, there never has been. They keep to themselves." Everyone knew that.

"Oh, I just thought it was strange! The moon holds power, I've read!" She curtsied. "I won't keep you much longer! And I need to return before Master Reinig begins searching for me." Before I could respond, she was swiftly walking towards the tea shop.

I had more questions and felt inclined to follow her, but I knew I needed to gather Raiku so we could venture home to prepare. I exhaled, hating to ruin Raiku's fun. I ticked my tongue and watched as he perked his head up from sniffing a flower bed. I gestured for him to come, and he excitedly bounded towards me.

"Come, Puppy!" Calling him that was a habit I could never break, even as he got older. I rose to my feet as we made our way through the town towards our home.

I continued down the path that led to the back kitchen gardens of the house. I let out a hearty burst of laughter as Raiku excitedly made his way to the chicken coop and he began barking at them. By this point, the chickens were familiar with him and didn't even act startled. I took a moment to lower myself by one of the raised beds and took a small bit of chamomile. It's fragrance reminded me of the herbal tea my mother would brew in the evening to help me sleep. A sudden familiar voice cut through the air.

"Idrial! Ya got any idea what time it is? Ya shoulda been dressed by now!" The voice cut through the air, pulling my attention from Raiku. I looked up to see Francie, our beloved cook. She was easily over twice my age and a Faun from Briarhollow, the House of the Meadow. She was kind enough, but still intimidated me a bit. She stamped her hoof at me.

I immediately shot up and turned to her. The other heads of houses would soon be arriving, and I looked a bit of a mess. Sand still clung to my skin and dress and my braided hair was an absolute disaster. I grimaced at the thought and nodded.

"Yes, I was just heading to my room to prepare myself," I lied. It had fully escaped my mind that officials were arriving so early that day. Typically they came in the evening, just in time for the first banquet. I suspected they traveled earlier to avoid running into any undesirables.

"Ya best hurry up now. Ain't got much time, and them ladies are waitin' on ya," she scolded. Her eyes narrowed as she saw my equally sandy dog happily trotting towards us. She ticked her tongue in disapproval and turned back towards the kitchen door.

I patted Raiku's head and followed a distance behind Francie. We rushed through the kitchen before she could yell about an animal in the kitchen and quickly escaped upstairs to my room.

I was fortunate to have one of the largest of the 12 rooms in my home. Our house colors are yellow and white, but I find them too loud. I was able to convince my parents to allow colors from some of the other houses, to show support. The ornate wood of my large bed posts were dark wood, with sunflowers carved into the headboard. I chose the dark green of the forest house for the fabrics all throughout the room. My wardrobe and desk shared the same wood of the bed so it gave the room a warm and cozy feel. The large golden chandelier proved to be a chore to move, and so it remained.

The oversized, sandstone fireplace was already lit and cast a warmth throughout the room. On top of the mantle, I had trinkets from neighboring friends. A needle felted red Poppy flower from the House of the Meadow, a lion carved from a shiny black stone from the House of the Mountain, and a wooden flute from the House of the Woods. My favorite was a large seashell from my closest friend from the House of Tides. They were gifted to me shortly after my parents' disappearance, a show of friendship and support. I smiled at them, reminded that I would see them shortly. But first, I needed to get myself clean.

The bathroom was the size of another room. The floors and tub itself were made of white marble and the ceiling had a gold tile pattern, etched with sunflowers all over it. As my maids filled the bath with hot water and fragrant oils of citrus and lavender, I stared out the large window to see the gardeners working on the final touches for the event. They had created giant floral arrangements to flank the pathways and increased the amount of golden torches. Everything was so golden and white. I exhaled nervously as I removed my damp clothing and lowered myself into the tub. I closed my eyes and delighted in the warmth as I washed the morning off.

After I scrubbed my skin raw and poured the oils all over my skin, I felt fresh and reluctantly left the steamed bath. I stepped out and wrung out the excess water from my hair.

I turned around at the sounds of footsteps to see Wren and Aelion, standing in front of my wardrobe, holding towels and garments. I gratefully grabbed a plush towel from Aelion and wrapped it around my body. They had been my lady's maids since I could remember. They gently curtsied and asked if I was ready for preparations. I nodded and followed them into the washroom attached to my room. I glanced back at Raiku, who had jumped on my bed and was fast asleep.

Aelion, a kind older woman, ran a bristled brush through my damp hair as I stared into the fireplace. She softly hummed an unfamiliar tune. I was faraway in thought when her soft voice slid into the air.

"Your parents would be most pleased with you."

I felt my heart lurch forward. It was as though she had known I was thinking about them. "I like to think that."

"Has there been any word on them?" She began to plait my hair.

I tried to shake my head, but she pulled the braid tight. "No, I had hoped something would come up once word got out I am performing the ritual."

She gently brushed the side of my cheek as she pulled back more hair. "I still cannot help but wonder why they disappeared at such an inopportune time. Right before your Trials."

"The thought crosses my mind every day," I admitted.

She continued to braid my hair, pulling aggressively every so often. "I have known them a long time. I am sure they had their reasons."

A sigh escaped my lips as Wren walked around the chair and faced me. "We must paint your face." She pulled her mousy brown hair away from her aged face and tied it with a ribbon.

I groaned. I loved the gowns and having my hair done, but having my face done was not my favorite. It felt heavy on my skin.

Wren chuckled. "You are the heir to the Sun House, afterall." She grabbed a brush and started painting my eyelids with a glittery gold. "You must shine."

I giggled. "I would rather be back in the sand."

"Francie told me you came back looking like a ragged thing." Aelion handed Wren another brush and she pulled a light pink over my cheekbones. "And I have been tasked with transforming you into something remarkable. Which isn't hard to do." She winked at me.

I glanced over at Aelion. "Well fortunately for me, I won't suffer for long." I smiled at the two warmly.

A few hours later, I found myself staring at my reflection in a giant mirror that spanned floor to ceiling on half of the wall. My handmaids did a fine job presenting me as a member of the high court. Framing my face were two golden braids pulled around the sides of my head to meet the rest of my hair that cascaded to my mid-back in soft curls.

I ran my hands down the side of my gown, the soft white fabrics having their own shimmer. The bodice was stunning, I had to admit. It was covered in gold filigree with sunflowers on the shoulders. I liked my arms to remain bare as longer fabric felt constraining. I slipped the simple golden heels on my feet and placed a golden lion silhouette pendant around my neck. It was my mothers and had an opaque white stone at the lion's eye. Aelion, smiled as she looked at me.

"You clean up well. Much better than the sandy sea creature we found earlier." She grinned at me as I scrunched my face. I glanced over to see Raiku smiling with his tongue out in approval.

"Well, thank you for bringing me back to the sun elf I am." I opened the door and stared out the hallway. "And now to go play the part of high society."

With a large exhale, I mentally prepared myself to join the banquet room downstairs.

Chapter Two

The grand ballroom stood like a jewel at the edge of the shoreline. Sunlight poured in through tall, arched windows, spilling hues of gold and pink from the sunset across the pristine floor of polished marble, so smooth it nearly mirrored the mural above. The pillars—each carved from veined stone the color of fresh cream—rose high and proud, gilded in fine gold leaf that shimmered like starlight whenever the candlelit chandeliers swayed overhead.

I glanced up to admire the masterpiece of a ceiling. A sweeping mural stretched from wall to wall, telling the storied legacy of the Six Houses. Each House was depicted with its own divine sigil—a crab sitting in pink coral, a golden lion standing at the shoreline, a fox laying on a thick tree branch, a horse running through a poppy field, a ram on a mountain, and an owl flying before the moon. They danced in a swirling sky of colors, their energies intertwined in harmony. I deeply inhaled the familiar air of salt and gardenias as I pushed forward.

My heels clicked along the white marble floor as I walked past the large golden pillars to see the vast room filled with finely dressed people of importance. Despite having been born into this world, every social event put a pit in my stomach. I steadied my breathing to calm my pounding heartbeat, my eyes scanning the room for a friendly and familiar face. My gaze landed on a group of winged people and my face softened. I hurried across the room, exclaiming, "Raewyn!"

A woman turned towards me, her face lighting up as she realized who said her name. She pushed her chestnut brown hair behind her pointed ears and raced over to me, pulling me in a tight embrace. "Idrial! I am so glad to see you!"

She twirled around to show off her gown, gently flapping her ivory wings. Her chiffon gown was pale blue, the color of the House of Tide, and had a stunning silver bodice where the patterns mimicked the gentle swirl of the ocean tides. The fabric on her shoulders had brooches in the shape of a seashell with small aqua stones. Her hair was pulled back in a large braid and tucked in a soft bun at the nape of her neck. Her pointed ears were decorated with silver seashells that matched her brooches. She had added iridescent beads to her soft, feathery wings.

My face broke out into a grin, feeling the nerves dissipate. "You look stunning as always! No crab decor today?"

She rolled her vibrant blue eyes. "It's ridiculous, really. I don't know why we couldn't have something more elegant, like a starfish or a manta ray."

I laughed. "Unfortunately we don't get to choose what represents us."

She nodded as she grabbed two glasses containing a bubbly liquid from a nearby servant carrying a golden tray. She handed one to me and raised hers up before lifting it to her lips. The best part of these banquets were the beverages, and we wasted no time before indulging. The texture of the drink danced on my tongue and warmed my throat as it went down.

"Have you seen Eldrin?" She asked, trying to seem casual.

I felt my cheeks warm as I took another drink. "Ah, I have not. I just arrived. I was a bit delayed in my preparations."

"The sea was particularly lovely today, wasn't it?" she asked, seeing my nerves return. She knew how I cleared my mind and where I escaped to. She could probably sense it from the short distance to her island.

"It was. Raiku and I rather enjoyed the morning in the sand." I was about to continue until I heard a deep voice sound over the crowded room. The Grand Magister Vaerith was at the front, ready to give his welcome speech. Raewyn and I turned towards the front to give our undivided attention to the dark-haired man on the front steps. His voice boomed over the crowd.

"It is with great pleasure that I welcome you to our Stone Summit Banquet, the first of many in years. It is an honor to host you in the resplendent halls of Calenor, the grand House of the Sun. Tonight, we gather not only to rekindle old friendships but to forge new alliances—ones that will serve the future of our kingdom.

"While the shadows of the past may seem to have faded, I remind you all that they are never truly gone. We stand at the cusp of a new era, one that I intend to help shape with strength and vision. The days ahead are an opportunity for us to remember why we are here: to nurture the earth, yes, but also to ensure that our lands remain unchallenged by rivals who would seek to disrupt our balance. Together, we will reinforce our position, fortify our power, and secure a future where no one dares to stand against us.

"So, as we celebrate, let us not forget the true purpose of this gathering. It is not just to revel in our past victories, but to set the stage for the inevitable rise of a new order. May we all walk away from this banquet with a clearer understanding of our shared interests—an understanding that will shape the course of the years to come."

The crowd slowly clapped, though many exchanged confused glances. His speech was welcoming enough, but something felt a bit ominous. Vaerith looked directly at me and gave a slight nod. My heart began to race. "Let us welcome our most vibrant Princess, Lady of the Sun, Idrial." He motioned for me to step forward. I handed my glass to my friend and made my way towards the front.

I stared at the crowd before me, colors from all the different regions blending together. I cleared my throat and began. "Thank you all for taking the time to make your travels to the House of the Sun. It is so good to see so many of you after many long years. It is my privilege to welcome you to the Stone Summit, and I greatly look forward to reconnecting. The next three days shall be dedicated to celebrating our fellowship and the noble qualities that render our kingdom unparalleled. It is your allegiance to the throne that allows our lands to thrive. There will be plenty of talks of trade routes and battles, but for tonight, I invite you to indulge in the great feast we are about to enjoy together and to delight in life's pleasures with friends." I lowered myself into a curtsy and the room erupted into applause. The servants came out in droves, carrying large platters filled with our dinner.

I had emphasized to the kitchen that we serve food that represents all the factions. There were large platters filled with lemon and garlic fish from the Vespara, the House of the Tide, richly seasoned potatoes and carrots from our friends in the Briarhollow, and sage-buttered mushrooms from the Thalrien, the House of the Forest. The Meadow's harvests had been particularly abundant this year, and there were also large wooden bowls filled with peppery greens and tomatoes in a light herb and oil sauce. Our drinks were filled with sweet honey mead from our friends in Evercrest, the House of the Mountains. This particular drink was my favorite as it had a slightly tart berry flavor to it, and if I were not careful, I would start rambling things of embarrassment. Large fluffy rolls of bread accompanied each table in a woven basket and cloth.

I moved towards the large table at the front and was seated in the center. I had two guards not far behind, and I nodded to both as a thank you. I always felt awkward being constantly watched, but since I was the first in line for the throne, it was part of the position. I thanked the servant who set my plate of food before me and filled my golden goblet with the mead.

I looked up as my younger sister sat to my left. She delighted in parties and her face was flush from her fluttering about, socializing with all of the young suitors. She was not terribly far behind me in age and always looked astounding. She chose a stark white ball gown that had a very subtle golden lion embellishment stitched into the bodice, its tail wrapping around her left side. Her golden hair was in tight curls that flowed over her shoulders. She wore golden sunflower earrings that dangled from her ears.

"Idrial! Your welcome speech was lovely. I know you despise public speaking, and you sounded absolutely regal." Her glow was extra vibrant as she took a large swig of her goblet.

"Ah, thank you, Allisara. You look lovely, yourself!" I grabbed a roll and smeared cold butter on it. "Have you seen our brother?"

She squinted and looked at the crowd, searching for him. Lucien was the spitting image of our father in an older boy's body. He had sandy blonde hair and startling blue eyes. As with all of the descendants of Eledrinna, our eyes had the unusual golden ring around the pupil that spread into the bright blues of our eyes.

As though he could read our minds, he appeared from behind. He clumsily took his seat to my right and immediately grabbed a roll.

"The food is always the best part of these events," he stated, shoving a large piece of bread in his mouth.

Allisara raised her eyebrows at him. "You might want to eat a little less like an animal."

He shrugged and scooped a large helping of the salad onto his plate. "We never get to eat like this, so I have to hurry." He paused for a moment and looked at Allisara. "Where is Bronwyn?"

Her cheeks slightly flushed. "I have not seen her yet. I had expected her to be here by now, honestly."

I grabbed Allisara's hand in her lap and smiled at her. "I saw her in town this morning. She was buying tea." I carefully watched her reaction.

Allisara cocked her head. "Odd. Why didn't she just come to our kitchens? She knows she is welcome."

I shrugged and took a bite of a roll. I chewed thoughtfully for a moment, not wanting to worry her. "Perhaps she also wanted the sea air."

My sister smiled, her face brightening again. "Yes! I know that does me good before something terrifying."

I took a bite of the salmon when I heard a man's throat clearing. I looked up to see a gruff man with black hair tied in a knot in front of me. I set my fork down and smiled politely.

"Good evening, Master Demarian." He was the Head of the Mountain and wasn't exactly my biggest fan.

"How are you going to do the Stone Summit tomorrow? You haven't been trained." His deep, rolling accent spilled over with judgment.

"The same as it has always been done. I assure you will not be disappointed. The order will be the same, and the Stone Summit Ritual will be done as is tradition." Despite my calm outward demeanor, my heart was racing and my hands began to feel clammy.

He snorted. "I should hope so. It's been too many years since we have had the ceremony. You wouldn't want to disappoint your parents."

Allisara rested her hand on my lap and smiled at him. "Demarian, I assure you will not feel it is any different than previous years. My sister is fully capable of such an important ceremony. The mages have been providing excellent training. Thank you so kindly for sharing your concerns and bringing such delicious mead with you. You and your house have truly outdone yourselves this year."

I was grateful for her ability to charm any snake at that moment. He was not an easy man to have a conversation with, and she always confronted controversy with ease. His face softened as he nodded. "Yes, it was a particularly good year. Let's hope the years ahead continue." He slightly bowed and walked away.

I let out the breath I had been holding. "Thank you. I don't know why they have to be so confrontational."

"He is just a bitter old man who doesn't know how to hold a conversation with anyone else but the goats and rams," my sister responded.

I chuckled softly and took a drink of my mead. I looked up as I noticed a new group of people enter the room. They were the Mage Scholars from The Institute of Celestial Order. I looked over at Allisara, whose eyes searched the group to find Bronwyn. She must have seen her as she abruptly rose and hurried over to them. Laughter broke out amongst the group, and I knew my sister had said something amusing. I watched them for a moment, making note of the man I had been searching for. He wore his dark curly hair lowly pulled back, except for a few wild pieces left framing his face. He had a rather friendly face as he drew his goblet to his lips. I studied his body, surprisingly muscular from lifting stacks of books and conjuring runic spells all day. His fairly long sleeved, velvet jacket covered him to just above his knees and was barely buttoned up at the right side. The sleeves of his black jacket narrowed and reached down to just above his wrists, and were decorated with a single thread lining from top to bottom.

The jacket had a rectangular neckline which revealed part of the silken dark purple shirt worn below it and was worn with a large cloth band, which is held together by a silver ornate pin. The cloth band was the symbol of scholars, an eight point star.

I must have been staring for a bit too long because my brother's voice cut through my thoughts. "What are you looking at?"

I turned to him and saw he had been following my gaze. He glanced over at me and asked, "Why not just go over to Eldrin? You don't have to stare like that."

I cleared my throat and rubbed my arm with my hand, as though to calm the light shining from my skin. I hadn't realized my glow had magnified. "Oh, hush. I am just enjoying the party, and watching everyone socialize is refreshing." I smiled at him.

He squinted his eyes and then shrugged. "It has been a bit, hasn't it?"

Since our parent's disappearance, we hadn't hosted any large parties or festivals. There was too much to be done in their absence and I honestly just didn't have the emotional capacity to celebrate anything. There was also my desire to avoid prying questions that had no answers. Unfortunately, my brother had to suffer. He was young when we had the last party and could only remember a few. Now that he was older, they would be easier for him to enjoy. And he could now understand their significance to the kingdom. His soft chuckle broke the thoughts of my wandering mind.

"I remember one Winter Festival where it snowed half of father's height." He paused to take a swig of his mead. "We woke up and all of the outside was covered, and it was still coming down. The ocean had even begun to crystalize. It was so strange to see, and I think it was the first time I had ever seen snow! Everyone who was in town had started to panic, but mother and father took it as an opportunity. I remember seeing them dive into the snow in their nightclothes. Their laughter fills my mind every time I feel winter's breath."

I laughed at the memory. "Yes, I remember we all put on the warmest clothes we had and everyone there from the festival ran outside and played all day. And the hot baths we had that night were the most marvelous!" There was something absolutely magical about sinking into a warm, fragrant tub when your skin is so chilly and dry from being outside all day. I closed my eyes and inhaled deeply, grateful for a peaceful reprieve from the noise of the party.

With my eyes closed, I could pretend I was at a party where my parents were still here. I could pretend everyone wasn't eyeing me, waiting to see if I failed. I couldn't see the hint of sadness on my siblings' eyes, despite their attempts to mask it. I didn't have to acknowledge the weight of the realm resting on me. And I didn't have to feel how terrified I was to perform the Summit. Instead, I could stay blissfully neutral and enjoy the slight buzzing from the mead inside my body.

A gentle hand suddenly rested on my forearm, breaking me out of my reverie. I opened my eyes to find my brother had slipped away and Eldrin had taken his place. His violet eyes shone as he brushed the back of his fingers against my cheek. I leaned into the movement, the scent of plum wine and leather filling my senses.

"I would be remiss if I did not get a dance with the Princess of the Sun." He winked. I rolled my eyes at the mention of the outdated title, but rose to my feet.

"Ah, well, I could never say no to such a handsome and powerful mage." I took his hand and we made our way to the other dancers.

The violins begin a slow and warm piece, soon joined by the cellos. I looked into the soft face of my love, his eyes glinting.

"You look as radiant as Eledrinna herself."

My cheeks warmed. "I believe that is sacrilegious to say," I joked.

He chuckled softly. "Not when it is the truth." He extended his arm and twirled me as the music swelled. "We were immortal once. It's not too far off."

I laughed. Long, long ago, the people of Terrathis were immortal, or at least lived longer than could be traced. But at some point, that gift started to wane, and the Sun Elves began to die off. Now, we live a human lifespan. No one knows what caused the shift or when it happened. Only old records have given us that insight.

"Stay with me, Light." He touched his fingertips to my chin briefly before spinning me. "Your mind wanders often."

"Luckily I have you to anchor me back down."

"Every time," he said. "I will always bring you back to me."

My face broke out into a grin as he tightened his grip on my waist, pulling me closer. The music was nearing its end and we wanted to savor each moment before our duties pulled us away. We let ourselves get lost in the feeling of our leading hands clasped together and our other hands wrapped around each other. Suddenly, nothing existed but the quiet rhythm of our heartbeats. I closed my eyes, feeling him spin me and effortlessly catch me. The music slowed to an end and he gracefully cradled me in his arms and leaned me back into a dip, where he gently planted a kiss on my lips.

Reluctantly, we broke away, bowing and curtsying as customary. I turned to see Raewyn approaching me. She offered a quick nod to Eldrin.

"The instruments are ready." She glanced over at a large, raised wooden platform, separate from the quartet's stage. Golden lanterns lined the edge of the stage where a harp and several stringed instruments rested, waiting to be played. I inhaled deeply, knowing the next part of the tradition had arrived. Eldrin squeezed my hand in encouragement.

I nodded and cleared my throat before making my way to the stage. I stared out at the crowd, all the patrons having gathered to watch. Most of the faces had a softness, the kind that comes with experiencing a collective familiarity. A few had a scowl on their faces, as they likely hoped my voice would squeak or I would stumble my words. I kept a warm smile on my face, pretending my heart wasn't pounding and my knees weren't shaking with nerves. Within moments, several others came to join me, collecting their instruments in their arms. The soft music swelled as I opened my mouth to sing the song of the Presentation:

In the dawn of time, a single ray,

A spark of light in the morning's sway.

Eledrinna fell to earth, a gentle kiss,

Awakening life in a golden bliss.

~

Oh, the Sun Stone shines, a gift so divine,

From the heart of the sky, to the roots of the pine.

In the Woods, in the Mountains, in the Meadow so wide,

In the Tide and the Moon, our spirits abide.

~

From the sun's first drop, the Woods did bloom,

Whispers of leaves, a soft, green room.

Mountains rose tall, with strength in their core,

Each stone a tale of the light they wore.

~

In the Meadow, flowers dance in the breeze,

Every petal, a promise, the earth's gentle tease.

The Tide rolls in, with a shimmer and glow,

A song of the sea where the wild currents flow.

~

But shadows fell deep, as the Moon turned cold,

The moon stone whispered secrets untold.

A yearning for power, it twisted the light,

Once a beacon of hope, now cloaked in the night.

~

So let us remember, as the seasons turn,

The light of the Sun Stone, forever we yearn.

For in every stone, in each land we roam,

Lies the heart of our earth, our true, sacred home.

As the last high note faded from my voice, I felt a sudden drop in my stomach. The natural glow of my skin abruptly ceased. I felt my bones vibrate and my body began to shake ever so slightly. I looked at the faces before me, all clapping and smiling. Some raised their goblets in praise of the song. Only a few from the Sun House stared at me with perplexed expressions. I cleared my throat and curtsied before exiting the platform. The strange feeling remained as I made my way towards the table and took a generous drink of my mead. My body warmed a bit and I turned to face Allisara. She had an odd look on her face and I know she also felt something was off.

She plastered a smile on her face. "Do you feel that?" She grabbed my arm and forced a laugh, looking around as others raised their goblets towards us.

"I did. Something has happened, though I do not know what." I was glad she also felt the change, though it made me more anxious.

"Do you think it's the Sun Stone?" She said, quietly.

I pursed my lips and exhaled through my nose. It had crossed my mind, though saying it out loud felt a lot more jarring. My eyes quickly searched the room until they landed on the goal. I squeezed my sister's arm and pulled her with me, moving towards the group of scholars. I lightly tapped the shoulder of the man with curly brown hair I had been staring at earlier.

"Eldrin," I said quietly. He turned and looked at me, his eyes softening when he saw my face shrouded in worry.

He politely excused himself from the group and moved towards Allisara and I. "Is everything all right? Your song was lovely."

I tightly pressed my lips together and subtly shook my head. I lowered my voice so much he had to lean in to hear. "Something is off. I am concerned about the Sun Stone. Did you see it today?"

He straightened, his violet eyes staring straight at me. "Yes, I did. We prepared it and left it in the tower under the protection glyphs."

He glanced over at Bronwyn, who was staring at us out of the corner of her eyes. Meeting my glance, she quickly turned away from us, continuing in her conversation with the others in her group.

I squinted curiously for a moment before turning my attention back to Eldrin. "I need to see it tonight."

Allisara cleared her throat. "We are not able to get to the tower, Idrial. It is too high and there are too many protections. It descends when the glyphs have cleared."

Eldrin nodded, glancing over his shoulder at the other scholars. "Yes, this is true. However, I can bring Idrial to its level. She is the heir for the Kingdom, and she has the blood to allow her entry." Seeing the confused look on my face, he continued, mildly uncomfortable. "Before your parents disappeared, they had us perform a ritual in secret that would pass on access to you alone. Only you and the appointed Mages have the ability to access the high tower. I can take you there, but we must wait until later this evening to prevent concern."

"We will visit *that* later." I sighed, more questions forming in my mind about my parents. "But now, I at least know I can see it"

"Perhaps seeing it will put your mind at ease. I am sure it is perfectly safe," Allisara offered, though her wavering voice did not convince me.

Eldrin nodded, not seeming convinced. "Come find me at the end." I nodded and he offered a smile. Despite my worries, his warm, familiar face calmed my nerves. As he gently rubbed my upper arm, I felt my skin's glow return, though faintly.

I spent the rest of the evening moving about to the different lords and ladies of the realm. I did my political duties of engaging in conversation, inquiring about the year's crops, as well as the various children that had been born. I commended the Meadow people for the meal their labors had provided for us at the banquet. I was able to engage in a light debate with the Scholars about various historical events. And I was even able to dance with a few of the visiting lords. After what felt like an eternity, the party was beginning to die down and the music was playing slowly. People had begun to retire to the guest rooms in the palace and the servers had removed all the empty plates.

I was seated at the head table, sipping the last of my mead. It was custom for the Lady of the house to be the last in the room. Raewyn approached my table, resting her elbows in front of me. Her bright blue eyes sparkled from the alcohol, but her brow was furrowed in concern.

"What are you plotting?" She queried.

I raised my eyebrows and took a sip of my drink. "What do you mean?"

She licked her lips and leaned closer to me. "I know you. Something is happening. And you," she pointed at me. "Are about to break some rules." She straightened. "I want in."

I coughed and set my drink on the mostly empty table. "I don't know what you are talking about." My eyes darted to a sunflower centerpiece to avoid eye-contact.

"Oh, fuck off. I know you better than anyone, *including* your beloved Eldrin." She sat on the edge of the table and watched the remaining people awkwardly shuffle around the dancefloor. "You felt something after your song. Something happened."

I sighed, feeling my defeat. "Okay, fine. Allisara and I both felt it." I paused as Raewyn twisted her body to look at me. "Something happened to the Sun Stone."

"What?" She exclaimed, jumping to her feet. She expanded her wings slightly.

"I don't know what! It may be nothing. But... something happened. Something is wrong. Eldrin is going to take me to see it."

She knitted her brows together. "How can you? You're not a mage."

I sighed, slightly exasperated by my friend. The alcohol was making my head spin. "While you are correct, I have been informed that my parents did some sort of secret ritual so my blood, as the descendant, could get into the tower."

Raewyn's eyes widened so far I thought they may roll out. "Well, that's not suspicious."

"I know. I know how it sounds. I can't think of that yet." I rubbed my temples. "That is a later issue."

"I suppose so. How can I help?"

I dropped my hands to the table, suddenly feeling worn out. "I don't know. Clear this room so I can finally go do questionable things?"

She nodded and stood, turning towards the vast room, spreading her wingspan to its fullest. She let out a loud, trilling sound with her tongue, getting the attention of everyone. "Thank you all for coming! The party is over. The light fires will be turned down and all of your alcohol will be poured into the bushes if you don't leave now."

I stifled a laugh, staring at her. She shrugged as we watched people disgruntledly filing out of the massive room. She looked down at me and winked. "I love you. Go do your shady shit."

I smiled widely. "I love you."

CHAPTER THREE

y mouth was completely void of any moisture as we made our
way through the halls. I smiled and nodded politely as we passed
a group of guards, hoping they couldn't see my body shaking slightly with
nerves. Every so often I exhaled slowly out of my mouth, hoping to calm
my racing heart. As we turned through a corridor leading to a massive
staircase, Eldrin stopped and turned towards me, grabbing my hand in his.

"My sun beam," he softly said. I felt my racing heart slow. He gently
kissed the tops of my fingers, sending electricity through my skin. I could
see the faint glow of my skin return.

"Eldrin," I quietly responded. "What if something happened?"

He stared into my eyes, a gentle look on his broad face. He placed a hand
on my cheek. "Then we will sort out whatever has happened. But let us
first investigate before letting our minds wander."

I smiled, a puff of air escaping my nose. "You are right. It may be nothing."

He nodded and squeezed my hand before turning towards the stairs.
"We will go to the highest location in the palace and make our way to the
tower. From there, I will show you how to enter the tower." He took the
first step of the stairs and looked at me, waiting for me to show signs I was
following.

The staircase curved in a large circle and narrowed as we continued
upwards. The stairwell was lit with sun orbs suspended above us. I had

never been to the height of the palace before and was rather intrigued by the small, round stained-glass windows that appeared every so often. They all had yellow, orange, and red glass that formed the shape of a lion, each window a different pose. On the windowsills sat various empty glass jars, collected with dust and webs. I quietly wondered what their purpose was as I passed each one.

The click of my low heels echoed against the stairs that had at some point turned from wood to stone. I suddenly wished I had changed my clothes, or at the very least, my shoes. The stone steps were less even and bowed in the center from centuries of use. The railing had disappeared, forcing me to run my right hand against the concrete wall. I felt the jagged texture beneath my palm to be satisfying and distracted me from the unease building in my stomach. I was so wrapped up in my own thoughts that I didn't notice when the stairs ended. I tripped and fell upwards as my feet landed on the platform at the top.

Eldrin turned and looked down at me, a look of amusement on his face. "We have made it to the top."

I playfully glared at him. "Yes, I realize. Thank you." I took his extended hand and rose to my feet, brushing off the bits of dirt and pebbles that clung to my dress.

I looked around to see a small, circular room with a simple wooden door. The room was completely empty and void of any windows or light. I summoned a small orb of light in my hand and placed it in a dusty golden lantern that sat on top of a table next to the door. I stared at the door as though I expected a ghost to appear. My nerves increased again, and I felt that uncomfortable pit in my stomach. I anxiously peeled away at the skin around my nails, a terrible habit I had. Eldrin stood patiently by the door, letting me take a moment for myself, before he pushed it open.

The bright moonlight spilled into the empty room, enticing me through the door. I brushed past Eldrin and feigned confidence, walking through it. I found myself on a large battlement made of the same sandstone of the rest of the palace. There were short, stone walls to prevent anyone from immediately falling over the edge. I found this oddly comforting. To the left were several large, wooden crates. I don't know why, but I had to peer inside of them.

"What are you doing?" Eldrin asked, his voice steady.

"I was curious," I sheepishly responded, closing the crate. They were empty and I was a bit unsatisfied at my findings.

"Is this important right now?" He queried. I could tell he was only partially annoyed as he was used to my relentless and often inappropriate curiosity.

"I am delaying, obviously." I glanced at the crates. I gestured my hand forward. "We may press on."

He raised his eyebrows at me but said nothing more. He continued towards the tower.

My eyes widened as they followed the vast height of the sandstone tower. I never quite realized just how high it reached into the sky. We were already several stories from the ground, and the tower seemed to go endlessly upwards. At its highest point lay the Sun Stone, hopefully still safe.

We walked to the end of the battlement, and Eldrin pressed his hand against the stone tower. He closed his eyes and softly spoke incoherently. He stared at the space before him, his eyes glowing violet. He began moving his hands before him, drawing invisible patterns in the air. Suddenly, several runes appeared, the violet light illuminating the night. He pushed the runes towards the stone. Without looking away, he said my name. I stepped forward and he abruptly grabbed my hand, pressing it into the glowing runes on the wall. I felt a great power pulsate through my veins. The glow of my skin briefly turned purple and a gasp left my mouth. My entire body felt as though lightning soared through it. Before I could say anything, the stones dissolved into an opening. Eldrin's voice broke through the string of thoughts swarming through my mind.

"Idrial, we can now enter. Come quickly, for it will not stay open much longer." He grabbed my hand and pulled me in.

As soon as I stepped through, it closed with a loud popping sound. I shook my head, as though forcing the sound out of my mind. Conveniently, there was a questionable wooden chair next to the door, and I lowered myself in it. I was only partially worried it would collapse under my weight, but it seemed sturdy enough.

"Is that what Arcane magic feels like?" I gasped, staring up at Eldrin.

His face broke out into an unexpected grin. He looked absolutely delighted. "Yes! It's so rare I get to show outsiders, and only in special circumstances. It is a bit jarring at first, but after some use, it feels like a warm hum." He stared at the wall where the opening had been just moments prior. He seemed rather proud of himself, if I wasn't mistaken.

He cleared his throat and straightened, adjusting the opening of his leather coat. He planted a soft kiss on my forehead and beckoned for me to follow him to the center of the darkened tower. It was at that moment I realized I was in another empty, circular room. There were no windows, yet a golden light softly illuminated the room. I could feel the pulsating magic of the sun within my blood and realized the Sun Stone's magic was nearby.

But something about it felt off, which made my stomach drop. I could feel the blood draining from my body, a cold wave rushing through my veins. I quickly looked at Eldrin to find the color had drained from his face. I opened my mouth to speak, but he held a hand up to keep me still. He took a few steps forward towards the center, where a large sun motif was engraved in the sandstone. He knelt down and placed a hand on it and drew a pattern over the stone. It glowed a soft purple and a pillar began to emerge.

He took a step back and as it grew to waist high, he cursed. He glanced back at me, a look of worry on his face. "The stone should be here. I don't know how this happened." He returned a sharp gaze to the empty pillar. He stroked it with his hand, as though to summon what was missing. After a moment, he let his hands drop to his side.

"We need to call a council. Fortunately all of the leaders are here, though this is not the event I had hoped for." He exhaled deeply as he turned towards me. "We need to discuss things first."

I had pulled Raewyn from her room and into the library, where we found Eldrin already pouring over texts in his study. Raewyn lounged in the corner chaise, a large book in her hand. I paced the floor, my hands on my head in anguish.

"I cannot believe this has happened," I said, having repeated the phrase multiple times.

"We will figure this out," Eldrin comforted, though his tone held doubt. He didn't lift his eyes from the massive text that read Warding Your Stone.

"What do you expect to find in there?" Raewyn questioned. She held a similar text, reading Protective Arcane Wards.

He sighed softly and looked over at her. "I expect to find *anything* that may explain how someone without Arcane magic could *possibly* remove Wards and steal the Sun Stone undetected."

"This states Counter-Warding," Raewyn spoke up. "Perhaps someone used some sort of a counter spell that would neutralize the effect without activating any sort of alarm?"

Eldrin shook his head. "No, they would need to know how to put them back when they finished their task."

I glanced over Eldrin's shoulder at the book before him. I pointed my finger onto a page. "They could have redirected the energy? And then put it back?"

Eldrin propped his elbow on the table and rested his chin between his thumb and index finger, as though contemplating the possibility. After a moment, he shook his head. "No, it would show a shift. Bronwyn and I made sure it was stable."

"Not stable enough, evidently."

I sent Raewyn a sharp look, who was holding the book directly above her head.

Eldrin slammed his hand on the table. "Why are you here if you are going to just make snide remarks? Be of use or leave."

"Because this is *bad*, as in immediate threat to all of Terrathis bad! And you were responsible for this. You literally had one job." Raewyn was sitting up now, staring at him.

Eldrin opened his mouth to speak, but I held my hand up. "This is not helpful. We are all tired and worried and still mildly drunk. Let's be nice." They were so similar in many ways, and occasionally butt heads. I smiled.

Raewyn rolled her eyes but said nothing more of it. She sat up and looked at me. "Would Bronwyn have any idea of this? I know she is your sister's lover. Perhaps you could talk to her."

"I don't believe she is powerful enough to have any inkling of this. Though, she didn't even react to it missing, even though she is a Sun descendant." The thought had crossed my mind earlier.

"Do we find this suspicious?" Raewyn sat up, watching for Eldrin's reaction.

"If I am being truthful, I don't know. She is an apprentice of the Mages, just barely graduated." Eldrin ran a hand through his unruly dark hair. "I will need to speak with the other Head Mages about this, but I do not believe it necessary to include everyone at this time."

"So, what now?" I asked. The sun was beginning to rise in the distance, and I knew we would have to present information to the council.

Eldrin stretched his arms upwards. "You're the Lady of the Sun. What do you think?"

I glanced over at Raewyn, who eagerly waited for my answer. I looked back at Eldrin. "I do not think the answers will be found in Calenor."

Chapter Four

The wood of the rectangular table seemed to stretch for miles before me. The massive stone fireplace crackled comfortably, a contrast to how I felt inside. Large tapestries adorning our crest of sunflowers filled the beige stone walls with color. The chamber blazed with midday light, shafts of gold pouring through high arched windows. The light felt wrong today; too bright. I had worn a relatively simple yellow dress that flowed from top to bottom and had a round neckline. The light fabric of my dress cinched loosely at my stomach and spilled loosely to my feet. The fabric was only broken up by a brown leather belt worn fairly high around my waist. I knew I needed to breathe, so I chose my pieces carefully to allow for nerves bubbling in my stomach. My sleeves were longer than my arms and wide, their flow broken up well above the elbow where they were divided by small, decorative bands.

So many familiar, yet intimidating faces stared at me, waiting for me to speak. My throat ran dry and I found myself picking at the skin around my nails. This was the last place I'd like to be. Yet, I had no choice.

I slowly stood to my feet, taking a drink of water given to me by Eldrin. He sat next to me, and nodded in reassurance. He still wore the same black and purple vestments from the night before and had a tired look on his face. He had retreated to the tower to study the echoes of the wards, even after Raewyn and I retired to steal a few hours of sleep. I inhaled deeply through my nose and gently exhaled through my mouth before speaking.

"I want to thank you all for coming to this last minute council. Unfortunately we have had an emergency occur that requires immediate attention." The eyes of every one of Therrathis' leaders stared at me. I paused for a moment before continuing.

"The Sun Stone has been taken from the tower."

A hush fell over the table like ash.

Cendric, Captain of the Radiant Guard, rose to his feet, his face dark with disbelief. "Gone? How can it be gone? It has rested in the Sanctum for seven hundred years without incident."

"Oh, Goddess Solira," Fiora of the Meadow whispered. "How do you know?"

"Eldrin took me to the tower after the ball last night, and I saw for myself." My worried eyes peered around the table at the concerned, and angry, expressions. "We spent the entirety of the night trying to sort it out, but I am afraid I believe it is no longer within the city walls of Calenor."

Demarian abruptly rose to his feet and slammed a fist on the table, yelling out, "This is an act of aggression! An act of war! Your parents would have never let it come to this!"

"Yes, but they decided to leave, didn't they," I hissed the words out, feeling the sting of his words. "Unfortunately, you have me as your future Queen."

Demarian scoffed and leaned backwards, crossing his arms over his chest. "Not without a Sun Stone."

"I agree," growled Asher, Lord of the House of Woods. "This is an act of aggression. The House of the Moon has always hungered for power they do not earn." He stared at me with piercing green eyes.

I raised a hand to quiet him. "I assure you, the Mages are investigating it as we speak. We do not want to throw blame before we have all of the information." I cleared my throat. "We know it was taken just before last night's banquet, and it had been heavily warded yesterday morning.

Cendric spoke up "The Radiant Guard will be sent out to inspect anyone who is attempting to leave. Other safety measures are being put in place, as well."

Magister Vaerith had remained silent until now, looming by the fireplace, fingers steepled beneath his chin. His robe shimmered subtly in the light with woven silver threads reflecting the light of the fire.

He stepped forward with deliberate grace.

"There is another possibility," he said, voice smooth, and all eyes turned.

My entire body tensed.

Vaerith circled slowly, like a teacher among errant students. "Perhaps this was not an act of war... but of release."

Demarian snorted. "Release? What nonsense—"

Vaerith did not look at him. "We speak of the Sun Stone as if it were merely a jewel. A symbol. But it is power incarnate. Old power. Caged for centuries in the heart of a sanctum none dared question." He turned towards the window, gesturing to the tower that now sat empty. "And power, like light, is not meant to be contained forever."

"You're suggesting the Stone *wanted* to be stolen?" Lady Fiora's tone was incredulous. She fidgeted with a red poppy necklace, the flower of her House Meadow.

"I'm suggesting," Vaerith said softly, "that perhaps it is a mercy. That something older than we understand has been stirred. That the world, in its infinite wisdom, has removed a crutch we have leaned on for too long."

A thick silence followed.

Lord Asher slammed a water goblet on the table. "This is dangerous talk. We do not speak of sacred relics like toys tossed from a child's hand. That stone is the anchor of Terrathis' stability." He glanced around the table at the others.

"And anchors," Vaerith replied, "are also weights. They hold us still when the tides shift." He looked directly at me. "Perhaps now, we will learn to swim.

I flattened my palms against the table, leaning forward as though to brace myself. "Regardless of why it was taken, it must be found."

"Of course," said Vaerith with a courtly nod, though there was something unreadable behind his smile. "If only to see what it has become."

An explosion of voices rang out as everyone suddenly began discussing their own opinions. Suggestions were made from simply waiting for it to return, to taking to the skies with a dirigible to search the land. Another thought was that it was obviously the House of the Moon and we should march up to their doorstep and demand it be returned. But, given they are on the opposite side of Terrathis and we had no proof, that was shoved off to the side. The other house leaders went on like this for quite some time, to the point I felt I wasn't needed. I absently sent small droplets of light in the water goblet before me, mesmerized how they shone through the glass.

Naia, the leader of the Tides, slowly rose after awhile. She was an ethereal woman, her dark brown hair in gentle waves falling down her shoulders. She had striking blue eyes, almost too bright to look at. Her expression was gentle on her narrow face as she brushed her hands against the silk cloth of her pale blue gown. Her vast, white wings were folded against her back. She cleared her throat, garnering the attention of the table.

"Idrial, what is your plan?" Her voice was gentle, but with authority. I looked up quickly and smiled, grateful to finally be included.

"I believe we need to venture into the realm to find the stone. I unfortunately do agree that it is no longer within the Sun City's walls." I hadn't said it out loud before this moment, but I could feel its magic waning. "I had considered going north to the Oracles to see if they had any knowledge."

My body relaxed as I saw several nods around the table. Except one.

Demarian's gruff voice called out, "And what if they don't? This is a vast land, and we can't have a youngling like you traipsing aimlessly." I flinched at the slight.

Eldrin stood abruptly. "Remember who you are speaking to. She is no youngling, but the future ruler of this entire realm, including the mountains. You were invited to be a part of the conversation, but I will not tolerate insults to her."

"Of course you would defend her as her lover. I assume you want to go with her?" Demarian narrowed his gaze.

Eldrin shook his head, ignoring the attempted jab. "I cannot go with her. I must stay here and study the echo of the magic in the Sun Tower." He glanced over at me and I gave him a sad smile. I was disappointed, but knew he was right.

Asher spoke next, "You certainly cannot go alone. I must return to my people in Thalirien, and I am sure the others feel the same." The orange light of the fireplace danced along his dark skin.

Raewyn, who had been sitting quietly next to her mother, rose to her feet. "I will accompany you. I know the land and the waters. I have been to the Oracles."

My heart dropped at her words. I had a feeling she would volunteer to come, though I knew this would be a difficult journey for her. My eyes closed briefly, absorbing the idea. Raewyn and her mother had gone to the Oracles after her father had suddenly passed several years prior. He did not wake one morning, and there was no sign of illness nor struggle. And so, the two women made the treacherous journey to the frozen mountains.

As much as I hated to admit it, Raewyn would make the perfect travel companion. There was a heavy pit in my stomach as I nodded slowly, my attention turning to Naia.

Naia squeezed her daughter's hand and nodded. "Yes, Raewyn will go with her. Our ties to the water make it easier for us to pass through frigid conditions. She is well-prepared and can keep Idrial safe."

Fiora, a woman of short stature, tapped her cloven hoof loudly to get the attention of the table. " I will make sure to prepare provisions for their journey. We want it known that the Meadow House contributed to this." Her dusty brown hair bounced lightly, its curls still finely formed from the night before.

Demarian scoffed, but saw he was outnumbered. "Then we need to mark a map for her." He pulled a scroll out from under the table and rolled it out on the wooden surface. He placed a glass on both ends to keep it from curling. "She will have to go through the Vorhi Mountains, which is a four days' journey. Evercrest is just at their entrance. When they arrive, we will give them lodging and food so they may rest. We will also provide them with weapons that can withstand the cold." He squinted at me for a moment. "Do you know how to wield a weapon?"

I laughed coldly. "Yes, I have been trained in longswords and bows, thank you. I can also fight from horseback as well as on foot." He didn't need to know I was terrible at swordfighting. I looked over at Raewyn, who was clenching her fists in frustration. "Raewyn is extremely skilled with a spear and an expert at throwing knives." She smiled at me and sat back in her seat, casually crossing her arms over her chest.

Demarian scoffed but said nothing further about it. He looked down at the map and traced a pathway with his finger. "There is a road that leads directly from here to Evercrest. It's a common trade route, so you shouldn't run into many issues. An occasional bandit or bear, but that is all." He smiled amusingly. "I am sure neither would be a problem for a spear-wielder."

Raewyn straightened. "Yes, we are both very skilled, so I have no concerns."

Demarian raised an eyebrow and looked at the map once again. "There is a large cave that houses our weaponsmith and other tradesmen. You are welcome to utilize anything there." He stood straight, smoothing the grey wool jacket he wore. "My home is carved into the mountainside of Evercrest. You can stay there and house your horses there while you gather yourselves." His voice was harsh and contrasted his words, but I knew he was at least genuine in his offer.

While he was a frustrating man, he at least was hospitable. The history between the Tide and Mountain Houses was rough. The Mountain folk were uncomfortable by how those of the Tide House had wings, as well as the water magic they held. I felt there was something more between the houses, but I could never quite find that out. Tide magic was usually rather lovely, though I supposed it could be deadly. I witnessed how Raewyn could conjure a bubble of water in her hands and throw it with great ease. She could also summon rain, but that only happened when she was experiencing strong emotions. I had not yet witnessed it, but I had a feeling our journey would reveal that in time.

I was broken out of the thoughts spinning in my head, hearing Asher say my name. "I am sorry, can you repeat yourself?" I sheepishly asked.

He stared at me for a moment, his dark green eyes narrowing slightly. "I was inquiring about your plan when you get to the Oracles? They do not just speak to anyone."

I paused for a moment. I hadn't thought of that. Fortunately, Naia spoke for me. "Raewyn has already encountered them and will let her in." Naia gave me a look that made me feel there was more to it than that.

I cleared my throat and straightened my back. "Yes, I do not believe entry will be a problem."

I turned to Fiora and Adair. "Do you have anything that will protect us from the cold?"

Fiora nodded. "Aye, we can brew a few things to help keep the shivers away, and provide you with medicinal tinctures."

Demarian's loud voice added, "We have furs and proper boots. Your summer clothes won't get you very far. Can your horses handle the cold?"

"Though the horses from Calenor are accustomed to the warmer weather, they have been all over Terrathis. They will be fine," Eldrin offered, gently resting his fingertips on mine.

"Then it is settled," Naia said. "Raewyn and Idrial will venture forth to see the Oracles. There they will hopefully find the answer to who stole the Sun Stone. We all should make our way back to our own cities to do what we can. We have never gone without the stone in its rightful place, and especially just before the Rite of Vitality. We do not know the effects it will have and so we must do all we can do to protect our own people."

Vaerith stepped towards the table, rubbing a hand over his thick, dark beard. "Ah, to the Oracles?"

Raewyn spoke abruptly, "I have been there before. I can help guide her."

Magister Vaerith chuckled. "I have no doubt you will be useful to her." His old eyes looked down at me. "I only wonder who will take care of Calenor and its people while you are in the wild?"

I inhaled deeply. That hadn't crossed my mind, and I felt a sudden mixture of guilt and concern. "Allisara and Lucien are too young and not prepared for the duty." My eyes slowly glazed over the other faces at the table.

"It is written that in the absence of all qualified royals, the Grand Magister may take temporary governance," Asher stated flatly, his eyes darkening as he carefully watched Vaerith.

I never fully understood why, but many of the other leaders were not a fan of the Magister. Any time I asked Eldrin, he would briefly mention he wasn't an honorable man, and then would change the subject. I looked up at Vaerith to see that effort was being made to maintain a neutral face.

"Then I shall take proper care of Calenor while you are on your mission." His lips turned upwards at me. "I would like to have a word with the Princess? In private."

Panic flooded over me and I looked from Eldrin to Raewyn. Eldrin gently kissed the top of my forehead and whispered, "You are safe." Raewyn squeezed my hand before she walked away, her sapphire eyes filled with reassurance.

The council chamber emptied slowly, with the sound of murmured politics echoing throughout. I moved to stand by one of the tall arched windows, my gaze fixed on the sunlit courtyard below. Servants bustled around as they made the travel preparations for the leaders of the Houses.

Behind me, soft footsteps cut through the silence like a needle through silk.

"You stood your ground well today," said a voice, smooth and deep, "like a flame that has learned the shape of its lantern."

I didn't turn, trying to keep myself neutral. "Magister."

"Lady Idrial," Vaerith replied, the faintest note of a smile curling in his voice. "You didn't expect me to request an audience, did you? Everyone left so quickly."

"I expected everyone to clear the room. They don't like decisions outside of their kingdoms. It only causes delays."

"True," he said, drifting closer. "But I loathe an audience. And I've always found farewells more honest than decrees."

I turned to face him then, trying to keep my expression unreadable. Vaerith was resplendent as always—silver threads glinting in his dark robes, his hands folded neatly behind his back. There was something theatrical about him, as if every motion had been practiced in a grander, unseen mirror.

"I didn't expect your support," I admitted. "Not for this."

He raised an eyebrow. "You mistake me. I supported the moment. The drama of it. You, standing alone, lit from behind like some mortal statue of dawn. Magnificent."

"I didn't do it for spectacle."

"No," he said softly. "You did it because you burn. And the council forgets that about you. The sun produces fire. Fire doesn't ask permission."

A silence settled between us, not uncomfortable but charged. I studied him, his poise, his amusement, the way his shadow never quite moved in time with his body. There was always something off about Vaerith, something that didn't fit within Calenor's golden order.

"You said in the chamber," I began slowly, "that the Sun Stone's disappearance might be... a mercy."

"Indeed." He smiled again, more fox than man. "Magic that old grows tired. It longs for movement. For change. Perhaps it wanted to be stolen."

I frowned. "You're personifying a sacred relic."

"I'm listening to it," he said, stepping past me toward the window. "All power yearns. The gods certainly do."

He didn't look at me when he said it, but I felt the words land in my chest like a weight. The gods. The implication hung there, unspoken but not unnoticed.

I let the silence linger an uncomfortable length of time. He turned back to me, folding his arms. "You've always felt it, haven't you? That there is more than the light we're told to worship. That the world bends behind the veil, and we've only been shown one sliver."

I drew in a quiet breath. "And what would you have me do? Abandon the sun altogether?"

"No," he said softly. "I would have you chase it. Beyond the horizon. Into places the council won't name and the old maps pretend don't exist." He paused. "And if you find more than the stone—if you find something that doesn't fit the story they've fed you—what then?"

"I don't know," I admitted.

"Good." His eyes gleamed. "Certainty is the grave of curiosity. May your path be crooked, Idrial. The straight ones are easy to trap."

I studied him again. There was a flicker in his gaze, too ancient, too deep. Like he was laughing at something far older than both of them. I noticed it every so often, but tried to ignore it. The light caught in his eyes, and for a heartbeat, I could've sworn I saw stars there.

"I don't trust you," I said finally.

"I would be insulted if you did."

And with a slight bow, he turned and walked into the corridor. His footsteps faded into the stone like ink into parchment, and I remained staring out the window as the last of the light slipped past the tower.

I did not realize until later that I had never heard him open the door.

Chapter Five

I paced the floor in my room, echoes of the conversation reverberating through my mind. I needed to refocus on the journey before me, but I felt unsettled. I sighed, throwing open my wardrobe doors. I needed to prepare clothes and provisions for the journey but I was at a loss for what to bring. How much food did I need? The clothes I owned were mostly for parties and recreational horseback. I doubted they would suffice for the frozen landscape we would soon find ourselves in. I fell back onto my large bed and stared up at the mural painted on the ceiling.

It was a beautiful work of art that had been there for centuries. The ceiling was covered in bright paint, depicting the sandstone city along the water's edge. The artist had decided to paint the city at sunset, an unusual choice considering we were known for our vibrant midday sun. I stared at the bright colors of orange and yellow mingling that cast a shimmer across the city buildings. My eyes fell on the largest tower, where the Sun Stone once was well-protected. I closed my eyes and put my hands over my face. A large exhale left my lips as I heard the door open.

"Idrial?" I heard Raewyn's voice softly speak.

I slowly sat up and smiled slightly at my friend. "Come in, please." I pat the bed next to me.

She obliged and took the spot next to me, elegantly crossing her ankles. She fidgeted with the soft blue silk of her gown. "The mountains are not so cold, and our sparring clothes will be sufficient until we reach Evercrest." I smiled more genuinely. She could always know what I was worried about. "Eldrin has said he will enchant us and our horses to withstand the cold a little better. So perhaps it won't be as bad."

I nodded. Of course Eldrin could perform runes to help against the elements. I hadn't thought of it before. "Yes, that would be helpful." I paused to choose my next words carefully. "How did you and your mother survive before?"

She cleared her throat and straightened. I knew the question brought up dark memories from that time and I hated to ask. But she knew it was important we were both prepared. "Ah, well my mother has much stronger powers over the water than I do. She was able to use it to sort of insulate us against the frigid conditions." She chuckled. "Granted, that meant we were wet most of the time, but it kept us safe." Seeing my confused expression, she elaborated. "Water cannot go below a freezing point, and so by maintaining moisture, we were able to stay in that temperature, even when the frozen mountains were well below freezing."

I nodded with understanding. "That honestly sounds miserable, but I suppose it's better than freezing to death."

Raewyn stared at me for a moment, a thought brewing. "Can you not warm yourself with whatever sun power you have?"

I smiled softly. "To a point, but of course, I have never tested it."

Raewyn nodded, a bit dejectedly. "Ah, well maybe we will get lucky."

"Perhaps so," was my only response.

She rose to her feet and glanced around the room. "Well, we need to gather our things. I suggest taking your sparring and horse-riding clothes as well as any cloaks you may have. Fiora is in the kitchen preparing us provisions to get us to Evercrest. She is making us several medicinal poultices and tinctures for medical emergencies." She had moved towards the door at this point. She glanced back at me, a wide smile on her lips. "Think of this as an adventure with your closest friend, rather than some doomed errand." With that, she disappeared through the door.

I sat in my bed, eating from a plate of apples and warmed soft cheese. It was late and the sun had set several hours prior, but I could not sleep. I had packed a brown leather bag gifted to me by the town's leatherworker. He had carved a sun and lion on the bag, the symbols of my city. I was grateful for the gift and would take the utmost care of it. I had several books open across my bed as I felt the need to take in as much information of the Vorhi Mountains and the frozen Morelia Mountain pass. There was not much known of the Morelia, other than the Oracles who lived there. Raewyn said she would tell me more information once we began our travels, which would at least pass the time.

I raised my hands above my head, stretching widely. I looked at the large candle on my night table, half melted from use. I went to reach for another apple when my door opened suddenly. Startled, I shot up to sit straight on my knees. The door closed behind the figure to reveal Eldrin. I relaxed and sat back down.

"Here for a late night snack?" I waved an apple slice in front of him.

He stared at the books on the bed and then at me. "Yes, but not that kind."

My eyes widened as I felt my heart suddenly race. I moved the plate to the night table and slowly pushed the books to the side of the bed. "Oh?" Was all I could ask.

"You are about to roam around unknown territory. I do not know when you will be back, and I want to make sure I am remembered before you leave." He was removing his velvet black coat and hanging it on the doorknob. "Something to keep you warm for your frozen travels." He was untying his black boots and winked at me. We found ourselves quickly in each other's embrace as we fell into the night.

The soft sunlight fell through my windows, casting shadows on my floor from my curtains. I had been up since the sun rose, but remained snuggled warmly against Eldrin's chest, reluctant to move from the comfort of his arms. After a short time passed, I sat up, my back against the wall, and stared into the rising sun's rays. Anticipation and fear rose as the previous days' events passed through my mind on repeat. I questioned the task before me and my ability to succeed. I doubted my own abilities and turmoiled if I were fully equipped. Perhaps I should have listened to the doubts of Demarian during the council.

As if reading my mind, a gentle voice interrupted my thoughts. "You will find the stone."

I looked over to see Eldrin staring at me, his fingers softly brushing my arm. I smiled at him and nodded. "I suppose I don't have a choice but to succeed."

He propped himself up on his elbow, his hand cradling his head. "I have several wards prepared for you. To keep your water and food from freezing."

"I hadn't even thought of that," I muttered. I stared off into nothing, wondering what else had not occurred to me. I chewed the inside of my lip anxiously.

"There are more people helping you than you realize," Eldrin said softly. "You do not need to have all the answers."

I exhaled aggressively through my nose. "But I feel much better when I do." I smiled jokingly at him.

He playfully swatted a pillow at my shoulder. "Thinking like that is going to stress you out the entire journey. As well as Raewyn." He sat up and swung his legs over the side of the bed. He took a moment to stretch, his flexed back muscles facing me. I was always impressed by the physique of the mages, though I suppose they had to remain at a certain level of strength and overall wellness in order to perform such physical spells. My musings briefly took my mind off of my stresses, though I realized I had been staring at his bare body for a bit longer than intended.

"You already explored what you see." He smiled coyly.

"If only we had the time for another round, but unfortunately I need to make myself presentable." I rose to my feet and looked at him. "Which also means you should, as well."

He nodded slowly and held me close, pressing my head against his chest. "I promise you will be just fine. I love you, my Sunbeam." He reluctantly broke the embrace and began gathering his garments. "I have several things for you and Raewyn. Stop by the library before you leave."

"I love you, too." I soberly responded, as I watched him slip out my door.

My maid caught the door before he closed it and entered. She curtsied and smiled at me, cradling dark clothing in her arms.

"Lady, I have instructions on how to dress you. It is not quite the fantastic appearance we are used to, but it will keep you safe and is practical." She laid the bundle of fabrics on the bed. One by one, she unfolded them and held them up to me, beginning the process of helping me dress.

The reflection in the mirror looked quite different than I was used to. My maids had braided my hair from the top of my head to the side so the golden braid rested over my shoulder. It was durable and would keep out of my face for the journey. My normal exquisite attire was replaced with simple linen brown pants, a white linen shirt, and a yellow ochre wool vest over it. My brown leather boots were lined with fur and I knew I would be grateful for the sheep's wool socks given to me by the Meadow people. I had a dark red cloak I would carry with me until it became cold enough to need. My maids made sure to also attach a golden lion clasp to hold it in place around my neck. I felt nearly naked, being dressed so plainly. I would dearly miss the beaded and lace gowns. With a heavy sigh, I turned towards the door and made my way to the library.

Chapter Six

The grand library was perhaps the darkest place in the entire palace, but it still had a dim golden light casting throughout stained glass windows. I had always been fond of the designs as each one was massive and depicted various lions reading books in different poses. It was meant to be regal, but I found it humorous.

My boots were heavy on the white marbled flooring as I scanned the room for Eldrin and Raewyn. I saw no sign of them and distracted myself with a nearby table, covered in large texts. One was open to a brittle map of the northern mountains. My fingers gently brushed over the slight texture of the symbol depicting the Oracles' location, Calenveil Cave. My heart raced slightly as images of my path ahead flashed through my mind. There were glimpses of a stoney mountain, golden light burst around sparse gray trees. The scent of iron was thick in the air, mingled with the fresh scent of snow. Before I could follow the blood scent in the vision, a gentle voice broke my thoughts.

"Idrial."

I opened my eyes to see Eldrin standing before me on the other side of the table, concern in his bright blue eyes.

My face relaxed into a gentle smile. "Just a forward vision." I gestured down to the map.

One of the gifts from the Sun Stone were forward visions, though I found they weren't always helpful and often ambiguous. It could show you glimpses of a possibility surrounding certain circumstances. In this case, touching the map triggered a possible situation on our journey to the mountains. I pushed the images out of my mind as I reached across the table to place my hand on Eldrin's.

His eyebrows raised but he just nodded. "Ah, well I have a gift for you." He came over to my side of the table.

He reached into his robe pocket and pulled out a breathtaking amulet. At its center was a large, faceted amethyst stone that seemed to pulsed with a soft inner light. Surrounding the stone were delicate motifs of stars and various symbols. I ran my thumb over the stone as I looked up at him.

"This is beautiful. And functional?" I queried.

He grinned brilliantly and nodded. "It is! It is imbued with protection and guidance spells. And it does something else." He winked at me as he turned it over.

There was another small engraving in the open back of the stone. My cheeks warmed as I recalled its purpose.

"Eldrin! I cannot summon you to my bed in the middle of the mountains!" I held my hand out to him, as though to return the amulet.

He laughed. "Oh, no it's an altered version of that sigil. This one only connects us through dreams. I mean it as a way of communication, but if you want to have *those* types of dreams with me, I won't say no."

A loud laugh escaped my lips as I playfully pushed him. I handed the amulet to him and turned my back towards him. He brushed my braid over my shoulder and gently kissed the nape of my neck before putting the amulet around my neck. I held it in my hand and stared down at it for a moment before turning to face him. I pressed my lips against his, softly running my fingers through his hair. The moment did not last long before a voice interrupted.

"Oh, did he give you the sex amulet yet?" Raewyn was walking towards us, an amused look on her face. Her clothing echoed mine, though in dark blues and greys.

I rolled my eyes at her, the smile remaining on my lips. "Yes, he gave me the protection amulet."

She threw something small and furry and white at me. I awkwardly caught it in my arms and stared at it. "What am I holding?"

Raewyn pushed a small blade into the belt of her grey traveling boots. "It's to keep you warm as we go further north. I got them from a merchant this morning. It's a shoulder wrap. You'll put it under your cloak around your neck."

I nodded and put it in my brown leather bag laying on the table next to us. I turned to Eldrin. "Didn't you say you had something for Raewyn as well?"

He smiled and looked down at her boot where the dagger was placed. "I already did. Grab your blade."

She raised an eyebrow but obliged. She held it out to him skeptically. It was quite beautiful with a curved, steel blade with runes etched into it. The cross-guard was an intricate design of waves that seemed to crash towards the blade. Raewyn handed it to me and I ran my fingers over the dark blue leather wrapped around the hilt. The pommel was a whale fin, with tiny blue stones at the tops.

"Did you lift this from my armory?" Raewyn queried. "This is for merchant's wives to guide them home from sea, historically."

Eldrin nodded, and gently tapped the runes. "I placed an enchantment specific to you two. If you two are separated, you will always be able to find each other through the light." Both of their eyes widened at the sight. He gestured to Raewyn and handed her the blade. "Go to the other side of the library and set this on the ground."

She walked backwards to the other side of the vast library, not wanting to miss anything. Soon enough, I could barely make out my friend across the massive, oval space. Suddenly, a soft glowing line appeared on the marble floor, stopping just before my feet.

Raewyn got closer to me, the golden glow brightening from the blade. Her eyes were wide as a soft chime could be heard from the glowing knife. "What sort of trick is this?"

Eldrin smiled. "May you never be separated, but this enchantment will guide you back to each other. The sigil will allow only the two of you to find each other. Anyone else who holds it will find it just a dagger."

Raewyn looked at it again, and flipped it in her hand before putting it back in her boot strap. "Not tide nor time can part us. But I am grateful to have this."

CHAPTER SEVEN

After a lengthy embrace, Eldrin parted from us. The sun was higher in the sky than I had expected. I wanted to leave earlier in the day, but we got caught up in the farewells of the household. The longest, most tearful goodbye was to Raiku. The large, fluffy dog aggressively nuzzled my face, his tail wagging enthusiastically. Eventually, we found our way to the stables where two horses were already saddled up and fully packed. I shifted the brown leather pack on my shoulder at the sight. *This is happening,* I thought.

The horses were slightly smaller than the others in the stables, which made them more agile for the mountain terrain. I went towards the nearly white horse, its silver mane and tail swishing in the gentle breeze. I glanced over to see Raewyn stroking the cheek of a lovely mare, its coat matching the color of sand and its mane and tail a few shades darker.

A stocky, jovial man came out of the stables, wiping his hands on a dirty rag. He pointed to the horse next to me. "That is Lumina." He moved his hand towards Raewyn. "And that is Nimara. They are strong horses used to long distances and the mountains you will take. Treat them well and they will return the favor."

We nodded and almost simultaneously mounted our horses. I gently squeezed the sides of Luminara with my calves, prompting her to move forward towards the path, into the fields that lay beyond my sunny home.

My heart leapt to my throat as we pushed forward. I had never left the safe walls of Calenor, except to run around and swim with Raewyn at the Tide House. I kept glancing over my shoulder, seeing the large sandstone palace slowly disappear. Everything I had ever known and loved resided in those walls, and I was leaving it. As though reading my thoughts, Raewyn spoke.

"You will come back."

I looked over at her, the sound of our horses' hooves clopping on the ground. "I know. I just feel unsteady."

"I would be surprised if you weren't. I am sure leaving your city in the hands of the Magister is no easy thing." She slightly flapped her wings, stretching the tendons.

"It's not only that," my voice trailed off. I felt like a child admitting my feelings. "I've never left. I don't know what to do without the safety of the guards and the familiar places. How do I talk to strange people?"

Raewyn laughed. "You talk to strange people all the time at balls!"

"Yes! But that's different. It's easier when I am surrounded by so many *other* people that I *do* know! And I always have Eldrin and you."

A comforting smile grew on her face. "You always have us. I am with you. And so is Eldrin." She pointed towards the amulet around my neck.

"How are you not afraid?"

She shrugged. "We have each other. When I drift, you anchor. When I crawl, you carry." She paused for a moment. "But, I am afraid. Sure, I went to the Oracles but my mother was with me. And that gives a sense of security." She paused for a moment. "I'll miss my bed. And the food."

I chuckled. "I will definitely miss the food."

"We will be fine. We are powerful and resourceful. You have been trained for years by the greatest of scholars and warriors and mages. And I am scrappy." She reached forward and stroked her horse's mane. "And we have these two. They have seen a lot of Terrathis."

I sighed heavily. "And now, we shall, too."

The dusty road was rather uneventful and the terrain became more and more repetitive. I found myself unnerved by the vastness of the grass fields that extended on either side of the road. It left me feeling exposed. The wind from the coast became more and more distant as we moved further from the coastal city I loved. The grass around the path became taller and fluffier, which also brought on loud insect noises that seemed to pierce my eardrums.

I directed my attention to Raewyn. "Where were you last night?"

She kept staring straight, but a mischievous smile sprawled across her face. "Why do you ask?"

"You slept in your traveling clothes." I nodded my head towards her body.

Raewyn flapped her wings softly, stretching them slightly. "I had a debt to collect."

I rolled my eyes and smiled. "And who was your victim this time?"

"I never caught her name. But she lost a game of cards to me the night before the ball." She looked over at me, her grin wide. "She was one of those sea thieves people never can seem to catch."

"Rae! You're supposed to report people like that," I exclaimed, laughter heavy in my voice.

"Oh, I made her pay, don't you worry." She winked at me and looked ahead.

A soft smile grew on my lips. "I'm sure you did."

Raewyn cleared her throat. "Do you think Master Vaerith will take care of Calenor in your absence?"

I inhaled deeply, her words echoing my own concerns. "I have no choice but to trust him. The other leaders don't trust him, and I find him unsettling."

She nodded, staring at the path before us. "I find him rather sinister and selfish." Raewyn brushed a strand of hair behind her pointed ears.

"Fortunately we will only be gone a few months." I tried to sound hopeful, but I had a pit forming in my stomach.

My horse stopped abruptly, kicking up a cloud of dirt around me. Raewyn's mount followed and let out a startled whine. I tried to calm her and looked around to see what caused the movement. Suddenly, three Kobolds erupted from the tall brush, their small, red scaly forms rushing towards us. They brandished rather crude weapons, one with a slingshot loaded with sharp rocks, the other two with broken spears.

"Evil House of Sun!" The Kobold released a slingshot, causing Raewyn's horse to rear in alarm.

"Damn Kobolds!" she shouted, her large ivory wings unfolding in great splendor. She swiftly leapt off her horse, grabbing her spear. She shoved it into the chest of one of the Kobolds. It let out a shrill cry as the life left its eyes, falling unceremoniously to the ground.

I grabbed my bow, the rich, dark wood ornamented with small inlaid designs of gold sunflowers. I jumped off my own horse, my boots landing in a cloud of dust and dried grass. My hand held the soft leather of the grip as I nocked an arrow and swiftly released it, watching the tip fly straight into a Kobold's eye. It let out a horrific screech and retreated down the path, the arrow still trapped in its skull.

"You'll pay for your houses' lies!" He snarled, dust swirling around him as he frantically tried to move away. He threw a stone at me as he raced away, hitting my forearm.

My heart pounded in my chest as I ran after him, trying to retrieve my arrow. I hadn't expected him to run away. The creature made a horrible garbling sound as he left a trail of blood on the rocky path.

I halted abruptly, dust clouding around my feet. *What does that mean?* I mentally queried. I turned around and made my way back to our horses. I walked over to Raewyn, who speared one in the chest as the other ran into the tall grass in fear.

She wiped the blood from her spear on her shirt and stepped over the body towards me. "What did they mean?" she asked.

"I do not know." I glanced down the pathway. "And now I've lost an arrow."

My friend smiled gently. "You finally made good use of your archery lessons, at least."

I placed my bow back in its place on Lumina and glanced up at the sun, which was getting close to descending.

"We had better find a place for camp soon. Though," I looked around at the vast plains, "I don't really see much cover." The brief encounter left me a bit shaken and confused.

Raewyn licked her lips, following my gaze. She mounted her horse and I followed suit. "We should keep moving for a little longer." I nodded as we carried on.

We eventually did find a small line of brush where we felt safe to rest and the horses had access to a small pond for water. The sun disappeared over the horizon as we enjoyed the dried fruit, bread, and cheese Fiora from the Meadow had packed. After several hours of light chatter, we were ready to turn in.

I lay on the thick blanket and rested my head on my hands. I found myself quickly falling asleep.

Lips gently pressed against my cheek, and a smile grew on my face.

"Eldrin," I softly purred. I looked around the dream state. Of course it was his study in the library. There was a soft, golden glow all around.

He lifted his head from my skin, his hot breath lingering. He grinned. "I waited a day before contacting you."

I lifted my hand to brush his curly dark hair behind his ears. "I miss you."

"We will see each other soon enough. How have your travels been?"

"I shot an arrow into a kobold's eye today."

Eldrin's eyes widened. "Kobolds? Did you get hurt?" He frantically examined me as though any injuries would translate through this dream state.

I waved a hand dismissively. "Oh, no, not at all. Raewyn is quick on her feet and took out one with her spear and scared the other. All I lost was an arrow." I decided not to mention the comment the creature had made.

He pressed his lips together in concern. "There have never been Kobold's on that route. Did you happen to see any merchants traveling?"

I narrowed my eyes, recalling the past two days. "No, actually. We haven't seen anyone." That was odd. I pressed my lips together. "They referred to me as liars and thieves. I don't understand."

Eldrin inhaled sharply. "Not everyone is a friend to the House of the Sun. There are forces beyond our walls who would rather see Calenor burn."

My eyes widened. "I don't understand. What have we done?"

"History isn't always what it may seem. Just remember that other people have different versions of what you may know." He rubbed his eyes with his left hand. I could tell he had not slept. The wards kept him awake.

I chewed on my inner lip, wanting to press him for more information, but decided against it. I was also fatigued and knew I needed to get some sleep. I knew I could always revisit that, or perhaps Raewyn knew something.

"So, how do I keep safe, then? If I have unknown enemies?"

He stared off into the distance. "Keep your senses sharp. And remember that I am always with you."

I told Raewyn what Eldrin had said, but she suggested it wasn't something to worry about at that time. Truthfully, I don't think she knew either, but didn't want to come across as ignorant. The following days felt the same and I was getting antsy. Eat, ride, sleep, repeat. Even the terrain stayed the same and I almost worried we were going in circles. Eventually, on the third midday, we saw mountains form in the distance. The ground beneath us transitioned into stone and pointed trees were becoming taller and sturdier. My chest tightened with nerves as Evercrest neared.

Chapter Eight

My mouth opened as I sat on my stationary horse, staring up at Evercrest. Perched high on a mountainside, Evercrest was far more beautiful than I had expected. My eyes trailed high up to the wooden homes that blended with the surrounding stone. We moved through the front gates, and followed the winding grey pathway, adorned with iron railings and copper flickering lanterns. The warm scent of herbs and meat wafted through the air and I felt my stomach growl in response. Massive forges and workshops lined the street where skilled artisans worked on their craft. Their dark eyes peered up at us from beneath dark hair, particularly narrowing at the sight of Raewyn. A group of large, fluffy sheep ran past us, their handler not far behind. As we followed the stone paths towards the top, it opened up to a large stone platform where it was an obvious place for music and dancing and other community gatherings.

There was surprising lightness in the air. Given Demarian's rather abrasive personality, I had expected that was the way of the entire city. I glanced over at Raewyn, who was clearly having a different experience. She had tucked her wings in as tight as she could. We halted our horses in the middle of the hub and stared at each other.

"Are you all right?" I whispered.

She chewed her bottom lip and looked out over the expansive land below us. After a contemplative moment, she sighed.

"I am not welcome here." She tucked in her wings, as though she could conceal them.

The wind chilled my skin and I hugged my arms as I looked around at the small merchant carts on the edge of the platform, all filled with flowers, baked goods, and handcrafted jewelry. I made eye-contact with a flower merchant and she gave me a tight-lipped smile before glancing back down. Several of the others were staring uncomfortably at Raewyn.

I exhaled deeply, absently stroking the silver mane of Luminara. I had known about the prejudice between the Mountain and Tide people, but had never experienced it like this. I could feel Raewyn stiffen and worried she would bare her teeth if provoked even the slightest. I glanced up to see an ornate archway just up a curved flight of stairs. I prompted my horse to move towards the steps, nodding my head at Raewyn. Wordlessly, she followed.

I slid off of Luminara, my hips and legs aching from the journey. I glanced up at the vision before me. The archway was significantly larger than I had expected, now that I saw it in person. I could make out stone carvings of rams and sheep in the black stone. What caught my eye was the massive statue of a towering man. It depicted a muscular figure rooted into the ground. His legs appeared to merge with the stone, his surface cracked and jagged intentionally. My eyes followed up to his face where I was met with a stoic, angular look, his features carved sharp and enduring. Deep-set eyes made out of polished obsidian gazed outward. His arms were stretched outward, one hand gripping a stone staff with an obsidian orb, and the other held palm-up, as though to offer strength to those of us below him.

"Ah, that is Tharundar, the Stoneheart! He's a sight to see, indeed." I turned to see a stunning woman standing near the archway. She was a few heads shorter than me but could probably easily take me in a physical brawl. She smiled and approached, beautiful furs wrapped around her broad shoulders. Her caramel eyes glittered as the light from a nearby lantern flickered.

"I am Thalira Draelor, mate of Demarian, Lady of the Mountains." She lowered her head in a bow, exposing her obsidian braided bun.

Raewyn stood next to me, and I could feel the tension rising from her. "A pleasure," she stated.

I did a slight curtsy, not knowing their customs. "Thank you for housing us. We are very appreciative."

Thalira smiled and abruptly took Raewyn's hands in her own. "I am also glad you are here. The hospitality is extended to you." She lowered her voice. "We are all the same under the Sun Stone."

Raewyn's wings relaxed and a smile warmed her face. "You have a beautiful city. My mother and I did not pass through here when we came north before." She gestured behind her at the expansive view overlooking the fields. "I could never imagine waking up every morning and seeing this."

Thalira beamed, laughter emitting from her. "Oh, that is kind. Each city has its own beauty." She patted Nimara on the side. "Now then, let's get these horses tended to and you ladies in the warmth! I am sure you are not accustomed to this chill."

The evening meal had been rather uneventful, though the food was quite remarkable. It was heartier food than we were accustomed to: a rack of lamb in a mustard and herb sauce, roasted garlic turnips, butter and brown sugar carrots, and goat-cheese stuffed rolls. Demarian had not joined us as he was out helping a farmer retrieve lost rams. I could not imagine him being generous with his time, but I was grateful for the escape from him. His wife was excellent company, as was the warmed berry mead that accompanied our dinner.

After an incredible meal and several evenings of sleeping on the ground, I was grateful to lay in a cozy bed. The rooms Raewyn and I were provided far exceeded my expectations. There was a large, grey stone fireplace in the corner of the stone-walled room. The floor had diamond patterns in varying colors of wood. The bed had the softest, fluffiest beige blanket, and on top a maid laid down a thick and heavy black blanket.

"It's sheep's wool," she explained, and tucked me into the warmed bed. Finally feeling safe and blissful, it didn't take long before I fell asleep.

A hand slivered up my thigh, his thumb gently caressing my skin. He firmly pressed his lips to mine, his other hand gathering my hair on the back of my head. I softly moaned into his lips, bringing my hand up to his chest. His hand made its way up my cotton nightgown and slipped close to my more sensitive parts. I felt heat intensify as my legs slightly parted.

He leaned me back on a purple chaise lounge in his study. His lips against my cheeks, he murmured, "I miss you."

Breathlessly, I whispered back, "I miss you, too." I pushed my hips towards his hand, beckoning his fingers.

At my movement, he exhaled hot breath into my ear as he gently slipped a finger inside. I let out a small gasp as he moved it around, finding the most sensitive bundle of nerves.

Eldrin gently nibbled the tip of my ear as he stuck another finger inside, his movement quickening.

"I can tell you missed me," he mused. "You're so wet." He moved his other hand to play with my breast, both feelings heavier with his touch.

I moved my hips against him, beckoning him for more. "I want you," I whimpered.

A sly grin formed on his face as he peered down at me, heat in his eyes. "I'm not done playing with you." He pushed two more fingers inside of me, stretching me. He moved his hand rhythmically, pushing me further and further into the intense feelings forming. Within moments, I felt myself building and building until I finally found release, sending shockwaves through my body. My golden light erupted, filling the dream space that was his study.

He continued to push his fingers inside me, sending another pulse of orgasm through my body, my cries of pleasure ringing out. He suddenly stood up and removed his linen pants, revealing a sizable and eager cock. Eldrin gently pushed my knees apart and leaned into me. He cradled my head in his hands and gently pushed himself inside of me. I let out a loud moan as his girth completely filled me. I spread my legs out as far as they could go to accommodate his size.

He let out a low growl and quickened his pace, thrusting deeper inside of me. Whimpers of pleasure escaped my lips as he pushed the rest of his length in. I could never get over his size and how it seemed to fill my entire body. My body shivered as I climaxed again and again under his body. My orgasms came pouring one after another until he finally came at the same time. He cried out in pleasure and his body collapsed onto me, careful not to crush my body. He kissed my cheek before rolling off of me.

A few moments later, after cleaning ourselves, we found ourselves draped in each other's damp, warm bodies, a thin blanket covering us. I rested my head on his chest.

"So, is this the true intention of the amulet?"

He smiled. "It is definitely a perk. I was intending on simply seeing how you are doing, but then I saw your beautiful body laying there. I figured you needed a release after the journey." He kissed the corner of my eye.

My smile widened. "I could never say no to you." I traced the dark blue whirlpool of ink on his chest. It was a mark of arcane magic, showing our galaxy and stars.

He brushed my hair with his hands and kissed the top of my head. "I will let you rest now."

Chapter Nine

"He's making good use of the amulet, it seems," Raewyn stated, a sly grin on her face.

I nearly choked on my porridge. We were sitting at a long wooden table, eating a hot breakfast. "What?"

"I could hear you. And I am sure half of this place could, too." She waved around her metal spoon, gesturing around the room.

My cheeks warmed as I pushed a blueberry into my food, sinking it to the bottom of the bowl. "I didn't realize it translated into real life." I was mortified thinking about the servants who had come into my room in the middle of the night to stoke the fire. Would they tell Demarian or Thalira? My thoughts raced as I shoved berries into my mouth.

Raewyn let out a loud laugh. "Friend, I am sure you are fine. If anything, people are probably jealous." She winked at me.

I nervously chewed the inside of my bottom lip and turned my attention to the large, wooden door at the end of the hallway, hearing it open. Demarian and Thalira waltzed into the great hall.

"Good morning!" Her warm voice rang out as they took a seat not far from us on the long, wooden table.

Demarian nodded to me. "I trust your journey was uneventful?"

"We did encounter some angry Kobolds," I quickly stated. "But it was mostly just dusty trails and tall, itchy grass."

Demarian unexpectedly laughed, startling me a bit.

"Oh, yes, it does get rough on that path. Kobolds, hm? A bit unusual, but not unheard of." Demarian nodded to the servant who put a plate of eggs, sausage, and potatoes in front of him. "Well, I am glad to hear it was a fairly easy journey." He paused and looked at me seriously. "The easiest part of your path."

The ominous tone in his voice took me aback and I rested my spoon in my empty bowl. I smiled softly and took a sip of my water. "Ah, well, I am glad to have some easy parts." I chuckled, not fully feeling it.

Thalira ticked her tongue at her husband, slicing her strawberries into slivers with her dulled knife. "Oh, now, don't be so dreary. They are perfectly capable of making their journey in one piece!" She spread soft cheese on a thick piece of toasted bread and laid the strawberries methodically on the cheese bread. "It is treacherous indeed, but you have sure-footed animals and the best supplies from us!"

I looked over at Raewyn, who was smiling again. She seemed much more at ease around Thalira. "Yes, we are most grateful for your assistance in this! This is the last bit of comfort I expect for quite a while." Raewyn's voice tapered off a bit.

I glanced out out the singular massive, arched window. It overlooked the town out into the fields and beyond. The sky was grey and just looking at it gave me a chill. I rubbed my bare arms with my hands, attempting warmth. I looked over at Thalira to see her smiling sympathetically at me.

"I know you are not made for the cold, but perhaps we can help." She rose to her feet and gestured to Raewyn and I that we should follow. She turned to her husband. "We will see you in a few hours, my heart."

Demarian shoved a large piece of bacon in his mouth and waved us away. "Ah, begone with you, women. I'm sure you don't need my help with whatever it is you are doing."

Thalira chuckled and ushered us out the large doors.

The Lady of the Mountain pulled us through the town center, stopping at most of the merchants. She scolded anyone who showed disdain towards Raewyn, explaining she was an honored guest. It was nice to see how highly regarded she was by her people, as well as how far her kindness extended. She made personal conversation with every single merchant, asking about their children or their recently ill family members. And it showed in the energy of the market. Her presence alone filled it with life. It was apparent she is the life source of this city. The thought warmed me, my gold light emitted brighter from my skin.

Raewyn glanced over at me, her lips widening. "I have not seen you this brightly shining in quite some time."

"It is always a pleasure seeing another leader love their people. I have never seen the interactions before, as they always come to Calenor." It was the one thing I resented about my station: I was not to leave the city walls. My father claimed it was too dangerous.

Thalira, who was speaking with a furs merchant, turned and waved us over. "Come, lovelies. You must touch and feel."

The merchant was a woman who very clearly worked hard every day. She was older and her hair had more silver than black. Her skin was ashen and her hands were calloused. Her dark brown eyes held more life in them than most had seen and were quite intense. Despite this, she still had a friendly, though gruff, way about her.

"You two are far from home, eh?" She shoved a large, brown fur coat into my arms.

I awkwardly cradled it. "Ah, just from Calenor. And Raewyn here is from Vespera."

The woman also shoved another grey fur coat into Raewyn's arms. Fortunately for her, she was prepared and more elegantly held it. She quickly slipped it on and stroked the long fur. "Yes, my mother is Naia."

The merchant nodded, pointing to her wings. "Ah, yes, yes. I see her in you. Welcome to our city. These are some of our strongest fur coats, imbued with Arcane magic that will prevent it from getting wet." She looked at Raewyn. "There's one large enough to fit your wings."

My eyes widened as I looked at Thalira, who was absolutely beaming with pride. "These are all gifts to you, from the House of the Mountain." She looked down at our shoes. "We should also replace your boots for more aggressive terrain."

A few hours later, we were absolutely exhausted. We had successfully replaced our boots with water-resistant boots that had a textured tread on the bottom. We also each grabbed a beaded bracelet; Raewyn took a black obsidian crystal for protection, and I was drawn to a cool, green stone that was said to bring luck. Thalira had also shown us a magnificent tavern that had the most delicious and creamy vegetable soup. The secret, apparently, was goat milk and leeks. I never had goat milk before and was pleasantly surprised at the mildly sweet flavor.

The three of us were sitting in a cozy den, the stone walls lined with tapestries of rams and white foxglove flowers. The stone fireplace was well alive, warming our sore bodies. Raewyn and I were not used to the tiered city with its steep pathways. We were embarrassingly out of breath on the ascent back to the Thalira's home.

The sun was setting behind the horizon, casting a soft blue hue in the room. Raewyn held a large copper mug in her hand, a ram engraved for the crest of the House of the Mountains. We were enjoying their infamous hot chocolate. Thalira smiled warmly at us, obviously pleased with the day.

"Well, I certainly feel much better about your journey forth." She took a sip of her own copper mug. "Now that you are better prepared for the cold. Your horses are also being fitted with more suitable shoes, and wool blankets have been given to keep them warm as well. That, paired with the sigils given by Eldrin, should be more than sufficient."

I nodded and drained my mug. "I am most appreciative. I will be honest, we were not expecting such hospitality from you. Demarian has never come across as... warm."

She chuckled, resting her mug on the black wood table next to her. "Ah, he is grumpy and a bit bitter. But he means well. Truth be told, he was ecstatic after your meeting. He has wanted the House of the Sun to see our beautiful city."

Raewyn tilted her head slightly. "Has no one ventured here? It is not *that* far."

Thalira's eyes grew sad. "There is much unknown to you both, but yes, the people of Calenor keep within their walls, sometimes venturing to Vespera by the tides. But within the past centuries, they have become more and more withdrawn." Seeing my widening eyes, she added. "Oh, you are most accommodating when we are invited within! Your most recent ball was exquisite. All houses used to hold fantastic balls and host political meetings, but roughly 150 years ago, they ceased. My mother used to love them. She would tell me about them when I was younger."

I found myself rapidly tapping the plush armrest of the large, grey chair I was curled in. Something about that fact felt greatly uncomfortable, though I could not figure out why. I glanced at Raewyn to see if she showed any signs of the same discomfort. She did not, of course, as she was always much better at hiding her emotions.

"What made them stop?" I queried.

Thalira smiled sadly and lifted her mug to her lips. She paused to take a sip before speaking. "Ah, that is not my story to tell. I believe your journey will reveal that to you soon enough."

I narrowed my eyes in curiosity, but said nothing. It was apparent she was not going to explain anything further, and I wasn't about to push it. I could not stop the questions from swirling around my mind nonetheless. Seeing my discomfort, Thalira rose and affectionately stroked my hair.

"Not all hidden history is frightening. There are just a lot of other people involved, and it would be best explained by someone else, and in a time where you are ready to receive the information." She made her way to the door. "You both should get to sleep soon. You have a long journey ahead of you."

We both nodded and obliged with no argument.

I awoke the next day feeling more refreshed than I had in over a week. Between the preparation for the Stone Summit, the stress of losing the stone, and our journey north, I had not slept well. It was a mix of the heavy food and drinks and the quiet reprieve of the warm bed. I was used to the bustling of servants early in the morning and the bright sun shining through my windows. But here in Evercrest, the halls remained quiet, there were no windows for the sun to shine through, and the Tide gulls weren't squawking loudly. It made me uncomfortable at first, not having access to the outside. But after the first night, I realized there were advantages to it.

I sat up in my warm bed, stretching my arms above my head. A wide yawn escaped my mouth. I moved to my wardrobe when a soft knock sounded at the door.

"Hello?" I called out.

Raewyn entered, fully clad in her traveling gear, with the addition of the colder weather garments we procured the day prior. She had her dark brown hair woven in a braid, wrapping around itself to create a secure bun at the nape of her neck. Stray wisps delicately framed her soft face. In this lighting, her hair had an almost raven-like depth while revealing subtle hints of warm caramel. I always loved the contrast we created when standing near each other.

She threw a packed leather bag on my bed and sat next to it. "I am surprised you slept so late! Another magical night with Eldrin?" She winked.

I clutched the amulet at my neck and playfully threw a sock at her. "No, I did not. I was just comfortable and was actually left alone by servants for once."

Raewyn grinned. "Yes, better leave that for the wilderness when you're feeling lonely." She tightened the laces on her black boots.

I rolled my eyes and finished getting ready. We made idle chatter as we went through the stone corridors, lined with magnificent arches, and reached the main hall. Thalira and Demarian were present, each holding a small pouch. Demarian still made me nervous, but I felt a little more at ease around him than I ever had. His more jovial manner in our time here was rather startling, but welcome. He also had warmed up to Raewyn, able to put his prejudice aside. She was still on guard from him, however.

"Ladies! We have packed a bit of food for you for the journey, as well as some medicinal herbs should you need it." Thalira handed me the leather pouch and gestured for Demarian to follow.

"Yes, we wouldn't want you out wandering the mountains without something for frostbite or even an animal bite," Demarian said, handing Raewyn the pouch.

She eyed him warily, but still took it. "We are most appreciative of this, and of your hospitality. Perhaps maybe your people won't be so cold to the next person from the Tide that graces your halls."

My eyes widened slightly and my mouth dropped. She had said it so pleasantly it took Demarian a moment to react. Before he could speak, Thalira clapped her hands together.

"Ah, yes! We should love visitors! Now, we shall make for the outside and be united with your horses, yes?"

We stepped outside into the overcast light to find our horses, freshly groomed and well-cared for. They were already fully packed and eagerly waiting to be out in the world. I approached Lumina and gently stroked her cheek. She leaned into the touch and let out a soft snort. I smiled and turned to Thalira.

"We cannot thank you enough for your hospitality. Perhaps some day soon we can have a grand feast with all the other Houses in your halls!" I curtsied until Thalira abruptly pulled me into an aggressive hug.

"Oh, that would be lovely!" She pulled apart from me and stared into my eyes. "Do be careful," she lowered her voice. "And do not fully trust what you know."

I opened my mouth to inquire further when Demarian clapped a hand on my shoulder. "Follow the Switchbacks when ascending the steepest points of the mountains. Those trails will keep you going the right direction."

I thanked him before mounting Lumina. I looked over at Raewyn, who sat on top of Nimara, and nodded. We were ready to begin our ascent into the Vorhi Mountains.

Chapter Ten

We made stops every few hours to let our horses and ourselves adjust to the elevation. The pressure made my head hurt and I was grateful for the herbs provided to keep it at bay. We had been fortunate to find streams to fill our waterskins several times and to care for the horses. Occasionally, we came across minimally sloped areas where we could make our camp. Idle conversations passed the time, but both of us had our own thoughts whirling in our minds. It wasn't until after a full day of traveling that Raewyn finally spoke about the conversation with Thalira.

"What history is she speaking of?" She asked, poking the freshly made fire with a stick. I had used the last bit of sunlight to burn some fallen logs and leaves.

I stared into the flames solemnly. "I do not know, truthfully. I have read in the library that there was a great falling out between the houses at one point in our history. But the Sun Stone is vital to all life, and so repairs had to be made." I squinted. "I don't recall how they repaired the damage done. I believe that to be part of why there is still tension between the Tide and the Mountain."

Raewyn nodded thoughtfully. "Yes, I have never quite believed the explanation that the Mountain House fears our water powers." She held her palm out and a small bubble of water formed. She smiled distantly and stared at it before gracefully closing her hand, the bubble disappearing. "Who could ever hate that?"

A soft laugh escaped my lips. "Perhaps our mothers when we would use my light beams to turn your water bubbles into steam."

Raewyn let out a hearty laugh. "Oh, maybe dinner parties weren't the best time for that."

I nodded, the smile remaining on my lips. "Perhaps not." I stared off into the distance, hearing the sounds of wyvern's screeching in the distance. A shiver ran through my body. I gently rubbed my arms with my hands and pulled a fur over my body. Raewyn looked at me, sympathetically.

"Can't you use your Sun powers to warm yourself?"

I shook my head. "I honestly tried earlier, but the sun is not as strong up here. I need to limit what I do as I am sure it will only worsen as we go north."

She sighed and slowly bobbed her head in agreement. "Do you think it is also partly due to the Stone missing?"

I chewed the inner part of my bottom lip. "I do. And that is what worries me. If I am already feeling its effects, then I can't even imagine how the city is faring."

Raewyn moved to sit on her knees next to me, her hand gently grazing the grass next to my feet. "I am certain we will find out answers soon enough."

"Yes, but the Oracles can only *possibly* point us in the right direction of where it is. Beyond that, we need to actually locate the stone." I finally voiced the worry that had been swirling in my mind for the past month. "What happens when we leave the Oracles?"

Raewyn shifted slightly. "Well, I suppose we will go back to Calenor. Depending on what information they give us, we either study books or a map, or we contact the other Houses again."

I made an incomprehensible noise at the idea of having another Council. I glanced over at our horses, who were fast asleep, standing. The higher we went in the mountains, the smaller the clearings for rest became, and they had to adjust to the space given. I was grateful for the enchantments from Eldrin to keep them warm. The air was feeling crisper, and the wind had picked up greatly. I was particularly pleased with the fur-lined boots from Evercrest.

"Where have you gone?"

I snapped my attention back to Raewyn, her foggy green eyes staring at me. "What?"

"Your mind wandered far for a minute there." She glanced at the dying fire. "Perhaps we should get some sleep." I nodded and obliged.

"I would assume the fancy dances stopped simply due to the war. It was centuries before Therrathis was no longer fragmented." Eldrin sat in a wooden chair, looking over a large, opened text on the table before him.

I idly stroked the arm of the large, plush chair in the corner of his study. "I would assume they would resume them to keep more peace?"

He shook his head. "The leaders at the time were more concerned with repairing the trust and security of their own people." He paused for a moment, his dark blue eyes darkening. "Truthfully, your parents' disappearance is what began the unification of all the Houses."

I snapped my attention to him. "How so?"

He sat back in his chair, resting the back of his head in his hands. "The other leaders were concerned for yours and your siblings' well-being. My personal belief, they also wanted to ensure you were capable of keeping the Sun Stone safe."

I inhaled sharply. "Well their trust was misplaced, obviously. Considering it went missing in my care." There was a slight bite to my words.

He sat up instantly, regret filling his features. "I didn't mean to insult you. I simply meant they wanted to be part of the protection of it, whether it was an altruistic move or selfish." He walked over to me and knelt down before my chair, resting his hand on mine. "You have done well in keeping your city safe." He gently kissed my hand.

A soft smile grew on my lips. "You think too highly of me."

He gently stroked my cheek with the back of his hand. "Not nearly enough."

"How is my sister? And my brother? Are they faring well under the Magister?" I had been nervous to ask before, but I had begun to miss my siblings.

He pressed his lips together firmly. "The Magister has been a bit difficult, and your sister has been challenging his decisions."

My shoulders rolled back as I sat up straight. "What decisions?"

Eldrin rubbed his eyes and sighed. "I do not want to burden you with things you cannot control." He exhaled, seeing my stern expression. "Magister Vaerith has been trying to convince the guards to close the gates to anyone not born of Sun Blood."

"I beg your pardon? Why would he do that?" My eyes widened, and I worried I had made a horrible decision in leaving Calenor.

"Idrial, he is not a good man. Nothing will come of it as their loyalty is to you. But I fear he is spreading misinformation to isolate the citizens of the Sun." He brushed a loose strand of hair behind my ear. "We will keep your city safe in your absence."

I relaxed my shoulders, realizing there was nothing I could do at this time. I watched as he rose to his feet and perused a nearby shelf. He pulled a scroll from a corner and returned to the table, spreading it out.

"I did find some useful information for you."

I joined him, staring at the map of the mountains he pointed at. "You are about to cross from the Vorhi Mountains to the Morelia Mountains. Your journey will become more challenging after you traverse the Paldor Pass, which is just a day's ride away." He moved his finger where the map transitioned the mountains from stone to snow. "There used to be a settlement in this pass before a dragon took it over."

My eyes widened, the gold rim around the pupil taking over more of the blue. "Excuse me? A dragon?"

He laughed. "It is long gone as this happened even before the war. But there are recent journals from travelers stating remnants from the town remain, such as rough lodging and some edible vegetation that comes back each year." He straightened and looked at me seriously. "It is in a bit of a valley, and we do not know who or what lives there. I recommend approaching with caution."

"My love, I am approaching everything with caution." My lips turned upwards slightly. "If you recall, I have barely left Calenor. Just to Vespera to visit Raewyn."

He gently brushed a strand of hair out of my face. "Just be a bit more alert. My world would shatter without you in it.

I leaned in to firmly kiss his lips. He leaned into me, his hands running through my hair. A moment passed and he pulled away from me, planting one last kiss on my forehead. "I need to let you sleep."

I sighed, knowing he was right, and felt myself pulled back into the cold mountains.

CHAPTER ELEVEN

The next morning, I immediately told Raewyn about the pass and the old settlement. She stated when they came through the mountains before, they had not ventured into the pass as they did not know what it was. Her mother was more cautious after the death of her husband.

"We need to find a place to wash ourselves. We are ripe!" Raewyn crooned, smelling her underarm.

I crinkled my nose at her. "Not in this cold!"

Raewyn glanced at the stream that had been running alongside our path for some time. She grinned and leaped off her horse. She jerked her head towards it, a mischievous grin on her face.

I rolled my eyes and climbed down from Luminara. "The cold is not my friend!"

"But I am!" She giggled. "Besides, can't you warm the water with your magic?" She removed her boots and socks.

"I *can*, but I don't want to disturb the balance of nature," I shivered, my feet bare and cold against the hard grass.

"Ugh, it will be fine for ten minutes. There haven't been any creatures around anyways." Raewyn stood before me, her perfectly curvy figure void of any clothing. She spread out her wings fully and flapped them gently.

"Oh, fine!" I removed the last of my clothing and stepped into the frigid stream, the water reaching my ankles.

It was deeper in some parts and we moved a bit down until the water rose to our knees. Shivering, we gently lowered ourselves into the water. I placed my hands on the surface of the water and focused for a moment, calling forth heat from the light. Within a few moments, the water around us heated and bubbled slightly.

A great sigh of pleasure emitted from Raewyn's mouth as she leaned back to lower her hair into the water. I watched as she rubbed the warmed water over her face in absolute delight. I looked down at my own legs and rubbed the dirt off them in the water.

"I never want to leave this again," Raewyn exclaimed, sitting up suddenly.

"It feels so much better than freezing on the backs of horses!" I agreed.

Raewyn opened her hand to show a small square of soap. She rubbed it in her hands, the smell of sea salt and lavender wafting towards my senses. She quickly moved the fragrant soap over her legs, chest, and abdomen before handing it to me.

"Of course you brought soap." I grinned, using the soap over my dusty, chapped skin.

"Well, we can still have some semblance of hygiene!" She rinsed herself off.

"I'm not complaining, not in the least."

We splashed around for a bit longer in the warmed water, feeling revitalized and clean. Reluctantly, we pulled ourselves from the warm water and scampered back to our camp, giggling and shivering. I made a small fire with wood and leaves nearby. By the time the sun was setting, we were mostly dried, our soaked hair tied into thick plaits; Raewyn's hair wrapped into a low bun and mine in a simple braid over my shoulder. My clothes felt dirtier now that I was clean, but I had no other option. Raewyn pointed out after the fact that we should have also cleaned and dried our garments, but the damage was done and we had to suffer. We ate a meager meal and spoke of idle things before we turned in for the night.

"I have a surprise for you." Eldrin stood before me in his study, his face bright.

"A surprise?" He had tapped into my dreams to meet with me. I hadn't intended to speak with him that night, but he was insistent.

He opened the door to his study and a large, golden dog came barreling through. My heart leaped as I saw my beloved Raiku. "Oh! Oh! Raiku!" Tears streamed from my eyes as I knelt down to pet him.

Raiku gently licked my cheek, his entire body wiggling with excitement. He pawed at me and I threw my arms around his neck, sobs erupting from my mouth. "Oh, I have missed you. I have missed you so much."

Raiku tapped his front paws on the ground, as though dancing from his joy. I kissed the top of his head no less than a thousand times before we were satisfied. I went and sat in the chaise lounge and beckoned Raiku to sit with me. He eagerly leapt onto the space beside me, a soft sun-shaped plush toy in his mouth.

I gently stroked his fur and felt myself glowing. "How did you get him into the dreams? I thought it was tied just between you and me? Is he actually here?"

Eldrin chuckled softly. "Ah, it took a bit more magic, but I must say, his fur is constantly everywhere. I realized your clothing and bag likely had his fur stuck to it and so I was able to use some here and tether it to you."

"I had no idea it would work like that!" I stated, once again kissing the top of Raiku's head.

"Truthfully, neither did I," Eldrin admitted. "But I felt you needed something bright, and Raiku has honestly been driving all of us mad."

I grinned sheepishly. "Oh, he has?"

"Yes. He cries all night and wanders around the house, sighing and letting out whines. He misses you." Eldrin sounded exasperated, but I could sense a hint of empathy in his voice. He stood, leaning his hand on the back of a chair.

I raised my eyebrows and looked down at Raiku. "Oh, my dear puppy, you don't have to cry. I will be home soon enough!" He wagged his fluffy tail a bit, just happy to be with me. I looked up at Eldrin. "How are things there?"

He cleared his throat. "Stable. Some of the other High Mages were able to calm down Magister Vaerith, and for now, he is only handling simple matters."

I nodded, idly stroking Raiku's fur. "That is good to hear." I paused for a moment. "Raewyn and I bathed naked in a stream today."

Eldrin stumbled a bit, nearly knocking over the chair. "In the mountains? Weren't you freezing?"

"Yes! But honestly, it was exhilarating. Raewyn brought soap, so we were actually able to get warm and clean." My body was vibrating with delight.

"Of course she did." She smiled and shook his head. "As long as you both are safe and happy. I just can't imagine that would be comfortable coming out of the water? You warmed it, I assume?"

"I did! It bubbled and all." I was beaming. For the moment, I could pretend I wasn't actually freezing in the middle of the mountains far away from my love and my furry companion.

Eldrin stroked my cheek and planted a kiss on my forehead. "Well, then I suppose I should just be pleased for you."

I nodded, grinning up at him. "Yes, you should."

The air suddenly turned sharp, wrapping cold air around me like a thick blanket. There was an unsettling stillness, broken only by the distant cries of large hawks above. The abandoned settlement before us stood as a haunting graveyard of the once abundant town. Weathered wood cabins stood, their tin roofs sagging with weight from years of snow and ice. The broken windows stared out eerily like hollow eyes. A few wooden cabins were partially destroyed by fire and others had only the stone foundation remaining.

The silence was palpable as our horses' hooves sounded against the cobblestone path. It was cracked and uneven and filled with wild weeds that reached out like skeletal hands. Vines took over a broken stone fountain of a ram in the heart of the town. I tilted my head upon seeing it.

"A ram?" I queried in a hushed tone. "You don't think this once belonged to the House of the Mountain?"

Raewyn halted Nimara, glancing around her. "Perhaps it was here before they had settled in Evercrest? I know my people wandered our island for quite some time before settling in what is now Vespera."

The sound of my boots hitting the stone seemed to reverberate off the mountains around us. Our horses eyes were wide, their ears raised and their breathing rapid, creating small clouds of fog before them. I gently stroked Lumina's cheek and whispered soft words of encouragement to her. I was not convinced by my own words, that nervous pit growing heavier and heavier. I walked over to a nearby cabin and gently pushed the wooden door open.

Dim sunlight cast faint shadows on the wooden floor of the cabin. This one was nearly untouched by the dragon, it seemed, though looters must have ransacked it over the years. Broken mirrors lay fragmented on the dusty floor and clay pots were knocked over, inedible food spilling out. The air grew colder as I stepped into the room, with Raewyn a few steps behind.

To my left was a black iron stove, and upon inspection, I saw it still had old, half-charred firewood in it. I gently placed my hand on the wood, causing it to emit a soft golden glow until sparking into a low fire. I closed the door on the stove and rubbed my hands together.

"At least we can have heat," I stated. I still could not shake the discomfort I felt.

Raewyn nodded solemnly. "The horses found some old water troughs filled, presumably from melted snow."

I pressed my lips tightly and looked around. There was a single bed, fortunately wide enough for two. I turned to see Raewyn brushing dust and debris off a small kitchen table near the stove. She placed her leather pack on its surface and pulled out some dried fish and figs. She set them on top of her leather pack and took a few figs for herself. I sighed heavily, having already grown tired of dried food, and took a few strips of the fish. It was overly salty, but it was sustainable.

We ate our meager meal and drank from our waterskins until the sun finally disappeared, leaving only the orange glow of the fire as our light. I ventured out once to check on the horses and to grab more firewood before we retired to the bed for the evening.

Chapter Twelve

The smell of damp smoke wafted into my nose. My eyes flashed opened to see flames engulfing the roof of the cabin. I sat up straight and looked at Raewyn, who was sound asleep. I shook her violently and she bolted to her feet, seeing what was before us. Outside of the cabin, I heard our horses screeching in fear. And another unholy sound. It was an otherworldly, high-pitched note that was right outside our door. I scrambled to my feet, grabbing our provisions and bags, and raced outside.

Our horses were running in circles and most of the cabins were on fire. *What the fuck?* I mentally questioned. A giant splash of water sounded behind me and I turned to see Raewyn forming massive water bubbles to try and douse the flames. They kept reigniting somehow. I turned towards the fountain and noticed it looked... off.

I ran the short distance towards it, throwing a hand forward, a ball of light escaping my palm. It crashed into something and illuminated the entire mountain pass in a gold light for a brief moment. And then I saw it.

A terrifying silhouette drifted above the ground, its form an unnatural patch of darkness. It hovered with an unnerving stillness, its limbs suspended by an unseen force, which made my skin prickle. Blackened bones twisted and coiled like charred branches, each bone fractured in places as though it had once been something far more solid—something that belonged to the living. It exuded a strong, putrid scent, like old, rotting flesh that had long since passed beyond the point of decay. I recalled the smell from the town's barns when they would find a dead animal.

My eyes widened as I took in the entirety of this... thing. Its ribs were sharp and jagged, and protruded outward. They creaked with every movement, a soft, ominous grinding sound echoing throughout the valley as it floated. The bones seemed to absorb all light, drawing all of my glow into their hollow depths, and the air around it thickened with a suffocating aura of decay and despair.

I looked at its face, searching for eyes. But I was met with only deep, empty hollow caverns. A malevolent glow radiated from within them, pulsing with an eerie, otherworldly light. A faint mist of darkness escaped its mouth, swirling and twisting around its jagged teeth, which were sharp enough to tear through Raewyn's steel spear. As it drifted forward, its form exhaled a soundless howl, bending the air in ways that made the ground tremble beneath its presence. I took a step back and glanced at my friend, who had gone pale.

Its movements were slow and deliberate, each gesture a grotesque imitation of life, as if the creature's very being was held together by nothing more than will and pure malevolence. The ground beneath it seemed to warp in its wake, darkening, withering as if the creature drained the life from everything it touched. The air grew even colder, the shadows lengthening unnaturally, as though it was both part of the night and something worse—something older.

In that moment, it was as though time itself had stopped, held captive by the floating, blackened, skeletal horror before me. And in that stillness, I could feel it begin to siphon my powers into its darkness.

A primal roar burst out of my mouth, scorching my throat with the ferocity. I pushed my wrists together and formed a large, golden ball of light in my hands before thrusting it towards it, causing it to fade briefly in its pain. I glanced over at Raewyn, who was holding her spear in her right hand. Her face was illuminated by the fires on the building, and there was nothing but rage on my friend's face. I watched in awe as she greatly flapped her massive wingspan open and lifted her body several inches off the ground. I turned back towards the creature.

"You do not belong here," the figure said, its whispering voice echoing all around me. "You must leave."

"We are trying to, you floating asshole!" Raewyn's raw voice carried in the wind. She threw her hand out, an aggressive stream of water shooting out of her palm and into the eyes of the creature.

He startled backwards at the impact, water droplets joining the shadows and wind around his skeletal form. "You cannot destroy me. I am Kha'laroth. I protect this valley." He threw a boney arm out towards me.

My vision was suddenly shrouded and I was staring into a black void. I squeezed my eyes shut and knelt down until I felt the broken cobblestone beneath my fingertips. I exhaled and pushed my palms together, focused, and then pulled them apart rapidly, revealing an orb of light. I slowly pulled them out further, increasing the size of the orb. Once I felt it was the width of my body, I shoved it forward, breaking the darkness around me. I opened my eyes wide to see the orb had crashed into Kha'laroth and combined with the water from Raewyn, creating steam.

Kha'laroth wheezed, obviously affected. I looked at Raewyn and we nodded at each other. Simultaneously, we formed our light and our water and pushed it towards him. They met near his face and combined into boiling water, and then steam. He shook his head and made a noise, the lightning in his eyes flashing.

"You cannot banish me, for my darkness is eternal."

It sounded as though he were laughing, which angered me even more. "You are wrong. Light will always pierce the darkness." I extended my arms out to either side, my fingertips stretched outward. I called to the light emitting from the flames around me and formed them into ropes towards me. With multiple tethers, I threw my hands forward. He screeched, his bones rattling in horror, as he recoiled.

I swiftly jumped to the side towards Raewyn as he flicked his boney wrist, shadowy tendrils shooting out. Raewyn reached out her hand towards him and began twisting the air around her, forming streams of water that danced and spun midair. She commanded them forward, crashing towards him like a wave in the sea.

Water splashed over his form, creating an icy frost over his bones. His shadows retreated and his body tried to wriggle free from the icy grip. The wraith freed himself and raised its skeletal hands. The air around him trembled as the shadows reached out and embraced my neck. My breathing became labored as their grip tightened. I felt my muscles growing heavy and the cold was creeping into my bones. Forcing my eyes open, they flashed a bright white light, causing the shadows to retreat.

"The darkest shadow is formed by the brightest light," he whispered, seemingly unaffected by my defenses. I stared at him for a very brief moment, my hand rubbing my neck.

Raewyn quickly grasped my hand and stared intensely into my eyes, raising her free hand. I quickly understood and raised my other hand as well, my fingers reaching towards the sky. Above our heads, a sphere of radiant water shimmered before we hurled it towards his chest. The sphere crashed into him, and for a moment, everything went silent. Suddenly, his bones shattered into millions of glowing shards. Raewyn and I lowered our bodies and covered our faces to avoid the shrapnel as bones, dust, and mist covered the area.

I slumped to the ground, my back resting on the hard stone. I closed my eyes and rested my hands over my chest, willing my racing heart to calm.

I inhaled and exhaled deeply a few breaths before rolling my neck over to Raewyn. She was lying next to me, her beautiful face covered in dust.

"I think I need to change my pants," she said lightly.

A hearty laugh erupted from me as I stared up into the stars. "I don't doubt the same for myself."

I pushed myself off the ground and looked around the pass. The flames had mostly died down and we were nearing darkness. With shaking hands, I sent out a small light orb and had it rest in the fountain, illuminating the town more. I glanced around, searching for our horses. When I did not see them, I clicked my tongue a few times. My pointed ears twitched, expecting the sound of hooves that never came.

Raewyn stood next to me, gripping her spear and brushing grass off her clothes. "I think we lost them. I am hoping they return to Evercrest." She looked back over her shoulder at the house we had slept in. "All we have left are the things we took inside. I don't expect our journey to ease up from here, and our food is lessening."

I split the light orb into two and sent one to follow Raewyn. The house fires had completely died, leaving the mountain pass in darkness, were it not for the light magic. Raewyn padded off into a wooden house on one side of the fountain, and I turned towards the other side.

I entered a house whose door had long since disappeared, whether it was a victim in the original battle with the dragon, or simply from the elements. I glanced around the room, only slightly startled by the foreign shadows cast on the walls. I opened several small clay canisters to find preserved herbs, as though it were waiting to be used. I lifted it to my nose and gently sniffed. *Farrowfew,* I thought. It was an herb meant to numb and help heal a burn wound. I took the small clay pot and shoved it in my bag.

I glanced around, looking for anything else of interest. There was a leatherbound journal covered in dust and soot sitting on a small table by the bed. I went and picked it up and opened it.

> I don't know what more to do. The Guardian Spirit has been getting more restless with each pass of the red dragon overhead. Endil is not worried, but I certainly am. Something feels amiss, yet I cannot leave my children nor take them with me. The leader assures us all is well, but I do not trust it. The dragon flies lower every week and the Guardian is becoming restless. I shouldn't be questioning the leader, but I regret ever coming here. I want to go home. I feel uneasy. Something is amiss.
>
> - T. Farlong

Farlong, I thought, *is the surname of the leaders of the Woods.* I stared at the writing for a moment before shoving the journal in my pack. I would have to revisit that when I returned home.

I checked the rest of the houses, finding various herbs, some sealed dried meat, and even a jar of sweet honey. It seemed most of the houses had been previously ransacked, leaving the bare minimum. I met with Raewyn near the fountain again, the sun slowly peeking over the mountains.

"I found mostly medicinal herbs, bandages, and this." Raewyn held up a dark amber bottle and let me sniff it.

I jolted back at the potent smell. "Oh, that whiskey has been sitting here." Raewyn grinned and put the cork back in before putting it in her pack.

We turned and looked at the mountains ahead of us, the silence spreading between us. "Well, friend, I suppose we'll take this on foot," I stated grimly.

CHAPTER THIRTEEN

The scent of old parchment and dust motes danced in the single shaft of moonlight filtering through the grimy windowpane as I stumbled into Eldrin's study. My heart hammered against my ribs, a frantic drumbeat against the serenity of this familiar space. I could not sleep and was in desperate need of my love. And a release.

I reached out, my hand passing over the surface of his oak desk. Where was he? Frustration gnawed at me. I yearned to touch him, to feel the rough texture of his beard against my cheek, to bury my face in the comforting warmth of his neck.

"Idrial, are you all right?" his voice, a low rumble that vibrated through me, sent shivers down my spine. He materialized beside me, his form shimmering into existence like heat haze.

I nodded. "Later," is all I said.

His eyes were intense and held mine captive. "My love," he breathed, his voice thick with longing, as though he knew exactly why I came. He reached for me, his fingers brushing against my arm, sending a jolt of pure electricity through me.

I stepped closer, my body aching for his touch. "Eldrin," I whispered, my voice hoarse with unshed tears.

He pulled me close, his arms encircling me, not like a protective cage, but more like a brand, possessive and urgent. I melted into him, the hardness of his chest a welcome anchor against the swirling emotions that threatened to consume me. I needed this.

His lips found mine, a searing kiss that ignited a fire within me. It wasn't gentle; it was demanding, a claiming. I clung to him, my hands tangled in his hair, desperate to lose myself in the sensation of his mouth on mine.

He tasted of plum liquor and spices, a familiar blend that sent my senses reeling. His hands roamed over my body, tracing the curves of my hips, exploring the sensitive skin of my neck with a bruising pressure.

I arched into him, my body craving the intimacy of his touch. He groaned, his hands tightening on my waist, pulling me closer until I could feel the hard ridge of his desire pressing against me.

"Gods, Idrial," he muttered against my lips, his breath hot and ragged. "You must miss me."

I traced the line of his jaw with my fingertips, my heart pounding a frantic rhythm against my ribs. "I need you," I whispered back, my voice trembling with anticipation.

He leaned in, his lips brushing against mine. "I need you," he growled, his voice a low, seductive purr, laced with a hint of something darker, more primal.

I nodded, my body trembling with anticipation. He turned me, my back to him, his hands sliding beneath my white tunic, not gently, but with a controlled urgency, exploring the silken flesh beneath. I gasped, arching against him, desperate for his touch. He found the silken cord around my waist, his fingers deftly undoing the intricate knot, the fabric falling away to reveal my bare skin.

My breath hitched as his hands cupped my breasts from behind, his thumbs swirling around my nipples with a deliberate roughness that sent shivers of pleasure and a touch of pain down my spine. I moaned, lowering my head, my body trembling with a need I couldn't deny.

He chuckled, a low, throaty sound, his hands moving lower, exploring the curve of my spine, the swell of my hips, his fingers dipping beneath the waistband of my breeches. I gasped, my nails digging into his shoulders as he found the silken folds of my undergarment.

"Eldrin," I whispered, my voice barely a breath, "please."

He understood, his eyes darkening with desire, but also with a hint of something wild, untamed. With a swift, decisive movement, he slipped the silken fabric from my legs, his gaze burning into me, claiming me.

I felt his eyes on me, burning into my very soul. I closed my eyes, savoring the sensation of his gaze, the anticipation building to an unbearable crescendo.

He leaned down, his lips trailing a fiery path down my neck, sending shivers of ecstasy and a delicious ache through me. I arched into him, my body pleading for release.

He reached for me, his hands finding the curve of my hip, guiding me closer. And with a slow, deliberate pressure, he slipped inside, completely filling me.

I cried out, a gasp that was part pleasure, part a sharp intake of breath. My body arched against his, the sensation of him inside me a symphony of pleasure and a thrilling sense of vulnerability. He moved slowly at first, his movements deliberate, savoring every inch of my response, but there was an underlying urgency, a barely contained force.

I leaned forward over the desk, my palms flat as he moved deeper, filling me completely. He groaned, his head buried in my hair, his movements growing stronger, faster, more insistent.

We reached the precipice together, our bodies trembling in unison, a wave of pure ecstasy, tinged with a delicious sense of surrender, washing over us. We cried out, our bodies convulsing as we reached our peak, lost in the blissful oblivion of shared pleasure.

He collapsed against me, his breath ragged, his body still trembling from the aftermath. I turned around and held him close, my arms wrapped tightly around him, savoring the lingering warmth of his skin against mine, the weight of him a comforting pressure.

"I love you," I whispered, my voice hoarse with passion.

"You have my love." He gently kissed my cheek.

He stepped away for a few moments while we tidied ourselves. He coughed slightly. "I assume you didn't come here just for that? Not that I am complaining, though I was not expecting you tonight."

I heaved out a sigh and sunk into the chair at his desk. I cradled my forehead in my hands. Now that I had extinguished my internal tension, we had to discuss what happened in the valley.

"Raewyn and I encountered a being I had never heard of before." I idly opened a book at his desk, not making eye-contact. "It was in a small, abandoned town in Paldor Pass, and was a terrifying being." I described the being we fought.

"You fought Kah'Laroth?" Eldrin's violet eyes were wide, pride peppering his voice.

"We did. He is gone from the pass, it would seem." I touched his arm. "Our horses ran away scared."

He lowered himself to the chair next to me. "Yes! They arrived at Evercrest last night! I received word from Thalira this morning."

A smile grew on my lips. "I had hoped they would. I am glad they are being cared for."

A sudden golden light shone through the window, casting a haze through the air. I could feel the warm sun on my skin. I had missed the feeling and intentionally sat in the path of a sunbeam. I had a feeling Eldrin had created that specifically for me.

"*How did you fight him?*" Eldrin gently stroked my arm.

"*We, uh, exploded him. Raewyn and I combined our powers.*"

"*You exploded him? With water and light?*" Eldrin drilled.

"*We did! I was honestly surprised it worked.*"

Eldrin pulled a thin, yellowed book from a stack and opened it. He thumbed through the pages for a moment before looking up at me. "*He was a Warden of the Pass, their guardian spirit. He was there to protect the town from any evil and to keep their land bountiful. He was an emissary of sorts from the first Sun Beam. She sent several throughout Therrathis to keep different regions safe.*"

I settled back in my chair, my face softening. "*So, what happened to the town? Why was he so evil?*"

Eldrin raised his eyebrows and looked up at me from the text. "*I would not call him evil so much as grieving.*"

"*Grieving what?*"

"*For centuries, he was tasked with caring for these people. He saw generations of the same families come and go. He was a part of every second of their history.*" *Eldrin lifted the book, showing a large green dragon breathing fire upon a village.* "*Until one of the Great Dragons somehow got in and completely obliterated the town. It does not say how the dragon made it into the valley. But I would imagine what you saw was the manifestation of grief.*"

I stared at the hand-drawn image on the page, the homes looking similar. Who had drawn this, I wondered. "*Why would he destroy anyone who comes to the Pass? We meant no harm.*"

His eyes softened as he took my hand into his. "*Some people show grief in silence, and others show grief in chaos and rage. Neither are wrong.*"

"*Perhaps, but one hurts other people.*"

He sighed softly. "Indeed. But I cannot personally fathom what Kha'Laroth experienced. It is not up to me to judge how he processes it. So, what can we learn from this?"

My chair creaked as I sat upright. He was always wanting to find a lesson. "I can accept something without understanding it."

He nodded and closed the book. "I do not believe you killed him, but perhaps banished him for some time. He may return to his village, or he may be gone forever. I do not fully comprehend how their life cycles work." His eyes glittered as he stared at me. "But I do know one thing."

"What's that?" I stared at him directly.

"You and Raewyn are incredible beings. To take down something like that with little training?" He squeezed my hand.

A grin spread across my face. "Thank you for noticing."

"Until next time, my sunbeam." He kissed my hand as I faded to waking.

The days passed slowly and were dreadfully repetitive. The air grew colder and snow began falling from the sky in large clumps. Every few evenings, I used the heat of my own sun to warm our bodies and melt the snow for water. Our food had run out after the first week since the encounter at the abandoned town.

The mountains were an unforgiving, still beast. It was constantly too bright, too quiet, and too cold. There was no sun, but we found ourselves squinting our eyes to see. As we climbed higher, we had to take periodic breaks to rest and adjust to the height. My ears kept getting muffled and I had to constantly work to break the uncomfortable feeling. Raewyn kept getting snow in her boots and her wings could no longer open without strain against the cold. We were both highly uncomfortable, not to mention the empty feelings in our bellies, and our attitudes were feeling it. After a few times of bickering, we decided it was best if we didn't speak. We just focused our attention on each step towards our destination.

The snow crunched under my feet as I moved down a slight slope. I looked up and gasped. Raewyn halted abruptly behind me and followed my gaze. We had reached Calenveil Cave.

I stared at the wide, open-mouthed cavern, a soft blue light emitting from it. I thought I could almost hear distant hollow bells coming from inside, but shook it from my head as we pushed forward.

The cave was dimly lit with no light source in view. The hall we walked down was just large enough for both of us to walk comfortably side by side. The walls were roughly reflective surfaces, which at first was startling before we realized it was our own selves we gazed upon. There was a constant feeling of being watched, though no eyes could be seen. I kept my voice low as I spoke.

"Eldrin explained what he knew of this place." She looked at me as I spoke, her face grim. "He said to refer to them only as They or Them. They hold the knowledge of what has happened, what is currently happening, and what is to come. They exist in complete neutrality."

Raewyn pressed her chapped lips together and nodded solemnly. "My mother would not let me come into this cave when we were last here. She wanted to speak to them alone. But still, it evokes hard memories."

I stretched my frozen lips into a semblance of a smile and grabbed her gloved hand, squeezing it tight. "I cannot thank you enough for coming with me."

She squeezed back. "I would never let you endure this alone."

We looked before us, where large ornate stone doors stood, seemingly embedded in walls of thick ice. I placed my palm on the door, a soft golden light pouring into the crevices of the door's design. Eldrin had warned me about a door that would need a taste of magic to enter. I took a step back and drank in the images before me.

Carved into the grey stone were fantastic depictions of all the Houses' crests: a crab, a lion, a ram, a fox, a horse, and an owl. I stared at the owl, who had a large wingspan in the dead center of the doors right next to the lion. The lion was the Sun crest, but I did not recognize the owl. Maybe the House of the Moon? Before I could think much further, the doors gently opened.

My senses were filled with a marine, metallic smell as the wind swept around us. My eyes stared at the long path ahead. Stretching before us lay a snowy bridge across the mouth of a vast, echoing cavern. The edges of the bridge were etched with intricate carvings that shimmered faintly. The ceiling above us seemed to shift into deep shades of midnight blues and indigos, swirling like a cosmic river. The stars pulsed in slow, rhythmic patterns, which cast an ethereal glow across the snow-dusted bridge. I looked down on either side of the bridge to see a river of silver mist that wound its way through the cavern floor and disappeared into shadows unseen. The air hummed with ancient power and I could feel that I was about to step onto a sacred pathway.

As my steps gently crunched against the hardened snow, a sense of peace overwhelmed me. In the distance, the sounds of violins and harps were playing the song of my house. I felt my face relax for the first time in weeks, and a satisfied sigh escaped my chapped lips. As I kept moving forward, I found my eyes drifting closed, feeling lulled into security by something unknown. Time felt nonexistent and I could no longer feel where my place on earth was. My skin prickled and I felt as though my body were being absorbed. I was in the middle of time and space and oceans. I floated in between anything that made sense. All sense of self was suspended and my physical being no longer existed.

The music swelled the further I went into the depths of In Between. I became seduced by the patterns of swirling colours in my mind's eyes of yellows and whites and pinks. My chest became full of love and hope and all that I wanted in life. A great smile spread widely across my lips and I felt my purpose restored once again. I remembered myself, my history, and my own body. Visions of my past floated through my mind, and some that I didn't recognize. I was lost in my own thoughts as the toe of my boot hit something hard. I fluttered my eyes open to see I had come to a massive, icy archway leading into an expansive room.

I looked over at Raewyn to see she had also felt some sort of transformation. Her body language showed restored confidence and purpose. As we passed through, I gently touched a finger to the archway, feeling the smooth, cool texture beneath my fingers.

The grand hall stretched infinitely, the walls and ceiling shimmering with the same ethereal, blue glow present in the halls. The air was crisp and comforting as the gentle winds seemed to echo within the cavernous room, a faint melodic hum present throughout. Columns of thick, translucent ice formed from the floor, each adorned with the same carvings alongside the bridge.

At the far end of the room there was a towering throne, sculpted from a single block of ice. Its edges had delicate Frostflowers that bloomed and faded with the melody. Its back formed an arch, containing the animals of each house, and the owl. The light from the high ceiling reflected against the throne, casting subtle rainbows throughout.

Seated upon the throne was the most ethereal being I had ever laid eyes on, neither male nor female, but a radiant presence that seemed to transcend all forms. Their body shimmered with a soft silver glow. Their features were impossibly beautiful, angular yet soft, with eyes that glowed like twin stars. Their hair flowed like liquid crystal, shifting through hues of ice and mist and cascaded down their back in soft tendrils.

A perfect stillness radiated from them, as well as an undeniable ancient power. Their gaze seemed to pierce through all aspects of reality, both inviting and daunting. We cautiously approached the throne.

"Welcome, Children of the World," a crystalline voice carried out.

I was unsure of the customs from here, so I lowered my body in a curtsy. Raewyn followed suit. "We thank you for your time."

A calm, otherworldly laugh rang out. "I am time." The Oracle uncrossed their legs, their gossamer fabric flowing to their naked feet. Every bit of their skin shimmered, like a light frost in the sun. "And I know why you come."

I pressed my lips together and exhaled, my breath lightly visible in a cloud before me. "Then you know who took the Sun Stone."

"I know what has, what is, and what is possible." The Oracle's words flowed.

I narrowed my eyes in slight confusion. "What is possible? Not what is inevitable?"

"To deal with mortals is to walk a path unmarked by fate. There are countless roads that may unfold, yet within these many ways, but a handful lead to the end you seek." The Oracle lifted their chin slightly with authority.

I pondered that for a moment. What did I seek? To find the Sun Stone, of course. "You speak as though I desire more than just this simple knowledge."

A knowing smile spread across their face. "Your kind ever hungers for more than mere knowledge. However, you have yet to discover what truly lies beyond your thirst."

I looked over at Raewyn, who stared down at her feet. This was a conversation I needed to have on my own. I exhaled slightly.

"Can you tell me what I need to know, then? To find the stone?"

The Oracle leaned back in the throne and seemed to ponder this question for a moment. "The Stone you seek bears a history shrouded in shadow, one you must first uncover. Yet, you are not yet ready to hear its tale. Before the path is clear, you must bear the burden of your ancestors' folly. The Stone shall not be given to you lightly, and you shall walk a solitary road for many moons. When the truth is laid bare before you, then, and only then, may your journey westward begin."

I blinked several times. "Westward? No, Calenor is South of here."

"Your journey forward is not." The Oracle turned to Raewyn, whose attention snapped up. "You must let go. Idrial's path forward is not yours. Trust yourself."

Raewyn glanced over at me, her eyes widened. "I will never leave her side."

The Oracle glanced past us. "You do not get to decide your fate."

My mouth hung partly open for a moment, not knowing what to make of that. I wet my lips and spoke again. "Where do we go next, if not south?"

"You must first awaken fully to your power, then you can press onward, but not without aid." The Oracle stared at me, the next words clearly only in my mind. *The fall you will face is not of the body but of the mind, the soul. The realm you grasp will crumble, and the sky you soar through will tear open, revealing the ruins of a forgotten truth.*

Then, without warning, the world tilted. The walls seemed to bend, to warp around me. The floor beneath my feet cracked with a deafening roar, splitting apart as the entire palace began to crumble. A sudden weightlessness surged, and I gasped, reaching out for something solid, but found nothing. The ground was gone, the palace shattering and spinning in a dizzying blur. I felt myself falling—no, *plummeting*—into nothingness.

But the fall didn't last long. I blinked, disoriented, and the next thing I knew, I was standing on the edge of a vast, floating island, high above a world I could barely comprehend. The sky stretched endlessly above and below me, a swirling expanse of blue and violet, dotted with clouds that seemed to ripple like ink. The ground beneath my feet became hard grass and ruined bricks. I glanced up and saw the Sun Stone glowing on top of a ruined building. I reached my hand out and walked forward.

A sudden, powerful force tugged at me, and before I could even react, a low, thunderous sound ripped through the air, one that was all too familiar. And then I was in the air, soaring high above the island's jagged cliffs, the wind howling around me as I clung to the back of a massive gryphon. It was Index! The blind Gryphon who guarded the library. His gold and blue wings beat with a rhythm that shook the sky itself, and I gripped his feathers tightly, the sensation of flight both exhilarating and terrifying. His violet moon eyes blazed ahead, unblinking, while its powerful talons dug into the air, carving through the space like a living storm.

But the sudden peace of the flight was short-lived.

The wind suddenly shifted, and I felt the gryphon's wings falter. The world around me blurred once more, the colors melting into a sandy, heat-heavy fog. The gryphon's roar vanished, and I found myself crashing into the ground, the rough heat of a desert beneath my body. The air was dry, the ground cracked and crumbling beneath me, littered with the remains of ancient, broken stone structures. The ruins sprawled out in every direction, as if this land had once been grand, but now it was abandoned, forgotten by time. I looked up to see several shadowy figures in the distance.

A strange stillness overtook me. The wind no longer howled; it was as if the very desert held its breath.

But that silence was shattered—shifting again, moving faster than thought—until I was back in the ice palace, standing in the middle of its frozen, crystal halls. But something was *off*. Something was wrong. The ice reflected back my image, but—*no*, not just my image. There were hundreds of them, stretching as far as the eye could see. Dozens of me—no, *more*—clones of myself in frozen poses, each caught in a moment, each trapped in time. The only sound was my ragged breath and the pounding of my heart.

I staggered backward, my breath freezing in the air as the reflections shifted, twisted, their eyes moving with me, following my every step, their expressions distorting as though they were alive— more than alive. They were *watching* me, all of them, their faces mirrors to my own fears. I could feel the weight of their gaze like a thousand hands reaching for me, pulling me in. But I wasn't afraid. Instead, I felt comfortable.

"You will see yourself as you truly are, reflected in a thousand shattered pieces. Only then will you understand the price of knowledge—and the cost of your choice." The sound of The Oracle's voice penetrated my thoughts.

I suddenly felt my stomach lurch forward as my body was abruptly lifted by some invisible force and I soon blacked out.

Chapter Fourteen

My eyes fluttered open to a stark white environment. We were outside again, right next to the cave. The snow was gently falling in a blanket around us and the world felt more peaceful rather than violent. There was a small fire glowing nearby with some sort of bird already seasoned and cooked waiting for us. I looked over at Raewyn, who was brushing snow off her pants as she stood. Her vast wings shuddered. She was clearly a little off-kilter until she saw the food cooking.

"Is this some sort of trick?" she queried.

I shrugged. "I don't believe so. Maybe a gift from the Oracle."

She scoffed. "Or maybe a sad apology for telling us absolutely nothing and then tossing us out in the snow."

I pressed my lips. I wondered if Raewyn had a similar, strange experience as I did. She seemed flustered, and I wondered what she had seen. I mindlessly picked at my fingertips and stared into the fire. I needed to mentally sort through what happened, but the sound of my stomach was louder than anything.

"Ah, well, it appears more is laid out before us. And with how empty our bellies are, I will not decline this!" Approaching the firepit, there was a white leather pouch nearby.

I opened it and peered inside. There were two vials of clear liquid, one labeled Fly and the other labeled Sunborn. "This tells us nothing," I said, passing them to Raewyn. I continued to look inside and pulled out some bread, a decent amount of dried fruit, and a small crystal spyglass. I held the cold, silver metal in my hand, rubbing my thumb over the etched runes. I noted that they resembled the runes all along the cavern. I put the contents back in the pouch, other than the vial labeled 'Fly', and handed it to Raewyn.

"I don't know if this is literal, but perhaps you should carry it. Since we are to be separated and all, evidently." I heaved a sigh.

Raewyn nodded and placed it in the grey leather pouch around her waist. She sat on a boulder near the fire and pulled the leg off the meat. "I don't know what to think of that visit, if I am being honest."

I joined her and took a leg for myself. I bit into it, savoring the warmth and decadent spices that filled my body. I could make out sage and lemon, and I had never before been so grateful for hot food. "I really do not know where to go from here. It seems we cannot go back to Calenor."

Raewyn nodded, hot juices flowing down her chin. She wiped it with the sleeve of her shirt. "I do not want to be the one to go back and say 'we went on our big journey and came back with absolutely nothing. Oh, we now go west somewhere, and also, we have to be separated?'"

I rubbed the bridge of my nose with my fingers. "What is west? I mean, furthest west?" I squinted, trying to recall the maps on the walls in the library.

Raewyn scrunched her nose, a snowflake landing on it. "The desert, some volcano I don't know much of... Nyxara." Her voice slowed.

I straightened. "I can't imagine we would have to go there." I paused for a moment. "Unless they mean that Lord Varyx stole the stone? The House of the Moon rarely becomes involved in anything outside of their own realm." I tried to ignore her mention of the desert, feeling a tug at its mention.

Raewyn placed her chicken remnants in the snow, unsure of how to dispose of it. "I will admit that had been a thought when you first presented it at the council." She cleared her throat and took a hearty swig from her waterskin. "The other leaders had suggested it before you entered. But we know how it is a delicate topic."

I nodded solemnly. "Indeed, that history is a bit muddled." I sighed softly, running my fingers over the amulet on my chest. I hoped Eldrin could untangle some of the Oracle's words.

He paced around the room, his hands clasped behind his head. "And they didn't say anything more specific than west?"

I sighed, exasperatedly picking at lint on the arm of the chair I had sunk into. I had spent the last hour explaining the entire conversation, and Eldrin kept picking it apart. I was almost regretting tapping into the amulet. A peaceful night's sleep may have been a better choice.

"The Oracle did not, as I've already said." I impatiently tapped my nails onto the arm of the chair, the bite evident in my voice.

His step faltered and he looked at me, his gaze softening. "My love, I do not mean to exhaust you. I only seek answers." He gently stroked my cheek with the back of his hand. "Can you tell me what they said, right before you were transported out?"

"You will see yourself as you truly are, reflected in a thousand shattered pieces. Only then will you understand the price of knowledge—and the cost of your choice," I quoted. I had replayed that over and over again in my head. I didn't tell Raewyn as I felt I needed to work it out some in my own mind.

Eldrin had sort of pulled it out of me. I never liked keeping things from him so it wasn't hard to do.

"Reflected in a thousand shattered pieces..." Eldrin muttered. He narrowed his violet eyes in thought, rubbing his mouth. "The cost of your choice is what I am curious about."

"Yes, what choice?" The question had plagued my mind.

I rubbed my pale blue eyes, the yellow sunburst having faded slightly. "And who am I truly? Do they refer to my family? My ancestors?" I paused for a moment. "What is the history of the Sun Stone? Is there something we do not know?"

He shook his head. "That is one thing your instructors were thorough on, teaching you of its origins." He turned towards a window, the light beaming through as though it were mid-afternoon. "The first drop of light fell from the sky and landed delicately onto the earth. The light took the form of a woman, Eledrinna, and from this, she formed what we know as Therrathis. The Sun Stone provides energy and life to all the other stones, keeping our lands prosperous and vibrant." He recited an old text I was well familiar with.

I cycled the history lessons more thoroughly through my head as though I could uncover some new meaning. A thought jumped into my head. "What of the House of the Moon?"

Eldrin snapped his head towards me, his voice shocked. "Why do you ask?"

I was startled at his reaction. "Why is there never any mention of the House of the Moon? When was their Moon Stone created? And what is their crest? Even the Summit Song does not mention their stone."

Eldrin looked vastly uncomfortable. "Ah, we do not have that knowledge anymore. Their destruction was ordered by centuries' past scholars. They ordered Index to take that information and dispose of it." He paused for a moment. "They have an owl."

I squinted my eyes. I knew Index and the other gryphons valued knowledge above all else. He could often be seen napping on the observatory tower or flying around the shoreline, catching fish that jumped out of the water. I could not imagine him taking sacred texts, containing what I would imagine is important history, and discarding them somewhere.

"Isn't all history important?"

Eldrin sighed and lowered himself next to me. He grabbed my hand and looked around before speaking in a hushed tone. "Listen, I don't believe he actually destroyed it. There are several scholars who believe they were hiding something." He straightened and spoke in a normal tone. "I can gather any information regarding that House."

I nodded and understood he was no longer alone. "So which direction do we go? I could not bear to face the leaders empty-handed."

He moved over to the table and looked at the map. "I personally would feel more comfortable if you could leave the snowy mountains, so I would recommend getting to the waterfall. You can take a boat there to Briarhollow, where Fiora will be glad to see you."

I smiled warmly at him. "I think you do love me."

He returned the smile. "If I were to lose you, it would be as though the sun left the sky. The world would fade to darkness and every step I took would be in a cold shadow." He pressed his forehead to mine.

"Then I suppose I must never leave this earth without you."

He lifted my chin and gently kissed my lips. "I will hold you to that, my sunbeam."

Chapter Fifteen

The next few days were spent in a cycle of walking, eating, sleeping, and picking apart the Oracle's words. We were fortunate that the only active weathering was soft, fluffy snowflakes drifting down every so often. Raewyn had to remove the water coating over her body as her wings kept stiffening from the ice sheet over them. She had attempted to coat my body in the same shield, only to find the Sun from within me prevented the water from freezing. It left me soggy the first time, which was not ideal in a snowy mountain pass. I was becoming aggravated again.

A dramatic sigh heaved out of my mouth, creating a plume of air. "I don't even know what we are doing at this point. We have no direction."

Raewyn glanced over at me, carefully stepping over some loose rocks littering our path. "Eldrin said to head to the Briarhollow; the House of Meadow."

"Yes, but for what purpose?"

My friend was quiet for a moment, choosing her words carefully. "Perhaps they will have more guidance than we realize?"

I stopped abruptly and turned to her. "What about? What could they possibly know?" My tone was more aggressive than I intended, and I winced.

"Therrathis history is vast, and while I understand you had the best instructors, they were still *only* from Calenor. It is important you seek knowledge outside of your own people." Raewyn's tone was gentle, though firm.

"Are you withholding information?"

Raewyn recoiled, clearly hurt from the accusation. "Idrial, stop. I know you are concerned for the Sun Stone. I am too. And I also understand that you are far from home and in an unending, miserable weather with little sun." She paused to grab my hand. "I am your friend and your ally, and you would do well to remember that. No, I do not have any more knowledge regarding our mission. But I *do* have a better understanding of the world outside Calenor than you do. And what I have learned is that it is important to learn from people different from you."

I paused for a moment, letting the internal heat die down. I gently squeezed her hand before nodding. "Yes, you are right. I don't mean to be so defensive. I just cannot help but feel I have let all of Therrathis down by losing the stone."

"You didn't lose it! It was stolen from a highly guarded tower," Raewyn exclaimed.

"Which is something else I have been considering. *How* did they get past the wards? Eldrin said nothing was changed, and the time on the wards had not altered since they placed them." I narrowed my eyes in thought.

She shook her head. "I have no clue." Raewyn paused her steps and looked at me. "Before we left, I went to Nalthera's Cavern." Her cheeks flushed slightly. Nalthera was the Tide people's goddess. Raewyn didn't really believe in the gods and goddesses as they are often presented, so it was a bit surprising she went.

I raised my eyebrows. "Oh?"

She nodded. "I threw a silver medallion into the cave pool with her statue. I thought perhaps it would bring us luck."

"I know you don't care for them," I softly said.

She swallowed hard. "I just think people rely on them too much. And I don't think they care about *us* as everyone makes them out to. I stopped praying to her once my father passed for no reason."

I gently patted her shoulder as we resumed walking. "You know you never have to explain it to me. I don't know what I believe in at this point." I stared up at the sky briefly. "I do know if Eledrinna still exists, I am currently frustrated with her for letting the Sun Stone be taken so easily." I hadn't said it out loud before, but I had felt it the past few months that we had been gone.

Raewyn smiled softly and nodded. "Who knows. Perhaps they will be so thrilled with us for finding the Sun Stone and restoring peace and prosperity to Terrathis, that they will come down here themselves and bestow gifts upon us."

I laughed, and she joined, knowing how absurd the idea was. I shivered slightly and rubbed my arms. Once again, the cloud-covered sun was fading beyond the mountains, and the little light we had was dimming. I attempted to pull my powers forward in order to warm myself, but it was no use. Without a vibrant sun, it just wasn't possible. I looked over at Raewyn, who had pulled her wings around her arms. They at least provided her with some insulation and blocked the wind.

We came to an opening on the narrow pass and gazed over the mountain peaks. In the distance, I noticed a strange-looking mountain. I pointed to it and squinted.

"What is that?"

The Tide people tended to have better vision, so Raewyn stared out for a moment. "Ah, it looks like a face?" She leaned forward. "A male face. Pointed ears."

I was startled. "Carved into the mountains? Who would commit such an atrocity? The mountains are beautiful as they are."

Raewyn shrugged. "Typically males in power, I find. They seem to show how powerful they are by carving themselves into rocks and naming big buildings after themselves."

I furrowed my brow. "Wouldn't people know how powerful they are just by the good things they do for their people? Why the need for some grandiose thing?"

Raewyn laughed dryly. "That is indeed the question. You would never want your face carved into a mountain or building?"

I coughed. "Absolutely not." I grinned. "Maybe they could make a giant statue of Raiku in my honor. Or carve his happy face into a mountain."

She laughed. "That would make a lot of kings mad, that's for sure."

We resumed walking, but I kept staring towards the mountain. "Whose face *is* that? I sort of wish we had a Gryphon to go explore."

"If we had a Gryphon, we wouldn't be soaking wet, freezing, and starving!" Raewyn exclaimed.

"I asked Eldrin if we could just borrow one for the trip, but he said they wouldn't leave Calenor unattended." I reached into my pouch and grabbed the last of my dried fruit.

"Not even for the Princess of the Sun?" Raewyn said, jokingly.

I chewed my fruit. "You vowed to never call me that!" I gently shoved her as she cackled at my expense.

"That is technically your title." She smirked.

I sighed and flipped my dirty braid behind my shoulder. "I know. Queen of the Sun has a nicer ring to it."

Raewyn nodded, choosing her next words carefully. "Have you and Eldrin found anything that would allow you to take your seat without the trials?"

I shook my head. I had also hoped the Oracle would have revealed something of that nature to me, but instead, I just went on an odd mental trip I was still sorting out. "No, unfortunately. There is still the Rite of Passing my parents were meant to do. But gods know where they are."

Raewyn sucked her bottom lip in thought. "One would think that finding the Sun Stone would allow you to bypass those laws."

I shrugged and kicked a loose rock on the ground. "One would think, but I would still need to come into my full power."

Raewyn opened her mouth to respond, but I would never find out what she intended to say because the ground shook violently, throwing both of us into the cliffside along our path. I crawled to my knees, examining a large gash on the outside of my forearm. I looked over at Raewyn to see her pushing her hands off her knees to stand, her wings extended and drooping. It appeared one of the segments of her left wing had broken. She sucked in the dry air and raised her hand to point forward.

I turned my gaze to the path ahead, the ground shuttering again, and a horrible crackling sound verberated through the mountains. Before us was a hulking frame of dense, compacted snow. Its towering body was segmented with rough edges that seemed to be sculpted by icy winds. Its surface shimmered faintly and veins of pale blue ice ran through its form, giving it a crystalline texture. I tilted my head back to see its head, which was a crude and imposing construct. I was met with a deep-set pair of glowing eyes, the pale blue haze pierced the increasingly heavy snowfall.

It trudged towards us, flakes of snow cascading from its body, the ground beneath its massive stone feet freezing with each step. It let out a loud bellow before slamming a massive, icy fist on the ground near me, knocking me back on my ass. Raewyn made to run towards me, but the golem hurled shards of ice towards her. She quickly turned her head to shield her eyes, but I could see the cuts along her face beginning to bleed.

I raised my hand and summoned an orb of sunlight, letting it erupt around the golem. It bellowed in pain, its voice like an avalanche. The glow in his eyes flashed as he charged forward, his arm swinging towards me. I rolled over and dodged his attack at the last minute, my movement less than graceful. I grabbed my bow and an arrow that had fallen nearby. I quickly held the tip, letting the light within create a flame. I swiftly fired it towards the golem. The arrow struck the golem's chest and I watched as it melted a chunk of its snow body into steam. It let out another roar of pain and slammed its fist into the ground again.

I scrambled over to Raewyn, who had grabbed her spear and threw it directly at the golem's face. He easily swatted it away, sending it off the steep side of the mountain. Raewyn watched in horror for a brief moment before shouting something unintelligible and sent a sharp stream of water towards it. The creature gathered the water and repaired the hole I had left in his chest. This infuriated Raewyn, and she screamed profanity at him before throwing nearby rocks.

Before he could retaliate, I pulled the power of the sun towards me and created a barrier of light and flame between us, vaporizing any frost coming from him. He slammed his fist into the mountainside, sending boulders cascading towards us. My light barrier quickly disappeared as I, once again, fell over. As she dove next to me, Raewyn released another swirling jet of water towards the golem. He was now fixated on her and slammed his fist into the icy ground, creating jagged sharps of ice jetting up around her. She attempted to fly upwards, even with an injured wing. She hovered just above the ground when massive chunks of snow and debris hurtled through the air, striking her directly. The impact knocked her off balance and her wings faltered as she struggled to regain control. The golem took this opportunity to raise both arms and crash down, sending shockwaves throughout the mountain pass. I watched in horror as the ledge, where a weakened Raewyn stood, crumbled and completely disappeared from sight, taking her with it. I held my breath, waiting to see her wings carry her back to me, but she never came.

She was gone.

The golem turned and looked at me, almost triumphant. A feral scream ripped from my throat as grief, rage, and anguish filled my entire being. A storm of light churned from deep within me. I planted my feet firmly on the ground, my glowing eyes staring directly at the golem. I pulled every ounce of the sun around me and within me forward until I was completely enveloped in a radiant glow. The intensity of the heat melted everything around me. This power was new, ancient, raw, and uncontainable.

I took a deep, shuddering breath, "You will not take me." My voice was sturdy as it echoed across the mountains.

The golem roared and rushed towards me, but I closed my eyes and let myself shatter.

"I am the blood of the first light that ever touched this earth, the daughter of dawn itself. You will not take me, for I am the storm that follows the sun's rise. You have faced shadows, but before you now stands the wrath of a thousand suns. Feel their fury, and know your defeat."

Heat and light exploded from within me, and I found myself completely engulfed in a radiant aura that blinded the golem. I quickly glanced down to see my skin had transformed, resembling molten gold. I slowly began floating above the ground, lifted by sheer rage and power, as waves of solar energy rippled outwards, melting the frost around me.

I raised my arms above my head, pure sunlight emitting violently from my body with no direction. I watched as the golem was ripped limb from limb, his body deteriorating before me. He attempted to crawl towards me with the remains of his icy body, but I was too vibrant. I spread my arms wide and the sun itself seemed to heed my call. The sky above broke open and a cascade of angry light poured from the space above me. With an ancient cry that shook the entire mountain, I unleashed everything within my being, sending solar flames that completely engulfed the golem.

The light gently faded and I lowered to the ground, defeated and distraught. I crumbled to the ground, my entire body numb and my heart tightly wound. I lay my head on the ground and the entire world around me went black.

CHAPTER SIXTEEN

"Our darling, come to the desert." A disembodied voice rang out.

"You must find the altar." Another voice...

A gentle hand touched my forehead. "She is not well. She must heal. She is not ready."

"Find us in the desert, our love. We will show you the stone and the Lights that have changed. You can restore this land that our Mother created."

"You are never alone."

"Trust the untrustworthy and you will find what you seek."

"Find me in the desert and in the sky, and we will restore..." The voice tapered off.

My eyes fluttered open, the weight of them almost unbearable. Every inch of my body ached and burned with an intensity I had never known. It reminded me of a summer where a stinging fish caught my leg and Raewyn had to rush back to her mother Naia to get a healing poultice. That same sensation reached deep into my bones.

Raewyn.

Her name echoed throughout every fiber of my being and into the greatest depths of my mind and my heart. I sat up, and a sob bubbled out of my throat, but no sound came forth. Searing pain shot through my body with the movement, and I immediately regretted it. I made a noise, and a figure at a nearby table shifted.

"Oh, dear, gentle." The figure wrapped a dark cloak around themself and moved towards the fireplace in the room.

I took a moment to evaluate my surroundings. I was in a small cottage, it seemed. There was a humble kitchen, a small round table with a bowl of fruit placed on top, a small stone fireplace, and the makeshift bed I occupied. There were two windows flanking the simple arched doorway, though the windows had wool fabric completely covering it so no light came in. The smell of sweet anise and cinnamon filled the air, along with the faint smell of cardamom. A gentle *hoo* caught my attention. I slowly looked to the corner at the foot of my bed to see a wooden perch. A small, black owl rested, curiously staring at me. I stared back at it, noting the tiny purple cape around its neck.

It met my gaze, its uncomfortably wide, blue eyes intensely. Without thinking, I slowly raised my right arm in a wave. It snapped its head to a tilt, letting out another *hoo*.

"Hush, Rune," an older woman's voice cut through the warm silence.

I turned to the figure, who was moving towards me with a red clay mug. She held it up to my lips and encouraged me to drink. Still in a daze, I took a sip, enjoying the source of the warm fragrances in the air. The warmth of the tea filled my body with delight. Until I looked up and saw the woman's face in the cloak. My heart sank.

She lowered her cloak, confirming what I had feared. She was undeniably from Nyxara, the capital city of the House of the Moon. She had unmistakable indigo markings of celestial swirls all up her violet arms, indicating she held a royal position there. I gazed up at her soft, silver eyes, her purple lips pressed together.

"Now, you can put your learned prejudice aside and let me continue to heal you, or you may leave into the unknown wilderness. The choice is yours." She set the hot mug on the table nearby and lowered herself in the chair. She crossed her ankle over the other and rested her hands in her lap, her aged violet face pleasant enough.

"Who are you?" My voice rasped.

She smiled softly. "I am Navarra. I was once a healer for the House of the Moon, as you may have discerned."

My head pounded and I closed my eyes momentarily. "Where am I?" My throat burned.

"You are in my home, at the top of the Eryndor and Vintar Rivers. I found you in the mountains in some awful shape." She took a sip of her own tea.

I stared at her, my eyes sticking with each blink. "I don't understand. I am far from the falls."

She nodded. "Indeed. That was roughly a fortnight ago. I had seen a strange light from the mountains while I was out hunting." She gestured to a countertop in the kitchen where lay out processed meat I could only assume was some sort of deer.

I furrowed my brow, my agitated brain attempting the maths. "Twenty days?"

"Yes, twenty days have passed."

"How have I slept so long?" A sudden thought pushed its way to my head and my hand flew to my neckline, grasping for the pendant. When I found it was not there, I frantically looked around my bed. "Where is my pendant? You must have found it with me?"

Navarra looked at me sadly. "Ah, the only things I found of yours were your leather pack and your bow, though it is quite splintered. And this." She grabbed a small, empty vial that said 'Sunborn.' The letters had worn off. "I wasn't exactly sure what it meant, but it was empty in your hand when I found you. I assumed it was important."

I was suddenly afraid because I had no memory of taking the potion. I didn't even know what the Oracle's gift actually did. My heart was pounding in my chest. I had no connection to Eldrin. Raewyn was gone. I was lost, and my only source of comfort was one I had known to be my enemy. Tears welled in my eyes. My heart suddenly felt empty.

I looked over at Navarra, her long ears twitching as though she heard my thoughts. I couldn't remember the powers the Moon folk possessed. *Could they mindread*, I mused. I rubbed my eyes, feeling the fatigue wash over me again.

"You may rest, my dear." Navarra's voice was soothing.

My head was spinning, and I lay back down on the pillow. I lifted my eyes to the ceiling and was astounded by what I saw.

Completely out of place for the ordinary shack, there was the most magnificent mural painted on the ceiling. It reminded me of the star maps Eldrin had in his study. There above me was painted a rich, dark blue with swirls of gold and silver creating circles and patterns. Small text sprawled all throughout, no doubt labeling the mapped out stars. I stared at the ceiling for a length of time before sleep pulled me back under.

Chapter Seventeen

"Easy, easy, you are safe," Navarra's warm voice brought me to a place of comfort from my nightmare.

I sat up, sweat dripping down my face. My clothes and hair were soaked and my eyes burned. I tilted my head to see her violet face, and was startled for a brief moment. I had to keep reminding myself the woman saved my life and she meant me no harm, no matter the history.

She gently brushed damp hair off my cheek, tenderly tucking it behind my pointed ear. I looked up at the ceiling and felt the sting of tears in my eyes. *I am alone. Raewyn is gone, and I have no connections to Eldrin or home. I miss my puppy. I am alone.* I brought my hands to my face and sobbed, my entire body being pulled into anguish. I didn't want to do this anymore. I wanted to go home.

Navarra pulled me into a tight hug, gently murmuring words of comfort. She rocked me as though I were a child. I wanted to pull away from her, but I had never felt quite so small, so fragile. I hated it. I hated every part of my existence. I had failed everyone. How could I face Naia, Raewyn's mother? The council had trusted me to do a simple task and I couldn't even do that.

Self-doubt wrapped around my mind like a dark cloak. I didn't even want to pull out of it. It felt easier to succumb to its grasp. Maybe if I just closed my eyes and let it take me...

"Idrial..." Navarra's voice was soft.

I snapped my worn eyes open and pulled away so I could look at her. "What?" My voice was hoarse.

"These feelings are the burdens of the living, and they are not to be cast aside." Her face was kind, and her eyes sparkled with sympathy. "But, your sorrow is not the mark of failure."

I darted my eyes towards the woman. "I don't like people reading my mind." I pulled away from her.

She chuckled softly. "I am not." Navarra slowly rose to her feet, tending to a whistling iron kettle on her stove. "But I have been where you are. Do not shy away from your grief, for it is but the shadow cast by a love that shone brightly. Don't see her passing as your failure. Her memory lives, undimmed and unbroken, within your heart. There is still light in you, and pieces of her live on within you. Do not let that light dim, for though the night seems long, dawn will come. In its glow, you will find that love's light never truly fades. Light lingers as a guiding star through all your days."

I watched as she poured more hot water into our mugs, releasing the potent fragrance. She set the kettle back on the stove and brought the mugs over, setting them on the table next to me. "The tea is still too hot. But in time, it will be easier to take in."

I knew she wasn't referring just to the tea. I stared at the swirls of steam floating above the mug. It reminded me of mine and Raewyn's powers merging. A shaky sigh escaped my cracked lips.

"How? How do I move on?"

"The pain of grief may linger, but it does not hold the power to dim your light. You will find within yourself a strength you have not met." She gently blew on the surface of her own mug before taking a sip. "Despite your pain, and your sorrow, you will find a way to shine brightly again."

I pondered her words for a moment. I could not ever imagine feeling this heavy, grotesque weight leaving my body. My throat was in a constant state of tightness and my heart felt as though it were gripped in vines. This felt endless.

"Have you lost someone important?" I reached for my mug, sensing it had cooled enough.

She took a sip before responding, her face neutral. "I have."

"Who?" I couldn't help myself. I took a drink, my stinging eyes peering at her over the rim of my mug.

"Everyone." She maintained an even face.

I lowered my mug, cradling it in my hands in my lap. I nodded in understanding, not quite feeling I should continue the conversation. She saw my discomfort and gently cupped my upper arm.

"We will not dwell in my grief. Let us work through yours." She rose to her feet. "You have a Sun Stone to locate, afterall."

My eyebrows raised quickly. "How do you know that?"

"I know more than I should." She winked at me and moved across the room to the sink. "Finish your tea."

I lay flat on the ground, my body sprawled across the earth as if it no longer belonged to me. The weight of the world pressed into my chest, and I could feel the cold, damp grass beneath me, its blades sharp against my skin. Bits of late winter snow lingered on the ground. I stared up at the sun, its harsh light an odd comfort to me. It felt as though the sun were watching over me, eager to help.

A gentle breeze drifted across my face, but it offered no comfort. It was hollow and fleeting, a cruel reminder that nothing could reach me now. My tears fell freely, tracing the contours of my face, soaking into my hair. My chest ached, a constant gnawing pain, and with it came the searing weight of all the loves that had slipped away in a moment.

Every fiber of my being screamed in agony and of guilt. The rage was a fire that burned at my insides, but it was nothing compared to the hollow, aching grief that consumed me. I wanted to scream and for my body to be torn apart.

I wanted to end it. To let go. Every bone in my body begged for release, for the relief of oblivion. But there was still that stubborn light within me that refused to succumb. I was digging my own grave, over and over again, burying pieces of myself with each breath I took, only to have the earth swallow them whole.

The agony of it was suffocating, like I was trapped in my own skin, my own thoughts, my own brokenness. The emotional whiplash was unbearable. My mind was a shattered mirror reflecting every failure, every loss, every regret. And yet, still, I couldn't stop the cycle. I couldn't find peace, even as I begged for it. I pressed my hands to my face, trembling, unable to hold back the primal sob that tore from my chest.

What had become of Eldrin? Does he think I am dead? How can I tell Naia that her daughter has died, taken by a snow golem? And for what? Our mission wasn't even fruitful. The Oracle hadn't even given us the information we actually needed. I sat up, suddenly feeling agitated.

"What the hell was it all for, then?" I asked no one in particular. I glanced around the clearing just outside Navarra's cabin. I looked over my shoulder to see her stepping from the doorway.

Navarra had been kind enough to help me lay outside. I felt stifled and needed to feel the warmth of the sun's rays on my skin. The fresh air was healing as I deeply inhaled, feeling it completely fill my lungs. I slowly exhaled as Navarra sat in front of me, curling her legs behind her waist. She reached forward and brushed the tears from my cheeks.

"It will get easier in time." Her eyes were soft.

"Will things get better?" I asked, hopefully.

She smiled softly. "No, they won't."

I raised my eyebrows in surprise. "No?"

She shook her head. "Life is not linear. It does not get better, and it does not get worse. It just does what it does."

"That makes no sense."

"Bad things will happen to you and around you. And so will good things. They happen in tandem *all* the time. What you have to decide is how *you* want to be during those times. Grief is important, but you cannot stay there. And joy is important, but you cannot always stay there. Everything is in balance."

I scoffed, bringing my knees into my chest. I rested my chin on them. "How do I decide what I want to be? Every piece of me is in ruins. How can I decide to be happy right now?"

"We decide *what* we are when we can accept what has happened to us." Navarra absently picked a small white flower nearby. "Your path, Daughter of Light, is not one of endless bliss, nor of endless suffering. There is a delicate dance between the light of joy and the shadow of grief. You will face trials that make your heart heavy, and you will experience triumphs that will allow you to glow. Both will shape you, but neither will rule you unless you allow them to."

I stared at her for a moment. "That honestly feels impossible."

"Indeed, it does." She reached forward and brushed a loose strand of hair behind my pointed ear. The motion reminded me of Eldrin. "Until you do it. You will find a way to just *be*. Don't force it, just let it come to you. Just as your magic has."

I stared into the thick grass as the wind swept over it. "I fear I have lost myself."

"Perhaps. Or perhaps you have lost the self that is made up of others' influences on you," Navarra gently offered. "Now you can rebuild yourself as you want to be."

I shifted to sit on my knees, my legs folded beneath me. I stared off into the trees around the perimeter, pondering that for a moment. "I suppose now I have no one to guide me, no one to tell me my next move. So, I decide now?" I looked back over to her.

She nodded. "You decide now."

CHAPTER EIGHTEEN

A few weeks passed and I could finally move, though with effort. My entire body had begun to heal, thanks to Navarra and her healing potions. Navarra helped me regain full functionality through breathing exercises and stretches. She also helped me get outside every day so I could meditate in the sun. Nothing could be done for the emptiness I felt at the loss of my Raewyn. I felt a constant hollowness deep within. And to be completely cut off from Eldrin left me feeling even more lost. I often found myself reaching to pat Raiku's head upon waking, but he wasn't there. However, each day became easier. My conversations with Navarra were becoming more comfortable. It was nice to have a friend.

I did wonder why she left, and how did she end up here? How did *I* end up here? What *actually* happened on the mountain with my magic? Why did Raewyn fall... I shoved that last memory from my mind. I still wasn't quite ready to think about it.

I sat on the foot of my bed, turning the empty vial around in my hand, waiting for some answer to come to me. Soft footsteps approached and I snapped my head up to see Navarra smiling softly down at me.

"You would like some answers, I am sure." She rested her hand on my shoulder.

I no longer needed to resist the urge to shrug her hand off. I had become comfortable with her, and a small part of me wondered if there was truth to the claims the House Moon were horrible people. I nodded and allowed her to help me rise to my feet. We moved over to the table and sat across from each other. She sat a clay mug in front of me, the simple fragrance of peppermint wafting from it. I grabbed it with my left hand and held it in anticipation.

"Where would you like to begin?" Her eyes were soft as she clutched her own mug.

I pondered this for a moment. "Why do you live here?"

I could tell that was not the question she was expecting, given the slight shift in her body. She settled her features into a soft smile. "The short answer to that is the Lord of the House of Moon. In my younger years, he changed and became feverish with greed and revenge."

I tilted my head slightly. "What changed?"

She shook her head. "I have thoughts about the matter, but I won't disclose that to you."

I understood wanting to keep secrets, so I didn't push it. "So you wound up in the middle of the mountains?"

"I originally came here with three other friends. We were part of the House court, and we each felt the same. And so we traveled East until we found this clearing. The spirits of the woods brought us here, and we found solace." She leaned back in her chair, closing her eyes. "That was fifty years ago. The others have passed on, and I am all that remains of us." I could hear the sadness ring from her voice.

"How did they pass?" My curiosity surprises me sometimes.

She opened her eyes, amusement dancing in them. "Most wouldn't ask such private questions." She sipped her mug. "You are not most." She paused for a moment. "Two were taken by illness, and the other drowned. That is all I will say of that."

I shrank into myself, feeling slightly mortified. "I didn't mean to pry." I was quiet for a moment. "You know who I am. Why are you helping me?"

She waved her hand at me. "We were not raised the same way. I have knowledge you do not, so I would not allow you to be taken by the elements because of bad history."

"What do you mean? What knowledge? I come from the greatest scholars in Therrathis!"

She sucked air between her teeth. "Who created your education system?"

"I would imagine the Magister's at the Institute?" I wasn't sure where she was going with this question.

"And they exist in the city of Calenor. Their funding comes directly from the capital, yes?" She stared intently at me.

"I believe so. I never quite thought of that." I was becoming increasingly uncomfortable.

"They would never allow knowledge to pass that paints themselves poorly, would they?" Navarra leaned forward.

My head was spinning as I set my half-consumed mug on the table. "I would like to believe they would give unbiased truths. For the sake of information."

She raised her eyebrows. "Things would be more simple if that were true."

I felt heat rise within. "What are you insinuating?"

"Sometimes," She sighed, choosing her words carefully. "People will alter historical accounts in order to protect their people."

"I cannot imagine the scholars would do such a thing! They have honor in their discipline." Eldrin would be aghast at such an accusation.

"I believe most of them to be good and want to preserve history and information as it is. However, power often breeds corruption. I know in the House of the Moon, several head scholar's loyalties came into question."

I tilted my head curiously. "Nyxara has their own scholars?"

"Oh, yes, indeed. Did you believe Calenor to be the only place that contained knowledge?" She leaned forward.

Embarrassment flushed my cheeks. "Ah, well, yes. I know our library and institute is the grandest."

"Because *they* tell you it is," She leaned back in her chair. "The scholars in our library said the same."

I pressed my lips together firmly. "I don't like how this is painting Eldrin." It was the first time I said his name out loud to her.

Navarra's expression softened as she touched my hand. "I am sure he is as honest as he can be. If he is a good scholar, he likely also has asked the same questions."

"He is indeed, the best scholar and mage." I knew I was being unnecessarily defensive, but I couldn't help it.

"Oh, my Light, let's move past this for now.."

I opened my mouth to protest, but realized I also wanted to change the subject for now. "So, what do you think of the vial?" The small jar from the Oracles sat on the table.

"Ah! I am glad you asked that. Where did you get it from?" Navarra grabbed the bottle and stared into it.

"The Oracles gifted these to us. I gave Raewyn the one that said Fly, though I am not sure where that is. It made sense that I take this one." I paused for a moment. "I do not remember drinking this, though."

She grinned, her teeth shining brightly in contrast to her violet skin. "I have a thought that can only be tested when you are more physically fit. But I believe you have come into your full Sun powers, and that it was to assist in your recovery."

My mouth gaped. "That takes a minimum of a years' worth of training under the tutelage of the greats. I never finished mine."

Her head shook excitedly. "In most cases, yes, but in cases where extreme emotions come into play, it can be fully unleashed. And..." She paused for a moment. "Magic of the natural world, the celestial world, is vastly different from the Arcane magic of the mages."

I sat up straight and stared at my hands, as though expecting the sun to shine out of my fingers. "So, what do I do now?"

"We test and we train."

Chapter Nineteen

"Ugh, this isn't working!" I shouted, throwing my hands down at my sides.

I stood in the clearing just outside Navarra's cabin. The ground had completely thawed and small fragrant purple flowers were popping up all over the clearing, and it finally felt warm enough to be outside. Rune kept me company from a nearby fencepost and watched through sleepy eyes as I failed at summoning my magic once again. My attempts at pulling out the new magic within me ended poorly every time.

"I feel like a damned child with this. I used to be *incredible*." I kicked a rock across the field.

I closed my eyes and exhaled, letting the moment of frustration pass through me. The years of training with the scholars resurfaced in my mind, grounding me. I focused, shaping my hands into a sphere, cupping them gently together. *Think of the warm light*, they had always said. *And become that light.* A deep breath filled my lungs through my nose, then escaped slowly through parted lips. My feet sank into the earth, my toes feeling the cool embrace of the grass beneath me. The tension in my face melted away, followed by my shoulders, until my entire body relaxed. My breathing steadied, and with each exhale, my thoughts began to fade, leaving nothing but stillness in my mind.

In time, I felt the space in my hands heat and slowly pulled them apart. A tiny, golden ball of light wavered there. I stared intently at it, the intensity of the heat increasing with each moment. It was barely the size of a large gold coin, but it was maintained. I steadied my breathing as I stared at it, feeling a sense of awe. I hadn't been able to hold my magic since the moment with the golem. It was as though the light within me fell with Raewyn. When I lost connection to Eldrin and my entire family. But I found it buried beneath the swirl of dark emotions.

A flicker of a smile ran across my face as I stared into the orb. Perhaps I could move forward and find my new purpose. I exhaled deeply, staring wistfully at Rune. *My journey has not ended. I have not ended.*

I turned at the sound of Navarra gently clearing her throat. She stood on the top of the short steps of her cabin with a plate of lavender and honey scones. I walked over to her and took one. It was still warm.

"I've been able to clear my mind enough at last." I took a bite of the fragrant pastry.

"Ah, so I see." Navarra smiled and sat on the steps, gesturing for me to her. She set the plate behind her and took a scone for herself. "I knew it would come to you."

I chewed thoughtfully and stared out at the clearing before us, my eyes following the flight of small birds near the forest's edge. "Navarra..." I was hesitant to ask, but I had begun to trust her over the past few months.

She turned and looked at me. "Yes, dear Light?"

"Before I awoke, when I first came here, I had a dream of sorts." I rested my hands on my knees and stared at the remaining scone.

"A dream?"

"Yes, well, I am not sure, actually." I fumbled over my words. *Why is this so hard?* "There were voices? They spoke to me about going to the desert."

Navarra looked at me curiously, tucking her white hair behind her pointed ear. "How did these voices make you feel?"

I furrowed my brow. "Feel? I suppose..." I looked around as though I would find the answer. "Comforted? They felt a part of me, really."

"Interesting." Navarra looked out before us. "What did they tell you?"

"They mentioned a Well? That I could restore something?" I squinted, trying to recall through the mental fog.

"I have heard rumors of the Altar in the Ruins of Arkanthys. It was once the grand temple of Eledrinna. Sometimes, lost artifacts suddenly appear there." Navarra pulled off a piece of her scone and fed it to Rune, who had perched beside us on the stairs. He ate it eagerly.

"Do you think the Sun Stone is there now?" My eyes lit up with hope.

"I think it is worth following those voices. It sounds as though past Lady Suns were guiding you." She patted my knee. "Thank you for allowing me this knowledge."

"So, I will journey to the desert, then." My voice was flat as the thought terrified me.

"Oh, not anytime soon. You must heal all parts of you first. Then you may be on your way." Her voice was stern, but had that motherly kindness to it.

"When will that be?"

A hearty laugh broke from her lips. "Ah, you will know when that time comes. You will know."

I stood near the top of a rugged waterfall, my feet steady on slippery rocks. The rushing water cascaded around me and the air was thick with mist. The deafening sound of the falls below helped me focus on my task at hand. Navarra had given me a set of simple, yet clean clothing. I wore a green tunic and dark brown breeches. My feet were bare as my toes gripped the rocks below.

I furrowed my brow in concentration and raised my hand towards the midday sun. The golden light reflected off the mist and cast soft rainbows all around me. My fingers trembled slightly, still recovering from my journey. It had been several weeks and I had only recently begun to practice my magic. My previous days' efforts made it evident this was not the practiced ease of someone well-trained, but rather the raw and undefined skills of someone learning their potential.

This new magic came forth in erratic, brief flashes of light pulsating from my hands. Any control I had of it previously was lost. This magic felt ancient and almost lost, not the carefully trained sun I had always known. A brief flash of light pulsated from my hands, but quickly disappeared. I sighed in frustration before attempting again. I inhaled deeply, paused for a moment, and moved my hands with more confidence, pushing my entire upper body into the gentle movement.

I whispered a word, barely audible over the roaring of the falls below me, and released the magic. A brilliant beam of sunlight pulsed out of my palms and pierced through the mist with ease. Moving my hands, the light began to take shape- an orb of sunlight, swirling like a miniature sun, suspended in the air just above my hands.

The water beneath me shimmered in the golden light, creating ripples across the surface. The leaves from the trees around me were bathed in light. For a moment, I stared at the orb. It felt different than the magic used to defeat Kha'Laroth in Paldor Pass. It was as though my magic and I were becoming acquainted with each other. I closed my eyes, feeling it pulsing through my body. It was starting to feel like an extension of me once again. For that brief moment, sorrow did not consume me.

I had barely slept, my mind replaying the moment Raewyn fell. I could have done something. I should have saved her. It should have been me. Every hypothetical scenario played in my mind like a cruel stage performance. Grief hit me every time I saw the birds in the trees, or heard the water crashing against the bottom of the falls. Every so often, I could swear I heard her rich, alto voice singing. My heart could not bear it most days. It took every piece of my entire being to open my eyes every morning, only to look up and see the celestial paintings on the ceiling.

And so, I would begin every morning, with another empty pit. I was completely cut-off from Eldrin and my home. Did he know I was alive? Did he think I abandoned him? What became of my beloved city? Did Raiku think I had abandoned him? The thoughts swarmed through my mind like restless insects every day.

A gentle cough broke me out of the tortuous mental cycle. I opened my eyes and turned towards the treeline to see Navarra. She had a soft expression and politely clapped.

"Lovely. Your ability to pull your powers fluidly has improved." She walked towards me, stopping at the water's edge. She reached out a hand.

I carefully took her hand and jumped towards the grass. I curled my toes in the soft blades. "It feels different."

She nodded, her gaze studying me. "It will. This is a deeper magic that no scholar nor mage could teach you."

"I don't understand that."

She patted my hand and watched as her owl, Rune, flew to a nearby branch. He let out a gentle *hoo* before closing his eyes. She led me to sit beneath the tree.

"Our world is much older than any of us can fathom. You know of Eledrinna, the Sun Goddess."

I nodded. "Of course, she is the creator of Terrathis."

Navarra smiled. "Indeed, she is. You are a direct descendant of her, as Lady of the Sun. The Mages are well-learned with Arcane magic, but not magic of the natural world. They can only teach you how to wield your magic in a very calculated, formal way. But natural magic is not formal, and while there is balance, there are no rules."

I curled my legs behind me, using my right hand to prop myself up. I played with the braid over my shoulder with my free hand. "How can there be no rules?"

"Nature, particularly the sun, is a force that flows naturally. It can be unpredictable and is limitless." She moved a loose strand of hair from her forehead. "It comes from within, which means it also moves with your emotions. You cannot study it, not truly. It is connected to you and your vitality and life. It is deeply personal, and each person's magic will show differently. You have been taught the basics and a more formal version of it, but that is not how you are connected to your power, and to Eledrinna." She smiled. "We are finding that now, hence why it feels foreign."

I nodded, feeling a warmth rush over my body. "Yes, I feel more awake than I ever had. I feel a constant rhythm inside."

"That will never leave you. Arcane magic is beautiful in its own way, but is much more calculated. We don't know its origins, so we cannot know its intentions. That is why Arcane magic is so much more easily corrupted. For ages, people have taken that and bastardized it. They attempt the same with natural magic, but the gods and goddesses wouldn't allow it." She pulled a hand-woven basket towards us and opened it, revealing various cheeses, bread, and grapes. Navarra grabbed a handful of grapes and gestured towards the basket.

I grabbed a small chunk of sourdough bread and a few grapes. "They no longer exist on our plane, though. How do they intervene?"

She raised her dark eyebrows a bit mischievously. "Oh, can you be certain of that? I truly believe Nyxar still has influence here. I may not have ever seen him, but I know he traverses here in some form." She looked up at Rune, who was clutching a small wand.

I shot my eyes to Rune and stared at him. "You don't mean?"

Navarra let out a hearty laugh. "Oh, my dear, no. Rune is simply a familiar of sorts. His lineage does go back to Nyxar, and his brother. It can be said that Rune comes from the first owls on Terrathis."

"Incredible," I mused. I chewed thoughtfully on the chunk of bread, my eyes never leaving Rune. He began pecking at a blue, pointed hat. "What do you mean, Nyxar's brother?"

"Ah, I forget you likely have but a page in your texts about the House of the Moon," she finished the last of her grapes and wiped her hands on the purple fabric in her lap. "Nyxion was his name. He was the second moonbeam to touch Terrathis, just by a few minutes. As such, he would never come to inherit a kingdom. Nyxar gave him a vast manor and land just outside of Nyxara. But it was never quite good enough."

"What happened?" I eagerly snacked on the grapes as she explained.

"No one truly knows. He disappeared at some point in our history. There are rumors, but nothing is solid. His manor lies vacant and nature has moved in."

"Why don't we see them anymore? When did they stop taking a form and walking these lands?" I licked my fingers, slightly sticky from the grapes.

"Because we are messy, dear Light. And the gods have their own mess to deal with." She leaned forward. "I believe they are coming back, though. Things have been unsettled for quite some time."

I opened my mouth to respond when something caught my eye behind her. Amidst the stillness of the woods, a soft glow caught my eye. A faded, violet rabbit shimmered like an ethereal wisp and hopped gracefully between the trees. Its fur glowed faintly in the dappled sunlight. I jumped to my feet, startling Navarra, and pointed at it.

"What is that?"

She abruptly turned around to see what I was pointing at. "What? There is nothing there."

I looked back where the rabbit was to see nothing. I squinted and looked around. Navarra had joined me, standing close by. She gently grabbed my arm. "I swear to you, there was a glowing rabbit."

Navarra lifted her chin slightly. "Curious. It is gone now." She patted my arm. "Perhaps we should get you some rest. You have been outside for a long time now."

I nodded and allowed her to lead me towards the cabin, with Rune flying above us. I glanced over my shoulder, expecting to see the strange being again. I sighed and crossed over the threshold into the cabin.

CHAPTER TWENTY

"**A**wake, dear Light." Navarra was gently shaking me.

I slowly opened one eyeball and looked at her. The indigo markings along her arms and chest were softly glowing. I opened both eyes to see the entire room bathed in silver moonlight. I sat up.

"Is something happening?" I glanced around for any sign of danger.

She grinned, her white teeth glinting. "Yes, it is. And you must see it!" She grabbed my hand and urged me out of bed.

We stepped outside, the summer mountain air wrapping itself around me, chilling my skin. The cotton hem of the white night gown whipped around my ankles as we raced down the steps of the cabin and across the field. Rune flew enthusiastically overhead, happy to have evening company. The entire clearing was covered in luminescent white flowers as the moonbeams lay in a blanket over the area. In the distance, I could hear the gentle croaking of frogs, and the low howl of wolves. Navarra held my hand as we continued running, maneuvering between the trees. I was grateful the grass beneath was soft as my naked feet thumped against it. We burst out on the other side of the treeline and stopped abruptly near a cliff's edge.

Navarra turned to me, breathless. "Look." She pointed outward, her eyes glowing a magnificent silver.

I followed her hand and gasped. We stood atop the cliff that looked over the Eryndor River. I stared out, my eyes scanning the valley and the distant hills. At first, everything seemed normal, but then I noticed it. At the edge of the forest, a faint glow appeared along the tree line, barely perceptible at first. I squinted my eyes to see more clearly. The glow gradually intensified, spreading outward in a slow, deliberate wave. It looked as though the earth itself was glowing beneath the moon's influence.

Navarra's eyes gleamed with pride as she explained in a hushed tone. "This is the *Moonfall*. It occurs when the light of the full moon aligns with the natural ley lines, magical lines, deep within Terrathis. These lines pulse with ancient power, and when the conditions are right, the land itself responds with a bloom of magic."

I stared out and watched as the glow spread across the land, from the forest's edge into the expansive farmland. The trees seemed to shimmer as though dusted with stardust, their branches bending and twisting in a response to a celestial rhythm. The fields below began to ripple, like waves on water, but the ground itself remained solid. It felt as though the very earth was breathing, alive with ancient energy.

The moonlight pulsed brighter, and I noticed that the rivers began to shimmer with the same light. The Eryndor River, normally a dark and steady flow, began to glow as though filled with liquid silver, its currents moving in intricate, swirling patterns. The light on the river seemed to draw itself upward, reaching out like delicate fingers in a yearning for the moonlight.

I turned to Navarra to speak, but she held up a hand to keep me still. I looked back out over the hills below. Small, ethereal orbs of light began to rise from the fields and forest floor. I looked around me to see we were also surrounded by the same small orbs. They darted and flickered, weaving intricate shapes in the air before fading into the night.

Navarra was watching me, her expression soft and knowing. "These are the Glowmoths. They are spirits of the land, born from the heart of the ley lines. They are the keepers of the land's memories, and when the moon reaches its fullest, they awaken to communicate with those who are attuned to their magic."

I shivered in awe as I watched the Glowmoths dance across the land. I could feel the very soil and stone beneath my feet breathing and well alive. I felt myself drawn into the magic, my own golden light glowing from my skin. I looked over at Navarra, who had the most pleased expression I had ever seen. Something shifted in me, and I had a thunderous realization. The Sun and the Moon worked together.

"When did Nyxion come to Terrathis?" I asked, Navarra. "I mean, in relation to Eledrinna and all the others?"

She turned from the stove and stared at me for a moment. Navarra turned back to the whistling kettle and silently poured it into two mugs. She carefully lifted them and set one before me on the table and the other in her normal spot across from me. She gently brushed a violet hand through her white hair before speaking.

"As you know, Eledrinna loved walking the land of Terrathis. But she felt she would love it more if she had a companion. And so, she lay on the ground and closed her eyes. This brought darkness across the land, the first time since she had arrived." Navarra paused to drink her peppermint tea. "And with the darkness, the moon shone freely again. Her eyes remained closed, and she reached out a hand to pull the moonbeam to earth. When she opened her eyes again, the two stood before her. Nyxar came first, and shortly after, so did Nyxion. She was immediately drawn to Nyxar, and the two became quick friends."

I pondered this for a moment and contemplated the revelation I had the night before on the cliff's edge. "It feels as though the Sun and the Moon magic are connected?"

Navarra's eyebrows flickered and a smile grew on her indigo lips. "Indeed, they are."

I sighed, and leaned back in my chair. "Then why are we enemies? What happened?"

"Greed and power led to The Light War," she stated, peering over her mug.

"Well, yes, I know of The Light War. When the House of the Moon broke treaties with the House of the Sun, and they betrayed us." The words caught in my throat as I remembered who I spoke to.

Navarra did not seem phased, luckily. "Yes, that is how your story is written."

"Are there other accounts?"

"What is it they say? There are always three sides: my side, your side, and somewhere between. That is often where the truth lies." She absently traced the rim of her mug.

I chewed the inside of my lip and stared into the pale yellow liquid in my mug. "I should find out what truly happened."

"Oh?"

"The historical claim is that House of the Mountain officials intercepted documents and plans showing a massive attack on Calenor. But if we always had a positive relationship with House of the Moon, why wouldn't we question that?" I sipped my tea contemplatively. "Why wouldn't we investigate thoroughly before making such great assumptions?"

"They very well may have, and it is just not accounted for. And don't forget, the death that set off the war itself." Navarra stirred a bit of honey into her tea.

I stared at her for a moment. "Battle at Cairnfall? Not to undermine the importance of life, but I never quite understood how one court healer's death would result in a massive war. That war tore about our Houses, and I am finding that perhaps things were not relayed quite honestly." I felt a bit gutted, but I was beginning to think things were not as they had seemed my entire life.

Navarra nodded solemnly. "There is something much more here, perhaps more sinister." She drained her mug. "I believe you have the ability to right whatever has been wronged."

My heart was pounding, but not with anxiety. I wasn't sure what this feeling was, but it felt like something more. Like something was happening. "I am but one person."

She set the mug down on the table. "You are heir to the throne of Calenor. Do you know what power that gives you?"

I closed my eyes and rested my elbows on the table. I rubbed my face with my hands. "I do. And so far, I have spent the last five years wasting it."

Navarra reached across the table and clutched my hand. "How did you spend your days? Since your parents left?"

My eyes flew open. "You know about that?" She nodded. I shouldn't be surprised. "I studied the past wars, and histories. I learned about the past leaders. I visited the temple of Eledrinna and prayed for my people. I tried visiting the townspeople and making sure they were cared for." I pressed my lips tightly. "I tried to be a good Lady for my people."

Navarra smiled. "Your people are *all* of Terrathis. You never left Calenor."

I swallowed hard. "I wasn't permitted to. I was told it was too dangerous."

"But now you have. And now, you get to choose how to help your people. *All* of us."

My heart dropped. "Us?"

Navarra chuckled softly. "When you take up your throne, you will be my Queen."

I stood suddenly, my chair scratching the floor. "Oh, oh no. I am not over the House of the Moon? They are separate?"

The look on the woman's face was soft with amusement. "My dear Light, under the current laws, House of the Sun rules the entirety of Therrathis. Nyxara is included in that, whether they want to accept it or not."

"What do you mean, under current laws?" I queried.

"Before the Light War, House of the Moon and House of the Sun were equals. They ruled in tandem; Moon took care of the West, Sun took care of the East. They would have meetings every season change at a different House location. Together, they would ensure each area was safe and thriving. Once a year, there would be a fabulous Light Ball that would alternate between Calenor and Nyxara. I hear they were incredible. Things were wonderful then, from the accounts I've read." Navarra placed her hands in her lap.

"So, why did the Moon House plan the attack on Calenor? What happened there?"

Navarra gently tapped her fingertips on the table. "There are a lot of unknowns in what caused the demise of harmony. People were dishonest, and sides were taken. Things happen quickly when deceit and power are involved." She paused for a moment. "The House of the Moon once was a powerful city and was well-revered. But now, they are vastly feared and cannot leave their kingdom."

My throat tightened as I paced the floors. I had never considered that. No one had thought to mention that. Were we so far into our hatred of the House of the Moon that we just simply left them out? Pretended they didn't exist. My mind was reeling. "If Varyx stole the Sun Stone, would that help him rule over all?"

Her eyes flashed a brief silver. "Ah, he may think so. He would be better off finding the lost Moon Stone."

I stopped and turned towards her. "I had not considered there would be a Moon Stone."

"Yes, we all came from the Stones. I personally believe part of the reason for the corruption in the Moon House is because they do not have their Moon Stone. And," she watched me carefully, "without the Moon Stone being part of the ritual, it has caused our land to slowly diminish."

I anxiously braided my hair. "I need to find it. I need to find the Sun Stone *and* the Moon Stone. We cannot have balance without both. I don't know how, but I will find a way to restore balance." I felt the fire within me glow as I leaned forward on the table. "I may not have been the greatest Lady these last few years, but I will be damned if I don't become the best Queen that every single House has ever had. I will find out what happened and unite us all."

Navarra clapped slowly. "There she is. You are the Queen of Terrathis, the Light of our World. You must now own it and show the world that light."

I bounced idly and wrung my hands, filled with a new energy I never had before. I was beaming and for the first time since the mountain three months ago, I felt happy. I felt fulfilled. I knew what I needed to do next, and I was no longer afraid.

Chapter Twenty-One

"The Arkanthys Desert is hateful," Navarra warned. She was packing a leather pouch with herbs and dried food for my journey.

"Thanks for the comforting words." I smiled grimly at her.

She ticked her tongue against her teeth. "I do not want you to be caught off-guard. There are things there you have never encountered before. Things even I have never seen."

I inhaled deeply. "Everything I have encountered since I left Calenor has been new and terrifying. What's a few more things?"

"Indeed, however, you did not have the magic you do now. And you can use the desert sun to your advantage. The greatest threat there is the Unsettled."

I shoved cotton pants into my brown leather bag. Navarra had restored the leather and repaired the tears. "That doesn't sound pleasant at all."

She gave a nod and walked over to a wooden cupboard, its surface marked by patches of chipped purple paint. She flung open the doors to reveal stacks of overflowing journals and loose papers. She peered at the mess until landing on one. Navarra delicately pulled out a large, green leather book. She cradled it in her arms and carried it over. She set it on the table with a thud, dusting flowing from it. I stared at the intricate pattern of leaves carved in the dark green leather. She undid the silver clasp holding it together and it sprung open. A rich, earthy aroma mingled with a muskiness as Navarra lay it flat. She thumbed through a few pages that had scrawled texts and drawings before landing on one.

I stared at the image before me. The sketch of the creature took up most of the page and had an elongated, wolf-like face, with sharp eyes and a glow the artist somehow captured. Its fur was wild and untamed, sketched with soft shading to create texture, giving it a sense of movement and life. The creature stood on his hind legs, its front paws seeming to form almost human-like fists. In ornate text sprawled across the top was the word 'Moonstalker- Varg.'

"Moonstalker, Varg?" I asked, my eyes not leaving the page.

"Moonstalker is its common name. It is one of the Unsettled. The Unsettled are various forms of souls and beasts that no longer belong. This book is a gift from an old Mage friend." She touched the page delicately.

"Wait, was this from his Runewalk?" I looked over at her. All mages went on a Runewalk, which was a year-long journey where all mages traverse the land, gathering important information in an effort to keep the library and school up-to-date with the latest discoveries and records. Eldrin said it was also important to experience history and see it firsthand.

"It is, in fact. He was one of the companions who followed me here," her voice softened.

"This is incredible," I whispered, staring back at the Varg. "And frightening."

Navarra nodded. "There are a few more in this one from his time in the desert. He said he hated that area the most."

"Because of the Varg and spirits?"

Navarra smiled widely at me. "No, because the food was dry and plain."

I laughed. "Oh, that is also understandable." I rested my hand on the table, leaning over the book. I turned the page that read Flickerbeast, but had no image. I read the text out loud "Ethereal, shape-shifting creatures that can appear briefly as distorted glimpses of former creatures, always in motion, always searching for meaning in their fractured existence. No one knows their true form. You'll know you've encountered one because of the teeth."

"The teeth?" I looked over at Navarra. She shrugged.

I turned to the next page. "Glimmerwraiths," I read. "This horror appears fragmented and inconsistent. It is semi-transparent, its form made up of shifting, flickering tendrils of shadow and light, like reflections on a dark pool of water. The creature is often seen as a humanoid shape, but this figure flickers and shimmers, as though it's not entirely real, but a fading echo of something that once was."

"The desert is a terrifying place," Navarra mused. "However, most of these fear the light. And that, my dear, is what you are."

I pulled my leather bag over my head, letting it rest on my hip. "You never did tell me your thoughts of the vial?"

"I believe the Oracles gave you and your friend the vials for that exact moment," her hands brushed my cheek as she worked on a tight braid in my hair.

"Why didn't they warn us? I could have prevented Raewyn's death." I felt a sting of betrayal.

She shook her head, resting my long braid over my shoulder. "The Oracles cannot interfere. They know things beyond our understanding. I believe they knew you needed to continue part of your journey alone. And I believe they gifted you the vials so you could come into your powers."

I chewed my inner lip. "Then what was Raewyn's for?"

"I believe you will find that answer down the road." Her voice quieted. "You are ready to continue on your path."

I smiled softly. "Thanks to your training and your kindness, I feel certain of my power." I gently closed the book. "I have something to show you."

She raised her eyebrows and followed me outside. The Spring sun was gentle and perfect for what I was about to show her. I motioned for her to stay on the wooden steps of the porch as I walked backwards to the middle of the clearing. I smiled and raised my palm to the sky.

The air around me seemed to shimmer faintly, and a soft golden light began to swirl around my hand like a delicate ribbon of light. With a graceful flick of my fingers, I guided the ribbon of light towards the sky.

From this, soft sun beams stretched down from the high sun as tendrils of sunlight broke through the clouds. As they descended towards me, they bathed the area in a soft, calming glow, making everything they touch appear more vibrant and alive. Flowers suddenly bloomed brighter, leaves shimmered, and the air became more refreshing as the beams filtered through the surroundings. The sunbeams didn't scorch or burn, but are a manifestation of the love I have for this woman of the Moon.

I slowly lowered my hand to my side, the sunbeams subsiding with the movement. I looked over at Navarra to see silver tears running down her lovely, violet face. She stepped into the clearing and pulled me into a full embrace. I felt overwhelmed by emotions and felt my own warm tears fall down my cheeks.

"My dear Light," she whispered. "You have the power to change everything."

"And so I will."

Navarra and I had a tearful goodbye the next morning. She had provided me with more than enough clothes, some of which were suited for the desert, herbs, medicines, and plenty of food. She mentioned the river boat had a lot stocked in it as well, so I could preserve the contents of my bag for later. I gave Rune a scratch under the chin, which was met with a soft *hoo*. He also seemed sad to see me go. I hoped one day to see them both again.

Navarra showed me the ideal pathway to climb down the cliffside along the falls. She told me there would be a boat named *The Wandering Whisker* tied to a sturdy tree a little ways past the bottom of the waterfall. I dismounted the last of the boulders, jumping into the soft, wet grass. I looked up at the waterfall, smiling at the rainbows cast across the thunderous water. I adjusted my leather pack, and walked alongside the Vintar River.

Sure enough, there it was. A small wooden dock extended from one side of a small houseboat, whose design was obviously built by the House of the Moon. The boat had a sturdy wooden frame of pale, weathered wood, giving it a subtle silvery sheen. The hull of the houseboat had intricate carvings, depicting phases of the moon, stars, and celestial patterns. A simple, low cabin sat at the center of the boat. There were lattice-like structures of thin, woven branches that framed the space, possibly to give more privacy. Small lanterns of glowing, silver crystal hung from the lattices.

I carefully stepped onto the deck of the boat, glancing around at the purple and blue cushions cast around, along with rope and other various fishing tools. My fingers gently grazed the large wooden helm on the deck. I pulled back the indigo curtain of the cabin, and stepped inside.

The walls of the cabin were unadorned, except for a few small shelves holding books, simple lanterns, and an assortment of small trinkets. There was a small table, perhaps used for meals or the crafting of simple charms. A hammock made from woven fibers hung near the back, which honestly sounded rather pleasant and reminded me of the shoreline by my home.

Near the back of the cabin was a small stone hearth, a small cast iron pot, and some firewood. There was another open shelf, holding containers of various dried herbs and spices. Hanging from a rope beneath the shelf were four fish, dried and seasoned. I exhaled deeply, ready for the next part of my journey. I removed my pack and set it on the table. I sat on a small stool and removed my boots and stockings, wanting to feel the breeze on my skin.

I returned outside and surveyed the deck once again, inhaling the cool, spring air. I looked around at the trees around me, noting their vibrant colors had changed. It was summer when I had left home with Raewyn. I shook my head, not quite believing how much time had passed. My fingers worked with practiced ease, untangling the knots that had secured the boat to the small dock. The twine felt rough against my skin, but this was a welcomed familiar feeling. It reminded me of home. My movements were slow and thoughtful as I was savoring the final moments of stillness. The rope gave a soft, protesting squeak as it loosened from its mooring. The small wooden boat creaked in response, as though stretching after a long period of stillness. There was a small tug, and with one final pull, the rope slipped free. The boat rocked ever so slightly, its hull shifting with the release, as if to acknowledge that it was now free.

I leaned over the railing at the bow of the boat and stared forward. I didn't know how far down the river to go, but Navarra told me to go on instinct. I had looked at a crude map she had and saw it passed by Briarhollow. I figured I could try to stop near there and restock. It would be nice to see familiar faces, and perhaps I could send word back to Calenor that I was safe. I inhaled deeply. *Do I tell them about Raewyn?* I wondered. I felt obligated to.

I looked down at the water rushing past the boat, splitting from the rounded point of the hull. It reminded me of my days at sea with Raewyn, and on occasion, when Eldrin would join us. I smiled, reminded of one of the songs we harmonized well to.

Oh, the winds are high and the waves do roar,

But the gryphons fly o'er the ocean floor,

With feathers bright and claws that gleam,

They sail through the skies, like a sailor's dream.

~

Heave ho, me hearties, and sing this tune,

With gryphons above and the rising moon,

We'll ride the storm, we'll brave the tide,

With wings in the air and the sea at our side!

My voice echoed down the river, the lilting sound resonating through the trees. I sighed, resting my chin on my folded knuckles. I looked down at my side, as though expecting to see my golden furry companion next to me, staring ahead. But he wasn't with me. Just as Eldrin wasn't with me. Just as Raewyn was no longer with me.

I suddenly felt alone again, and lowered myself to the deck. I curled my knees into my chest and rested my forehead on them. Painful sobs released aggressively from my body, its entirety shaking. My song had been replaced by sounds of grief echoing loudly down the river. I sobbed for what seemed like forever, unable to contain it. That heavy, yet hollow feeling had returned. Navarra had replaced a bit of that loneliness these past few months, and now I had no idea how long before I would see her again.

I turned my head to the side, resting on my knees, my arms still wrapped around my legs. I stared off into the passing woods and softly whispered to no one, "I can't stop shining. I won't stop my light."

CHAPTER TWENTY-TWO

I took a large swig from a dusty brown bottle. I had found a small stash of honey mead in the cabin and fully took advantage of it. I sat cross-legged on the deck, the entire world bathed in twilight. I had a lantern beside me and a book in my lap. It was a brown, clothbound book that were journal entries of who I assumed to be a previous companion of Navarra. At first, I felt a bit intrusive reading it, but after a week of sailing, I was going a bit mad. It seemed to be the journal of a Moon Mage, and I particularly loved his description of leaving Nyxara for the first time.

> I had thought the world beyond Nyxara's borders would be much like the land I have always known—a realm bathed in the quiet, constant embrace of twilight. Nyxara's skies are neither night nor day; they are a deep and contemplative shade of purple, hanging over us like an ever-present veil. The air, thick with the quiet hum of celestial magic, has shaped me, as it has shaped all of my kin.

> Yet, as I step beyond the gates of Nyxara for the first time, I find myself consumed by the strange, blinding light of a world *alive*. The air here feels foreign, sharper and more

pungent, and the overwhelming brilliance of the golden sun burns through the soft twilight haze I've always known. The heat on my skin is a sensation I did not anticipate. It wraps around me, much like the magic of my homeland, yet with a weight I've never felt. My eyes, accustomed to the dim, struggle to focus.

Before me, the landscape is no longer shrouded in a cool, muted dusk. The trees are *alive* in a way I hadn't expected, and they stand tall and proud, their green leaves vibrant against the bright, azure sky. Their colors *glisten* and it is as though the entire forest has been set aflame with life. The thick trunks stretch upward toward the sun with a vigor that mocks the stillness of Nyxara's shadows. The sight leaves me both awed and fearful. How strange it is to witness the world in full color, not merely in the shades of nightfall.

- Soren

I arched my back, stretching my arms above my head. I found his observation interesting. Did House of the Moon mages not do a Runewalk? She said they did. How had he never left Nyxara? I yawned and rotated my neck, stretching the stiff muscles. I went to turn a page when the jovial sound of music caught my attention.

I quickly rose to my feet, a bit unbalanced from the mead. I went to the side railing and stared into the forest. I saw bits of golden and orange light bobbing up and down, contrasting to the dusk light. I reached over to the large wooden wheel and willed *The Wandering Whisker* over to the shore. My body lurched slightly as it made contact with the riverbank. Eagerly, I grabbed the rope and tied it to a thick tree. I had no idea what I was chasing, but my curiosity got the best of me.

I was wearing a simple dark green shift dress, and I knew I blended with the woods. My feet tingled against the cooled grass. I hadn't bothered throwing on my boots. I slowly entered the woods, following the sound of the music and the lights. My face broke out into the utmost grin and wonder as my eyes laid on the scene before me.

Nestled throughout the trees were whimsical houses, no taller than five feet, blending seamlessly into the forest. They were soft and rounded homes. Even in the twilight lighting, I could see the roofs with their cheerful vibrancy, painted in bold hues of yellow, red, and orange. The walls were a beautiful mosaic of grey and brown stones, each one weathered by time and nature, giving the houses a timeless, earthy feel. What truly caught my eye, however, were the doors. Most were arched, their curves elegant and inviting, with intricate paintings of oversized, vibrant flowers. Each petal seemed to burst with color, their vivid pinks, purples, and oranges a stark contrast against the stone. In the center of it all, there were the most peculiar creatures dancing and playing instruments.

I moved towards a large tree, still a safe distance from it all, and watched quietly. They couldn't be more than two to three feet tall, and all looked like various forms of flowers and squashes. I blinked my eyes a few times, unsure of what I was looking at. There was a creature that looked remarkably like a carrot happily playing the fiddle. Next to it was a yellow squash playing a tambourine, and beside it, was a mushroom playing a small mandolin. There were about a dozen similar creatures, flowers and other things, all dancing and enjoying themselves. The orange lights I had seen were lanterns strung up across their village.

I rubbed my eyes, wondering what was in that mead. This could not be real. I opened my eyes again and watched them excitedly. Their energy was contagious and I couldn't help but tap my feet to their music. It was nice to see unbridled joy, despite the oddity of it.

I suddenly felt a sharp poke at the back of my thigh. "Ow!" I turned and looked down to see a Sunflower... being poking me with a sharp spear, its black eyes narrowing at me.

"Who are you?" it asked, its voice mildly high-pitched.

"I am Idrial, Lady of the House of Sun." I curtsied for some reason.

"There are no houses on the Sun," it said, warily.

"Oh, no, I am from Calenor, the capital of Terrathis." I was perplexed and wondered again what was in that mead.

It lowered its spear, evidently not deeming me a threat. "Capital what?"

"Capital city?"

"Cities aren't capitals."

My head was spinning. "No, Calenor is sort of in charge of all of Terrathis."

"No one is in charge of lands. It takes care of itself." The Sunflower crossed its arms over its chest.

Luckily, I didn't have to respond to that because a Mushroom walked over to us. It somehow had a mustache and spectacles. "You found a rare creature," he said.

"This giant creature knows nothing," the Sunflower complained.

"Excuse me! That is not true!" This was absurd.

The Mushroom let out a low chuckle. "The New Ones do not know much, but they cannot be faulted."

"I beg your pardon? My people have been here for a very long time. Since the first Sun Beam touched the earth!" Why were they getting under my skin?

The Mushroom and Sunflower exchanged looks and nodded. Finally, the Mushroom looked back at me. "We have been here since before Eledrinna and her friends arrived. But we welcome them nonetheless."

My eyes widened until they felt dry. "Before Eledrinna?"

He patted my hand. "How did you find us? Most cannot see."

I raised my eyebrows and looked around, still waiting for them to fade away. "I don't know. I was on my river boat and I heard music and saw your lights." I pointed to the general direction of the river.

The Mushroom nodded. "What do they call you?"

"I already told your sunflower friend, I am Idrial." This was insane.

The Sunflower stamped its foot. "I am *not* a Sunflower, I am Helia, a Daisy!"

I held up my hands to her. "My deepest apologies, Helia. You look like the giant Sunflowers back home."

"Giant?! I thought you said you were a Lady!"

"Helia, she didn't mean anything by it. She doesn't know better." The Mushroom looked up at me. "I am Myce, the Mayor of Bramblelite. We are the Poddarins."

"Ah, oh, pleased to meet you." I curtsied again. I glanced over my shoulder, hearing the music stop.

Myce followed my gaze. "Ah, come. The others would love to meet you. They only get to see Earthstriders such as yourself every few thousands of years."

I mouthed the word *thousands* in astonishment and followed the two towards the village. As I entered the small area, everyone froze and stared at me. Myce waved his arms around, as though to calm their nerves. Helia was still a bit huffy and kept side-eyeing me.

I suddenly felt incredibly giant. Other than the trees, everything was scaled down. Their firepit, their homes, the clotheslines, and their gardens.

I stared at their gardens for a moment, wondering what on earth they would eat. I turned towards Myce to see him gesturing for me to sit. I looked around, not wanting to sit on anything, or anyone. I found the curved base of a large tree and rested my back against it.

Myce raised his hand high, addressing the concerned looks of the Poddarins. Most of them had black, rounded button eyes, and they darted back and forth between Myce, Helia, and I. After a rather uncomfortable silence, he spoke.

"We have an Earthstrider visiting us. She means us no harm. She is a daughter of Eledrinna. Many of you remember her?" They all nodded, their eyes somehow widening.

My jaw dropped. They remembered her? "Oh, I am not her daughter, just her descendant."

The Mushroom Mayor turned and looked at me. "No, you are her daughter. I am sure of it. I have met you before." He turned back over to the crowd. I opened my mouth to explain, but I wasn't given a chance. "You know what to do."

The musicians nodded and began playing a melody. A familiar melody. It was the same as the Song of Time, the one I sang at the ball so many months ago. That felt like a lifetime ago, thinking back to it. I turned my attention back to the carrot playing the small fiddle, its melody much more vibrant and upbeat than the version I knew. The tambourine player had their eyes closed, a look of absolute joy on its gourd face. I smiled, recalling that same feeling. I hummed along, trying to keep up with the faster pace of the familiar song. I caught myself feeling a twinge of guilt for being happy. I pushed it aside. My friend and my love would want me to enjoy this odd moment. The Mushroom Mayor seemed to notice as he approached me, his little round, black eyes intent on my face.

"Oh, you are pained. You have loved too deeply, and so you have lost."

I pressed my lips together. "Yes, I have."

He nodded and looked at the musicians, who had stopped playing. They returned the nod and started playing again, this time a bit more somber music. He looked at me carefully.

"We play this when we are sad. We do not lose our own, for we are forever. But we have seen loss. And we sometimes feel sad for the trees."

A soft smile grew on my lips. "That's rather nice." I looked up at the musicians. "This feels nice."

His tiny hand gently pat my leg. "It's good to feel nice, even when sad."

The musicians slowed their song to the end and slowly bowed. I clapped along with the other dozen or so Poddarins. They slowly moved towards the firepit, leaving Myce and I to ourselves.

Not taking my eyes off of the flame, I dared to ask. "What do you mean, I am the daughter of Eledrinna?"

"She had a love before everyone came. It was her, the dark one, the other gods, as you call them. And us. And you were born from her. But you only come like this every few thousands of years. We don't know why. But we are happy to see you." He smiled.

I narrowed my eyes, taking in the new information. It seemed rather outlandish, but these sprites had no reason to lead me wrong. Or maybe I was too trusting and this was a trap. Or maybe it was the mead. My mind swirled. He seemed to understand what was reeling through my mind and spoke carefully.

"You appear to us when there is unrest. When things are about to happen."

I pressed my lips together firmly, trying to recall all the history my instructors and Eldrin tirelessly attempted to drill into my mind. "Then why did I not appear for The Light War? If what you say is true, why did Eledrinna not send me before? Why not give me the power to keep harmony?"

He was sitting next to me, and I felt we had this conversation before, in another life. "Ah, well, then what would be the point of living? If you have all powerful entities controlling everything all the time? What would be the purpose of Earthstriders?" He paused for a moment, looking at his small village. The others were enjoying a small feast. "I cannot tell you why you exist, the humans, the elves, the winged-ones. However, Eledrinna and the others felt it was important to let you live out how you must. Even if it means destruction, death, and cruelty." His thin mushroom mouth smiled. "But you offer more than that."

I turned my head to him, raising an eyebrow. "Oh?"

"Ah, yes! We didn't always have instruments! How beautiful the music you created. Some centuries ago, an elf from the House of the Woods came through and wanted to share his love of music with us. He had always seen us as a boy and spent time learning them all so he could make them and pass on his passion." He gestured to the instruments leaning against a tree trunk. "He built them to fit our size. And that is just a small bit of the lovely things your people have brought into the world."

I pondered this for a moment, still rather confused by the claim of my heritage. How could I be a direct descendant of *the* Eledrinna? Wouldn't I know? What of my parents? Is this why they disappeared? I anxiously tapped my fingertips on my knees.

"Lady of Light, there are always going to be more questions than answers. The important thing is to find out which questions *you* need to be asking, and which ones are a distraction." He rose to his narrow feet. His bodily proportions were strange, and I wondered how he didn't fall over.

"How do I know which is which?"

"I cannot tell you. But I can tell you that your instincts are right. You are the daughter of the first Light, and you have existed since nearly the beginning. All of those previous versions of yourself exist deep within you. You must find them." He bowed lowly. "Our time has ended together. But thank you for stopping by. We will come if you call upon us."

I blinked and looked around, the forest having returned to a normal state. I jumped to my feet, startled by the change. The little houses and the garden were gone. None of the little squash or flower sprites remained. The twinkling lights from their houses were replaced by the soft light of the moon glowing through the trees. My mouth hung open, not knowing what to make of it.

I made my way back towards my boat, wondering if I dreamt it all. I untied *The Wandering Whisker* from the tree and stepped on the wooden surface. My hands gripped the wooden steering wheel, slightly damp from the night dew. The wind gently teased my hair as I turned the heavy wheel to move the boat away from the riverbank. The sounds of the water lapping against the hull of the boat as I steadied in the center of the river. A sigh escaped my lips as I rubbed my hands over my face.

I grabbed another bottle of mead and made my way to the cushions on the deck. I took a large swig before plopping down on the pile of cushions. I laid back, resting my hands on my stomach and extending my legs out. The stretch was welcome and I relished in it for a moment before crossing my ankles. My mind swirled with everything Mayor Myce had said. If he even existed? That was truly bizarre. Did I finally reach a breaking point where I had to create strange creatures?

How could I possibly be the daughter of Eledrinna? What does that even mean? I am just Idrial. I exhaled dramatically out my mouth, followed by a frustrated scream. The sound reverberated throughout the woods on either side of the river, disappearing into the trees. My eyes glazed over the sparkling lights in the sky. I was grateful that Eldrin and I had spent so many nights laying on the domed roof of the grand library. He showed me how to read the stars. Judging by what was brightest, I realized it had been roughly ten months since I left home. So much had happened, it was overwhelming.

I was no longer that same person. I felt... better. Somehow, having lost everything gave me the space to find myself. For once, I wasn't influenced by what I was told to feel or think. Navarra showed me that perhaps what I had learned about the Moon House wasn't quite right. Oh, how painful that was. It made me wonder what else I had been told that wasn't entirely truthful.

And for once, I had to discern information on my own. I didn't have Eldrin to interpret. That part was hard, and would continue to be. I knew I didn't fully trust my own instincts. What if I were wrong about going to the desert? And once I arrived, what then? Would some magical thing direct me to what the voices said? And what about the idea that I am another version of the daughter of Eledrinna? Questions like this made me long for Eldrin and his books. I absently reached a hand to my chest, as though I would find the pendant there.

A movement in the sky caught my eye and I sat up, looking around for it. Flying around, I saw an ethereal hawk soaring above the river. It wasn't fully solid and reminded me of the violet rabbit I saw in the woods with Navarra. I squinted, my eyes following it as it swooped closer to my boat. It landed on the steering wheel and stared at me with glowing, purple eyes. It felt familiar, but I couldn't pin how. I slowly rose to my feet to touch it, but it quickly flew away before I could even take a step. I ran over to the bow of the ship and clutched the railings, watching it disappear.

What the hell is happening? I wondered.

I heaved out a sigh and retreated to the cabin to sleep off the bizarre evening.

Chapter Twenty-Three

A pungent odor wafted into my cabin, startling me awake. I quickly realized something was on fire. I struggled out of my hammock bed and scrambled outside. I looked around in a panic, trying to find the source of a fire. The smell reminded me of Paldor Pass, where we fought the Kha'Laroth. My heart pounded in my chest as my widened eyes looked to the forest line to see distant flames. There was a village on fire. I quickly steered *The Wandering Whisker* over to a questionably sound dock nearby. I leapt off the boat, my bare feet hitting the wooden surface, my white night shirt flowing in the morning breeze. My feet sank into the soft mud as I sprinted towards the forest, the wind whipping through the trees, carrying the distant smell of smoke.

My breath came in sharp, ragged bursts as I pushed through the bramble on the forest floor, my heart racing in rhythm as my feet pounded against the earth. As I neared the tree line, the woods parted before me, welcoming me into chaos. My footsteps quickened, desperate now, until the trees suddenly broke open, revealing the village just ahead.

Before me, a once calm settlement was now ablaze, the entire scene bathed in the red-orange glow of flames. Thatched roofs were alight, curling into smoke and ash, while wooden walls were being consumed in roaring flames. The hoofed villagers were running towards safety, others dashing back to try to save what little they could. There was a nearby group throwing torches onto the buildings.

I halted in the middle of the small village, watching the wood cabins burn. Fauns rushed past me, completely ignoring the questions I shouted. Smoke burned my eyes and my nostrils as I hurried through the village, trying to find someone to help. My eyes stopped at a smoke-filled barn, where a lavender-skinned woman stood, pushing various sheep and goats out into the open. I could make out a dark blue tunic peaking out beneath protective black armor made from hardened leather. Her silver eyes met mine and she shouted at me.

"Stop standing there and do something!"

Startled, I quickly obliged. I rushed over to her, staring into the chaos inside the barn. "What are we doing?" I shouted over the commotion.

She stared at me like I was an idiot. "Saving the animals!" She handed me torn cloth and motioned for me to tie it around my mouth and nose.

I fastened it and went inside. There was another woman, with beautiful olive skin and frizzy, dark hair. She was unlocking stables and pushed a donkey out towards the Moon woman. She glanced at me, her dark eyes peering over her own face cloth. I noted her pierced, pointed ears, realizing she came from the House of the Woods. She also wore black leather armor, but with a dark green tunic beneath. She impatiently grabbed my hand and pulled me towards the next stall.

I unlocked the stable and pulled the panicked horse, bidding it come with me. I had never encountered horses in such a state, and I was mildly scared. The wood elf moved on to the next stable and released that horse. I looked back at the horse I was working with and stepped to the side, as the woman had done. It let out a loud neigh before racing outside. We alternated unlocking the stable doors, the horses eager to escape. The smoke billowed even more inside, making it harder to see. The cloth wasn't filtering out nearly enough. By the time we finished, both the elf and I were coughing aggressively. She grabbed my arm and forcefully pulled me out, back towards the Moon elf.

We ripped off our cloths and stood for a moment. I braced myself with my hands on my knees, coughing out the last of the smoke. She looked over at me, her curly hair falling across her face.

"I'm Marowen. Pleasure to meet you." Her many hooped earrings jingled together as she nodded to her companion. "That's Elaria."

I straightened and looked between both of them briefly. "I am Idrial." I was a bit surprised when neither had a reaction to my name. It had no significance to them. I was about to continue when Elaria extended a finger to the other burning houses.

"We need to put them out." She looked me over. "Are you a Tide person? You don't have wings."

I shook my head. "No, I am from the House of the Sun."

Marowen looked disappointed. "That doesn't help us here."

"What started this? What happened?" I queried.

"Later. We'll explain later." Elaria was racing down the path towards the village center again.

I quickly followed, searching my mind to see how I could help. Sun magic was so close to fire. There had to be some way this could work. I stopped abruptly, a thought coming to mind. I wasn't sure if it would work, but I had to try.

I extended my arms, palms open, towards the fire. The sun magic coursing through my veins came alive and I could feel my skin glowing vibrantly. I willed the fire towards me. I felt an odd hesitation from the flames, almost reluctant to relinquish its power. I closed my eyes and compelled it, siphoning the flames as though they were part of me. The fire bent and shifted, flowing into me. The intense heat of the inferno diminished as the flames were pulled from the building. I stared down as my hands glowed with a fierce, golden light. The building before me was completely void of fire. I looked over at the two women, who were staring.

Marowen let out a victory shout and said, "I don't know who the hell you are or what that was, but do it again!"

Pleased with myself, I raced around the village, willing the flames towards me. After the fourth building, I began to feel fatigued, but I knew I couldn't stop. My skin was glowing and singed with flames. My white night shirt had turned grey from the smoke and ash. I was certain I looked like a complete mess. But my powers were actually helping, and I would not stop. A few remaining villagers stopped to watch me. These were my people, and I needed to help them.

I turned to speak to Elaria to find she had run down the cobblestone path and stood in the town center. She was shouting at the male fauns I saw torching buildings. I lowered my hands and quickly raced towards her, well aware of my stinging, bloody feet. My heart pounded in my chest and I could feel waves of nausea pass over me, but I swallowed hard and tried to ignore it. Marowen stood next to Elaria, who now stood with a dagger pointed at them. Marowen stopped abruptly and drew her bow and nocked an arrow, staring at the men threateningly.

"Why do you destroy your homes?" Elaria said through clenched teeth.

"Varyx won't take us. We'd die before he destroys us all." One of them shouted, stamping his hooves on the ground. "There is no food left. He has taken these people captive!"

"And so you'd rather burn it all down than fight back?" Elaria hissed. She stepped forward, raising her dagger. "How asinine."

Another faun spoke up. "I refuse to let them sell our things to pad their coffers! There's no hope!"

"There is *always* hope," I interjected. "Hope is lost when you believe nothing can be changed."

He scoffed and looked me up and down, no doubt taking in the burned and bloody mess I was. "What does a Sun Cur from the streets know about hope?"

My eyes widened, having not heard that slur in person. My younger brother had heard it in town once and asked what it meant. Our parents scolded him for using it. Before I could counter, Marowen released an arrow into the faun's thigh. He grimaced and lowered to the ground, clutching his leg. He looked up at her in anguish.

"What was that for?"

She shrugged and readied another arrow. "That was uncalled for."

"Mind your manners and you won't see any more blood," Elaria purred, putting her dagger in the sheath at her waist.

I raised my hands and shook my head. "I don't understand what is happening." I glanced down at the faun, who was reeling in pain on the ground. I stared at the other two. "Briarhollow is taken over? If that's the case, why burn down your homeland? Why terrify your neighbors instead of trying to reason?"

Marowen lowered her bow and turned to me, a pierced eyebrow raised. "You can't reason with imbeciles."

"Yeah, there's no point! We show them that *we* are in charge of ourselves! They can't have it if it's in ashes."

"Oh, shut the hell up," Elaria rolled her eyes. "This isn't the way to handle things."

"Do you know what the Moon Guard did to our people? To my *wife?*" The faun's dark eyes were wide with fear and anguish.

My voice shook, "What did they do?"

"They *raped* her in front of me. In front of our children. And then plunged each of their daggers into their hearts." His voice cracked as he knelt down beside his friend.

My skin went cold and my blood stilled as I lowered myself before them. "What are your names?" I tried to keep my shaking voice even.

"Alder," he responded. He nodded his head towards his injured companion. "That's Talon."

"What has happened here?" I gestured around.

Talon snapped the arrow off, leaving the iron tip still in his leg. He groaned and looked up at me. "Months ago, an emissary from the House of the Moon came to Briarhollow. She saw our crops were dying and offered Lady Fiora aid. I didn't trust her, but people more important than me did." He carefully dug out the tip of the arrow and threw the bloody piece beside him. I reached out to tie my rag around his leg. He flinched and narrowed his eyes at me.

"Let me help you," I softly offered. I could feel Marowen and Elaria tense behind me, but I didn't acknowledge them. "What happened then?" I cleaned his wound the best I could before pulling the rag around his leg.

"It got better, things did. For a bit. Food came back, the soil was better. And then the Moon Guard came through. Something about paying a debt and honoring their King." I let out a small gasp. "Then they started taking people, forcing them into caged wagons. If we didn't come, they killed us on the spot. Our kids and our ladies were killed. Something about them being useless." His voice trailed off.

I couldn't quiet the loud force of my heart against my ribcage. My head was swimming and I struggled to keep my vision clear. I sat back on my knees and pressed my fingers into my temples.

"You all right? Not the kind of news for a Lady," Talon said.

I opened my eyes and licked my lips thoughtfully. "This can't be." I rose to my feet slowly. "This cannot be my Kingdom."

Alder scoffed. "Your kingdom?"

"I am Idrial of the House of the Sun. I am from Calenor's palace." My voice held a confidence I did not feel.

Talon and Alder exchanged glances and then laughed. "Then what are you doing with this riff-raff?" They gestured to the other women.

Marowen shot him a harsh look. "We make our living honestly by taking from those with access. Royalty and the wealthy are easy targets because they don't think they can be tricked."

I made an uncomfortable noise but said nothing. Elaria side-eyed me briefly, before turning her sharp, silver eyes to the fauns. "Maybe find better ways to help your cause than destroy your homes."

"Why? You think anyone here will come back?" Talon helped Alder to his feet, careful not to put pressure on his injured leg.

"I will restore your home."

"You've got a lot of hope for someone who knows nothing about anything," Talon said simply.

"Then all I can do is learn." His words pricked at me, but he was right. The further from Calenor I got, the more I realized I knew nothing.

"Good luck," Talon said, not fully genuine. "We'll head back to the camp." He turned and looked at us, his gaze stopping at Elaria. "We'll keep that secret."

Purely out of habit, I curtsied and watched them hobble away, Alder supporting Talon's leg. I moved over to a nearby, half-broken bench, and cautiously sat on it. Every muscle in my body was screaming. As I had expected, my bare feet had hundreds of cuts on them. My white night shift was grey and the bottom half was burned. I finally took a moment to take in my surroundings. Various farm animals wandered around, bleating and crowing, unsure of where to go. I absently pet a dirty sheep that stood near me before realizing the two women stared down at me, their arms crossed.

"All right, now that they are gone, who are you really?" Marowen queried, a serious look on her face.

I looked between the two. "I am Idrial, from Calenor."

"So you said. You're obviously well-educated, but heir to the throne?" Marowen raised an eyebrow.

I let out a nervous, shuddering breath. My head was spinning. "It is true."

Elaria knitted her brows. "How did you get here? Knowing the Sun House, they would never let their most prized person out of the sandstone walls."

I pointed through the trees towards the river. "I was on a riverboat from the mountains. I smelled smoke and saw the flames. I wanted to help." I stared at the now distant figures hobbling away. "Who are they?"

Elaria cleaned a dagger on a cloth. "Men from the outskirt towns of the Meadow. They have been going to different villages and stealing and setting fire to their homes." She sheathed her dagger. "People lose their minds when in moments of panic."

I bit the inside of my lip. "I don't understand why they are destroying their own towns?"

Marowen shrugged. "In times of defeat, people tend to do stupid things. And as they said, they didn't want their possessions being stolen and sold to support the wrong side."

I stared at her. "So, because their leader is compromised, they are just burning it down? That makes no sense." I searched my brain for any mention of similar actions in my history lessons, but I found none.

"I'm sure they have lost everyone and everything. What more is there to lose?" Elaria wiped her hands on her pants, leaving a print of grey dust.

"You mentioned a boat?" Marowen extended a hand. "Will you bring us to it?"

I stared at her hand, momentarily enamoured by the swirling runes tattooed on her fingertips up to her shoulder. After a brief consideration, I grabbed her hand. I winced from the pain that shot through my entire body. Elaria noticed and reached into the black leather pouch at her waist. She pulled out a small vial of brown liquid and handed it to me. I eyed it suspiciously.

"If I were going to kill you, I would have shoved you into a flaming building," she said, a mischievous smile on her face. "It will help your pain."

Desperation was settling in, so I popped the cork and quickly downed the bitter liquid. Warmth poured through my body, and I rapidly felt a bit of the pain easing up.

"It's Sweetbark. You brew it, and it makes a tea that helps the pain." Elaria took the empty bottle back and shoved it back in her pack.

"Thank you. I didn't realize it would be so effective so quickly." I was astounded at how much better I felt.

"Eh, there's also a bit of alcohol mixed in, so that helps." She winked at me.

I let myself smile, mildly amused. We walked through the woods, the soft grass a welcome feeling on my feet. I was only slightly worried something happened to my boat and relief washed over me as I laid eyes on it. I stepped onto the dock and turned, hearing a low whistle.

"This is a fancy-ass boat," Elaria stated, her silver eyes wide. "And very obviously from the Moon House." She eyed me curiously.

"Ah, someone in the mountains helped me during some troubles," I chose my words carefully. "She gave me her boat to get to the desert."

Marowen laughed. "You realize you can't take a boat to the desert, right?"

"Yes, I know that!" I was a little irritated. "I intended to take the boat as south as I could and then head towards the desert on foot."

She waved her hand. "Don't be so serious. I assumed as much." She brushed past me and stepped on to the boat. Her fingers gently caressed the wooden railing near the steering wheel. Marowen looked up and gently tapped the hanging lights above the cushions before turning and nodding at Elaria. "One of yours?"

Elaria stood at the steering wheel, gently touching the markings in the center. She shook her head. "Nah, this has Moon Healer marks." She looked up at me. "It's warded by a Moon House healer. She tells the truth."

I furrowed my brow. Warded? Did Navarra add protection spells without my knowledge? I suppose that made sense. A cold wave washed over me as I missed the old woman, not for the first time. Sensing my mood shift, Elaria cleared her throat.

"You should probably bathe and change. You don't smell great, and I can see your breasts." She pointed at my chest.

I looked down to see my clothes had become mostly translucent, not to mention the left side of the chest was ripped, nearly exposing me. My cheeks warmed as I tried to cover myself. I was mortified.

Marowen grabbed a sealed bottle of mead and lowered herself onto the cushions. "It's happened to the best of us." She popped the bottle open, Elaria having joined her on the deck. "We'll wait for you." She took a big swig, obviously delighted from the noise that came out of her mouth. I smiled to myself as I disappeared into the cabin of the boat.

I grabbed a tan tunic, black pants, and a towel, as well as a soap bar made from rosemary and mint. I stepped back onto the deck and felt amused as I saw the women laughing with their whole bodies as they shared the bottle.

I was eager to join whatever was happening, so I rushed off the boat, set my clothes on the deck, and stepped into the cold river.

My entire body tingled from the chill that permeated my skin. I inhaled sharply while my body acclimated to the water. It wasn't *nearly* as cold as the creek Raewyn and I had bathed in, but it wasn't quite as warm as the hot baths from Navarra. I summoned my powers to gently warm the water around me. I didn't want to disturb the natural wildlife, and so I was careful to not let it warm too much. I exhaled deeply out of my mouth, then sucked in as much air as I could, before diving into the deeper part of the river.

It felt so good to be in the water. I hadn't really bathed or allowed myself to enjoy it since leaving Navarra, and it felt a bit like home. It wasn't the ocean, of course, but I felt I could almost hear the gulls calling in the distance and Raiku barking at them. Under the water, I could pretend home was just above the surface and Raewyn was there waiting for me. Under here, the Sun Stone wasn't missing, and I would spend the evening in the arms of Eldrin. But under here, I would run out of air. I reluctantly resurfaced, pushing my face through the water's tension. I quickly scrubbed my skin and hair with the bar of soap, feeling the grime leaving. I scrubbed my hair, my eyes closed, enjoying the warm sun on my face.

"Woah! What are you doing?" A surprised voice snapped my eyes open.

I looked up at the ship's bow to see Marowen and Elaria. Elaria was holding the mostly empty bottle, her arms draped over the wooden railing. Marowen was pointing directly at me, her mouth opened in shock.

"What do you mean? I'm cleaning myself as you suggested!" I suddenly felt shy and covered my chest.

Elaria waved the bottle. "Oh, we've all seen every species naked. You're not special."

Marowen laughed at her friend then looked back at me. "Yes, and why are you *and* the water glowing?"

I looked around to see the surface of the river was glowing gold. I looked down at my hands to see my skin had my normal glow that appeared when I was content.

"Huh. Normally only I glow. Not the things around me."

"Excuse me?" Marowen said, her eyes widening in glee.

"It is a trait of people from the House of the Sun." I shrugged as I made my way towards the deck. I grabbed the towel and quickly dried myself before putting on my clothes.

"Sure, but I've never seen anyone make a damned river glow," Marowen stated, her eyes following me as I boarded the boat again.

"Truthfully, that has never happened before," I admitted reluctantly.

Elaria eyed me, mildly suspicious. "You are royalty. You said so. Just *how* royal?"

I dropped the bar of soap and my dirty clothes. I turned to look at them. They were both leaning against the railing, their arms crossed. Their movements were similar, which led me to believe they spent a lot of time together. *No secrets from each other, either,* I mentally noted. I went to lean down to gather my things when Marowen stopped me.

"Listen, we really don't care about your status. We just want to make sure we are safe. We have others at camp, and we are vetting you to make sure you won't go and kill us all." She knelt down and grabbed my things. "You probably should throw these clothes away."

I managed a smile and nodded. "Yes, you're right." We stood square in front of each other, her dark brown eyes reflecting the light from my skin. It showcased the gold flecks in her irises I hadn't noticed before. I inhaled deeply. "I am heir to the House Sun, Ruler of Terrathis."

Elaria handed me the bottle. "It sounds as though you need this more than we do. That's a lot of weight on a person."

I tilted my head slightly, confused by their lack of... shock. "You're not intimidated?"

Marowen shrugged. "Why would we be? You're still the same person you were when you helped us free the animals from the barn."

"It's true. What are you doing here, anyways?" Elaria asked.

My shoulders relaxed. "That is an incredibly long tale that I will tell you at some point. But there is still much pain there."

They both nodded, evidently having been in that space before. I was grateful for their understanding. They felt refreshing, honestly. I could loosen up a lot with these two. Perhaps that is what I needed after an incredibly stressful year. I smiled at the thought.

Elaria lowered herself onto the floor pillows again. "I would like to know how you acquired this boat, however, seeing as it's made by my people." Her tone wasn't accusatory, just curious. Regardless, I felt an odd guilt wash over me.

I lowered myself beside the two women. "I was gravely injured in the mountains." They exchanged looks, but said nothing. "I awoke in a strange cabin at the top of Galenra Falls, and there was an older woman, an elf from the House of the Moon. She took care of me for many months and helped me regain my strength. Once I was healed, she sent me to the bottom of the falls to take her boat."

Elaria eyed me, her curiosity deepening. "What was her name?"

For some reason, my heart pounded. What if Navarra was an enemy of Elaria? What if they were relatives? I cleared my throat. "Her name is Navarra."

Elaria's pierced lips rose softly. "She survived, then."

My pointed ears twitched. "You knew her?"

"I knew *of* her. She was my great-aunt. I know she was the Healer of the House of the Moon until she left with others. My mother told me great stories before we left Nyxara."

I wanted to ask why they left, but felt that was a conversation for another time. My thoughts were confirmed when Elaria continued. "It's good to hear she is doing well. That was good of her to care for you." She paused for a moment. "I am surprised you weren't afraid of her."

My cheeks flushed. "Ah, I was uncomfortable at first. Calenor does a fantastic job of painting Moon folk in a poor light. But so far, that has been proven wrong."

"How many of us have you met, then?"

"Including you? Two, now. More than I ever have." I smiled warmly.

Elaria returned the smile and leaned affectionately against Marowen. "I am glad to contribute to a positive experience."

"Are you two a couple?" I suddenly blurted out.

Marowen laughed. "No, we have just been through hell before each other and with each other. You form a certain bond from that."

I nodded. "Ah, my friend of that depth has passed. But I understand a bit of it."

Marowen sat up. "That is hard, to lose a part of you." She gently touched a hand to my knee. I looked down at the tattoos that sprawled from her fingers to her upper arm. It was a beautiful blend of vines and foxes and Trilium flowers, all symbols from the House of the Woods. I absently traced one of the fox tails.

"Did these hurt?"

She smiled down at her ink. "A whole hell of a lot. Mostly at the fingers. It goes numb after a while."

"Why did you leave your home if you are so fond of it?" I couldn't stop myself from asking.

A surprised laugh burst from her mouth. "Wow. Well, I left because I was tired of being told what to do. I was the *best* archer Thalirien had ever seen, but because I am a female, I could never enter a tournament." She mimicked drawing back a bow string and releasing it. "They only wanted my skills when it was useful to them. And to put it simply, I got fed up and left. But it is still home to me."

My eyes widened. "Just like that? You left?"

She shrugged. "I did."

The sun was beginning to lower in the sky. I looked at my new companions, and glanced around. "So, what happens now?"

"Well, where are you trying to go?" Malowen asked.

"I need to get to Briarhollow and speak with Fiora."

The two exchanged nervous glances. "Briarhollow is not well. Fiora may not be willing to speak with you."

My brows furrowed. "We are allies? I saw her a year ago in Calenor."

Elaria pressed her lips together. "Let's sleep here tonight. Marowen and I will happily sleep on the deck. In the morning, we will take you back to the camp with the others. Briarhollow is not terribly far, and we will accompany you there."

I opened my mouth to inquire further, but realized the day had left me exhausted. I retired inside and curled into my hammock, quickly drifting to sleep.

Chapter Twenty-Four

The dirt path kicked up billows of dust under my feet as we made our way out of the forest. The sun was just peeking over the horizon, its warmth casting the field before us in a soft, orange and pink glow. I followed the two women as we came upon a massive oak tree. Beneath its sprawling branches, a man sat cross-legged on a rather tattered red blanket, a leather-bound book open in his hands. Upon further inspection, it appeared he was reading to a few curious squirrels that were perched nearby. His voice was enthusiastic and I swear the squirrels nodded, agreeing with whatever the book said. He wore a loose linen purple shirt with cotton black pants. His feet were bare, which somehow seemed fitting. There was a familiar feeling about this man, but I couldn't pin it.

My eyes drifted a short distance to the warm glow of a firepit flickering in the morning light. There stood a man with a rather imposing presence, despite the fact that he was cooking over the firepit. I studied him for a moment, noting his broad and muscular frame told me he once was a guard. He had shorter black wavy hair and he moved with precision. The sleeves of his white linen shirt were rolled up as he tended to a simmering pot hanging over the flames. A sweet aroma of its contents filled the air. My stomach growled in response, reminding me we hadn't eaten. I glanced around the campsite to see a few woven baskets with bundles of herbs, dried meats, and mushrooms from the woods.

What surprised me the most was their wagon. The canvas wrapped around was not the usual beige I was accustomed to, but rather a combination of red and purple and blue in great swirl patterns and starbursts. It was vibrant and cheerful. Colorful cloth banners fluttered from a rope tied between the wagon and the oak tree. My eyes briefly grazed over a lyre harp resting against a wooden crate that said 'BOOKS.'

Marowen stepped over to the man reading to the squirrels. "They are going to eat our food if you keep bringing them here, you know?"

He glanced up at her, adjusting his round spectacles that magnified his golden-brown eyes. "I'll ask them not to." He looked over at me, did a double-take, and quickly jumped to his feet. The squirrels scattered, nearly startled as I was.

"Idrial?"

My eyes widened as I stared at him. "Do I know you?"

"Yes! It's me, Calveris!"

I stared blankly at him for a moment, studying his face. He felt so familiar and had similar features as others in the House of the Sun. Obviously a scholar of some sort.

He brought his hands up to his head, and began pacing. "Does Eldrin know where you are? Why have you left Calenor?"

Marowen interjected before I could answer. "Wait, how do you know Idrial? Who is Eldrin?"

I stared at the man for a moment, studying his face. It was thinner and he had grown rather scruffy looking facial hair. It suddenly dawned on me who this man was.

I swallowed hard. "You were the High Curator of Fauna and Lore, weren't you? At the Institute of Celestial Order?"

He nodded enthusiastically. "Yes! Technically, I still am. I have just been away for a few years to study various creatures that have been popping up at random. There had been many reports filed to the Institute, and they asked if I would be interested in field work." He paused for a moment. "Of course, I didn't mean to be gone for so long! These ones," he gestured to Marowen and Elaria, "found me in a bit of a bind up near the Witches' Bog two years ago, and we've traveled ever since."

His explanation presented me with more questions than answers, but there was one most pressing thing I had to ask. "Do you have a way to contact Eldrin? Anyone back home?" My voice caught on the word home.

His features softened. "I do not. The communication device I had has long since broken. Moreover, I didn't have a reason to contact them." He stared at me, studying my face. "Why are you out here?"

I blew air out of my mouth. "I will tell you, especially because your companions have so kindly invited me here. But I would love to have food in my belly first."

He chuckled and nodded. He looked over to the campfire. "Alaric! Is there food ready yet? We have a guest!"

I stared at the man named Alaric. He also seemed vaguely familiar, but I couldn't place it. His piercing blue eyes stared intently for a moment, the look of past grief shrouding his features. There was such an intense sadness about him that my skin prickled. I felt Elaria's gentle hand on my arm. I looked over at her and she smiled. "Come eat with us and tell us your story."

We sat on logs around the campfire, which felt oddly comforting and normal. The boiled oats had dried figs and honey drizzled in with a pinch of salt. It was a warm welcome after eating salted meat and foraged berries for months. Alaric had also poured some liquid from a silver flask that turned water into a yellow citrus drink. It was wonderfully tart. After we were all settled, Marowen cleared her throat.

"So, what brings the Heir to Therrathis out here on a riverboat?"

I coughed gently and looked around at the eyes staring at me with curiosity. "I don't know how much to tell. So much has happened."

Elaria shrugged. "Tell as much or as little as you'd like."

I nodded and sat up, setting my wooden bowl on the log beside me. "Roughly a year ago, all the leaders of the different realms were in Calenor, my home. I was set to perform the Stone Summit." I paused for a moment. "We hadn't done it for quite some time due to my parents' sudden disappearance. But the leaders were concerned for their people and their lands, and so we decided to host one. The evening before the ceremony, the Sun Stone was taken."

Calveris gasped. "Were the wards not in place?"

"They were. Eldrin could find no trace of anyone tampering with them. He and the other head mages saw the Sun Stone on its pedestal that morning. He was beside himself upon discovering its absence."

He shook his head, adjusting his glasses. "There was no trace?"

"None at all."

"Incredible. Carry on."

"After a council with the other leaders, we decided it was best for my closest friend, Raewyn, and I to venture north to visit the Oracles. She is the daughter of the House of the Tide leaders and had been there before." I stopped abruptly as Alaric had choked on his bite. I stared at him with concern and curiosity for a moment, before he waved me on to continue. "We passed through Evercrest and made our way through the mountains. The Oracles, unfortunately, were not as helpful as we had hoped."

Elaria chuckled. "I find they bring more confusion than clarity myself."

"Truly. We left with more questions than we arrived with." I stopped speaking for a moment, realizing what happened next in our journey. I inhaled deeply. "We encountered a Snow Golem and... Raewyn was lost." I lowered my head, staring at my fidgeting hands in my lap.

"That must have been hard," Marowen softly said.

"It was. I destroyed the Golem and passed out." I decided not to tell them about coming fully into my powers. I didn't know them yet and wasn't sure how it would be received. "I woke up some time later where Navarra, a woman from the House of the Moon, had found me and took me in. She helped me heal and train back to health over two seasons. When the time was right, she let me take her boat, and I followed the river. And then I met these two." I gestured towards Elaria and Marowen. "And here we are." I smiled fondly.

"And here we are," said Elaria, eyeing me suspiciously. I could feel she knew I left out some key points, but she didn't press me.

"Where do you go now?" Alaric spoke up, his deep voice even.

"I am hoping to meet with Fiora at the House of the Meadow." I took a sip of the tart drink.

"When did you last speak with her?" Alaric's expression was neutral.

"At the council before we left Calenor." The way he asked his question formed a pit in my stomach.

"And you have had no contact with her since?"

I shook my head. "I had a pendant that Eldrin had given me before I left. It allowed me to communicate with him. But I lost that during my fight with the golem. I am hoping Fiora will allow me to send word back home that I am alive."

The four exchanged silent glances, which furthered the pit in my stomach. Something was wrong. After a long, awkward silence, Elaria stood.

"We will come with you to Briarhollow. But you must be warned: it is not what you expect. Not anymore."

I furrowed my brow. "How do you mean?

Marowen rose and extended a hand towards me. "It is best if you find out for yourself."

I took her hand and rose. We gathered our dishes and threw them in a bag while Alaric put out the fire. Marowen explained we would wash all the dishes when we came upon a creek. I was about to inquire about Briarhollow when Calveris came out of the woods with a large beast. It was the strangest looking thing, yet somehow beautiful. It was a massive horse-like animal, but had white fur with large black stripes. Its legs had white, fluffy fur that extended over its grey hooves. The most astounding part was the two large horns that jetted out of his forehead.

My mouth gaped open, staring at it. "What is that?"

Calveris grinned and patted the beast's side. "This is Bellar. He is a Valkor, one of the last of his kind. I found him up in the mountains near the witches' bog. He was injured and was nearly victim of the witches there. I think they wanted to eat him." He stroked Bellar's cheek. "He's a big help."

My eyes remained wide as I had never quite seen anything like him. He had rather gentle eyes for such a massive creature. I watched as Calveris hitched him up to the packed up wagon. The mage stepped on the wooden tongue on the wagon and climbed onto Bellar. He glanced down at us.

"Shall we?"

Chapter Twenty-Five

It was half a day's journey to Briarhollow. Calveris offered I ride in the wagon, but I found my nerves increased with each step and I needed to walk. The movement and the changing scenery helped ease my mind. I was anxious to arrive in Briarhollow, and my new companions' odd behavior towards it didn't provide any comfort.

As we came to the outskirts of the town, I immediately knew something was horribly wrong. The sun cast a warm light on the fields, but I felt a sickly hue to the air, an undercurrent of something wrong. The crops, while still abundant, had taken on a strange, twisted quality. The wheat grew too tall in some places, leaning over at odd angles, while the orchards had begun to rot, fruit hanging like unnatural lumps on withered branches. The scent of the earth, once rich and comforting, emitted a faint smell of decay.

The cracked roads beneath my feet made it hard to maneuver as we made our way into town. I glanced down to see discarded, dusk-hued helmets from the Moon Guards. I picked one up, staring at it intently. I ran my fingers over the crescent-shaped ridge on the brow. The small veil of chainmail on the neck was broken and missing pieces. I set it back down near a tattered, thick indigo cloak and continued on. The cobblestones were uneven, and overgrown with creeping vines that seemed to choke the life out of them. Various carts were pushed through the streets, but their wheels made a horrific grinding sound. I looked down at a cart covered in blankets that passed us.

"What is that?" I hesitantly asked.

"Death," Alaric stated. "That is all you will find here."

I glanced around at the people, who were known to be vibrant and full of life. It was an unsettling sight, as they now walked with hunched shoulders, eyes dull and vacant. Their clothes were stained, and they didn't even glance our way. I looked over at Marowen, who walked on the other side of Bellar, but she kept a straight face forward.

My weary eyes landed on a nearby cartstall, one I knew to be a baker. I saw the figure behind and recognized her.

"Briar!" I called, walking towards her. The normally vibrant faun was a shell of her former self. Her dark skin was ash and her green eyes were vacant. She looked at me, but there was no sign of recognition.

Calveris stepped beside me. "She won't see you. No one has their own mind here."

I looked at him. "What happened to them? This place feels wrong."

Alaric clutched his sword at his waist. "The entire town is dead. Not just the people, but even the very land itself has been poisoned."

"Poisoned?" I glanced around. "I do not see any signs of poison."

Calveris adjusted his glasses. "Without the Sun Stone in place, the land is more susceptible to evil. You are seeing the effects of twisted Arcane magic. It swept the minds of the people and tortured them until they could no longer think for themselves." He paused and looked around. "The ones still living now only exist haunted by those hallucinations."

Hot tears pricked at my eyes as the reality of his words set in. *Who did this? What twisted Arcane Magic?*

"We cannot linger here to mourn what has been lost," Elaria stated. "Even we are not immune to it. It is unsteady and could corrupt us if we are not careful."

"Can't we just find who did it and destroy them? Won't that heal the town?" I asked, hopefully.

"Oh, you will meet her. But she cannot be destroyed. Many have tried." Marowen's voice held a bitter tone. "And even if you did, it would not restore Briarhollow."

I said nothing as we continued forward. I knew there had to be a way to heal them. I was determined, perhaps naively so.

The market was eerily quiet, the only sound was the hooves on the street and our wagon rattling against the broken stone. Vendors stood still, their wares more grotesque than appetizing. I stared at them as I walked past, noting wilted vegetables, bruised fruits, and meats that seem far too dark for anything fresh. The air was thick with an unsettling sense of unease, as if every breath draws in more than just the usual scents of earth and produce. There were no children running and playing in the square, as I would expect. I looked around to see that instead, they lingered in the corners of the square, their faces pale and their gazes fixed on something unseen. Some seemed to be whispering, as though hearing voices that aren't there.

At the heart of it all stood the infamous great stone well, cracked and overgrown with dark moss. The water that once was pure now appeared stagnant, murky, as though it carried something toxic.

"I wouldn't drink that water," Marowen grimly joked. Marowen knelt down and picked up a few arrows off the ground and put them in her quiver.

We continued further west towards the house of the town's leader, Lady Fiora. I stopped abruptly and stared at the house before me. Where once the manor was clearly a beacon of prosperity, it now loomed like a darkened fortress. The whitewashed walls had begun to peel and crack, and the vibrant flowers that once grew in her garden were now withered husks. The scent of mildew and rot clung to the air, a stark contrast to the healthy growth that was likely to have surrounded her home. I looked around, listening for the sound of cheerful birds, but was met with silence and the occasional hollow creak of the house's timbers shifting in the wind.

"What happened here? Her estate is described in such vibrant ways in all the songs," I whispered.

Calveris dismounted Bellar and looked over at me seriously. "There is no way we could have warned you." He looked back at the house.

Alaric moved past me, pulling out the sword at his belt. "Do not expect to be greeted by friends. Whatever your past relationship was, it is no longer."

My body vibrated with nerves. My heart pounded in my chest and I felt my skin dampen. *What happened to my friend?*

Leaving Bellar with the wagon, we pushed through the iron gates and made our way towards the house. As we approached the gates of Fiora's house, my eyes landed on strange symbols carved into the stonework—markings that pulsed with an unnatural energy, as though the house itself was alive, feeding off something dark. The garden was a twisted mockery of its former beauty, the plants unnaturally contorted, their roots choking the earth. In the distance, the low growl of a storm could be heard on the horizon, though the sky remains clear.

I held back as we approached the few broken stone steps that led to the large, arched wooden doors. Elaria saw my hesitation and gently rested a hand on my arm.

"Your light within burns brighter than whatever evil is before us. Shine bright, Lady of the Sun." She winked at me before removing two daggers from her waist.

Elaria's feet were soft as they landed on the steps and she joined the others at the top. She nodded her head towards the door, as though encouraging me. I swallowed hard and moved up the stairs, wishing I had my bow. I saw all the others were well-armed and suddenly felt underdressed. I looked over at Calveris to see that he even had a dark wooden staff with a blue orb at the end. It was simple, yet seemed effective.

"Where did you get that?" I hissed.

"The wagon, of course!" He tossed it to his other hand and polished the orb with his sleeve. "She's reliable and sturdy."

"I am a bit worried that I am the only one not armed?" I looked at the group.

Marowen raised an eyebrow. "You *are* a weapon, remember? Your light power exists."

I opened my mouth to protest, but was cut short as Alaric pushed open the door and motioned for us to quiet. With a strong force, he shoved the door open to reveal a dark entryway.

We poured inside, and as the door closed behind us, we found ourselves in darkness. I sighed and held my palm up, summoning a small orb of light, illuminating the hallway.

I stared at the walls, unsure of what I was seeing. There were signs of verdant tapestries that depicted blooming meadows and serene skies, but they seemed to ripple with subtle disortions. The patterns warped like reflections on water disturbed by unseen forces. I reached out my hand to touch the surface, only to have Elaria aggressively bat my hand away. I looked at her and she shook her head.

"Don't touch anything," she whispered.

The hallway stretched unnervingly long. With every step, the space seemed to grow more labyrinthine. I suddenly felt we had been here for eternity. I was grateful for the light in my hand, though it created strange, sharp angles, as though the darkness didn't know how to behave around the light. The hall was filled with the sharp, electric smell. It reminded me of Arcane magic, but with a rotting smell intertwined.

With every door we passed, I swore I could hear Fiora's voice, calling my name in a tone too sweet, too pleading, to be real, only to fade into distorted laughter or whispers that sent chills down my spine. Strange images formed before me, and I couldn't focus on them. Fleeting images of meadow flowers appeared, but quickly wilted and turned to ash as soon as I reached for them. After what felt like eternity, we reached the end of the corridor. I reached for the handle but was stopped by Alaric.

"Do not trust anything in there. You may have come to this conclusion, but we are no longer in a peaceful Meadow House, but rather a House of Illusions. Nothing is true." My golden light flickered against his hardened face, casting harsh shadows. He appeared more intimidating at this moment.

I nodded nervously and watched as he opened the door. My entire body went cold.

Chapter Twenty-Six

Before me was a chilled chamber once reserved for Fiora's peaceful meditations. There were remnants of colorful, fluffy pillows all over the ground and shattered statues of animals. Slats of wood were broken on the walls, but no sunlight came through. In the dead center of the room, a mirror sat and reflected nothing but the emptiness of a cold, moonlit sky, despite the sun being high outside. Sitting on a small wooden stool facing us, was Fiora.

Lady Fiora herself had changed. I pulled my light away, the silvery moonlight the only thing remaining. Her normally black braided hair was loose and bushy. The bronze glow of her umber skin had faded. I could see her hooves had overgrown from lack of care. Her antlers had been cut off at her scalp. Tears pricked at my eyes as I took in the image before me. Where once she was a wise, kind leader, she now appeared as a hollow shell of her former self. Her once radiant smile had been replaced by an empty expression, and her eyes gleamed with a strange, distant look.

Without thinking, I stepped forward. "Fiora?"

She slowly lifted her head and looked at me with empty eyes. They grazed over the group beside me, not really seeing. They settled back on me.

"There is nothing for you here." Her voice was raspy and faded. My heart sank.

"I can help you. What has happened?" I went to rush forward, but was held back by Marowen pulling my arm. I looked over at her.

She shook her head somberly. "Do not approach."

I opened my mouth to protest when a silver voice broke the eerie silence. "She is no longer your friend, Sun Heart."

I looked behind Fiora to see a tall figure come out of the shadows. Illuminated by the moonlight, I saw she was from the House of the Moon. Her skin was a rich purple, almost black. Silver swirls gleamed all over her bare arms. She wore a black iridescent gown that spilled to the floor. Fabric loosely draped over her shoulders and the neckline plunged deeply, exposing her cleavage. I noted the silver pendant around her neck containing a large, round Moonstone. Her silver hair cascaded down her back in straight lines. She was beautiful and terrifying.

She slowly walked towards us, her black boots thudding on the wooden floor. As the woman approached me, I felt Elaria place a protective hand on my shoulder. Despite my heart thudding in its chamber, I stood firm.

"How do you know me?"

She laughed, but there was no humor in the sound. "My dear, anyone would recognize the Heir to the Sun. It was only a matter of time before you arrived here." She stood just a few feet before me. "I imagined you would believe you could save your friend here."

"That is what I intend to do." My voice was even.

"Hm," she sang. She calmly walked back to stand beside Fiora, who watched us with vacant eyes. "She is too far gone for you. There is only the light of the moon left."

My lips turned upwards. "Fortunately for me, the moon is only illuminated by the sun."

The woman's expression cracked for a brief moment. I heard Alaric cough behind me, stifling a laugh. She flung her silver hair over her shoulder.

"Indeed. Which is why you would be wise to help us and not become our enemies." She affectionately stroked Fiora's hair.

"You are already our enemy with what you have done to this place!" Marowen took a step forward, reaching for her bow.

She raised her eyebrows. "There is no need for battle. We are merely talking."

"Who are you?" I angrily queried.

"I thought you would never ask. I am Thalassa, Emissary to Varyx of the House of the Moon." Her voice had a hint of pride in it.

"What have you done to Briarhollow? Why are you here?"

She casually glanced down at her hand, as though she were bored of our conversation. "I merely offered Fiora a solution." She lowered herself in an ornate wooden chair. "You see, while you were traipsing about Therrathis, I was actually helping the people. This poor farming town came down with a horrible blight. Their crops failed, and people became sick. I simply offered help and healing." She looked over at Fiora, who was blankly staring at her. "She had no choice but to accept."

"No doubt it was *you* who caused the corruption," Marowen exploded.

She shrugged and smiled. "We will never know the cause, will we?"

I felt my body warm as my powers pulled to the surface. I could see my skin glowing gold against the silver light in the chamber. I heard the sound of steel behind me and knew Alaric and the others had drawn their weapons. Thalassa saw the movements and confidently rose to her feet.

"You should not have come here. The House of the Moon is not a place for the warmth of the Sun." Her voice remained even and calm.

"This is not the House of the Moon. You are in the Meadow House, who is under *my* protection."

"I am not fond of your cockiness," Marowen spat. I suddenly heard an arrow whip past my ear towards the woman.

As though she anticipated the attack, Thalassa held up a hand. I watched in horror as the arrow stopped a foot in front of her face and dissolved. She waved her hand, sending us to the ground.

Elaria expertly leapt to her feet, thrusting a dagger at the emmisary. She wasn't aiming for her face, and I watched as it embedded itself in her leg. Thalassa broke her demeanor and crouched down, a cry escaping her lips.

"You bitch! How dare you think you can overtake me."

Calveris raced forward, his staff extended towards her. Lightning beamed out of the blue orb. Thalassa pulled the dagger out with one hand and lifted the other. The lightning scattered, seeming to hit some sort of invisible shield. Blood streamed down her leg as she limped towards us.

"Your efforts are in vain." She sent out a blast of Arcane magic, the light of it blackened by corruption.

A nervous scream shook out of my mouth as I covered my face, bracing for impact. None came. I looked up to see Alaric stood in front of us, blocking the attack with his shield. It was only then I noticed the House of the Tide crest on the metal front.

"You can take me, but you will not have her," he shouted.

"We will see about that." Without a warning, she raised her hand, and the very air seemed to tremble. Shadows from every corner of the room surged forward, twisting, coiling like living things, and in their wake came a series of horrifying whispers that wrapped themselves around my mind.

"Are you so certain this is worth it?" Thalassa's whispering voice rang out in my mind, the words dripping with mockery. "Look at them, Idrial.

Your companions. They are already slipping away. Your power will not be enough to save them."

The room began to change. The walls seemed to ripple and bend like water in a storm. I glanced around at my new friends to see their faces contorted in pain and fear, their eyes dark and hollow. They were crouched on the ground, reaching out to me, their mouths opening in silent screams.

My breath hitched and my pulse quickened, and suddenly, the world around me blurred. The chamber now seemed filled with twisted shapes, like figures from a nightmare, their faces masked by darkness, their limbs stretching unnaturally long.

"Idrial, don't abandon us!" Calveris cried.

I spun toward him, but his form twisted in an instant, his face now a grotesque mask, skin rotting away to reveal the dark, corrupted essence beneath. "You've already failed us," he rasped. "You should have never come to us..."

"No!" I shouted, my heart pounding in my chest. I would not lose another friend. Not again. I stepped forward, trying to will the light within me, but I found the shadows were stronger, pulling me back.

The vision of Calveris vanished, but only to be replaced by more. An image of Raewyn on the cliff flashed before me. She was reaching out to me.

"Idrial! Why did you let me fall?" Her wings were broken and her body was covered in blood and bruises.

I reached out, tears streaming down my face. "I didn't mean to! I couldn't save you. I couldn't save you."

"You were my closest friend. I trusted you." Her vision disappeared before I could reach her. I fell to my knees, only to be swept into another vision.

The world whipped around me and I suddenly stood in my mother's bedchamber. I recognized it as the night my parents disappeared. The fireplace was lit, but instead of a warm glow, the flames were indigo and thrashing about. My mother stared at me, her bright blue eyes showing great disappointment.

"We had to leave you."

I gasped. "Why? Where did you go?"

"We could not bear to see you fail as our heir. We knew you would let down our kingdom. You are a disgrace to the Sun and Eledrinna. All of Terrathis will see you fall." She sat on the bed, turned away from me.

"Mother! I am sorry! I will not fail." I tried to walk towards her, but found my legs were bound and I could not move. The image disappeared in a purple mist.

Eldrin looked up at me from his desk in the library. He set the quill down and looked at me, disgust all over his face. "You mean nothing to me. You are a silly, stupid girl."

I squeezed my eyes shut, hot tears escaping. *This isn't real.*

"Of course it's real. You truly believe such a powerful mage and scholar as myself would love you? You were just a good body to keep mine warm." He casually dipped his quill in an inkpot.

"No, you don't mean that. You are my heart."

He laughed, the sound distorted in the illusion. "You were never mine. I never wish to see you again."

I was suddenly back in the House of the Meadow, my companions before me, each one writhing in agony, their voices echoing in my mind. Their distorted faces screamed in fear, accusing me, pleading for release. I had failed them just like I failed Raewyn. Just like I had failed everyone.

"Please stop!" I cried out, my breath was ragged as I fought to hold onto my sanity. I closed my eyes, focusing on the warmth I had carried with me for so long. The new intensity of light that was part of me.

As though they could sense my will, the hallucinations pressed harder. The room seemed to collapse in on itself, the walls narrowing, the ceiling lowering. I felt the floor beneath my feet become uneven, cracks running along its surface, revealing a darkness so deep that it swallowed everything around it. My legs trembled, but I held firm, refusing to let the darkness consume me.

"Don't listen to them," Thalassa's voice whispered through the chaos, now a soft, insidious hum. "They are already lost. They are nothing but shadows, illusions of your own making. You did this to them."

The light of Eledrinna flickered inside me. I could feel it weakening and faltering under the weight of the house's curse. I suddenly felt the sun's warmth slipping away, the darkness trying to drown my light.

My heart pounded louder in my chest, my fists shaking. I had to stay grounded. I *had* to—

With a deafening roar, I reached deep within myself, channeling every ounce of my sun-born power into a single, blinding flare of light. My entire being seemed to explode with golden energy, the warmth of a thousand suns rising up from my core. The shadows recoiled, screaming as the light cut through them like a blade through smoke.

The house groaned, the walls cracking and splintering as the force of my power surged outward. The hallucinations fractured, breaking apart in shards of dark illusion, leaving only the hollow, corrupted husk of the house around them.

Thalassa hissed, shielding her face from the light, but it was no use. The power of the sun, pure and unyielding, poured from me like a cleansing tide. The very fabric of the house seemed to burn away, its dark magic evaporating under the assault of my light.

"Idrial!" Marowen's voice was clear and real this time, cutting through the fading illusions.

My vision cleared. The walls of the house were no longer bending, no longer shifting into horrible shapes. The corruption that had choked the place now seemed to recoil as the sunlight poured through the cracks. Thalassa was crumpled to the ground, though her face was lifted towards me.

"Your light show is for naught!" she snarled, her face twisting in rage. I looked up to see her rising, and suddenly, there were five of her, walking towards me. One on the far right spoke.

"You may feel powerful now, Daughter of Eledrinna, but you will not win." That version disappeared and another spoke. "You will not find the Sun Stone. It is fractured." She was gone before I could blink. The remaining illusions cackled. I could no longer discern who was real. My head was pounding as I tried to sort them out. "We will meet again." My eyes finally adjusted to see they had all disappeared.

I stood still, breathing heavily, aware my body still glowed with the remnants of my power. "It's not over," I whispered, my voice fierce and resolute, the warmth of the sun radiating from me. "But we've taken the first step."

I rushed over to Fiora, who had been gathered into an embrace by Elaria. I knelt down and looked somberly at my new companion.

"Is she all right? Is she alive?"

Elaria nodded. "Yes, she is. The darkness has taken her for too long. She will survive in body, but her spirit will take a longer mending."

I let myself collapse to the ground and bent my knees so I could rest my forehead on them. My arms dangled beside me as I willed the world to stop spinning. I felt strangely dizzy and my heart would not stop pounding. Before I could get any words out, I felt the world around me blacken.

Chapter Twenty-Seven

"She is the Heir to the Sun, of course she's powerful." I heard a male voice speak.

"Yes, but no one is *that* powerful, not even an heir." Another voice, female this time.

"I have a theory." It was Calveris. "She may be the daughter of Eledrinna."

Alaric scoffed. "That is a myth. Stories told to children. Thalassa was taunting her."

I sat up, noting I was still in the cold chamber. Sunlight squeaked through the slats on the wall. I rubbed my eyes, my head pounding. It took a moment to get my bearings, when I suddenly remembered what happened.

"Fiora!" I shot upright.

"Don't move!" Marowen crawled over to me. "That display did a number on you."

I looked around to see my companions huddled nearby, drinking from silver flasks. Elixirs, no doubt. Or alcohol. I searched for Fiora but could not find her.

"Where is she?" I frantically queried. "Is she all right? Did Thalassa take her?"

"Now, now," Marowen calmly said, handing me her own flask. "Drink this again."

I obliged, feeling the liquid begin to work. It was the same healing potion they gave me previously. After a moment passed, I looked at her.

"Where is she?"

"We laid her down over there." Elaria pointed to a corner where pillows had been piled. I saw a figure under blankets. "She is alive, but asleep."

"Will she survive? Did we save Briarhollow?"

Marowen laughed, despite the grim situation. "You didn't save the town, no. This place will need the greatest healers. However, I do believe with Thalassa gone, it can begin the process."

I groaned and closed my eyes. "Where did Thalassa go?"

Elaria shrugged. "Back to whatever hell she crawled out of, I hope."

I heaved a sigh and laid flat on the ground. I stared at the ceiling, seeing the faded wildflower mural above me. The visions Thalassa had pushed into my mind lingered, chilling my skin. I had never experienced Arcane magic like that before, and I was afraid. Did Eldrin know the bastardization of his life? Tears clung to my eyelashes and the heaviness of his absence resurfaced. An anguished groan escaped my lips.

"Now, now," Marowen purred nearby. "We do not have time to suffer. We save that for later." She gently touched my hand on my stomach.

I opened my eyes and looked at her. "Ever since I left Calenor, there has been nothing but death and darkness for me."

She pulled me to a sitting position. "That has been here long since you ever came here. The world is not as bright as they would have you believe."

I pressed my lips tightly. "How did I not know of this?"

Calveris looked over at me. "They shielded you. The capital only wanted you to know how great and powerful it was."

Alaric rose and pushed his sword into its hilt. "Now is not the time to discuss this. We need to find the others."

I furrowed my brow. "The others?"

"Do you not think Fiora would have protected as many as she could? There was a point where she realized Briarhollow was lost and would have ordered as many to safety as she could." He extended a calloused hand. I grabbed it and let him pull my worn body up.

"Where are they? I saw no sign of life on our way in." I looked around, as though expecting to see fauns appear.

"Underground, Princess." He winked.

I scowled at the title. "Underground?"

"Every main capital has a stronghold where its citizens can go for protection. Calenor has one." He shrugged, rotating his shoulder. He winced at the movement.

"Yes, just barely South of the walls. It's enchanted to look like ruins." I placed a hand on my ribcage, feeling the sting of bruising.

"Correct. You are not the only city with resources, however quaint Briarhollow's may be." Alaric held his shield and wiped it with his untucked shirt.

"Since you seem to be an expert, lead the way." I gestured back towards the door.

Chapter Twenty-Eight

Elaria remained back with Fiora to tend to her wounds and spirit for when she awoke. The rest of us piled out of the decimated home. Calveris gave Bellar a carrot before we headed down a dirt path just beyond the town. We came across a field and Alaric abruptly stopped. He pointed at a wooden door hatch.

"In there."

I raised a quizzical brow. "In there? An entire town could not possibly fit."

Marowen smiled and shoved past me. "You would be surprised." She lifted the hatch and gestured down the stone stairs. "After you, m'lady."

I eyed the darkened stairwell suspiciously. It felt like a trap. Part of me was still wary from the illusions and I didn't fully trust my own mind. She looked at me encouragingly, and I summoned courage to make the descent.

The stairs went straight down, and I had to hold onto the walls. As I took the last step onto the flat, even stone, I looked around. Torches lined the walls, illuminating the empty hall. My body relaxed as I felt my companions beside me. The hatch closed, blocking out the last of the sunlight. I suddenly felt very claustrophobic.

Calveris walked forward. "They should be just this way."

As we made our way down the hall, I could hear distant voices and footsteps. Nerves formed in my stomach as we neared them. What would I find? How many were there? Before too many anxious thoughts could form, we turned a corner and the corridor opened into a large, stone room.

The ceilings were oddly high for being underground and there were wooden tables all throughout. Families sat scattered, seemingly comfortable. A few children ran past us, chasing a red ball. The smell of warm meat and bread mingled with the dust in the air. There were some burly fauns standing nearby, all with tin mugs in their hands. They stopped their conversation upon seeing us.

"Alaric! What brings you down below?" A faun with tawny skin approached us, brushing his curly dark hair from his golden eyes.

"Galen, we need to speak in private." Alaric's blue eyes were stoney and his face was grim.

Galen nodded and looked at the other two. "It seems we need to head to the War Room."

They have a war room down here? I silently questioned.

I followed them past the tables and we entered a room that had been made into a makeshift armory with a table in the center. Lining the walls were racks of rudimentary farming tools forced into weapons. Partially rusted scythes and rakes leaned against the walls, along with other implements I wasn't familiar with. Galen sat and gestured for Marowen and I to take a seat. Alaric and the other two stood around the table.

"What troubles above now?" Galen asked. "And who is this?" He looked at me curiously.

"I am Idrial, from-"

Alaric cut me off. "She is just a traveler from Calenor. We found her just outside of Briarhollow. She has been helping us."

That seemed to be a satisfactory answer as he didn't press it. "Welcome, Idrial. I wish it were under better circumstances."

"That is why we are here," Marowen answered quickly. "We met with Fiora."

A rather tall faun with tanned skin looked at us curiously. "No one meets with Fiora. She is lost."

"Yes, Merrick, she is. But we encountered Thalassa," Calveris said carefully.

Merrick whistled. "I'm surprised to see you lot, then."

"No one sees Thalassa and escapes," the third one said. He seemed a bit more sullen. I noticed his dark hair was greying and his face showed signs of age. He looked down at me. "I am Faelon. I used to be head of the Farmer's Guild here."

"Not anymore?" I queried.

"Not much to farm these days." He crossed his arms over his chest.

"Anyways, we were able to utilize a weapon we didn't have before, and Thalassa is gone." Alaric pushed through. "Not dead." He raised his hands before the others could interject. "She is banished."

Galen leaned back in the wooden chair, eyeing us curiously. "Must have been a rather mighty weapon to send her away." I looked down at my hands clasped in my lap, feeling their eyes on me.

"It was rather spectacular to see in action! I had never seen such power in many years," Calveris said, excitedly.

"What was this weapon?" Faelon asked, taking a swig of his drink.

"Ah, we cannot disclose that yet," Alaric said. "I don't want too many knowing of it just yet. For the safety of the people."

"Yes, the safety of the people." I could tell they weren't sold.

"Why are you down here and not helping above?" I blurted out.

Galen scoffed. "We fought for months. Don't think that because we are a farming town we are just simple. I can tell you're one of those high-brow elves. You wouldn't have your grand feasts without us." I squeaked out an apology. "Once the blight came through, we had to put all of our efforts into salvaging and preserving what we could. Some of us saw it for what it was: corrupted magic. But Fiora was too kind and didn't believe we could be overtaken."

"Don't paint her like that," Faelon said.

Galen shrugged. "I tell the truth. Once Thalassa and her Moon group came through, we realized we were overtaken."

"What of your warriors?" I asked in shock.

Merrick chortled. "You're looking at them."

I tilted my head and looked at Alaric, who seemed mildly embarrassed by my ignorance.

"What do you mean? I thought you were farmers?"

"We are. And The Hearthguard. We volunteer our efforts when needed. But there aren't any highly trained warriors here." I stared at him. No wonder they were overtaken so easily.

"Look, we do what we need to in order to get by," Galen said, seeing my expression. "We haven't been attacked in a millenia. Solira has long blessed us and with her Meadow Stone, we have never failed." He stared directly at me. "It seems the Stone Summit couldn't be performed last year at the capital. Once Fiora returned, we started seeing our crops slowly fail."

I swallowed hard. He had to know who I was with that statement. "That is unfortunate."

Before the conversation could derail any further, Alaric spoke up. "Yes, it is. But we believe Thalassa and her Moon Guards won't come back to bother your land again. You can start to rebuild."

Merrick raised his eyebrows. "I highly doubt that." He waved his arms, and that is when I noticed one of his ligaments was missing up to the elbow. He saw me eyeing it. "Unfortunate horse incident, years ago. Hazard of the fields."

My cheeks flushed. "Ah, I see that."

"What is it you want, Alaric? Surely you don't think we can just let all the people out. Their homes are destroyed. There's nothing for them here."

"So you remain underground and cower?" His voice was gruff.

"That's a lot of nerve for a banished high guard to say," Faelon retorted.

"Do not insult me because you hid away while your leader and remaining people suffered above," he spat.

Galen slammed his hands on the table and rose. "Get out."

Calveris nervously adjusted his glasses. "We didn't come here for personal issues. We believe it is safer for your people to return home. We will help rebuild, of course." He looked at Marowen and I, who were nodding enthusiastically.

Faelon rested a gentle hand on Galen's shoulder. "Perhaps they may be right. The immediate threat is done. Let's inspect the town and assess. Then we can decide what to do from here."

Galen's shoulders sagged. He rubbed his face with his hands. "Fine. If you think it's safe. We will gather a few others and head to the surface." She pointed at Alaric. "Not a word of this to the rest. I don't want to get their hopes up."

"Something we can agree on," Alaric responded.

We shuffled out, agreeing to meet on the surface after supper. I was eternally grateful when a woman offered to feed us. I realized we hadn't eaten since the sweet oats that morning. The sun was setting and my stomach was growling.

Marowen and I sat across from each other at a wooden table, eating a marvelous warm chicken and mushroom stew. It was filled with leeks and potatoes and onions. I was surprised at how flavorful it was, considering they must have limited resources down here. I caught hints of thyme and even lemon juice. I was curious where they acquired that. It was accompanied with a basket of warm sourdough bread that I happily dipped in the stew.

We ate in silence, savoring the flavors and grateful to let our bodies rest. I felt a twinge of guilt, knowing Elaria was likely eating more dried meat. Maybe I could somehow bring her some. I pondered the logistics when Marowen broke the comfortable silence.

"I don't know how we will restore the fields. None of us have that magic." She paused and looked around. "If anyone were to, it would be the Meadow folk."

I nodded, slowly. An idea had sprung to mind, but I was hesitant to offer it. I lowered my voice. "You lived most of your life in the woods, yes?"

She lowered her bread to her plate curiously. "I did, yes."

"Did you ever…" I paused for a moment. "Did you ever see sentient mushrooms and flowers?"

She wheezed out a laugh. "Did you drink their liquor?"

My face grew warm. It was a silly thought. "No! I did not!"

"What do you mean?" She looked at me with amusement.

"I…." I let out an exasperated sigh, keeping my voice lowered. "One night on the river, I had an encounter. At least I think I did."

"Go on." She took a bite of the stew.

"They called themselves Poddarins. They claimed to have been here before even Eledrinna touched Terrathis. I thought maybe they could help?" I hurried through the last sentence.

"Huh..." she said, almost distantly. I could tell she was searching her mind. "Tell me more about these Poddarins."

"I heard music one evening from my boat and saw lights through the trees. I docked my boat and followed the sound."

"There just happened to be a dock nearby?" she interrupted.

I hadn't thought of that. "I suppose so, yes." I paused in brief reflection. "If I could find them again, maybe they could help the Meadow restore the land? I am sure they have powers enough."

Marowen chewed thoughtfully. "And you weren't drinking?"

"No! Maybe a little," I responded, laughing. The movement hurt my sore ribs, but it felt nice to laugh. "I know how it sounds, but I promise you, it was nothing like that!"

She grinned at me. "I believe you." She pushed her bowl to the center, clearly sated. "All right, then, how do we find them again?"

"I don't know."

She tilted her head at me. "How did you find them before? Did you summon them somehow?"

"I have no idea. They just sort of... appeared by the riverbank. They were having a festival and playing tiny instruments."

"You do realize that doesn't help your sanity case?" She raised her pierced brow at me.

I dropped my hands to my lap and let out a dramatic sigh. "Since everyone is convinced I am the daughter of Eledrinna," Marowen choked on her water. "Yes, I heard you all. Since you all think I am her, perhaps I can somehow call to them?"

"Like some sort of goddess ritual? Be careful, the men will get spooked." She winked playfully at me.

"Will you help me?"

"This seems like absolutely nutter, but yes, I will help you."

"Please don't tell the others. Not unless it works?" I pleaded.

"And seem like a fool? Not a chance."

CHAPTER TWENTY-NINE

"Do you have an instrument on you?"

Marowen turned and looked at me, an incredulous look on her face. We had made an excuse to head to the forests' edge, claiming we needed to forage herbs for healing poultices. The sun had set and the only light was from the moon. It cast a dappled glow through the trees. In this environment, I didn't find it terrifying. It reminded me of my time with Navarra.

"Let me just pull one out of my ass," she joked.

I rolled my eyes. "I don't know if I need one, but I think in order to summon him, I need to play a song."

"What makes you think that?" She lowered herself to the ground, sitting crossed legged.

"When I joined their festivities, they played a song. It is the Song of Time, one that I have sung many times before at the Summit Ball." Marowen looked at me curiously. "The night before the Stone Summit, there's always a grand ball to celebrate the joining of the different realms. I took on the tradition of singing the song when I came of age. When I found the Poddarins, they played a different version of it."

"Ah, so you think maybe that could bring them to us?" Marowen idly made a chain with white flowers around her.

I shrugged, sitting on the ground next to her. "I don't see why not. If nothing else, you get a free performance."

She grinned. "Well, don't wait for my cue!" She gestured to me.

I inhaled deeply, bracing myself. It felt strange to sing this in such an informal space, to one person. I let the song begin on my tongue, closing my eyes. I held my hands in my lap, letting the music swirl around me. For a brief moment, I was back in my home, and I would open my eyes to see all those I knew and loved staring back at me. The breeze picked up, and suddenly, I was joined by other familiar instruments. I heard Marowen gasp as the last note left my lips, and I sprung my eyes open.

Before me was Myce and Helia, with a small fiddle and lyre. They strung out the last of their notes and bowed to Marowen. "Welcome!"

"Welcome? We summoned you! I didn't believe you existed," she exclaimed. Her eyes were wide and gleamed in the moonlight.

"We welcome you because this is our land. But we share." He turned to me. "You are wise to remember our song. We come because we know your heart is pure."

I smiled at him. "Thank you for hearing my call. I didn't know if it would work."

"It worked because we know you are good!" Helia chirped. She happily flapped her broad leaves.

I looked over at Marowen, whose mouth was open in shock. I could tell she was mentally convincing herself this was real.

"What can we do for the Daughter of the Sun?" Myce asked, his round black eyes filled with concern.

I glanced towards the direction of Briarhollow. "The land here is corrupted. We have banished those who caused it, but I am afraid the fields are beyond our powers. The Meadow people don't have the strength or magic needed to begin restoring it."

The two sprites nodded and exchanged looks. "Yes, we can feel it," Myce started. "There was evil here."

"Yes, deep evil," Helia glumly agreed.

Marowen eyed them. "Can you help them?"

They nodded enthusiastically. "Yes! But, they cannot see us. We will gather the others and work together."

"How will you do it?" I couldn't help but ask.

"That is ancient magic beyond your understanding. But, do you know how mushrooms work?" I swear his mushroom face smirked.

"Not exactly..." Calenor didn't really grow mushrooms. The sand didn't work well with them.

"It's an underground network, I think," Marowen spoke up.

Helia and Myce clapped enthusiastically. "Yes! Good job. Most of the mushroom system is underground. What you see above is just the part that makes more. I can call upon it and help heal the roots."

A huge sigh of relief passed my lips. "So you can do it subtly, then?"

"We have mastered subtlty. Not many know we exist," he stated. "We will do it slowly. The people need to feel the magic came from them."

"You don't want credit?"

"It means nothing to us," Helia said brightly.

I smiled. "That will surely lift their spirits."

"How long will it take?" Marowen asked.

"It will be at least a season to fully restore it. We cannot rush healing. As you know, Archer of the Woods." Myce watched her carefully.

She widened her eyes, her skin flushing. "Ah, yes." It felt she wanted to say more, but she remained silent.

That brought many questions to my mind, but instead I rose to my feet. "So, we just go back to them like this never happened?"

"You may do whatever you like with this information. But let the Meadow people believe they healed their lands. It will restore their faith in Solira and their magic."

"Why do the gods and goddesses not help?" The question had been pressing on my mind for quite some time.

"They won't interfere. They have their own conflicts." He paused for a moment, grabbing his fiddle. "You will also become intertwined with those, soon enough."

His words hit my gut like a force. "That is beyond me."

"It isn't!" Helia beamed. "You'll find out."

We rose to our feet. I slowly bowed towards them. "I thank you so much for coming. Your assistance will not be forgotten. I will find a way to honor you."

"Find the Sun Stone and restore the land. That is what you can do for us. The desert will hold what you have lost." Myce and Helia bowed and faded from our sights.

Marowen and I stood in the forest. She leaned a hand against a tree, as though absorbing the interaction. "I truly did not believe they existed."

I nodded. "I still don't fully, to be quite honest."

She laughed. "I have to tell Elaria of this. Calveris will also be fascinated."

I felt a twinge of guilt. "Do you think they will be upset we didn't include them?"

She waved her free hand in the air. "Nah, they will understand. I am sure Elaria has also been occupied in healing Fiora."

I bit the inside of my bottom lip. "I wish we could have brought her some stew."

"I believe Calveris was speaking with the cook and found a way to get some to her. I had the same thought." She smiled warmly.

We made our way back towards the village, and passed some of the farmers who were working tirelessly into the night to repair some homes. We stopped briefly to speak with them and found they had decided to keep the townspeople in the bunker for a few days more while they cleared debris, which, in a macabre way, included the dead. They had no choice but to take them to a field and burn them. There would be a ceremony in the days to come for those lost. There was a schedule made by Calveris and Alaric to rebuild homes and clear out fields. It would take some time, but I felt lighter knowing the Poddarins would be helping.

We entered Fiora's home, the previously eerie hallway now illuminated with the flicker of candles. The warm vanilla scent only mildly masked the metallic smell of the corrupted Arcane magic. As we entered the chamber, my eyes fell on Elaria and Fiora. They were sitting on pillows in the middle of the floor, eating the stew. Fiora had some warmth restored to her, and I felt a huge weight lift.

I rushed over to her and pulled her into an embrace. "I am so glad to see you!"

She laughed softly and set down her bowl. She returned the embrace, squeezing me tightly. I winced as my ribs were still sore, but I welcomed the feeling. "I cannot thank you enough, my dear."

I pulled away and looked into her eyes. She was soul-weary, but she was my Fiora. "I would do anything for you, my friend." I looked over at Elaria. "I could not have done this alone. I am fortunate to have found them."

Fiora gestured to Elaria. "Yes, she has been most attentive. If not a little pushy." She winked.

"I merely wanted you to rest longer before venturing outdoors!" Elaria exclaimed. I looked over at her to see she had bruises on her left jaw.

I gently reached over to touch it. Elaria rest her hand on mine before I could make contact. "It is all right. Thalassa did a number on us all."

I heaved a sigh. "She did that. But she is no match for us."

Elaria's smile widened. Her skin was magnificent in the moonlight. The violet swirls had a silver glow to them. Constellations seemed to peer out among the swirls. "She did not know we had a weapon."

"Yes, how did you banish her?" Fiora spoke up.

I looked over at Marowen, who was seated next to Elaria. She nodded encouragingly.

"Something happened to me on the mountains. After we left the Oracles, there was an encounter with a Snow Golem." I paused for a moment. "Raewyn was lost." Fiora's face fell. "I somehow became the Sun, and I believe I came into my full powers."

She gasped. "Without training?"

"I am still sorting it out myself, to be honest. But it seems in moments of pure emotion, I can summon it. I don't exactly have control over it, though." I sheepishly admitted.

Fiora smiled warmly and placed a hand on my knee. "That will come in time. I am sorry about Raewyn. I know she was your soul friend."

Tears sprung to my eyes at the thought. "I carry much guilt and grief there." I cleared my throat and straightened. "I will not burden you with my sorrows, for you have your own weight."

Elaria quietly interjected. "It is quite late, and we should all turn in for the night. We can reconvene in the morning when we are better rested."

I felt a wave of exhaustion pass over me and agreed. We piled more giant floor pillows in the center of the floor. Marowen grabbed blankets from various corners of the room and we created a fluffy nest. I laid my head down and felt my heavy eyes close. Sleep welcomed me into its embrace.

Chapter Thirty

The sound of hammers pounding against wood greeted me as we emerged from the house. The morning sun was golden and poured generously over Briarhollow, reminding me a bit of home. It was the same kind of sun I would run on the sands with Raiku. I lifted my face towards the warmth, basking in it for a moment. Fiora stood beside me, staring at her town. She leaned against Elaria, her body still weak. I noticed the shadows remained on her face, but a glimpse of hope had begun to return. The men had worked tirelessly through the night to repair the shops around the town square. There was still a long way to go, but it was nice to see progress.

We met with Alaric and Calveris at the dilapidated well. They were conferring with Galen on how to clear the water so it was safe for drinking. Upon our arrival, they turned and greeted us.

"Fiora! It is good to see you out!" Galen beamed.

Her face brightened. "It is good to see you, friend. I see you have been busy." She looked around, surprised at their progress.

He nodded. "Yes, they were getting restless and when I presented the opportunity to the surface and start work, most able-bodied people quickly volunteered. We are about to switch shifts so they can rest."

"You should see the fields," Calveris exclaimed. "We cleared a few last night and this morning, there were already sprouts."

Marowen and I exchanged pleased looks. She looked at him. "That *is* good news!"

Fiora stared at me. "I don't doubt our own magic, but that seems too quick of a turnaround. Especially considering the nature of the blight. And the missing Sun Stone."

Alaric leaned against the stone well. "Yes, it is a little strange."

I cleared my throat. "We have something to discuss, but not here in the open. We can explain over our midday meal."

"I would love to see the state of the fields," Fiora said, redirecting the conversation.

Galen nodded and leaned his shovel against the rotting wood of the well. "I can take you to them."

We headed past the town square and made our way just to the outskirts. Bellar was hitched up to some sort of contraption that had a massive rake attached. It seemed to be forming rows in the turned soil. It was hard to believe it had been overrun by twisted vines just the day before. The Poddarins worked quickly. I felt my body warm with gratitude towards them.

Fiora approached the edge of the bed and kneeled down. She delicately gathered loose soil in her hand and brought some to her face. She deeply inhaled the earth and tapped her tongue against it. She nodded and rose, clapping the remaining soil off her hands.

"This is possibly even better quality than even we could manage. I am most curious how that happened." Once again, she eyed me curiously.

"I am glad to see it is healing!" I walked over towards the next field and gestured. "I see the sprouts. Do you know what is planted here?"

The faun carefully lowered herself to the ground, laying on her belly. She propped herself up on her elbows and gently touched one of the sprouts. "It's hard to tell at such an early stage, but I believe it is Spinach. It is stronger in the cooler weather we are heading towards and grows quickly. There may be lettuce and other leafy greens mixed in." With the support of Elaria, she rose to her hooves.

Elaria gazed out at the field. "Did you not plant these before?"

She shook her head. "No, the last crop we planted was for warmer temperatures. We had just laid down many types of peppers and tomatoes." She pointed to the other field being tilled. "That was to be wheat. We store it so we can at least make bread all through the winter. It's our most abundant crop."

"Do you have anything leftover from last year?" Alaric asked.

She shrugged. "I haven't looked at the grain bins yet. I know Merrick was taking inventory of what survived."

"There is still time before winter sets in. We will ensure your people are fed throughout the cold months." Elaria reassured.

"I am very glad you all came when you did. I don't know what would have happened if this went on much longer." Fiora grabbed my hand. "Thank you for not giving up."

"My dear friend, I could never give up on you. I would have stayed as long as it took."

"Fortunately, it didn't take long," Marowen stated. "I think we need to let Fiora in on some things."

I nervously agreed. We left the fields and went back to the house, passing by fauns working tirelessly to fix their homes and their gardens. Their faces lit up as they saw Fiora and she gave a small wave. She was their hope, a sign of a true leader. We made our way towards her manor, and a smile tugged on my lips as I saw a few women fixing her fence and tearing down the ragged vines that took over.

Her dining room seemed to be the least touched by the curse, the tapestries still intact and their colors still vibrant. I idly touched one with the back of my fingers, feeling the rough textures. It was a beautiful image of what seemed to be the lifecycle of a poppy, their House flower. I lowered myself onto a wooden chair, wincing at the pain in my ribs.

"While we are quite the hard workers, nothing could have performed the speed at which the fields have returned," Fiora started, pouring herself a cup of hot tea.

I looked over at Marowen, who nodded encouragingly to me. After a steady exhale, I looked back at Fiora. "I sought the help of an ancient magic, one I am barely familiar with."

Calveris made a noise. "Forbidden magic?"

I shook my head quickly. "Oh, no, nothing like that." I rested my palms on the table, as though bracing myself. "They are a peculiar group, called the Poddarins. I met them months ago on my journey along the river. They say they have been here since before even Eledrinna."

Alaric's dark eyebrows raised. "Poddarins?"

"Oh! I have heard of them! They are more of a myth, children's stories. They are small sprites that protect the land." Calveris excitedly interjected.

"They are no myth. Marowen and I took to the wood's edge last night and I called to them. Myce, their leader, came. With another called Helia."

"One is a mushroom and the other some sort of daisy," Marowen chuckled.

Elaria burst out a laugh. "A sentient mushroom?"

"I know it sounds insane, but I promise you they exist!" I laughed and took a sip from the teacup before me. It was a warm, cinnamon and cardamom blend. "I told him what had happened here and he was willing to help. I do not know exactly what they did, but it seems to already be taking effect. They are working to heal the earth so your crops will have yields before the winter months."

Fiora sighed in relief, leaning back in her chair. "I have never heard of these Poddarins, but I am glad for that."

Alaric crossed his arms over his chest. "How do you know they have good intentions? If they have been here since before time, perhaps it is a trick to take back their lands."

"I didn't get that impression," I said thinly. "I don't think they are bothered by our existence."

He huffed and shrugged. "Time will show their true nature."

"Ugh, why do you have to be such a downer? We summoned them with music, for gods' sake." Marowen responded, her voice rife with irritation.

Fiora laughed softly, "I saw the fields with sprouts. They mean no harm. Nothing with ill intentions could create that."

"Did he say where they came from," Calveris asked, curiously.

"They didn't. Just that they have been here longer than any Earth-strider, as they called us. They seemed to be fond of Eledrinna." I traced the rim of my cup.

"With their help, we can restore Briarhollow and the surrounding towns," Fiora mused, her voice soft. "We have so much to do because of my failure."

"You did not fail," Elaria reached out and placed her hand on the faun's. "You did what you thought was best with the information you had at the time. You did not know Thalassa was corrupt."

"Deep down, I may have known," Fiora admitted. "But I saw my home was overtaken by a curse and my people were suffering."

"Yes, and someone came to you with hope. Someone powerful came to you with an offer to help." Marowen's voice was steady. "No one could fault you for that."

We sat in silence as we drained our teas. I stared into the cup, seeing the leaves gathered at the bottom of the cup. They seemed to form a shape. I lifted the class and tilted it slightly. Marowen looked at me.

"See anything?"

I handed her the cup. "It looks like a ship to me."

She studied it for a moment before setting it down. "It is a very clear ship. It appears you have a grand journey ahead of you."

I snorted a laugh. "You don't say?"

"Not just *any* ship," Marowen continued. "It seems you have a strange journey ahead of you."

"I doubt there are any ships in the desert," I grimly stated.

"Where are you journeying next?" Fiora asked, her warm eyes soft.

"I need to go to the desert. The Oracles and... dreams have been telling me to head there for answers about the Sun Stone." The nervous ball of energy returned to my stomach.

"What are you looking for there?" She asked.

I shrugged. "To be honest, I have no idea. I am hoping once I get there, I will find out."

"Well, we love flying by the seat of our pants," Elaria was brimming with excitement. "We have business there anyways and would love to accompany you."

I stared at my new companion and let my eyes wander to the others. They were all nodding with agreement. "You would come with me?"

"The desert is a perilous, unforgiving place," Alaric began. "We could never let the heir of Calenor suffer it alone."

"And there are so many areas that are unstudied! I could have a new discovery named after me! Think of all the creatures unknown!" Calveris clapped his hands together.

"And think of all the things that want to kill us," Marowen grinned.

"Ah, that is just part of the experience," Calveris offered.

I smiled warmly. For the first time since losing Raewyn, I felt I had true friends. I felt a pang of guilt sweep over me. I didn't want her to be replaced. But I also knew she would want me to have company. I exhaled and stretched my arms over my head.

"Well, I suppose we can stay here another night and then begin our journey south."

"You should probably bathe first. Have you looked at yourself recently?" Marowen carefully said.

"I suppose I need pointed to the bathing room, then."

Chapter Thirty-One

I stood before the large oval mirror on the wall, staring at myself in disbelief. I hadn't seen my own face since Navarra, and even that was in a very rippled mirror. I was astounded to see my eyes were sunken in, dark circles contrasted against my bright blue and yellow eyes. My cheekbones had grown hollow and my hair was dull. I was a shell of my former self. There was an ever present look of sadness and weariness that I never had before. Long gone was the princess with the bright skin and vibrant eyes. I cleared my throat.

"You look rough, lady," I said to my reflection.

I glanced around the bathroom, searching for soap and oils. The House of the Meadow bathing room was beautiful. The dark wood floors contrasted against the pale yellow walls. The bathtub looked as though they took down a massive tree and hollowed out the trunk. It was finely sanded and smoothed down for comfort. I glanced up to see large, wooden beams stretched across the vast room and in the center, was an iron chandelier. Lush greenery lined the walls close to the ceiling. There was a single, round window that allowed the sun to cast a golden hue in the room. I opened a cabinet to see amber bottles of oils and salts. I lifted one that read "Sandalwood." I grabbed that, along with lavender salts and made my way to the bathtub.

I sunk into the filled tub, letting the aroma-filled steam fill the air. I closed my eyes, exhaling. It felt nice to relax for the first time in months. My mind wandered with everything that had happened. I was shaken by the takeover from the House of the Moon. What was their plan? Why did they torment Briarhollow?

Eldrin had always talked of past wars and would mention how enemies used areas to their advantage. Briarhollow was the first line of defense towards Calenor. The river was useful in that it spilled directly to the south sea. I played with the bubbles in front of me. Maybe they were planning to infiltrate Calenor by boat? Is that what my tea leaves meant? I sighed in frustration. I was nowhere close to being a good leader. I knew nothing of war and battles. I was only good for balls and pretty dresses. Even with my newfound powers, I could not lead an army.

I rest my head against the edge of the tub, deeply inhaling. I felt tension melt away from my shoulders and the pain in my ribcage subsided a bit. It felt out of place, indulging like this, but I needed it. And the time alone. After some time, I felt my heavy eyes close and I drifted to sleep.

"You have become distracted. You must come to the dessert." That distant voice echoed in my mind.

"I needed to save Fiora..." I responded. I didn't know I could speak to this voice.

"That was by design... to keep you from us."

"Who are you? Why should I trust you?" I was feeling annoyed.

"We have lived long before you, and we are you."

"That is nonsense. What is in the desert?"

A pause. "You will find answers. And half of the Sun Stone... But it will not be without a trial."

Before I could react, I was pulled out of my sleep.

"Idrial?"

I was awoken by a soft voice. My eyes flashed open and I flailed, confused that I was floating in water. I took a moment to catch my bearings and I looked up to see Elaria standing over me.

"You startled me."

She smirked. "I noticed. You have been here for an hour. We became worried." She handed me a towel and looked away. "Were you dreaming?"

I carefully rose to my feet and grabbed the towel. "Yes, my apologies. I must have drifted there." I wrapped the towel around me. I wasn't about to explain the voices. Not until I unraveled them myself.

Elaria sat on a wooden stool. "I am sure it is the first time you have felt safe for some time."

I nodded. "It has been. Not since Navarra."

"When I first left Nyxara, I was constantly on guard. It took years before I felt comfortable in unfamiliar places." She idly picked at her nails.

"I had never stepped foot outside of Calenor. This is an awfully long way from home." I sighed. "I am out of my element."

Elaria shrugged. "Aren't we all? None of us knows what we are doing."

I found that oddly comforting. I paused before responding. "Why did you leave? What did you do there?"

She smiled sadly. "I was one of their assassins. The king would order me to take out any enemies. Usually it was based on conjecture and paranoia. But he paid well, and so I obliged."

My eyes widened as I grabbed a clean, dark green tunic. "An assassin?"

"While I am dangerous, I am not a danger to you." She winked and handed me tan breeches.

I slipped them on, setting aside modesty. "Why did you leave?" I asked again.

She inhaled softly, bracing her hands on her knees. "Well, friend, there were certain orders he asked of me. And I wouldn't do it."

My eyes widened. "What orders?"

"To kill the other house leaders, including yours." Her silver eyes seemed to swirl with memories of her deeds.

I snapped my head to hers. "I am currently the leader of the Sun."

She nodded, her face neutral. "I know. And I refused."

Fear gripped my chest as I braided my hair so it lay draped over my shoulder. "Couldn't he just give orders to another assassin?"

She grinned. "Oh, he most likely did. But they won't succeed. They aren't as good as I am."

I rubbed my eyes. "I suppose I am grateful for that. And to you." I paused for a moment. "You could have turned me in. How do I know you haven't sent word to him and this is a trap?"

She shrugged. "You don't know. You just have to trust me." She rose to her feet. "I have no ill will towards you or the other leaders. He is just corrupt and jealous."

I stared into the bathtub and watched the remaining water swirl down the drain. Ever since Raewyn and I left the mountains, I felt I was in a constant state of fear. Despite having found new companions, I felt that fear grow each day. And with that fear, the pain of losing Raewyn and not having Eldrin with me grew. They were my *safe* places, and I knew what to expect from them. While I was growing fond of this new group, I realized I knew nothing of them. Was I insane for entrusting them with my mission in the desert? Apparently half the Sun Stone is there.

As if reading my mind, Elaria gently touched my shoulder. "We will not hurt you. But we can only show you that. Just give it time."

I felt my body relax slightly. "It's just all new to me. Every single day is new."

"And we are here to help you through each day."

Chapter Thirty-Two

A week passed and we had spent our days helping the remaining villagers back to their homes. No more than forty had been spared, whether by death or captivity, but their small numbers didn't diminish the work done. Most of the houses and shops had been repaired to a functional state and the fields were beginning to flourish. The Poddarins' magic had taken full effect, and the crops they planted were up to my knees.

I sat on the center well's edge and stared at the few faun children running around, their hooves clacking against the broken cobblestone. That would take longer to repair. I was glad to see the young ones were rather untouched and didn't seem much phased. I could still see a sadness in their eyes that I knew even they didn't understand. How many of their friends were gone? How many had lost family members? Tears sprung in my eyes.

"They will remember this, but they will also remember your kindness." Fiora lowered herself next to me and crossed her ankles.

I looked over at her. "I couldn't imagine walking through Calenor and seeing this destruction."

Fiora's lips formed a thin smile. "You will prevent it from spreading, I am sure of it." She watched the children chase a ball.

"I am so sorry I wasn't here sooner. I am so sorry I didn't realize what was happening." Tears rapidly found their way down my cheeks.

Fiora leaned close to me. "Oh, my love. You didn't know. You were working on taking care of your own realm."

"But this *is* my realm. Everyone in Terrathis is under my care." I wiped the tears off my cheek.

Fiora's face brightened as she helped me wipe them away. "Yes, we are. And we are grateful for that. But the burden is not entirely yours. We are here to help you, as well as our own people." She grabbed my hand. "When your parents disappeared, they had not given you all the information and the tools you needed to rule a kingdom. You are ill-prepared for this, and for what's to come." I startled a bit. "That is not to insult you, but just to remind you. You have done the very best you could with the knowledge you have. And that is something to be proud of."

I pondered her words for a moment, the tears still falling freely. A sob escaped. "How do I learn? How do I improve so I know what to do?"

She gestured around. "You followed your heart. You took what you knew and you saved Briarhollow. You pulled in people you know and did what you thought was right. And it served you well." She tapped my chest. "Keep at that, and you will not fail."

My face softened as I pulled her into a tight hug. Fiora held me tight, knowing I needed the closeness. "You are going to do marvelous things, my love." Her whispered voice tickled my ear.

I pulled away slightly. "I have no choice now, I suppose." I looked over to see my new companions gathered near, staring at me. "And I suppose the time has come for us to continue on."

She patted my hand. "The desert is a fierce place. Head south and you will find the Ark Outpost. It is the last point of civilization before the desert." She nodded towards Calveris. "He will know the way there." She looked back at me. "They will help you. Trust them."

Her words reflected Elaria's, and I was comforted. "I cannot thank you enough for your kindness." I rose to my feet. "May your land be prosperous and your people find joy once again."

Fiora curtsied and I noticed the buds of her antlers had new growth. "You are always welcome here at Briarhollow." She rose and gestured around. "And next time you come through, it will be restored to its vibrancy once more."

I pulled her in for a tight embrace. "You are the vibrancy." I felt her arms tighten around my waist.

I reluctantly pulled away, feeling Marowen's hand on my arm. I looked up at her and nodded. Fiora squeezed my hand before I made my way towards the wagon and my friends.

Chapter Thirty-Three

Bellar was strapped to the front of the wagon and he graciously let me ride him. My body was weary from the last month, really the last few months, and I was glad to sit. They offered I sit in the wagon, but I wanted to feel the sunshine on my face. After all the time in the mountains, I would never take this warm feeling for granted. I inhaled the fresh air, noting the trees around were beginning to turn yellow. The breeze was warm, but had that underlying feeling that autumn was around the corner.

Calveris walked alongside Bellar and I, humming a jaunty tune. I smiled softly, enjoying the sound. I missed music and I recognized it as one of Calenor's. He was looking at a map, peering over his glasses every so often so he didn't stumble.

"Where is that?" I looked down. It was a part of Terrathis I wasn't familiar with.

"Ah, it is a closer look at the desert and outlying areas. We are roughly here." He pointed to the upper right edge. "And the Ark Outpost is here." He dragged his finger diagonally down towards the middle. "And the desert is all here." He circled the bottom left area that just had ruins and depictions of sand. "But! We are heading here!" He pointed to a place just south of Briarhollow called Pipwick.

I squinted as I stared at it. "Pipwick! I've never heard of it. Why are we going there?"

"It's a most fascinating town! It only exists for festivals and celebrations! No one lives there, but it has incredible structures for shops and taverns." Calveris folded the map and tucked it into his purple robe. I smiled, the color reminding me of the mages at home.

"So, people built an entire town just for parties?" I queried.

"It seemed better than destroying towns during holidays, no? The crowd out here can get a bit more unruly, so some centuries ago, they created Pipwick."

"And why are we going there? I should think getting to the desert is a bit more pressing than a festival." I chewed my lip nervously. I couldn't afford another delay.

He looked up at me, his eyebrow raised. "Well, in fact, you have yet to tell us *why* you so desperately need to go there. Of course, us being treasure hunters and seeking knowledge, we are happy to come along. But you really haven't given us much insight as to *your* purpose there."

I pressed my lips together. Calveris was someone I had known for a very long time, even a bit distantly. Surely, I could trust him. I stared at the fluffy fur between Bellar's ears. After an uncomfortable length of time had passed, Calveris spoke softly.

"Idrial, we just want to help you. But if we are going to put ourselves in danger, we would like to know the reason." He patted Bellar's nose and gave him a carrot. "However, the reason we are going to Pipwick is for the Emberfall Festival!"

My head turned so quickly, the bones in my neck cracked. "Emberfall? Already?"

He nodded. "Indeed! 'Emberfall marks the fading of the summer fire and the beginning of autumn,'" he quoted.

"I saw the leaves were turning. I knew it was coming up. I just hadn't realized it was so..." The words trailed.

"You left Calenor before Emberfall, didn't you?" His voice was even, as though he understood the weight of the realization.

"Months before. This means I have officially been gone for over a year." I rubbed my eyes. "I believe Raewyn and I made it to the Oracles around this time, but I cannot be sure. The mountains confused my sense of time."

"Ah, yes. They are not very kind for that. Very little light and a chill that never leaves." He glanced up at the sun. "This is the correct kind of weather, in my opinion."

I raised an eyebrow and cocked my head. "Correct weather?"

"Yes! The sun is warm, but not blisteringly hot. And the air is just cool enough that I can stand to be in its path for a long period of time. Nothing is too aggressive one way or the other." Bellar brayed, seeming to agree.

I laughed. "I suppose I can see that. What of Calenor's weather? Did you find it disagreeable?"

He waved a hand. "I am not one to sit in the ocean, but the breeze was pleasant. But, here we are, talking about weather as though we are acquaintances." Calveris chuckled.

"Fair enough. So, why are we going to Pipwick? Other than for the Emberfall festival?"

He shifted uncomfortably. "Well, we do need coin. And it is running low." He glanced behind us at the wagon, where the rest of our companions sat. "Marowen has The Kaldris Deck, and she uses it at festivals to pad our pockets."

I raised an eyebrow. "I haven't heard of those in years. I remember when I was younger, a druid from the Woods brought one to a ball and offered readings." I giggled at the memory. "Mother was so angry. She said it was nothing but party tricks and a bastardization of the gods."

Calveris smiled. "Oh, I am sure she did not like that. She never liked the magic that didn't align with hers."

"I never quite understood that. Our goddess, Eledrinna and their god, Sylvorith, aren't that much different. Their intentions are generally the same. And besides, all the deities came because of Eledrinna. I feel she would want us to love them equally?" I sighed and twisted my waist, loosening the tight muscles around my spine. "I suppose I never understood the divide. It was never meant to be this way."

Calveris stopped walking and motioned for Bellar to follow. "Oh, I agree. Religion should never be divisive but rather more about community and education. We could all learn from each other, no matter the beliefs. But we become corrupt and stuck in our own ways. And sometimes, other peoples' beliefs challenge our own." He held a hand up, gesturing for me to get down. We had been riding for several hours and my bones were stiff. I ungracefully slid off Bellar. I would never get used to his size.

"Do people feel that way about Arcane magic?" I asked, brushing the dirt off my brown tunic and tan breeches.

"Oh, yes, even in Calenor. Some think that magic that has to be studied isn't real. That if it isn't gifted to us by the gods, then it shouldn't exist." He readjusted the bridle on Bellar's face, loosening it. "The funny thing is, we don't even know where the Arcane magic came from."

I remembered Eldrin telling me something similar, years ago. That Arcane magic seemed to just appear millennia ago. The origin was never found, and after some time, the mages stopped looking. Eldrin suspected they feared if they discovered the origin, it would cause discourse between them and the Houses. And so, they stopped their search.

"Eldrin had spoken of that before. Do you have any idea where it came from?" I asked, not really expecting an answer.

"My thoughts? I believe Arcane magic came from the cosmic dust that settled around when Eledrinna and Nyxar landed on Terrathis. The Sunbeam and the Moonbeam coming here couldn't be without residual effects." He shrugged and walked towards the back of the wagon where Marowyn was exiting.

"Why have we stopped?" she asked, looking around.

"Idrial's backside was hurting," he gestured back at me.

I jumped, my cheeks turning red. "Oh! I thought Bellar needed a break?" I walked closer to them.

He laughed. "Ah, I saw you twisting and turning. That's about when my ass starts hurting. Bellar isn't an easy ride."

My face was hot as I looked down. Marowen laughed heartily. "Idrial, we have all been there. Come into the wagon. You should get some sleep, anyways. It's a day's more ride before we get to Pipwick. We will wake you up when we stop for an evening meal."

I stretched my arms above me, feeling my muscles loosen even more. Ever since I had come into my full powers on the mountain, I felt my joints hurt more and my muscles became quickly fatigued. I just assumed it was the extra strain from all the climbing in the mountains, as well as my emotional state. But even after days of resting, I found my body didn't function like it used to. I sighed as I climbed into the wagon and found it was a lot more spacious than I had considered. I quickly realized it must have been enchanted. I blinked a few times, taking it in.

The inside bloomed with impossible space, and was incredibly warm and welcoming. The curved wooden ceiling arched high above, and had lovely glowing lanterns strung across the beam. The walls were lined with shelves and crates overflowing with books, some bound in cracked leather, others sealed with wax runes. A few hovered just off the ground, gently rotating as if searching for attention. I was reminded of parts of the library, and I felt a smile tug at my lips.

I looked around to see bundles of dried herbs hanging from the rafters, tied with twine—lavender, mugwort, juniper—that released a mix of earthy and floral aromas. Wooden drawers labeled in a careful hand hold rarer ingredients: powdered beetle shell, moonlight resin, dreamroot. No doubt these were things Calveris had discovered on his travels.

A small hearth flickered with blue-green flame, enchanted never to smoke or scorch. Beside the fire, a fold-out writing desk was littered with parchment, quills, vials of ink, and pressed leaves used as bookmarks.

Near the rear of the wagon, nestled beneath a tall, round window, were a pair of cushioned benches draped with soft throws and fur, facing a low table carved with sigils. Alaric nodded at me, lifting a steaming teapot from a table and poured it into a mug. He handed it to Elaria, who was sat on the bench, an open book in her hand. Alaric poured another mug and extended it to me.

"It's chamomile. It calms you down, which you appear to need." A smile spread across his normally solemn face.

My mouth hung open as I took in the space. "This is beautiful. I had no idea it was so... cozy?" I took the hot mug of tea.

"I'm sure if you had, you wouldn't have suffered on the beast," Elaria said playfully. She closed her book, placing a stray stem of rosemary in it.

"Oh, the company was fine. But my bones are paying for it." I made my way over to the bench beside Elaria and sat, my body sinking into the cushions. My aching body nestled into the corner and leaned against the oversized fluffy pillows. The tea was warm in my mouth and the sweet flavor was quite welcome.

Alaric sat down at the writing desk. "We were most fortunate when we came by Calveris. He noted our shanty little wagon and did some incredible magic to create this." He took a sip of his tea and gestured above. "We were at each other's throats by that time. Mostly from being in uncomfortable spaces for too long. It's fortunate we found him in Rathgar's Mire when we did."

Elaria chuckled. "For all of our sakes. He was to be eaten by witches."

I looked over at her, my eyes wide. "Eaten?"

She smiled mischievously. "Does the princess not know of the Witches of Rathgar?" She leaned against the back of the wagon. "They are cannibals. Calveris had wandered too far into the Mire trying to rescue Bellar. And they caught both of them." She took a long drink of her tea. "Luckily, the two made such terrible sounds we heard it from miles away. So we decided to check it out."

"You just… knowingly ventured into the cannibal's house? For curiosity?" I pulled my legs onto the bench and curled them behind me.

Alaric sighed, though a look of amusement was on his face. "These two never could set aside curiosity. Fortunately, it worked out for all of us."

"Except for the thing you lost," Elaria said, her eyes darting towards him.

He pressed his lips together and shook his head quickly. "Not yet."

I stared at the two in silence, suddenly feeling uncomfortable. "You don't have to share anything with me. We all have our secrets."

Elaria turned to me. "Indeed we do." She rose to place a soft, blue blanket over me. "You should get some rest for now." I handed her my half-consumed cup of tea. The last sound I heard was the soft thud of the mug being set on the table.

Chapter Thirty-Four

The abrupt sound of laughter woke me with a start. I was in a room lit only by violet lights, which reminded me of Eldrin's eyes for a split second. I sat up, rubbing my neck. I slept in an awkward position on the bench and my upper body ached. I twisted my back and sighed of relief at the multiple cracks that resounded through my spine. I found myself frustrated because I never had this issue before. I stretched my arms high above, nearly hitting a hanging lantern, before rising to my feet.

As I walked towards the back entrance, I hesitated. I could hear the sound of a lyre being played and laughter erupting. I felt so heavy inside and didn't want to bring a stormcloud to their enjoyment. If I were honest with myself, I had felt weighed down since I left the riverboat. While I was glad I had helped Fiora and I found these new friends, I missed my old life. I wanted nothing more than to run in the hot sand with Raiku beside me, chasing the sea gulls.

Tears sprung to my eyes as I felt that ache. Layered on top of it was the absence of Raewyn. I felt guilty in the moments I found happiness. I wished she were with me to experience it. Eldrin would be fascinated by all the things I have seen. But instead, he is back in Calenor, having moved on, no doubt. It had been a year since I left and I was sure he considered me dead. It made me wonder which of my siblings took on my role. Neither were trained, and neither really wanted it. I cleared my throat and looked around at the enchanted wagon. There was no use in staying in sadness when there was obvious joy just outside. I wanted to be part of it, but I still felt that hesitation.

I took the few steps down until my feet touched the short, bristly grass. Night had fallen, and they had made a rather impressive bonfire. Calveris had a lyre and was playing a very familiar, upbeat tune. It was one we sang often in the summer months at festivals. His voice was deep and rich as it rang out the happy tune.

"O leave your cloak, your boots, your name,

And chase the waves in sunlit flame.

For tides remember songs of old,

In every grain of moon-washed gold."

I sat beside him on the log, joining with the harmony.

"So pluck the lyre, let joy take wing,

And to the sea your spirit sing.

For summer's heart beats loud and free—

A tale upon a silver sea."

He strung the last chord and looked at me, grinning as he adjusted his glasses. "Oh, wonderful! It has been too long since my melody intertwined with another voice!" He paused as the others clapped, and raised their bottles of liquor.

"I haven't heard that one in years!" I smiled, feeling the darkness from before lifting. It was nice to hear a song from home. "I didn't know you were musical!"

He laughed and handed me my own amber glass of whatever home-brew they had. "Ah, us scholars aren't just good for our tricks and books!"

I took a swig and nearly choked. Whatever this was, it was not good. It was rich and bitter, and its pungent smell wafted up to my nose. I swallowed it, despite wanting to spew it out. "Ugh, what is this?"

Marowen let out a heart laugh and took my bottle. "It's ale, my friend!" She took a large swig. "It will bite ya, but you get used to it."

Elaria let out an uncharacteristic giggle. "After a bottle or two, you don't even taste it!"

I shook my head, trying to rid my senses of the taste and smell. Alaric chuckled softly, handing me a silver flask. I raised my eyebrows at it warily.

"It's Skara." I relaxed my shoulders and took a drink of the familiar alcohol.

"What the hell is Skara?" Marowen asked, throwing sticks into the fire.

"It's a clear liquor made by the House of the Mountains. It comes from Frostroot." He paused for a moment, watching me down a good portion. "It tastes like juniper and mint."

"That sounds pleasant. Why haven't you shared this before?" Elaria eyed him curiously. "You've been holding out on us with the good stuff!"

"We have had a small barrel of it this entire time." Alaric gestured a thumb towards the wagon.

Marowen's mouth dropped and she stared at Elaria. They both fell into a laughing frenzy. "Impossible. There's no way I missed that."

Alaric shrugged and took back his flask. "I mentioned it before, I am sure." He settled back onto his log across the flames.

I felt the Skara making its way down my throat, warming my heart and my body. I smiled, watching the two dissolve into laughter, patting each other's laps and playfully shoving each other.

"It's okay to enjoy life again," Calveris softly stated, his eyes forward on the fire.

I turned my head to him. "Why do you say that?" My voice was low.

"I can feel you hesitate to be happy. Raewyn and Eldrin would not want you to keep from your joy." He gently strummed on the lyre an absent tune.

I pressed my lips together. "My heart misses them."

"I expect it does. But does that mean you should keep from living?" He gestured to the women in a laughing fit. "They, too, have suffered. But eventually, they found their way back to this."

"That feels so far away," I slowly say, staring down at my hands.

"Your path isn't what you expected, but you can lay down the rest of the stone."

I pondered his words for a moment. "It feels like too much at times."

His laugh surprised me. "Of course it does! Because you're trying to do it alone."

"I feel I am alone."

"You're not. Look around you. We don't let just anyone into our family. You are good at your core." He smiled at his friends. "We keep those people around."

Between the Skara really hitting me and Calveris' words, I felt a bit lighter. I chuckled softly. "Well, I suppose I am glad for that."

"You will find your laughter again, I am sure of it." He gestured a hand towards the other three, who were all retelling stories of their meetings. "Especially with this group."

At that moment, Marown threw a pebble towards Calveris. "Hey, remember when you almost got eaten by witches?" She laughed hysterically.

He sighed, though had a look of amusement on his face. "I do. All for the sake of research and knowledge."

"Are they really cannibals?" I ventured to ask.

"Do you really not know of the Witches of Rathgar? I thought you were joking about that!" Elaria asked.

I shook my head. "Not much. In Calenor, they are just a scary story to tell the children. My father used to tell us about them so we wouldn't try to sneak out at night. But I always thought it was made up."

"Oh, ho, I wish," Marowen said. "We have no idea how Bellar made it up there. Usually they herd closer to Briarhollow. But bleeding-heart Calveris here apparently discovered his plight and went to his aid, only to be captured."

Calveris' cheeks were red as he rubbed his hands on his face, jostling his glasses. "I never want to be hung upside down for as long as I live."

My eyes widened. "Excuse me?"

Elaria sunk down next to me, forcing Calveris and I to move over. "That's how they bleed out their meat."

"This is absolutely a nightmare of a bedtime story," I said, chills forming over my skin.

"It wasn't easy to cut him down. He was sobbing and pleading with all the gods." Marowen recalled the memory as if it were a pleasant stroll in a garden.

"Wait, why didn't you just use Arcane magic?" I looked at Calveris curiously.

"Arcane magic is blocked in the swamp. Always has been." He shrugged.

"I didn't know that was possible." The liquor had taken full effect, and I felt the outside world spinning. I was about to speak again when I saw a glimmer behind Alaric in the darkened trees. I sprung to my feet and pointed.

"That! Do you see that?" An oddly iridescent deer moved swiftly through the trees. It had that same purple glow.

They all stood and watched where I pointed. Marowen laughed and placed a hand on my shoulder. "That Skara gets to you, doesn't it?"

I looked at Calveris. "I keep *seeing* these animal... lights." The alcohol made me lose my words.

He raised his eyebrows. "Animal lights?" He pondered it for a moment. "Are they translucent and violet?"

I jumped and clapped, relieved. "Yes! I have been seeing them all over the place for months! Am I haunted?"

A knowing smile tugged at his lips. "You are not haunted. Let's just say you are protected."

"Protected by what? Woodland spirit animals?" Elaria asked, sarcasm in her tone.

"Something like that." He winked at her.

I furrowed my brow and lowered myself to the log again. "I just wish I could catch one."

Alaric poked at the fire with a stick, sending sparks flying upwards. "Some things aren't meant to be understood until the right time."

I looked up at him. "Fine, you all may keep your knowledge. Just know that if a giant, purple glowing lion attacks you, it's not my fault."

I was met with laughter and I found myself joining in at the thought. We sat around the fire in comfortable silence for quite some time after that. Elaria and Marowen soon dozed off on the grass, curled up near the fire. Calveris and Alaric spoke quietly about some historical artifacts they had recently found. I lay down on the flat part of the log, my arm as a pillow. I stared into the dancing flames until my eyelids became heavy and sleep took me.

Chapter Thirty-Five

The grass still smelled sweet from the meadows we had passed, and the fading sun painted long shadows across the hills. We had set camp mid-afternoon the following day, letting Bellar rest after the long haul from the House of the Meadow. Marowen sat by the fire, her cards spread before her, though her sharp eyes flicked more often toward the clearing than toward the deck.

Alaric stood opposite me, having insisted on improving my swordsmanship. He held two wooden practice swords. "Your grip's too tight," he said, offering one out. "You'll tire yourself before the fight's even begun."

I arched my brow. "I thought I was supposed to *hold* it. Not coddle it."

A grin tugged at his mouth. "Hold it like this—firm, but flexible. Let the blade do the work." He stepped closer, adjusting my hands on the hilt. His fingers brushed my knuckles, warm and deliberate. I felt the heat crawl up my neck but refused to look away from his vibrant eyes.

"Better," he murmured, his voice low. "Now, try again."

I swung, clumsy but determined, and he parried easily. Our movements quickened, wood striking wood in sharp beats. I lunged again, overbalancing, and Alaric caught me by the wrist, pulling me close before I fell. The contact sent a strange jolt through me. My breath caught, his grip lingering a fraction longer than necessary.

A throat cleared by the fire.

Marowen didn't look up from her cards, but her tone sliced sharper than any blade. "If you two are done dancing about, we could use that firewood I asked for." Her green eyes flicked briefly to Alaric—cold, unreadable. "Or does swordplay make you forget your ears?"

Alaric's grin faltered, and he stepped back from me, tossing the wooden blade to the ground. "Guess we've been dismissed."

I pressed my lips together, watching him disappear into the shallow woods. I looked over at Marowen, who was still staring at the cards before her. Elaria and Calveris were tending to Bellar and didn't see the exchange.

"We were just practicing," I offered. I wasn't sure why she was upset.

She didn't look up at me. "You need to stay focused on finding the Sun Stone. You cannot let yourself be distracted by a *man*!"

My mouth gaped open. "It was just a friendly thing. There is no distraction here." I crossed my arms over my chest and lowered myself beside her. "I am loyal to Eldrin."

Marowen pursed her lips, and before she could say anything, Elaria and Calveris returned. They had a basket containing potatoes, carrots, and a skinned chicken from Fiora. Elaria skimmed Marowen and I, noticing something was off, but said nothing. Calveris quickly covered the chicken in rosemary, oregano, and salt before posting it over the fire.

I leaned forward and helped Elaria cut up the potatoes and carrots. We threw them in a thick iron skillet with the same herbs and let them sizzle over the fire. I looked up at her.

"Why is Marowen so testy?" I queried.

She pressed her lips together, responding in a low tone. "Alaric has mentioned he is fond of you." My eyebrows raised. "Apparently, it goes back even to your time on the coast. Marowen doesn't want to see him hurt."

"I won't hurt him."

She shook her head and turned me towards her. "You won't intend to. But he is troubled. You have a light people are drawn to. And I don't just mean your powers."

I pondered this for a moment, feeling uncomfortable. "But my love is still with Eldrin."

"I know. And Marowen knows, which is why the flirting concerns her." She pushed the food around with a wooden spoon, the fragrance filling the air."

"I'm not flirting!" I tried to keep my voice low.

"Not intentionally," she spooned the food onto a clay plate and handed it to me. "Just be careful, with your heart and his. It's easy to fall in love with someone you are constantly around. Proximity affection and all that."

I chewed my lip thoughtfully. "He is a kind man. I feel I know him."

She shrugged. "He is from the Tide. I am sure you do." She filled another clay plate and handed it to me.

I took the filled plates over to Calveris and Alaric and quickly handed it to them, not making eye-contact with Alaric. He muttered a thanks before I retreated back to Elaria, who had two other filled plates.

"You're a good woman, Idrial. But sometimes kindness can be mistaken for something else." She smiled at me with great affection.

I took the plates over to Marowen and lowered myself next to her on the ground. I handed her one and she thanked me. After a tense moment, I spoke.

"I didn't know."

"That you were an object of affection?" She asked simply.

"I've only ever held Eldrin's eyes. I never considered others." I took a bite of potatoes, the warm herbs filling my mouth.

"I am sure you have. You just don't notice." She smirked at me, stabbing a carrot with her fork.

"Perhaps. But I don't want to mislead Alaric." The entire thing made me uncomfortable.

"He believes in you. Not just with his heart, but as a Queen. We all do." Her eyes sparkled with tears.

I chewed a piece of chicken thoughtfully. "I don't believe in myself."

She laughed. "That much is evident. But I think you will get there." She pushed her food around on the plate. "I can imagine being pushed into this harsh world has been quite a shock. You are likely just looking for some sort of comfort."

"Perhaps so. What if I am... falling for him?"

"You need to stay focused on what we are doing. And if your heart is still with Eldrin, then it is just a fleeting feeling. But one that could do great damage to Alaric." She glanced over at him, who was in a deep conversation with Calveris and Elaria.

"I could never betray Eldrin," I said, firmly.

"Then just be careful, friend."

Chapter Thirty-Six

Pipwick was less a village and more a stage set brought to life, nestled in a verdant valley rimmed by flowering trees and winding brooks. As we walked through the cobblestone paths, I was hit with the strong scent of roasted meats, sweet wines, and fresh herbs. We followed the cobbled paths through colorfully painted stalls, whimsical tents, and timber-framed cottages—each one adorned with ribbons, lanterns, and bright orange and yellow banners.

Calveris had explained there were hardly any permanent residents, and they were mostly performers, artisans, and traders who had nowhere else to be and preferred it that way. He said that some claimed the town was blessed by gods of revelry or chaos, because strange things often happened here—plays that summoned real ghosts, feasts that never ran out, and jesters who seemed to know your secrets.

I found it odd there was no town guard. Instead, there was a puppet theater on every corner and jugglers in the streets. Pipwick seemed entirely untouched by age like other places. Marowen had to guide us after a while as maps are unreliable, and the only way to find Pipwick is to follow laughter, music, and perhaps a paper lantern drifting on the breeze, as she said.

We had passed beneath its ivy-wrapped archway and entered a place where reality seemed to bend. Bunting fluttered across narrow lanes and its buildings rose surprisingly tall for such a frivolous place, crafted from warm, weathered stone. I noted the brightly colored thatched roofs were dyed every color you could imagine.

The architecture was solid, enduring, as though carved for permanence—but everything else about Pipwick was fleeting. Streamers looped from gabled windows. Painted shutters flapped open to reveal stages rather than sitting rooms. Doorsteps doubled as altars, musical stages, or platforms for dramatic proclamations. No building seemed to have a single purpose; each was a theater waiting for its next act.

Music drifted on the breeze, as if the wind itself were in on the joke. I was enamored by the jugglers tossing flames beneath the eaves of honey-stone inns, and painted mummers danced through the streets in silk and bells. The scent of spice cakes and salted meats hung in the air, blending with the musk of incense and the faint tang of fireworks.

"Who founded this place?" I asked, my eyes taking in all the strange sights.

"No one really knows. Some believe it was a gift from the god, Vaelros," Calveris explained. Seeing my confusion, he continued." "He was the brother of the God of the Moon, and the second moon beam to touch Terrathis. He was known as a bit of a trickster god. Not much else is known of him."

I had never heard that name and was curious why he wasn't in our history. I pondered this for a moment, passing a baked goods stall. I noted the brightly colored confections that had an iridescent look to them. I made a mental note to return there. Our caravan kept down the path until we reached the southern edge to a crescent-shaped grassy space. We passed under another wooden archway that read, "Wanderer's Hollow." There were other traveling troupes setting up their wagons and tents. In the center was a towering maypole wrapped in every color ribbon. The wheels slightly sunk into the wild thyme growing freely. Marowen quickly rushed to pull out a wooden sign that read *Fortunes Told, Wonders Shown, No Fee Too Strange* in large, looping script.

We pulled out the brightly colored pennants and tied the wagon to worn, stone markers. Marowen and Elaria set up a sage green canopy beside it and hung up lanterns that flickered softly with violet mage-light. She set up a round table in the center, draping a black velvet cloth over it. She made a few minor adjustments and stood back to admire it.

"Ah, it feels nice to be Madame Virella again," she said proudly.

"Madame Virella?"

She brushed some grass off her black pants. "My magical persona. I do readings of the Kaldris deck here."

"I didn't realize you were actually a seer? Or is it just for coin?" I posed the question carefully.

She laughed. "People reveal a lot when they think you know everything. I just interpret that based on their reactions to the cards." She pulled a large deck out of a wooden box on the table and shuffled them. "Sometimes people don't know what they want to know until they see it."

I furrowed my brow. "What do you mean?"

She gestured to the wooden chair in front of the table. I took a seat, and she lowered herself in the seat opposite me. She shuffled the deck and set it flat on the table. "Split the deck."

I obliged, awkwardly removing the top half and set the other half on the deck. She fanned out the cards and told me to pick one. I did and set it face up, revealing a card with a painted armored figure carved from stone. He was guarding a mountain pass. It read The Stoneheart Sentinel.

She smiled. "This card usually appears to someone who has a strong feeling of duty."

I nodded. "That makes sense. I need to find the Sun Stone to save Terrathis."

She smiled and had me pull another card. The Kaldris Ascendant. A cloaked figure dissolved into starlight, its arms raised as celestial forces swirl around them. "Alignment with destiny. It shows you are on the right path."

I shifted in my seat. "Perhaps it means I am on the right path in fulfilling my duty." I pulled out a third card. The Drowned Voice showed a figure submerged in deep, dark waters, eyes open, mouth agape in silent song. This card made me uncomfortable.

"Ah, ancestral ties, particularly to hidden meanings." She stared at me with a neutral expression.

I swallowed hard. "The Poddarins told me I am the daughter of Eledrinna. Maybe it ties into my duties." I stared at the cards for a moment before sighing. "I see what you mean."

In one fell swoop, she shuffled the cards together and packed them in the wooden box. Closing the lid, she said, "You see what you want to see. Or maybe there is something divine here. I never know." She set her palms flat on the box. "Do you believe you are the daughter of Eledrinna?"

I chewed the corner of my lip for a minute, staring at the tattoo swirls on her hands. "If I accept that as truth, it changes everything."

Marowen spun a silver ring on her finger with her thumb. "What would change?"

I looked up at her. "My relationship with my parents, why they left." I swallowed hard, hesitantly offering my truth. "And I am not nearly that important to be something so ancient."

Marowen chuckled softly. "You realize you are to be Queen of Terrathis one day?"

I rubbed my pointer finger on the tablecloth, not making eye contact. "I know. But being a Queen is different from being the daughter of a deity..."

Marowen shrugged, her dark curly hair flowing over her shoulders. I noticed she had a bright pink ribbon braided through the underside of her hair. "It doesn't have to be different in a negative way. Think of all the good you could do being a goddess *and* queen!" She grinned at me.

I laughed through my nose. "Well, if it turns out to be true, then I will sort that out. For now, I am just Idrial."

"Are you making her uncomfortable?" Elaria walked up with a large turkey leg in her hand. She took a hearty bite of the meat. "You should know better."

Marowen grinned and shrugged. "She was curious." Marowen rose to her feet and peeled a chunk of the turkey meat off the bone. She quickly downed it and wiped her hands on her clothes.

Elaria offered the turkey leg to me and I shook my head. While the wagon was comfortable, the jostling about turned my stomach. I also felt oddly nervous being in Pipwick, despite how vibrant and light the place felt. Perhaps that's why I felt nauseous. It contrasted my cloudy mind.

Elaria poked my arm. "Just enjoy being here. Not many from the coast get to travel here."

"You should go see Bronze!" Marowen said, her mouth full of turkey.

"Who is Bronze?"

"Pipwicks' delightful blacksmith. He is a fairy from the sky islands and is one of the best!" Elaria beamed.

My mouth gaped. "He is a what from where?"

"A fairy from the sky islands," Calveris entered the tent. "They don't often come down here, but Bronze wanted more."

"More of what?" I asked. I hadn't considered there were inhabitants on the sky islands.

"They are Wind Shepherds. They tend to the air currents and jet streams. That's partially why the islands float around." Calveris had suddenly become very animated while explaining. "Some of them are Cloud

Gardeners. They shape the clouds. And occasionally, they give them a nice squeeze when they feel we need extra rain in an area."

My eyes widened as I stared up at the cloudless sky. "I had no idea. So, why is this Bronze fairy here?"

Marowen shrugged. "He wanted to be a blacksmith. And he certainly is the best, perhaps in all of Terrathis."

I pondered that for a moment, more questions coming to mind. "Well, I do need a dagger. I don't have any weapons going into the desert."

Marowen laughed. "You *are* a weapon! What are you skilled with any-ways?"

My cheeks flushed. I didn't want to tell Marowen, the highest skilled archer, that I used a bow. She stared at me impatiently. I cleared my throat. "A longbow is what I am most proficient in."

Marowen made a sound of exclamation. "The best weapon, of course! There is also a fantastic Bowyer here!"

I squinted my eyes at her. "Why are there weaponsmiths here? This seems like a land-of-never-ending-joy sort of place."

The wood elf shrugged. "They have to make a living somehow." She gestured to the table. "Just like we do. Which reminds me that I need to transform into Madame Virella!" She disappeared into the back of the wagon.

I chewed my lip thoughtfully as I gazed at my surroundings. Alaric had ventured off earlier to find food and Calveris was sitting on the ground outside the wagon, reading a book. Elaria tossed the scraps and bone of the turkey leg into a nearby metal bin. She licked her fingers.

"Let's go find Bronze! His lovely wife may be around, but I would watch yourself with her," Elaria warned, her tone still light.

"Oh? How so?" I asked, as Elaria looped her arm in mine and pulled me forward.

"Kolili is so sweet, but rather mischievous. She likes tricks and games." Elaria steered my body to take a dirt path to the left.

I raised my eyebrows as my brown boots kicked up dust before me. It was obvious it hadn't rained in quite some time, and part of me wondered if this place was enchanted to not rain. Passersby raced down the path and I noticed they had gossamer wings. They giggled and chased iridescent bubbles that floated freely in the air.

I couldn't help but smile. "This place is lovely. I've never seen anything like it."

"I am sure you had fine festivals in Calenor!" Elaria popped a bubble that passed by her face.

"We do, but they always have the underlying feeling of formality. I would love to bring something so carefree to my home." My skin warmed at the thought, and I could see my glow softly emit from my arms.

Elaria noticed as well, and didn't say anything. But I could sense she was pleased. "I am sure you could make that happen. A princess surely has connections." She smirked.

I rolled my eyes. "I'm sure I could manage something."

We came upon a row of merchants, all in their colorful stalls. We approached a large, open building that smelled of steel and fire. A large man had his back turned towards us, and I immediately noticed large, shimmering copper wings. I noticed one seemed to be replaced with a makeshift bronze wing. It didn't flutter as well as the other. I cocked my head, taking in the peculiar man before me. A bright blue tunic contrasted against dusty, brown linen pants. His thick, brown boots kicked up more dirt as he shuffled about the smithery. Sweat-glistened arms lifted a large metal sword from the fire, the tip glowing with heat. He turned and rested it on a large anvil. He paused to rub his red beard, adorned with tiny blue flowers.

He hit the end of the sword with a hammer and grinned. "Welcome! I am so glad you are here!" He looked up at us, his round face red from the heat. His voice was almost lyrical and warm.

Elaria quickly curtsied and I followed. "Hello, Bronze! I have heard incredible things about you from our companion, Calveris!"

He finished hitting the glowing sword and dunked it in a large barrel of water. With a hiss, steam rose from the barrel. Bronze wiped his hands on a dirty rag around his waist. "Calveris is marvelous! Any friend of his is certainly a friend of mine." His wings flapped enthusiastically. He looked at me. "And to be graced by the presence of a royal from the Sun House is an honor!"

My cheeks flushed. "How did you know?"

"My darling, you have the glow of the sun and the eyes of a sunrise." He came over and shook my hand with great vigor.

"I have never met a Sky Fairy before," I blurted out.

A laugh bellowed from him, shaking his entire body. "I can imagine not. We are quite rare on the ground."

"Idrial here needs a dagger," Elaria stated, picking up an ornate knife on the table next to her.

He nodded. "Oh, yes, of course! I have plenty already made, or if you are looking for custom, I am happy to help."

I pressed my lips together. "I don't think I have the coin for this. I lost everything in the mountains."

He cleared his throat, his face remaining neutral. "Those mountains will take much." He waved his hand and retrieved the sword from the water barrel. He put it back in the flames, letting it reheat. "Calveris has done much for me, and I am happy to gift his companion a dagger fit for a queen." He winked, the blue paint on his eyelids emphasizing his honey eyes.

I cleared my throat, tucking a blonde strand behind my ear. "I am honored you would do such a thing."

He waved a hand again, shoving the glowing blade back in the water barrel. "Anything I can do to help!"

I was about to ask what he would make when I found myself surrounded by a cloud of rainbow glitter. It filled the air around Elaria and I.

"Kolili!" Bronze exclaimed. "Not at our guests!"

I heard a giggle as the glitter fell to the ground. Once it cleared, I found myself face to face with a faun. She had bright blonde hair and painted lines on her chin. Around her neck were multiple scarves of bright colors that contrasted against the black cotton dress she wore. She danced a little, clearly excited.

"Oh, Bronze, it's just simple sparkle!" She held her hand up in a circle and blew through it. Bubbles formed and flew through her hand, swirling all around us.

"I am Kolili! I am so excited to meet you!" She curtsied low, holding her skirt out and revealing her hooves. She had painted those bright green and yellow.

"I am making her a dagger! She is from the House of the Sun!" Bronze beamed with pride.

Kolili clapped. "Oh! I can tell! You are glowing so beautifully!"

I murmured a thanks, feeling awkward. "It is hard not to shine in such a wonderful place."

The faun danced a circle around me. "This place is magical! I love the Emberfall Festival!"

I smiled at her and looked around at Bronze's table of wares. There were many beautifully crafted swords, daggers, and maces. I was impressed with his work. His reputation held up. My body suddenly went cold as my eyes caught the familiar glint of blue stones. I brushed my fingers over the leather hilt and looked at Bronze.

"Where did you get this?" My voice was shaking.

Kolili stopped moving, feeling the sudden shift. Her eyes widened and she looked at Bronze, who was staring at me curiously.

"Ah, I found it from a traveling merchant on the other side of the river. It was earlier this year. It took quite awhile to polish and clean." He watched as I carefully picked it up, brushing my fingers over the familiar Runes. My heart pounded in my chest and my head began to spin. I lowered myself to the straw-covered ground, carefully holding the dagger.

Elaria placed a hand on my shoulder, concern in her voice. "Idrial? What is that?"

I looked up at her, my eyes welled with tears. "This was Raewyn's dagger. Eldrin gave it to us with Runes so we could always find each other."

She inhaled sharply and looked at Bronze, who was very obviously un-comfortable. "You found this from a merchant?"

He nodded. "Aye, he said he found it in the mountains near a stream."

I rose to my feet, ignoring the nausea that washed over me. "Was there anything else? Did he see anyone?"

Bronze shook his head. "He didn't mention anything. Just said he had never seen the Runes before. Neither have I."

I ran my fingers over the etched Runes, as though it held answers. "How much for this?"

"It seems to have emotional importance, so it is my gift to you."

My shoulders sagged as a heavy sigh left my mouth. I knew it was unlikely, but this gave me a slight bit of hope. Maybe she had somehow survived. I looked up to see Bronze handing me a brown leather scabbard.

"I had this made to fit the dagger. It will keep it protected from the elements." His eyes were soft as he watched me.

"I cannot thank you enough. This dagger means the most to me." I blinked a few tears away.

He bowed. "Then it is my pleasure to give it to you."

"Do you know where we might find a Gredda Marn?" Elaria hesitantly asked, not wanting to break the moment.

Kolili jumped and clapped. "She's by the woods!" She pointed down the path. "She is scary, but can be nice."

Bronze raised his eyebrow. "What do you want with her?"

I looked at Elaria, the question also in my mind. Elaria didn't look at me. "We need protection for where we are going. I have heard she can deliver."

He crossed his arms over his broad chest. "She can, for a price."

Elaria shrugged. "We have coin."

"That is not the price she will ask of you."

The pit in my stomach grew. I really didn't want to vomit the festival food here. "What price, then?" I ventured to ask.

He tilted his head. "It depends on her mood and what you can offer."

Elaria touched my hand and nodded her head towards the path. "I am sure we can deliver. We thank you for your help."

I curtsied slightly, thanking them again, before making my way towards the wood's edge.

Chapter Thirty-Seven

We came upon a large canvas tent held up by bleached driftwood and antler spires. The canvas was a worn patchwork gray and blue. Windchimes made from bone and etched glass danced in the breeze, giving off low clattering rather than a bright tone. The entrance was a veil of moss-colored veils and old netting. Outside was a sign that said The Rustling Veil. I looked at Elaria, who pointed her chin forward.

The smell of distant rain and dried chamomile hit my senses instantly. The round room was dimly lit with glowing jars and candles that drifted aimlessly throughout the air. There were wooden shelves standing, filled with flasks that glowed and seemed to whisper. I stared at one round flask that seemed to have shadows flickering inside.

My feet met a soft rug and I looked down to see it was an animal hide. Placed on it was a worn oak table, covered in scratches and ink stains. Behind it was a wiry woman, hunched over. She had a bird's nest of faded copper hair, and her fingers were covered in small silver rings. Her robes were half-mended and she was adorned with bone charms around her neck. She looked up at me, her eyes inked a solid black.

"Ah, you have seen the edge of dreams?" Her frail voice withered.

I frowned. "I am sorry?"

"Your thoughts fray like sun-rotted rope." She lowered herself onto the stool.

She turned to Elaria. "You were wise to bring her here. If she stepped into the desert without these, she'd hear a voice in the dust. And she'd kneel to it smiling."

Gredda opened her aged hand to reveal obsidian wrapped in silver wire. I could faintly make out an unfamiliar carving on its surface. "You will need these to keep your mind sharp in the ruins."

I swallowed and looked at Elaria, whose expression was neutral. The silver markings on her face had a faint glow. After a moment, she spoke confidently. "Name your price."

The woman waved her other hand. "Ah, straight to the point, I see. You are familiar with us."

"Who is *us*?" I asked before I could stop myself.

She cackled. "The Rathgar Witches."

A gasp shot out of my mouth as I took a step back. "I have heard of your kind."

"And nothing kindly, I am sure," she grumbled. "I don't eat people anymore. There is a reason I left."

My cheeks flushed, feeling a bit of shame. "I am so sorry. I didn't mean to offend."

"If you think I can be so offended by such a young, naive girl, then you are mistaken. After the horrors of my life, nothing can touch me." Gredda's eyes peered into me.

"What can we offer you for this?" Elaria impatiently stated. I could tell she was uncomfortable and wanted to leave.

She tilted her head at my companion. "A memory. A nice one." She looked at me. "From you. I have not traveled to Calenor."

I coughed uncomfortably, suddenly feeling my mind void of any memories. I couldn't recall anything. "I don't know how to give it to you. Or even what memory."

She tapped her long, gnarled fingernails on the table. "How about a dance? Surely you have a lover."

I pressed my lips tightly, not wanting to relinquish anything with Eldrin. We have had over a dozen dances together, so it shouldn't be that difficult. But his memory was fading from me, and I could barely remember the lines on his face. To give up a fond memory of a dance and laughter with him was a great sacrifice.

As though reading my thoughts, she grabbed a square flask and put it in front of me on the table. "Just a part of a dance, then."

I looked over at Elaria, who nodded in encouragement. After a moment, I agreed. "How should I do this?"

"Wait," Elaria said. "Hand us the charm."

Gredda laughed, a rather shrieking sound. "You are not new to dealings with us, I see." She held out the obsidian and I quickly took it. "Look into the bottle and focus on that one memory. Hold it steady."

I closed my eyes and drew up a memory from years ago. Eldrin held me in his arms as we twirled around the balcony during one of the most magnificent sunsets. It wasn't during a ball, and the only music playing was a violinist in the street below. The air was warm and the breeze was cool. We had spent the day in the library, as he had been encouraging me to study past wars. I had become restless and needed to feel the breeze on my skin. Being cooped up all day had made me depressed and he had felt guilty for it. He brought me to this balcony to see the sunset, when he suddenly scooped me in his arms. I laughed and felt the darkness of the day disappear. And soon, this memory slipped out of my mind and was replaced with nothing.

My eyes flashed open as I looked down at the jar. In it was a swirling sparkle of gold and violet. Both of our magics combined. Despite no longer having that memory, I smiled. Seeing it in a physical form brought me an odd sense of peace. I looked up at Gredda, who was putting a cork inside. She examined the color.

"Ah, yes, this is exactly what I have been looking for." She melted yellow wax and poured it over the top to seal it.

"What will you do with it?" I asked, my eyes not leaving the liquid.

"I will find out when the time is right."

Chapter Thirty-Eight

The wooden bench dug into the bones of my backside as we watched two men on horses run into each other with wooden lances. I winced every time they made contact with a shield, sending their poles splintering into pieces. The crowd cheered as the green knight dismounted his horse. His grin was wide and brilliant as his arms raised, gazing at the jovial crowd around. He turned towards a box in the center of the audience where a man and a woman linked arms. They were dressed very ornately and had bedazzled crowns upon their heads. The woman was covered in stunning fabrics of shimmering coral overlaid with gold filigree. It reminded me of the gowns I once wore. The man was adorned in similar clothing, even his fine shoes were gold. I smiled and clapped with the rest of the onlookers.

I glanced down at my own clothing, happy to see a bit of home. I had found a corset-maker, and she had a beautiful cream-colored corset that was embroidered with sunflowers and leaves all over. Marowen produced a dark green skirt to pair it with. I felt lovely for the first time in months, with sunflowers strung throughout my loose hair.

"Sir Retland of the Woods has proven himself once again as Pip-wick's finest warrior," the announcer's voice reverberated in the arena. "But he has one more opponent before he can claim victory.

Sir Retland bowed. His lips were moving, but his voice was lost in the cheers.

"And now, Sir Alaric of the Tide has come to try his chance as our reigning champion," the announcer's voice boomed with pride.

I sat up straight and looked at Marowen beside me. "Alaric is dueling?"

She nodded, taking a bite of a large pickled vegetable wrapped in a cloth. The smell of vinegar wafted through the air, stinging my nose. I wrinkled my face at her.

"It's a pickle. You should try it." She pointed it towards me. I shook my head, and she shrugged, taking another bite. "He tries every year. Last year, he almost won, but he fell off his horse."

"That's a bit embarrassing," I mused, staring at Alaric as he climbed onto the back of a large black horse.

Elaria laughed. "Oh, don't bring it up to him. It haunts him." She took a swig of her spiked cider.

We turned our attention back to the tournament as the men lined up on opposite sides of the barrier, a tilt-yard, Marowen explained. I sat on the edge of the bench and watched nervously as they raced forward. Retland lowered his metal helm over his face just before making contact with Alaric's shield. They slowed their horses to the ends of the fence and turned around.

"Did he win?" I asked excitedly.

"No, it's best two out of three," Elaria said, rising to her feet. She started clapping and shouting.

I watched intensely as Retland was given another lance and the two readied themselves. They both lowered their helmets once again and kicked off their horses. They raced towards each other and Alaric steadied his lance towards Retland's helmet instead of the shield. With finesse, he shoved the helmet off his opponent's head, sending it crashing to the ground. I couldn't hear it, but Retland's lips formed a curse word as he slowed his horse. His attendant quickly retrieved it and handed it to the man. He aggressively shoved it over his head as the two raced towards each other again.

Retland thrust the lance forward, and Alaric blocked it swiftly with his shield, sending wooden shards into the air. Retland angrily threw his lance onto the ground as he jumped off the horse. He ripped his helmet off and yelled at Alaric, who was raising his arms above him in victory. The crowd had quickly risen to its feet and was cheering in an unruly manner that made me slightly uneasy.

"Sir Alaric has been declared this year's winner!" the announcer's voice once again boomed over the arena. Alaric dismounted his horse and walked in front of the well-dressed couple. He bowed lowly, his lance still in hand.

"Blessings are bestowed upon you, Pipwick's most fearless knight," the woman declared, a wide grin on her angled face. Her features shared similarities with the House of the Woods.

I pondered this for a moment and glanced around at the crowd. I tried to separate the individual faces and really look at them. I don't know how I missed it before, but it seemed people from all over Terrathis were here. Winged people from the Tide, the glow of the Sun people, and even the House of the Ram were present. I was surprised to see druids from the Woods shapeshifting so flippantly as though it were a magic trick. It brought smiles and laughter as one man transformed into a large, vibrant bird.

I leaned forward, resting my chin on my clasped hands. My elbows dug into my thighs as I looked down at the arena. Alaric was walking towards us.

"Champion! I am finally the champion of Pipwick!" he proudly declared.

Marowen and Elaria clapped for him. Marowen leaned against the wooden railing. "Oh, Sir Alaric! How could we ever be worthy of your presence now?"

Alaric rolled his eyes at her jest and turned towards me. "Idrial, what did you think of the joust?"

I joined Marowen on the railing. "That was intense for a festival. But it was fun."

He bowed and raised his right hand, producing a yellow rose. He held it up to me and I felt my cheeks flush. "What is this for?"

"The champion gets to pick anyone they'd like to sit with at tonight's dance. I am not one for dancing, but I would love your company." His bright blue eyes glistened with hope.

I looked over at Elaria, who shrugged, and then back at him. "Well, I would be honored to sit with the Champion of Pipwick."

Chapter Thirty-Nine

I picked at the skin around my nails as I watched the dancers before me. They flowed effortlessly around a giant maypole, the colorful ribbons flowing in the breeze. The bright sound of fiddles and a lyre filled the air, along with chatter and boisterous laughter. The sun was setting and the earth was flooded in twilight, though we were well-illuminated by floating lanterns and several bonfires. The smell of wood and damp soil drifted through the air, mingled with copious amounts of alcohol. Raewyn's dagger felt heavy at my waist, and I found myself glancing down at it, hoping to see a glimmer of the gold path that would lead me to her.

My skin glowed ever so slightly as the warmth of laughter filled the air. Marowen and Elaria were nearby, chattering excitedly with Kolili. The spritely faun was sharing in what appeared to be cherry handpies. I took a bite of a flaky tart. The spiced cherry hit my mouth and I briefly closed my eyes. I licked a bit of the vanilla almond cream off the top. It was unnecessarily good.

I felt a presence lower next to me on the large tree stump beneath me. I looked over to see Alaric. Every time I looked at him, I felt a strong sense of familiarity, though I could not pin it.

"How are you enjoying the fair?" he asked, brushing a bit of powdered sugar off my cheek.

"It is unlike anything else I have ever experienced. It's absolutely magical." I finished off my pastry and wiped my hands on my skirt.

Elaria had given me clothing from their wagon. She said they kept an excess of clothes and accessories, just in case. She handed me a pale blue linen dress that hung just above my knees. I appreciated the thin straps that held it up over my shoulders. It was lightweight and comfortable in the warm air. The white corset with blue flowers was a little tight, but I didn't mind. And I was honestly grateful to feel lovely again. Marown had encouraged me to get my hair braided with ribbons, and so I had a single long pleat going from the top of my head all the way to my mid-back, with a blue ribbon woven in.

"Not one for dancing?" he quietly asked, not taking his eyes off the dancers.

I stared at him for a moment, his question catching me off guard. "Not much these days."

"I've never been one for parties," he said in agreement.

"Even as the Champion?" I playfully nudged him.

He smiled. "I am made more as a warrior than a partygoer."

Silence stretched before us as we watched the flame dancers twirl their batons in the air. Something had been eating at me, and I finally ventured to ask, "Do I know you?"

He turned, his sapphire eyes piercing. "Do you?"

I recoiled slightly at his response. "I... don't think so? But you seem familiar."

A smile formed on his lips, but didn't reach his eyes. He brushed his dark hair back. "We have met, though I didn't expect you to recognize me."

My eyes wandered back to my fingers, which I noted were bleeding from my anxious picking. I licked the blood from my thumb and wiped it off on my dress. "I am sorry. Could you remind me?"

He shifted, stretching his long legs in front of me. "Where do you think I am from?"

I looked at him, examining his face. "You share similar eyes as her."

"Raewyn."

I swallowed hard. I thought of her every time I looked at him, though I did not want to admit it. The dagger suddenly felt heavy at my side. "Yes. You share the same eyes as the people of the Tide."

"Indeed."

"But..." My voice trailed off, as I couldn't stomach continuing. "No wings."

He studied me carefully before taking a swig from a silver flask. It had the crab emblem from the Tide. "Not anymore," he offered the flask to me, but I raised a hand to reject it. My mind was already spinning.

"A cruel and vicious punishment." Alaric's voice was steady, but it had a hint of sadness.

I knitted my brows, trying to recall him. I felt I should know who he was, especially considering he was missing wings. I closed my eyes, recalling the palace of Vespera. Eldrin always taught me to mentally walk through spaces and keep track of details. He said, as a leader, it would be beneficial. I pulled forth memories of the palace across the water from my home. I found myself back in the glistening halls, the floors a mosaic of blue agate and white quartz. The halls were arched with scallops at the top and the columns were made of mother-of-pearl. Raewyn's mother always scolded us for touching them, claiming we would ruin the iridescence. I forced myself to remember the faces of those I passed. My eyes flashed open as I suddenly recalled who he was.

"Alaric..." I said, my voice soft. The jovial music in the background contrasted the conversation, leaving me with an odd feeling. It felt wrong to be speaking of such tragedies in a festive place.

"The Captain of the King's Guard of the House of the Tide," he said flatly. "And tortured and banished." A faun walked by, offering us a pipe. We both declined awkwardly. This was hardly the place for this reunion.

I swallowed hard. Five years previously, he had been accused of treason and he was stripped of his title and banished. His wings had been removed as punishment. "Raewyn was so upset."

He snorted a laugh. "I am sure. Her father was cruel in his decision." His voice was bitter. "I can't say I was sad to hear of his passing."

"Why didn't you say anything sooner?"

He shrugged, crossing his arms over his chest. "I wanted to see if you would remember." I opened my mouth to defend myself, but he waved a hand. "Once I realized you were involved in your own grief, I didn't expect any sort of recognition. And, truth be told, I wanted to see if I could trust you."

"So why did you? Trust me, that is?" I picked at the loose bark on the stump and rolled it between my fingers.

"You showed no fear when you saw Fiora was in trouble. There was no hesitation. That is the mark of a good and selfless leader." His sapphire eyes stared into mine. "That is the type of Queen I want to follow."

I didn't know how to respond, and a long silence stretched before us as we watched the dancers. Fire Breathers had joined in, spitting the flames from their mouths. "That was unfair, what they did to you."

"Aye, it was." He stretched his arms above his head. "But, I was found by this group." He nodded towards Marowen and Elaria, who were dancing nearby. "And for that, I am grateful." He glanced over at me. "I was surprised to see you with them."

A chill washed over me, sending my arms to smooth the raised hairs on my arms. "I am thankful you let me join. I would think you would have ill feelings towards me."

"If I were to hold everyone accountable for the wrongdoings of their superiors and family, I would never enjoy another's company again. You were young and had no control over anything. And neither did Raewyn." He made a motion to touch my knee, but instead dropped his hand. "She visited me in the cells."

I shifted slightly, pulling a leg under me. "I remember. She had me help sneak food from the kitchens."

"Ah, she did. I was grateful for that." He paused and looked at me. "I am sad to hear of her passing."

I exhaled forcefully and rose to my feet. I couldn't have this conversation anymore. "Let's dance. We shouldn't be so sad around all this joy."

He chuckled and raised his hands, shaking his head. "Oh, you are welcome to, but I don't dance."

I shrugged. "Suit yourself!"

I bounced towards Marowen and Elaria, trying to shake the heavy feeling from my chest. They laughed and each reached out a hand, bringing me into their dance. We bounded around in circles, twirling each other every so often. I closed my eyes, focusing on the movement and the music. But the haunting cries of Raewyn as she fell lingered in the back of my mind. The music stopped, and we slowed our dancing. As if sensing my grief, Elaria pulled a large horn off her belt. She flipped the copper top off and handed it to me. I peered inside to see a brown liquid that smelled heavily of bourbon. I quickly took a large gulp, letting the liquid warm my insides. It burned for a moment and ended on a sweet note. I handed it back to her and wiped my mouth with the back of my hand. The musicians started another song and we danced until the moon was high in the sky.

Chapter Forty

"Ugh, I am never drinking again," Marowen groaned.

I rolled over, feeling the grass bristle beneath me. The sun was warm on my face and I knew it was well into the morning. I forced my eyes open, the light hitting them like fire. My head exploded. Begrudgingly, I sat up and rubbed my eyes. I looked around to see we had fallen asleep on the ground near the maypole, and we weren't the only ones. We danced well into the night drinking and laughing. Eventually, the solemn memories had faded, and I found myself lost in the festivities. I vaguely recalled trying to juggle balls of light in my hands.

"It was your fault," Elaria stated. Her violet skin appeared paler and her silver eyes were a dull grey. "This is almost as bad as the Frostheart Festival."

Marowen laughed, the sound hoarse. "Ah, it was all worth it. How was your first Emberfall Festival?"

"I think you were trying to kill me," I grumbled, feeling my stomach growl.

"That's how you know you did it right!" Elaria laughed. She grabbed the side of her head and squinted her eye. I was glad to see I wasn't the only one with a pounding head.

"No surprise here," Calveris said. I craned my neck to see him walking towards us with a large platter. It had slices of bacon, rolls, and scrambled eggs. He sat down next to me and placed the platter before us.

Marowen crawled over and grabbed a roll. She took a small bite and chewed it forever. I watched her as she carefully ate, pausing every so often to ensure it didn't come back up. She clutched her stomach.

"Did you bring water?" she asked weakly.

Calveris sighed and pulled out a large skin, handing it to her. "You ladies never learn, do you?"

Elaria shook her head, bacon in hand. "One day of feeling like rubbish when you have an incredible night? Nothing is trying to kill us here."

Calveris grinned. "Are you sure about that? You seem near death's door."

Marowen tossed a bundled up rag at him. He laughed as he dodged it. "Well, eat your breakfast and clean yourselves up."

"Where were you last night, anyways?" I asked. I realized I hadn't seen Calveris at all.

He adjusted his glasses before taking a piece of bacon. "I tend to the animals at these. All of the loud noises and irresponsible people tend to put them in a bit of danger." He saw my expression fall. "Oh! No need to have guilt! I keep them in an area far enough away. The more nervous ones get a bit of an enchantment." He held a hand out and a soft purple glow emitted. "An old charm to soothe them for a bit of time." He quickly closed his hand, snuffing out the glow. "And it sort of recharges them for their next journey."

"Speaking of," Elaria shifted to sit on her knees, "we should make our way out of town. We need to get to the Ark Outpost."

A sickly feeling washed over me, and not from the alcohol. "How far until then?"

"Roughly four days," Calveris stated simply.

"Four days!" I cried. "And from there, how far is Arkanthys Desert?"

"I suppose it depends on a lot of factors." He thoughtfully chewed his bacon. "How far into the desert are we going? How many things will try to kill us?"

"I won't let a desert take me," Marowen spoke up, rising to her feet. She brushed off a few small sticks that stuck to her knees. "It would be far too embarrassing for someone from the Woods to get taken down by a bunch of sand monsters."

Calveris peered at her over his glasses. "Most have never been explored. There are ruins near the southern part, but it is not recommended to go there. It is a death sentence to most."

"I think I need to go there."

Calveris threw his hands up at me. "Did you not just hear me?"

I slowly stood up, my head spinning. "I know. But I am not most." I looked over at Marowen, who grinned. I turned my attention back to Calveris. "You don't have to come with me. None of you do." I looked at each of my companions, trying to keep my gaze neutral.

"We will come with you." Alaric suddenly stood beside me. I hadn't even heard him approach. I looked at him, seeing he had changed into a white tunic, emphasizing his muscular build. He wore brown breeches and thick brown boots. He looked more casual than I had ever seen him. He saw me staring at his clothing.

"We are about to go into a space where the sun is unrelenting. Dark clothing attracts the heat." He paused and looked at my disheveled dress. "I might recommend you change into something more practical as well."

The way he looked at my body warmed my cheeks. I looked away, turning towards the direction of our camp. A strange feeling tugged at my chest, but I willed it away. I felt the warmth of Marowen and Elaria next to me.

"Is something going on?" Elaria asked in a hushed tone.

I quickened my pace, but they matched my stride. "I am just trying to get to the desert."

Marowen grabbed my arm as I took a step up to enter the wagon. She looked at me, her dark brown eyes narrowed. "I warned you, do not lead him on. While you are used to the warmth of friendship, he is not. And he may misunderstand."

I shook her off. "I have no intentions with anyone. I cannot help if he misinterprets things." I pulled the curtain to the side and entered. Unfortunately, Marowen and Elaria followed.

"We know your heart lies with Eldrin, but the way you talk to Alaric sometimes seems like more than friendship. And he is picking up on it." Marowen handed me a light blue tunic and cream colored pants. "We saw you with him last night."

I set them on the table beside me and yanked my dress over my head. "I don't know if I will ever see Eldrin again. He may even think I am dead and have moved on himself." The tunic had a wide neckline, and Elaria had to pull it tight.

"Eldrin still knows you live," Elaria stated.

"How could he know that?"

"You know when your other half has been ended," she responded, keeping her eyes on tying a knot on the nape of my shirt.

"Why are we even talking about this right now? If Alaric has concerns with how I interact with him, then I expect him to discuss that with me directly. Otherwise, I have more important matters to handle." I yanked on my pants, wincing at their stiffness.

"Idrial, like it or not, you are our princess and will soon be Queen. Alaric was a *guard* at the House of the Tides. He was the *Captain* and had everything stripped away due to an injustice in the system. He sees *redemption* in you. He sees a part of him coming back." Marowen grabbed my shoulders and stared directly into my eyes. "We *all* see a redemption in you. All of us have been cast out or chased out of our homes because we don't fit their narrative. And now we have come to know you. You are the embodiment of justice and kindness. And I hope to gods damned that you keep this when you take your throne."

I was stunned. I hadn't considered the weight of my status in reference to them. I had been so focused on getting the Sun Stone and saving Calendor that I forgot the people in front of me were part of it all, too. Hot tears pricked at my eyes as I turned to find my boots. I cleared my throat.

"You all have shown me nothing but kindness and patience. You have allowed me to heal, to laugh. I don't know what kind of ruler I will be. I don't even know if I will survive that long." I laughed bitterly. "But I promise you that I will fight for you. I will do whatever it takes to give you back your voices." I looked at Elaria, who had a soft expression on her violet features. "I can't give him back his wings, but I would be honored if he, and all of you, stood by my side if I do ascend to the throne."

Marowen took my hand in between hers. "When. We won't let you fail. But you need to understand our own personal stakes."

I nodded. I felt a surge of energy flow through me. I was more determined to get the Sun Stone back to its place and to right many wrongs.

"To the Arkanthys Desert, then."

Chapter Forty-One

The music faded behind us.

No more floating lanterns, no scent of roasted honeyfruit or enchanted incense. Just the dry scrape of boots on cracked earth and the relentless glare of the sun at our backs. I didn't look back, letting the festival linger as a dream. We traveled in silence for the first few hours, partially due to the headaches that remained from last night's festivities, and partly due to the weight of what lay ahead. Calveris had mentioned the Arc Outpost was less than a day's journey from Pipwick.

We spent most of the day idly chatting, taking turns riding in the wagon to rest and pretend we weren't reaching the grueling desert. Calveris and I spent time pouring over Navarra's compendium, studying her notes. There were many creatures Calveris had never heard of, and I could see his spirits were lifting from new knowledge. Marowen, Elaria, and I spent time sharpening our blades and telling stories from our homes. I hadn't realized it had been years since either crossed the borders of their homes. Eventually, the ground turned from grass to dry earth.

The wind was dry and sharp, scraping dust across the cracked earth as we crested the last ridge. Before us, nestled in a cleft of red stone and shadow, stood Arc Outpost—the final flicker of civilization before the desert claimed the world.

It didn't look like much from afar. A low, squat structure built into the bones of an ancient cliffside, its sandstone walls shimmered faintly with arcane wards that buzzed faintly in the air. I noticed a faded cloth banner hung above the entry, its language unreadable to me, though the image of a coiled serpent and a chalice made its message clear enough: *Drink here, if you dare.*

As we approached, the scent hit my senses immediately. Not just food and spice, but something subtler: heated scales, exotic herbs, and the metallic tang of magic. Crystals embedded in the archway pulsed softly as we passed beneath it, registering presence, not identity.

Inside, the tavern was cooler than I expected, and quite a relief. The walls curved like the inside of a shell, smooth and naturally formed. Strange incense smoked from bowls carved into the walls, warding off desert sickness and unfriendly spirits. Tables were shaped from petrified wood and low to the ground, designed for patrons who coiled rather than sat.

I was startled to see the being behind the bar. He was long-bodied and scaled with sinuous grace and gleaming black eyes. His voice was almost melodic, tinged with a hiss, and he moved effortlessly behind the bar. I looked around to see more serpentine figures, some gliding upright on their tails, others slithering silently across the cool stone. Jewelry of copper and bone adorned their bodies, and their service seemed impeccable, if unsettlingly quiet.

"What are those?" I whispered to Alaric.

"They are the Esshka, the last of their kind," he whispered back, leaning towards me. "They are nothing to fear."

Behind the bar stood another, one I could tell was the proprietor of the place in how she carried herself. Her scales were a magnificent pale gold and her gaze ancient. I watched as she interacted with her patrons. She didn't speak unless spoken to, but her presence was commanding.

I glanced around the tavern to see its patrons were a mix of desperate travelers, weather-bitten guides, and quiet mercenaries who nursed drinks like lifelines. A map wall stood in one corner, scrawled with notes and shifting routes across the desert—a living thing that changed by the hour.

And at the heart of it all, the air hummed with that unspoken promise all adventurers chased: *One last comfort before the wild. One last place to turn back.*

"Sashara! It is so good to see you!" Calveris opened warmly, making his way towards the bar.

The serpent woman looked up at him, her angular face sharp and almost too symmetrical. Her large and lidless eyes snapped to me, shimmering gold. As we approached, I could see her skin wasn't covered in rough scales, but more like smooth porcelain with faint patterns that seemed to shimmer in the dim light.

"Calverisss," she hissed. "You have not been here in many yearss, and now you bring friendsss."

He laughed as he seated himself at the bar. "Indeed. I have gathered quite the group." He beckoned us to join him. I felt I had no choice.

I awkwardly sat on the stool beside him, folding my hands neatly on the bartop. I could feel the eyes of the other Esshka boring holes into the back of my head.

Sashara extended her long, sinewy arms towards us, setting short clay mugs in front of us. I glanced to my left to see Elaria idly tracing the rim, not seeming to be bothered by the strangeness that surrounded us.

"You have never brought royalty here before." She eyed me suspiciously, pouring emerald liquid into my mug. I glanced down at the magnificent color.

Calveris raised his cup before taking a hearty drink. "She is quite special, she is. We are heading to the Ruins." Those around us ceased their conversations and leaned in to hear more. Calveris either didn't seem to notice or didn't care.

"The Ruinsss are a death sentence. None survive their puzzless." Sashara looked at me. "I don't poison my paying customersss."

I carefully took my mug in my hands and lifted it to my lips. I was surprised to find it had a bright melon flavor to it. There was a tart finish to it that I found surprising. I could tell it was heavy on the liquor and worked to simply sip the beverage.

"I told you," she stated, her eyes wide at me. "You are foolissssh for going into the ruins."

"Perhaps so, but I have to save Terrathis," I said, determination filling my voice.

She let out an otherworldly laugh. "Terrathissss is beyond ssaving. There isss no hope here." She turned away to clean a glass.

I recoiled as though she smacked me in the face. "I can save Terrathis! I can find the Sun Stone and restore it!"

Sashara whipped her head around. "What do you mean, find it?" Her vibrant gold eyes stared at me intensely as she leaned over the counter.

I chewed my inner lip and glanced over at Calveris. He gave a short nod, as though to say she were safe. I looked back at the serpent and lowered my voice. "The night before the ritual, the Sun Stone was stolen from the tower."

Sashara quickly leaned back and opened her mouth. The dim lamp above her caught the glint of two sharp fangs that peered out. "Ssstolen?"

Calveris raised his glass of amber liquor to his lips. He took a sip and stared into it. "Which is why we are out in this lawless place." He peered up at the bartender over his spectacles, as though a silent warning.

She grabbed a rag and wiped the counter. "I sstill think you are foolsss to go into the desert, but I can sssee the dire need for it." She glanced at the door. "I recommend the Coil Plaza, before you go." She slithered away.

"I could use venom for my arrows," Marowen idly stated.

Calveris drained his glass and rose to his feet. "We make our way to the Coil Plaza, then."

The heat shimmered above the sandstone walls of the Arc Outpost like restless ghosts, but the Coil Plaza was alive with motion. The plaza's ground was a mosaic of polished stones arranged in spiraling patterns, a serpent swallowing its own tail in an endless loop. Around the spirals, stalls and shade-cloths of deep indigo and bronze flapped in the breeze, their edges weighted with rattle-bells that hissed with sound whenever the wind caught them.

Serpentine merchants coiled languidly behind low tables, their scales glimmering like sunlit armor. I watched in awe as their elongated bodies moved with hypnotic grace, looping over one another. The air was thick with spice and dust, and the cloying scent of something metallic, perhaps venom.

"Keep your purse close," whispered Marowen, her voice barely audible over the din. "Places like this have more fingers than a sand-spider has legs, even if half of them are claws."

She wasn't wrong. A lean, mottled-scaled serpent coiled beside a table stacked with glass vials of sun-amber liquid, each stoppered with wax and marked with symbols burned into the glass. He smiled—or something close to it—as he ran a forked tongue over his lips.

"Sun venom," he hissed softly, holding up a vial so it glowed like fire in the light. "For poison or pleasure. A drop in water, and you'll see through the desert's lies. Too much, and…" He trailed off with a sharp grin, making a slicing motion across his neck.

My eyes widened as I stared at the vial. *Sun venom,* I thought. That felt oddly personal. But I shook it off as just being paranoid. Elaria grabbed my arm and pushed me forward to the next stall.

Not far off, another merchant offered contraband desert maps, drawn on cured lizard-hide and sealed with obsidian ink. I stared as a hushed argument broke out between two buyers. I couldn't help but eavesdrop, my curiosity never quelled. It appeared to be over a route that promised safe passage through the sandstorm-wracked canyons of the south.

Near the center of the plaza, a low ring of stones formed the "Inner Coil," where the shadiest deals took place. A heavy-hooded figure—a serpent with scales so black they drank in the sun—slid forward from the shadows of an awning. "Artifacts," he rasped, lifting a cloth from a small table. Beneath it, pieces of shattered metal and bone glowed faintly, etched with runes that pulsed like they had a heartbeat. "Found in the deep ruins. Touch, and you'll feel the voices. Not cheap."

Alaric walked a few paces behind, and I was fully aware of his every movement. Any time a merchant got too close, he was quickly by my side, his sword partially drawn. Calveris had to calm him down, claiming he was the greatest threat in the square. I smiled, being reminded of my old guards that followed Raewyn and I around the halls. She often got annoyed and tried tricking them into leaving. It never worked.

We pushed through the crowd that was a tangle of travelers and serpents alike: mercenaries with dust-crusted boots, cloaked traders whose faces stayed hidden, and a few outlaws carrying weapons they weren't supposed to. There were unofficial serpentine guards, draped in silver collars, watching with half-lidded eyes but didn't interfere. The Coil Plaza ran on its own rules.

Elaria lingered at a merchant selling shards of desert glass, glowing faintly with trapped heat, while Marowen was drawn to a table where illegal charms lay scattered like playing cards. The charms were carved from bone and sealed with dark resin, their faint whispers just audible when the wind shifted.

"Wards against the House of the Sun," the seller murmured. "Banned in half the cities, but here... you'll find no law."

Marowen's hand quickly flew to mine, squeezing it before I could say anything. I lowered my eyes, and we quickly moved on and stood beside Elaria, her gaze caught on something in the scatter of trinkets. She lifted it and held it in her hands. A shard of silverstone gleamed faintly. Its surface bore the crescent-mark of her people—the crest of the House of the Moon—worn but unmistakable.

I arched an eyebrow. "You look like you've seen a ghost," I said, my voice low but edged with curiosity. "Isn't it just an old emblem?"

Elaria crouched closer to the table, brushing aside a faded cloth. "This... this shouldn't be here," she whispered. Her tone was almost reverent, though tinged with fear. "This stone was carved in the Lunar Forges. Only the Moon Houses know the secret of shaping it. How—" She looked sharply at the merchant, a wiry serpentine figure with greenish-gold scales and eyes like fractured glass. "Where did you get this?"

The merchant's tail flicked lazily across the stones, making a dry whispering sound. "Does it matter, moon-girl? It's for sale. A relic from old bones, pulled from the sands near the dead canyons."

Elaria's jaw tightened. "That's impossible. The House of the Moon never traded our relics, especially not to black markets."

"Then it must have been stolen," Marowen said, leaning closer with a smirk that never reached her eyes. "The question is... by who?"

The serpent tilted its head, unbothered. "The desert does not care who dies in it. I find, I sell. That is the way."

Elaria reached forward, almost snatching the shard, but I caught her wrist lightly.

"Careful," I murmured. "This isn't the House of the Moon. It's a pit full of teeth. If you show you want it too much, he'll triple the price—or worse."

Elaria exhaled sharply, forcing her hand to unclench. She straightened, trying to mirror my calm. "Fine. What do you want for the shard?"

The merchant's smile widened, forked tongue flickering. "Two silver suns. Or... something better. I trade in rare things. Memories, sometimes. Or secrets."

"Secrets?" My voice dropped like a blade. I had already spared one memory and wasn't eager to give up much more. "You'd better be careful whose secrets you try to take."

The serpent hissed softly, unafraid. "The moonstone is old. I feel it hum. It knows stories. Perhaps stories you would pay dearly to keep hidden."

I could almost hear Elaria's heartbeat as it pounded in her chest. I could sense the artifact wasn't just a relic. It was resonating with her, faintly glowing as though calling to her bloodline. The swirls on her skin began to emit a soft glow. "I'll pay the silver," she said, fumbling with her pouch.

The merchant slithered back, coiling lazily. "Oh, silver is dull. I want something sweeter. Tell me..." His gaze cut to Marowen, sharp as a fang. "You carry a shadow. The desert likes shadows. Trade me one of yours."

Alaric suddenly stepped forward, his hand moving subtly toward the hilt of his blade. "Or we take it."

The serpentine guards nearby shifted, their spears tapping the ground like rattling tails. The merchant's smile sharpened further, enjoying the tension. "You could try. But the Coil does not favor thieves."

Elaria stepped between them. "Stop. Alaric, this is my home's blood in this shard. If we have to bleed for it, I will."

The standoff was beginning to draw too many eyes. I kept my eyes lowered, suddenly aware of just *how* evident my heritage was. A few serpentine onlookers had slithered closer, curious to see if blood or silver would be spilled on the mosaic coils of the plaza. Alaric's hand was still close to his blade, his dark gaze fixed on the merchant like a wolf sizing up prey.

Then, a voice cut through the tension, smooth and warm as desert wine.

"Now, now," said Calveris, stepping out from the crowd with an easy smile. "Isn't this a little uncivil for a market? We're all friends here, aren't we?" His dark hair glinted under the sun's light, his indigo tunic subtly stirring despite the still air.

The merchant's slitted eyes narrowed. "Friends pay their due."

"Oh, certainly," Calveris said, his tone light as if they were discussing the price of sweet dates. He leaned over the table next to Elaria, his gaze flicking to the shard. "But surely you can feel it too. That moonstone... doesn't quite belong to you. It wants to return home."

The merchant tilted his head, amused. "Stones do not speak."

"Oh, they do," Calveris replied with a sly grin. I watched in surprise as he raised his hand casually over the table, fingers tracing lazy, meaningless-seeming patterns in the air. At first, nothing happened. Then the shadows under the awning shifted ever so slightly, elongating like serpents, coiling softly around the merchant's table.

I felt Elaria stiffening, as we all sensed the subtle pulse of magic. It was a trick so quiet it didn't even smell of magic, just a ripple in the air like heat off stone. The silver shard began to hum faintly, a pale light blooming along its etched crescent, responding to the magical current.

The merchant's forked tongue flicked nervously. "What… is this?"

Calveris leaned closer, his voice dropping to an intimate, conspiratorial tone. "The stone is alive with memory. And memory is dangerous when bound. Wouldn't you hate to have it start… remembering you?"

As he spoke, the crescent symbol on the shard flared with cold light, casting the serpent's own shadow on the ground in the shape of an open-jawed snake, its fangs inches from his throat.

A hiss escaped the merchant, his coils tightening reflexively. "Tricks," he spat, though his voice wavered. "Mage tricks."

"Perhaps," Calveris said with a shrug, letting the illusion linger just long enough for the fear to settle in. "But what if the House of the Moon marked this shard to curse any who dared take it? A curse that…" He let the words trail off, the air growing cool around the table. "…lingers."

The merchant's eyes darted between Elaria's intense stare and Calveris's calm smile. His hands twitched, then retreated from the stone. "Take it," he muttered. "It is… too loud. Too old."

Elaria's breath left her in a rush as Calveris scooped the shard into a piece of cloth, wrapping it carefully. "You drive a hard bargain," Calveris said cheerfully, tucking the bundle into Elaria's hands. "But truly, you've saved yourself trouble. No one wants a piece of the Moon's wrath."

The merchant hissed low, but said nothing more. The watching serpents lost interest and drifted back to their business. We began making our way back towards our wagon and Bellar.

Elaria looked up at Calveris, her knuckles still pale from clutching the relic. "You didn't have to—"

"Yes, I did," Calveris said, his tone suddenly softer. He glanced at the shard, then at her. "That thing belongs to you, not to some snake counting coins." Then his grin returned, mischievous and bright. He adjusted the frames on his face. "And besides, I never could resist a good bit of theater."

I smirked, tension bleeding from my shoulders. "Theater. Right. Next time, remind me to bring a mage when I go haggling."

A sudden commotion broke out by the square's edge. Two serpentine traders coiling violently around each other, hissing and striking.

"These water-stones are counterfeit!" One cried. I watched as he threw round, blue stones at the other. "These are useless!"

"What are water stones?" I whispered, as we slinked past the crowd.

"Life-saving here," Calveris stated. "They can help summon water."

We pressed on, avoiding other altercations. The crowd surged like a living creature, whispering bets or stepping back to avoid the conflict. No guards came. The plaza thrived on spectacle. Having filled our rations, and then some, we knew it was time to head into the Arkanthys Desert.

CHAPTER FORTY-TWO

"According to the old accounts," said Calveris, breaking the silence. "This region was once a riverbed. Long ago, the land flourished. Shade trees, springs, even herds of golden deer." The three of us walked alongside Bellar, letting Marowen and Elaria sleep away the pain in their heads.

"And now?" grunted Alaric. His face was hidden beneath a sun-veil, but his voice still held the gravel edge of command. "Now it cracks beneath our feet and swallows the dead."

Calveris glanced away, fiddling with the rolled parchment at his side. "Well, yes. Now it's... less hospitable."

"I see that." I shielded my eyes, scanning the distant dunes. The sky shimmered, heat distorting the horizon like a veil of melted glass. "Keep your hoods up. We can make it to the Pillars before nightfall."

"Assuming they haven't sunk further into the sand," said Alaric. His tanned skin glistened faintly with sweat, but his pace never slowed. I could tell being so far from the water weighed on him already. "This place eats memory. Don't count on old landmarks."

He dragged the toe of his black boot through the dust as he walked. The thin trail he left behind wilted, the sand blackening for a heartbeat before returning to its pale gold. His magic was dying here. I could see it in his eyes, but I said nothing.

By midday, we reached the top of a ridge. Before us stretched a sun-bleached basin surrounded by bone-like rock formations. At the center stood the ruins of a shrine, half-swallowed by sand.

"We'll rest there," Calveris said, already descending. He pulled on Bellar's lead, careful not to slip down.

As we approached, the shrine's carvings came into view—solar spirals, gryphons, and a crown wreathed in flame. All around them were various runes. I felt something stir in my chest. The symbols were familiar. My mother had drawn them in the margins of old stories, always with trembling fingers. I once asked what they meant, and she simply said they were old runes of Eledrinna. This was once a shrine for the Sun Goddess.

I knelt beside a cracked offering bowl and brushed away the sand. Inside lay a piece of red stone, no larger than a coin. Still warm.

"Someone's been here," I murmured.

Calveris crouched beside me, taking the stone piece from me to examine it before returning it. "Recently." He pointed to a footprint in the dust. Not theirs. Smaller. Unshod.

Alaric eyes narrowed. "Ghostly desert children. Or worse."

"Worse?" I asked.

"There are things born of too much sun and no shadow, the Unsettled." He glanced at Calveris. "Navarra told you about them."

I nodded. "She gave me her book that explained their encounters."

"I would be most interested in seeing that," he said, closing his fingers around the stone sliver.

"What is this stone?" I queried, rising to my feet and brushing off bits of sand.

"Carnelian. It once was thought to be the stone of artists. If worn, it would give your creative abilities more power." Calveris smiled softly. "It is likely this place held music festivals to worship."

The sun had fallen below the horizon like a coin dropped into molten bronze, and still the desert radiated heat. The sand glowed faintly under the twilight, holding on to the memory of the sun's fury. That night, we camped in the lee of the shrine. None of us felt comfortable, being so exposed.

Marowen built a small flame from dried root bundles she'd brought from the Woods. The fire was pale green and cracked like bones in winter. Calveris passed around water skins while Alaric stood watch, still and silent. Elaria cleaned her blade with an oil that smelled like crushed moonsage.

I sat apart, the piece of Carnelian warm against my palm.

"You're thinking too loudly," Calveris said, settling beside me.

"Do you always listen where you're not wanted?"

"It's why I'm still alive." The scholar watched the fire, his voice softer than I had ever heard it. "Do you really believe the Sun Stone is here?"

I didn't answer right away. My eyes gazed into the fire until they burned.

"I don't know, truthfully," I said. "But I have to hope those visions, or whatever they were, were real. Because without the stone, we will all fall."

Calveris made a quiet sound, whether in agreement or worry, I couldn't tell. "Just remember that you were born for this. The magic of Eledrinna flows through you. You wouldn't be given this responsibility if you weren't capable."

A gust of hot wind swept through the camp, and for a moment, the fire bent toward me as if drawn to me.

Elaria looked up from her dagger and glanced around. "The desert heard you. Maybe it wants you to come for it."

I closed my hand around the stone.

"Good."

Chapter Forty-Three

I shot up from a fitful sleep, once again tormented by the visions from Thalassa. I feared my sleep would never be the same again. The sun was just peeking over the horizon, and I looked around to see the sand outside the camp begin to *shift*. It wasn't loud, and there was no dramatic tremor. Just a hiss—like wind through dry grass. And then a *scraping*, deliberate and steady, that looked over at the others, who also sat up straight, awoken by the sound. And then, it *rose* all around the perimeter of our small camp, the dunes broke apart like crusted ice. Pale limbs thrust upward. Figures emerged—no sound, no roar, only the gritty rasp of sand sliding off bone-dry skin. They were gaunt, lean things, made of cracked flesh and shale. Their eyes were empty pits beneath smooth white masks, crescent-shaped mouths curled permanently open, as if in warning or hunger.

Calveris was already moving. With a flick of his hand, a thin arc of lightning sprang into the air, cracking like a whip above our camp. Shouts erupted. Bellar reared back and screamed. "A Skarnling!" He shouted.

A Skarnling lunged towards me, and I quickly rolled sideways, sand exploding where I had previously stood. I grabbed my small blade in one clean motion. I instinctively struck the creature's side, causing it to let out a horrible shriek, a high rattling sound, and it crumbled back. I knew it wasn't dead.

"Salt," Calveris called across the chaos, parrying a clawed hand with a shimmer of magic. "They're vulnerable to salt—"

"I don't *have* salt!"

"Use the dried rations! The meat!"

I glanced over to see Marowen quickly tear open one of the supply crates with the heel of her boot, grabbing a strip of preserved venison. As one of the Skarnlings lunged again, she hurled the salted meat into its chest. The reaction was immediate—steam burst from the wound like breath from a furnace. The creature collapsed into ash.

Elaria screamed. Another Skarnling had grabbed her, dragging her in blankets into the sand.

"No!" I sprinted forward, diving and catching the assassin's wrist just as the creature began to vanish beneath the surface. My fingers closed around fabric, then skin. The ground beneath her gave way—until an arrow coated in oil and salt streaked past my shoulder, striking the monster in the head.

Marowen. Her face was unreadable, but she stood in the desert wind, her empty bow string shaking.

Breathless, I hauled Elaria free from the sand and stumbled backward. With a fluid leap, Elaria was behind another Skarnling—daggers flashing. Her curved blades bit into the creature's spine, but it didn't bleed. Instead, sand poured from the wounds, and the thing spun unnaturally, arms scything. She ducked under the blow and buried one dagger beneath its chin. A hiss—then collapse.

Three Skarnling had slipped towards Alaric. Even from my position, I could see his face drenched with sweat as he wielded his large sword, slashing at them. He was outnumbered. I attempted to move, but a sandstorm was picking up and I struggled to fight against its strength.

Elaria appeared again—*above* it this time, leaping from the wagon. She drove both blades down into one of the collars of the monster, using the momentum to slam it flat. But it twisted, shrieking, and nearly threw her.

Marowen shot another arrow straight into its skull.

"You owe me," the archer muttered.

Elaria grinned, panting. "Put it on my tab."

I ran past Marowen, my dagger in hand. I lunged forward, thrusting my blade into a Skarnling's face. It screeched and turned to dust. I suddenly heard a giant roar. My heart jumped into my throat, and before I could turn to look at it, a *ginormous* brown bear leapt past me.

"What the hell is that?" I watched in horror as it grabbed a Skarnling with its giant paws and easily ripped its head off with its teeth.

Elaria calmly stood beside me, slowing her breath. "That is Marowen."

"The BEAR is Marowen?"

"She's a druid!" Elaria said simply. We watched as Marowen easily took apart the group of desert monsters.

"Most elves from the House of the Woods are druids. You knew that!" Calveris was rushing by my side, his staff in the air.

My heart raced as I watched the mage and the bear dispatch the remaining Skarnlings. Calveris quickly weaved violet runes in the air, creating a current of Arcane Magic. Symbols flared around his wrists, white-hot. The sand beneath the creatures turned to liquid glass, then exploded upward in jagged, glowing spears.

The earth rumbled again, a deeper tremor this time, like something vast turning in its sleep beneath the surface. My heart leapt into my chest.

Alaric's grip tightened on his blade. "Something else is coming."

The sand behind the rockline erupted—this time with violence. A jagged claw burst forth, followed by a chitinous bulk that glistened dark red in the morning sun. A creature emerged like a buried nightmare—part insect, part stone, with eyes like molten glass.

I recalled a page from Navarra's journal. *The Burrowmaw is a colossal predator of the desert, feared by travelers for its ability to emerge from beneath the sands without warning. Its form is a disturbing fusion of living insect and the raw geology of the desert itself, as though the creature were born from the stone and sunbaked earth.*

"A burrowmaw!" Elaria cursed, backing toward me. "They don't come this close to surface light unless—"

A chorus of *clicking* erupted across the camp. From the ridges, long, serpent-like creatures began sliding down the dunes—mouths fanged, tongues flicking with heat-sense. Their skin shimmered like hot coals, and as they moved, the sand melted beneath them.

"They're being *pushed* toward us!" Calveris shouted over the roar. "This isn't random—it's like a purge!"

I turned in a slow circle. Our perimeter was folding. Even as they struck the Skarnlings down, *more* monsters crawled from beneath the dunes. Elaria had taken a hit, her arm bleeding. Alaric fought with his back to us, as though trying to protect his companions.

And then—

A *sound* split the air.

A piercing, high-pitched *cry*—not human. Not beast. It rolled across the sky like thunder caught in a blade.

Every head turned upward.

"Do we have to fight that, too?" Marowen cried, back in her human form. She released double arrows into the mass of insect creatures.

Against the rising sun, a shape descended—winged and massive, golden feathers catching the light like fire. The gryphon dove in a steep arc, talons outstretched. Its rider leaned forward, cloak billowing, hands already moving in swift, ancient sigils. My heart stopped for a beat, not believing what I was seeing.

Eldrin.

The gryphon hit the burrowmaw with devastating force—talons digging deep, beak tearing through the carapace. Sand erupted with his landing as Eldrin flung a bolt of lightning magic into the creature's open wound. The desert lit up white as if the sun had *answered* him directly. He leapt off Index's back and stood in the midst of the chaos. He waved his large, ornate staff above his head and chanted. We were surrounded by bright blue rings of magic, runes dancing all around. He then drove the staff into the ground, exploding all of the runes at once.

Everything around us shrieked and immediately burst into blue flames.

His wild violet eyes found me. Even from a distance, I saw the change in him: sunburnt skin, windswept robes, and a sharpness in his gaze I had never seen before.

We hadn't spoken in a year. And now he had suddenly fallen into our war and saved us.

Index let out a loud shriek of joy into the suddenly quiet desert. Despite not having sight, I knew he could sense me. Eldrin moved in a fluid motion, already summoning a protective shield of light around us.

"Stay in the light! It will protect you!" he commanded, voice steady, charged with magic. Outside of the magic barrier, more deadly creatures screeched and fought against it.

I stood, frozen in place. Sound had been replaced by a loud ringing, and my skin felt as though someone poured ice water over me. I stared at him, not believing what I could see. I met Eldrin's eyes across the wreckage. My blade dripped with dark ichor. My breathing was ragged.

"Eldrin."

He stepped closer, the memory of a thousand nights in his eyes.

"I have torn apart the earth and the skies to find you. I have ripped open the mountains and flattened trees to reach you," he said, his voice hoarse. He lowered his staff to the ground, his breathing shallow. I opened my mouth to speak, but found I had no voice.

Without warning, he pulled me into his arms and held me tightly until I thought I would lose my breath. I melted into his familiar arms, tears streaming down my face. I pulled away, desperate to see his face. He brushed a gloved hand against my cheek, wiping them away. I gently touched a healed scar on his cheek and wondered about the story there. I didn't have time to ponder before he pulled my face towards his and pushed his lips onto mine. We kissed with a fervor, a hunger. Neither of us thought we would ever see each other again. I could feel the eyes of the others on me, but I didn't care.

I was home again.

Chapter Forty-Four

The firepit was long dead and our belongings were scattered around the camp. Calveris was soothing Bellar and offering him carrots he had purchased from Pipwick. Alaric and Elaria were cleaning their blades, covered in ooze and dust. I watched as Marowen worked to repack the rations in a fabric roll, the efforts not seeming to work out as she wanted. Index was curled next to the wagon, seemingly glad for a reprieve. The desert was unsettlingly quiet, and all I could hear was the labored breathing of my companions. Eldrin and I sat a short distance from the group, not wanting to be apart.

I watched silently as they worked on their tasks, wishing they hadn't come. Every day they were with me, a new danger presented itself. I pulled my knees to my chest and rested my chin upon them. A sigh escaped my lips.

"My Sunbeam," Eldrin quietly murmured. "You have found loyal friends. You did not force them into this."

I closed my eyes, my lips turning slightly upward. It felt so good to hear his voice again. To feel it vibrate in my chest. I turned my head, resting my ear on my knees. "I do not deserve such loyalty. Look where it got Raewyn."

He inhaled deeply. "It is a heavy burden to have people so invested in you that they are willing to risk anything."

"I don't want it anymore."

He gently brushed a loose strand of dusty hair from my face. "You don't have a choice. You are not only their friend, but their Queen."

"Not yet. I haven't earned the throne yet." Another thought that frequented my mind.

"I believe you have. Perhaps not in the most traditional of ways, but you have." He brushed sand off the stubble that had formed on his chin. It was strange seeing him so unkempt, but I found it all the more alluring.

"How did you find me?"

He extended his legs out in front of him, leaning into a good stretch. "Several nights passed, and I didn't hear from you. At first, I thought perhaps you hadn't slept. But then I knew something had gone wrong. I spent a month weaving tracking spells and sending them out to you. Just when they would see you, it felt as though you disappeared."

"Tracking spells?" I asked curiously.

"Did you ever see critters that didn't belong? In the woods or the water?"

My mind went back to the ethereal violet animals that seemed to follow me. I sat up straight, turning towards him to sit on my knees. "You sent those? They were beautiful, but I thought I had lost my mind."

He let out a throaty laugh. "I had hoped they would bring you peace and you would realize they were from me!"

I shook my head. "I thought I was going insane from grief or something." I paused for a moment. "What do you mean I disappeared?"

He shrugged. "I can't explain it. After the first one, I stole Index and flew through the mountains. I landed in a clearing in the woods." His lips upturned. "I met Navarra. She is quite a remarkable woman."

Memories flickered in my mind of the old woman who saved my life. "She is. I would no longer be here without her help."

"Indeed. She told me what happened to you and Raewyn," his voice trailed off, grief shrouding his face.

I nodded, a heavy weight pressing against my chest. "She helped me through my mourning. And helped me train with my new powers."

"Your new powers?"

I inhaled sharply, lowering my gaze to the sand. "I don't know what happened. After Raewyn fell off the mountain, something filled me, and I became an entirely different being. It was as though I *became* the sun. It's how I survived the golem."

He pondered this for an uncomfortable length, staring out into the distance. "You are the daughter of Eledrinna. You became all of your past selves in that moment."

I recoiled slightly. "How do you know?"

He rubbed his eyes with his fingers. "Idrial, I need to tell you something."

The weight on my chest deepened and reached my stomach. "What do you know?"

"I had my suspicions after your parents disappeared. It felt too clean, too purposeful. So, I went to the Banned Archives and found your family's history. The history they kept locked away." A look of guilt flashed across his face.

"You could have been exiled for going there. How did you get past the Archive Demon?" For a moment, my curiosity was greater than any of the other feelings swirling around.

"Ah, that was not an easy task. But now is not the time for that." He twisted the silver ring on his finger. It held the sigil of the Celestial Order of Mages. "What I found is that Eledrinna had a daughter. And when she was born, the goddess imbued her with eternal life. And she lived for thousands of years. But when the House of the Moon became corrupt and split, her life began diminishing. It is when our ancestors began losing their long life." He stopped for a moment, choosing his next words carefully. "Eledrinna did what she could to save her daughter, but the magic didn't work how she expected. She passed away. When the next royals of the House of the Sun had a daughter, she came back in that form. That is how she continued her long life, through others."

I stared at him, my mouth hanging open. I coughed abruptly, sand having gathered. I grabbed my waterskin and took a hearty gulp. "Did my parents know?"

"I believe that is why they left, even before your trials. They must have found out and perhaps went to go find more information."

I wiped water off my lips with the back of my hand. "What information? And why leave without warning?"

He shrugged his broad shoulders, his curly dark hair resting on them. "I like to believe it was to protect you. If anyone else knew, it could put you in danger." He rested his hand on top of mine in the sand. He opened his mouth to speak, but closed it.

"What is it?"

He stared idly into the desert. His eyes glazed over with the same look he would get as he poured over thick leather tomes in the library.

"My love, I think you can unite our country. Moon and Sun once ruled together."

I scoffed. "They are corrupt. Their spoiled prince wants nothing but war. You didn't see what happened to Briarhollow, to Fiora! How could I want anything to do with them?"

He lowered his arm by his side. "Yes, I did. It was the last place I looked for you. I spoke with Fiora. She told me what their emissary did, and I saw the remnants of their terror."

I dropped my hands and exhaled, my heart quickening. "I just... I can't. Why would you even think that?"

"I believe things will unfold in time. When it does, you will have to make the decision to let Terrathis fall or unite us." Feeling me recoil, he pulled me close to him, his hands gentle on my arms. He stared into my eyes with such an intensity I could barely stand it. "I believe the House of the Moon discovered certain information, and that is why they have acted out. Why they are trying to take over. They don't want you to gain power over their ranks."

"And why they took the Sun Stone?"

"I believe there is more to that reasoning, and part of me thinks your mother is involved." I began to protest the accusation but he continued. "I think she had to act in order to protect it. And you."

"So she could still be alive? Her and my father?" I had long assumed they were dead and didn't want to hope again.

"I don't know. But I believe we are intertwined in a centuries-old plan by the gods. We have become their pawns in games they could not work out themselves." He spoke in a hushed tone, as though they were listening.

I glanced around suspiciously for a moment. "What do I do? How do I fix everything? There is too much broken."

He gently stroked my cheek with the back of his hand. "We continue towards the ruins to find the Sun Stone. And then we will make a plan."

I leaned into his hand, grateful for the familiar warmth. "I am glad you are here with me. Here at the beginning of everything."

Chapter Forty-Five

The desert night stretched silent and endless, a black sky strewn with white stars that burned like shards of ice. The dunes gleamed faintly under the pale crescent moon, their ridges etched in silver. A low wind hissed across the sand, carrying with it the chill that seeped into the bones and the faint rasp of distant movement. I sat with my knees curled behind me, listening to the soft sounds of Eldrin breathing. I knew I needed to sleep, but my mind raced.

My eyes stared into the low campfire, its embers glowing like a wounded heart in the darkness. My companions laid scattered about, the belts on their packs swaying with the breeze. The scent of smoke and sweat mingled with the dry, dusty air. Suddenly, another smell intruded, musky and feral.

Without warning, a guttural snarl broke the stillness. Out of the black horizon came large, shadowed figures. Their forms were half-hidden by the shifting dunes, first seen only as moving shadows, then as hulking silhouettes with eyes that glowed like molten gold. I squinted to see them better. They moved low and fast, claws cutting into the sand without sound, muscles rippling beneath bristling fur that shimmered under the moonlight.

One leapt from the ridge above, teeth bared, and landed with a thud just beyond the fire's circle of light. Another slunk around the flank of the camp, its breathing heavy and animalistic. Their howls rose like a cruel choir, echoing through the dunes, drowning out the wind. I quickly shook Eldrin awake, my eyes not leaving the beasts.

The firelight caught their features—elongated muzzles wet with saliva, jagged teeth gleaming like ivory knives. I recognized them from the journals: the Varg.

With a flash, Eldrin was on his feet, his staff in hand. I looked across the firepit to see the glint of Alaric's sword reflecting the moon's light. One of the three Varg turned and lunged for him. Sand sprayed as his claws tore into the ground. I scrambled to my feet, soon joined by Marowen and Elaria.

"Can't we just have some peace?" Elaria groaned, her daggers ready in her hands.

Marowen shouted a warning to Calveris, who was running towards his staff. He dove into the sand, his hands making contact. He rolled to his back and pointed the staff towards the creature. Blue lightning erupted from its orb and stunned the wolf-life creature.

Eldrin's voice cut through the chaos like a sharpened blade, his hands tracing intricate symbols in the air. The violet runes flared to life, glowing with an eerie, otherworldly light that pulsed in rhythm with his heartbeat. He planted his staff firmly into the sand, and the ground around the campfire shimmered as arcane circles burned bright beneath his feet. With a sudden roar, violet tendrils shot forth, snaking like serpents through the night air, lashing at the nearest Varg with a searing, magical bite. The beasts snarled, their flesh smoking where the runes struck, and several staggered back, howls twisting into pained growls.

Not far off, Calveris raised his hands to the storm-darkened sky, his eyes crackling with raw energy. Blue lightning arced from his fingertips, zigzagging in furious, jagged lines. With a sharp clap, he slammed his palms downward, sending a surge of electric fury rippling across the sand. The blue bolts danced and twisted, striking two Varg at once with a roar of crackling power. The beasts convulsed, their bodies spasming violently before collapsing in twitching heaps, fur singed and smoking.

I watched as the mages moved in tandem, their magic a deadly dance amid the howls and snarls. Eldrin's violet runes pulsed in cascading waves, ensnaring and burning, while Calveris's lightning arced unpredictably, striking wherever the shadows moved too close. Each blast and rune left scorched marks in the sand, painting a streaked battlefield glowing with violet and electric blue.

As the pack faltered, shaken by the sudden onslaught of magic, Eldrin's voice rose in a chant, weaving a final binding rune that erupted beneath the last snarling Varg. The beast was trapped in a cage of glowing violet light, struggling futilely as Calveris's lightning cracked overhead, promising swift and final judgment.

Beside me, Marowen swiftly applied venom to the tip of her arrow before pulling it onto her bow. She carefully aimed it at another Varg racing towards us. It whistled past and landed directly in the beast's chest. Elaria leapt towards another, landing both daggers into its head. It swiped hard on her shoulder, leaving deep gashes in her violet skin. She cried out but kept moving.

"Idrial! The sun! They cannot survive in the light!" Calveris cried out, pointing towards another group of Varg coming towards us.

I nodded and pushed my palms together. I closed my eyes and focused, trying to draw my power. Being in the hot desert sun had grown the intensity, and now I was about to unleash the sun's fury.

"Protect them!" I shouted at Eldrin. He nodded and held his staff above his head. A shimmer of violet fell upon each individual, and I knew they were safe.

My body hummed and vibrated as I raised my arms above me, releasing the solar energy. The desert sky flared bright as a second sun, blinding and burning. Waves of golden light pulsed outward, turning sand to glass and igniting dry brush. The werewolves howled, their fur singed and smoke rising where the light touched.

In a voice not quite my own, I rang out, "By Eledrinna's eternal blaze, you will not take us!"

A blinding corona ripped from my hands, and a solar storm filled the desert. It was as bright as midday, and as hot. The ground beneath me trembled as I watched the scorching radiance melt the claws and sear their flesh. I felt my heart pounding in my chest as a wave of nausea filled me. I closed my eyes, knowing the earth was coming closer.

"Idrial... we feel you. You will be healed."

"I am so tired." I didn't want to leave this dream state.

"You are so close. You have found the Carnelian stone. It is for you."

"What is it for?" I asked, my voice sounding unnatural.

"It will bring you courage. Keep it with the Obsidian from the witch. You will enter the ruins with a clear mind."

"Who are you?"

"We are always within you. We are part of you."

I tried to look towards the voice, but I was surrounded by blinding, golden light. "What is in the ruins?"

A pause. "There is a deep nightmare that has taken over. Trust your companions. Trust yourself."

I awoke to the soft touch of Eldrin's fingers on my cheek. I fluttered my eyes open and looked up at his face, covered in sand and worry.

"That was quite the display," he murmured. Relief poured from him and I slowly sat up.

"Are we safe?"

"Thanks to the powers of mages and the sun," Marowen said. She was sitting on the ground.

The sun was beginning to rise and cast a warm glow across the dunes. I took a mental inventory of everyone, including Bellar and Index. I was relieved to see they were all safe. My skin was damp from sweat, and I could smell an odd burning scent. I grabbed my braid to find the bottom few inches had been charred and were coming loose.

"If you wanted a haircut, I could have helped," Elaria joked. She crawled over to me and redid my braid. It wasn't perfect, but it would hold up better.

"I, for one, am tired of this damned desert trying to kill us." Marowen was laying out her arrows, taking inventory.

"The Arkanthys Desert is relentless. Sashara did warn us," Alaric stated. He sat at a close distance, sharpening his sword.

"Sashara?" Eldrin looked over at me, curiosity playing in his eyes. "At Ark Outpost?"

"You know her?" I asked.

He rested his hand next to my leg. It was difficult not touching each other after so long. "Yes, all Mages encounter Ark Outpost and the Esshka during our Runewalk. It's part of exploring different cultures and races." He took a hefty swig of his waterskin.

"They seem to hate the House of the Sun," I said quietly. That had been bothering me since we left.

He smiled sadly. "Even if you do everything right, people will still hate you. The important thing is to stay true to your own values." He brushed a loose strand of hair from my face, letting his hand linger. I savored the touch. "You are a kind and just woman. And you will lead with that."

My lips turned upwards in a soft smile. I wanted to ask him about home, but I was afraid to. He briefly mentioned that Raiku was well and missed me, and that my siblings were well but very obviously ill-equipped to run a city. I felt there was more to it, but I couldn't be distracted. I needed to focus forward.

CHAPTER FORTY-SIX

The sun was high and relentlessly burned into our skin. Even the cotton fabrics over our skin couldn't keep it out. My skin stung with the burn of the hot rays. I never had a sunburn before, and it felt mildly embarrassing. Eldrin had shown me how to tuck the brown linen fabrics of my ankles into my boots to keep the sand out, so I at least had that. We had walked tirelessly for days, taking turns in the enchanted wagon. It had been a day since any of us had spoken, as we had grown irritable from the heat. I walked alongside Ballor, who I could tell was not a fan of the sand.

Every so often, I thought I caught a glimpse of ruins, but it turned out to be something Calveris called a mirage. *The desert plays tricks on your mind,* he said. I glanced down at my boots, the rich brown leather covered in dust and sand. I yearned for a bath with fragrant oils. I missed my dog, and I missed the ocean. I tried not to let my mind wander too often to those comforts, as it only made their absence more known. I was glad to have Eldrin back, at least.

He spent the first day telling me bits of his journey. He had spent a year flying around on Index in search of me. He spent a few nights with Navarra, and she told him what she knew. I wanted to tell him more of my powers I came into, but I wasn't sure how to fully explain it. Every time I used my sun powers, it felt different. It felt ancient and somehow *golden.* I looked up at the skies, expecting to see Index flying around. Elaria and Marowen had begged Eldrin to let him stay. He could be useful and scout ahead for the ruins. But Eldrin reminded them he was blind, and he also needed to return to Calenor to let my siblings know I was alive. Every time I asked how things were back home, he got quiet and said it was functional. I knew something had happened, but I didn't press it. For now, I needed to focus on the mission ahead.

I yawned and stretched my arms above my head, feeling a slight tension release in my shoulders. When I opened my eyes, I squinted. I swore I could make out tall structures in the distance. I rubbed my eyes, hoping it wasn't another mirage. The image stayed. I looked up at Calveris on Bellar's back to see he was staring wide-eyed in the same direction.

"Are they real?" I asked, my voice coming out gravely.

He nodded. "I believe we have found them." He looked down at me. "Do you feel anything? Any sort of connection?"

I paused for a moment and felt for any sort of vibrations in my body. I shook my head, slightly defeated. "I do not. Surely if they were the old ruins of Eledrinna, I would notice something?"

He shrugged, the white linen scarf around his head and shoulders shifting. "Not necessarily. These ruins have lain dormant for centuries."

I glanced back at the wagon. "Should we alert the others?"

"Not yet," he said carefully. "We don't want to get their hopes up. They seem to be but a few hours away." He took a swig of his waterskin and then offered it to me.

I took it graciously, having not consumed anything for hours. I had been too lost in thought. "What will we find there?"

He smirked. "Hopefully, the Sun Stone."

I playfully pushed his leg. "Other than that."

"Who knows, truthfully. It could be empty, or it could be riddled with more desert monsters." He gently stroked Bellar's neck.

"Or maybe dragons."

We both laughed. Dragons no longer existed in Terrathis. After the great war between the gods, the dragons moved to another continent. No one knew why exactly. All we had were artists' depictions and old stories.

We walked in silence for some time and the ruins became closer. We crested the final dune just as the wind shifted, and there it lay—half-buried in the golden sands, like the bones of a fallen god.

The Solareth Ruins stretched across the basin like a shattered crown. Pale sandstone pillars jutted from the earth at crooked angles, some broken in half, others still upright, their surfaces smoothed by centuries of wind and grit. A once-grand causeway, lined with statues of sun priests and celestial lions, led to a collapsed ziggurat, its upper tiers swallowed by sand. Sunlight caught the remnants of inlaid gold in the stones, making them glimmer faintly, as though the ruin itself still remembered how to shine.

Above the entrance, half-buried in shadow, was a weathered relief: the sun with five rays, each ending in a different symbol—crab, ram, horse, fox, and a moon. Several had been chiseled away.

The air suddenly grew hotter. Unbearably hot. As if the temple still held the heat of the sun trapped inside it, unwilling to let go. We stopped, and I turned towards the wagon. My companions were already emerging. They stopped short and stared up at the vast ruins, complete awe covering their faces. I looked at Eldrin and he nodded, coming towards me.

"We must enter, carefully and quietly," he said, his voice low.

Calveris dismounted Bellar and stroked him gently, allowing him to lap up water from a clay pot. "You stay here and stay hidden," he murmured softly. I could tell it pained him to leave him out here exposed.

My heart pounded in my chest as we walked towards the entrance. I felt a wave of nausea came over me, but I forced it down. The moment we stepped past the threshold, it was like walking into a breath held for centuries. My hands began to shake.

Inside, the halls were wider than expected, though many were collapsed. High ceilings arched like ribcages above, and beams of sunlight pierced through holes in the stone, illuminating ancient murals: a civilization of sun worshipers cloaked in gold and white, bowing to a radiant disk suspended between twin obelisks.

My eyes scanned the room, noticing that some things had decayed. Some murals had been scorched. Others defaced. A long-dead struggle lingered in the broken altar, the shattered brazier, and the blackened marks of fire where nothing had burned in centuries.

"Where do we go?" I asked, my voice echoing.

Marowen stood next to me, her bow in hand. "We explore, I expect."

"Should we split up to cover more ground?" Calveris asked, his eyes scanning the vast room.

"That is never a good idea," Alaric stated, gently touching a sand-covered chest. His voice was low and he didn't dare open anything.

I closed my eyes, the feelings of anxiety replaced with an odd sense of familiarity. I inhaled deeply, starting to feel the connection I had hoped for. After a moment passed, I opened my eyes and pointed down a darkened hall. "There. We go through there."

No one questioned me, and we quietly made our way through. As the pass darkened, I created a small ball of light in my hand. The sound was eerily quiet, except the occasional sound of sand shifting. The hall was long and winding and spilled out into a vast room. The smell of metal and heat filled my senses. I stopped abruptly and held my arm out to stop my friends from continuing. There was a steep drop into complete darkness below. Marowen kicked a small rock into the pit, and we waited to hear it land, but the sound never came. I looked across the empty space to see another platform that led to a door. I looked around for a broken bridge or some way to cross, but came up empty.

I looked over to see Eldrin and Calveris speaking in hushed tones, pointing to the pit. I approached them with questioning eyes.

"This is a failsafe, to keep the unnecessary people out," Eldrin said at last.

"Out of what?" Elaria asked, obviously uneasy to be so high up.

"Whatever is over there. Which means we are on the right path," Calveris flatly stated. He turned to me. "This is Eledrinna's temple. Your light is the key."

I threw my hands up. "I have no idea what to do here."

"Cast a light wave or something," Marowen offered.

I furrowed my brow. "I don't know if it works that way."

"Either way, this is your ancestor's place. They called you here for a reason. They wouldn't give you a dead end." Eldrin gently brushed my arm.

I sighed, perhaps a little too dramatically. I walked a foot away from the edge and stared out. My fingers fidgeted at my side, peeling back the cuticles. I closed my eyes and pulled forth my powers, summoning the brightest light I could. I heard Marowen gasp behind me and opened my eyes. I looked down to see there was a small square illuminated in gold over the pit. My eyes found Eldrin, who nodded hesitantly. I swallowed and took a careful step forward. I was surprised to see the path solidified into sandstone and illuminated another square ahead.

"Do you think it's safe for you all?" I asked, my voice shaking. I was wildly aware of the vast distance between me and the unknown ground beneath me.

"Well, I suppose we will find out," Calveris said, almost cheerily. He took a careful step forward onto the path behind mine. "It seems stable as any. I trust you," he encouraged.

Single file, and very slowly, we all made our way to the other side of the cavern. As much as I wanted to sprint across, I didn't know if the stones were temporary, and I had a constant mental image of all of my companions' falling to their doom behind me. After what felt like an eternity, I stepped on the last stone. I was about to step off when Eldrin shouted a few paces behind.

"Don't!" I froze, remaining on the last stone. I tried to look over my shoulder at him. He continued. "We don't know if the path is only tied to your magic. We need to dismount strategically."

I looked down at my feet. How could we all get to the other side if I had to remain on this tiny square? An idea sprung to my mind and I carefully dragged my foot to the right. As I had suspected, another gold square illuminated and turned to stone. I sighed in relief and stepped over. I looked at Eldrin a bit smugly.

"I don't need you for everything, you know." Despite how terrified I felt, I smiled at him.

He smiled, though it didn't reach his full face. I knew he was terrified of open heights. I watched as he followed Marowen off the last stone and onto stable ground. Alaric was the last to exit the path and I leapt off my stone. We watched in horror as the path did immediately disintegrate and fall into nothingness.

"I am glad you waited for us," Elaria said, her voice shaking slightly.

I nodded, a lump in my throat, and laid down, my hands resting on my stomach. I wanted to feel a flat surface against my back, no matter how jagged the ground was. Marowen and Elaria joined me as the men stood near the doorway. I could sense Eldrin was eager to push on, but I needed a moment.

We feel you here. You are on the right path.

The air snaked around my ears, sending shivers through my body. I stared up at the endless ceiling. That first challenge seemed straightforward enough, but I had a sinking feeling it would only become more difficult. I reluctantly pushed myself up and looked around. Elaria deftly got to her feet, feeling my movement. She looked down at me and offered a hand.

"Time to move?"

I nodded and grasped her hand. "Time to move."

Chapter Forty-Seven

The next room was surprisingly cooler, something we all welcomed. It looked like a rather average room. It reminded me of the holiday rooms at the palace. They were more or less rooms filled with things only used during festivals. Raewyn and I used to run around them, pretending the statues were following us if we looked at them. We made it a game to hide from them, squealing as our imagination ran away from us.

As we made our way into the chamber, it opened like the heart of a buried monument. Fine sand coated the floor in rippling drifts, as though the desert itself had crept inside to claim it. I smoothed the chills that formed on my arms as I glanced around. Four statues, half-buried and worn by time, stood sentinel around the room. I approached the nearest one, gently touching its stone face. Each figure was cloaked in the faded armor of some forgotten sun-guard, their stone faces eroded and featureless, their shields and armor covered in a layer of dust.

I turned to the center of the room where Eldrin and Calveris were looking upwards. There was a single circular opening that pierced the ceiling; a perfect oculus that allowed a wide cone of sunlight to spill into the center of the chamber. The beam shifted slowly, as though marking the hours, sending a pale glow across the sand.

"What do you make of it?" Calveris asked Eldrin.

Eldrin shook his head, glancing upwards and then towards the door. "It's some sort of riddle." He extended his hand towards the doorway.

Opposite the entrance loomed a massive door of gold-burnished stone, etched with a great sun motif: long rays curling outward, inlaid with fragments of polished metal. At its center, set like the eye of the sun, was a perfectly smooth mirror, dark with age but waiting for light. Despite the layer of dust, it was still magnificent.

"The arrangement of these statues seemed deliberate," Elaria mused, circling them. She pointed her dagger towards each of them. "They all face the center."

Alaric brushed a pile of sand off the top of one. "What purpose does this serve?"

Marowen sneezed and rubbed her nose. "Probably to keep people out. I don't like how they are watching us."

Alaric knelt beside one of the figures, brushing the grit from its shield with a calloused hand. "This isn't just decoration," he said, his voice low. "Look how smooth the surface is. Like a mirror." He glanced up at the column of sunlight, frowning. "Why would they put mirrors in a place like this?"

"Could be used to blind intruders," Elaria offered.

Eldrin moved to the other side of the chamber, straining his neck to see the sun motif above the door. He pointed up at it. "This is most likely a mirror."

I closed the distance between us to get a better look. "What an odd mechanic."

Calveris remained in the circle of light and shifted around, looking at each of the statues. "Somehow we have to make them all face the door?"

I chewed the inside of my lip. "Maybe I can use my magic here again? It worked before."

"That would be too easy," Marowen stated. She leaned against a stone pillar, resting her bow in her lap. "But it's worth a shot."

I conjured a small amount of light, not wanting to blind anyone in the dimmed room. I threw it at the motif above the door and it bounced off as though it were made of rubber. My eyes widened as I watched the ball of light roll across the sand and then snuff out into nothing.

"*That* is new," I stated in surprise. "It's never maintained form before."

"That could prove useful later," Alaric noted.

Calveris crouched to examine the shield nearest him where the ball of light had ended. He squinted, glancing between the statue and the door. "Wait," he said slowly, "What if they're meant to direct something?"

Eldrin followed his gaze, his violet eyes narrowing in thought. He moved toward the beam of sunlight, positioning himself in the column and then turning to see where the light caught the shield. A faint golden gleam danced across the opposite wall. "A reflection," he said. "If the statues could turn, the light could be aimed."

Alaric rose to his feet, brushing sand from his palms. "You think we need to line them up? Bounce the sunlight into the door?"

"It's worth a try," I replied, already gripping the edge of the nearest statue's shield. It groaned faintly under my strength, sand grinding as the figure shifted ever so slightly on its base. As I turned it, the beam of light caught the mirror and scattered across the room like a blade of gold, striking the wall and making the sun motif on the door shimmer faintly. I felt a hint of triumph.

Elaria stepped back, scanning the other statues. "The sun will start to set soon."

"Then we have to be fast," Eldrin said.

Alaric, grinned, the old soldier in him relishing the challenge. "A puzzle of light and time. Let's get to work."

Marowen and Elaria each stood at a statue, and Alaric and I took the others. Calveris and Eldrin stood by the door, ready to take on anything that may come through. The four of us looked at each other and nodded.

The first statue groaned as Alaric rotated its angled shield into the sunlight's path. A clean, narrow beam cut across the chamber, landing near the second statue. Dust and sand hissed as the beam warmed the air, the heat of the desert sun concentrated and sharpened to a blade of fire.

"Careful," Eldrin warned, his eyes intense on the light burning away the top layer of sand where it passed. The grains popped and cracked, sending tiny curls of smoke into the air. "That's not just sunlight anymore. It's focused. Strong enough to... gods, it could cut through flesh."

Elaria squinted at the beam. "Wonderful. So if we misalign this, it'll slice us apart. Fantastic."

Marowen tested the second statue, pushing against its shoulder. The stone shifted reluctantly, scraping against its base. "We'll just need to keep clear of the light," she said, straining to angle the mirror. "Easy enough."

The moment she adjusted the shield, the beam shifted and slashed across the floor, grazing within inches of Elaria's boots. She cursed and leapt back, glaring at her friend. "Easy, she says."

"Sorry," Marowen muttered, sweat running down her brow. She nudged the statue again, slower this time. The beam connected, bouncing to the third mirror. Another flash of searing light cut through the air, making the room feel like a forge.

I moved to push the third statue but stopped as a faint rumbling echoed above us. Dust sifted down from the ceiling, and a section of wall opened, revealing a panel of ancient bronze mechanisms. They began to turn with an ominous grinding sound.

"What did you do?" Elaria asked sharply.

"Nothing," I said, teeth clenched. Panic setting in, I looked at Eldrin who had gone pale. "I think... we're on a timer."

Eldrin's eyes darted upward. The sunlight, once steady, had shifted by a fraction, dimming as a faint cloud of dust crossed the oculus above. "The beam's moving," he said. "If we don't align all four statues before the light leaves the circle... the mechanism will lock."

"And then what?" Elaria asked.

As if in answer, a row of slits opened in the walls with a sharp *clack*. Sand began to pour out in steady streams, flooding the floor faster than a heartbeat. Alaric leapt forward and immediately started digging, shoving sand away from the base of my statue. His efforts were in vain, and it did very little to help.

Elaria spun towards me, eyes wide. "Tell me you know how to stop this!"

"I don't!" My voice cracked, echoing against the high walls. Marowen fumbled with the nearest statue, trying to twist its shield. The metal squealed as it caught the sunlight, scattering a faint beam across the wall, but nothing happened.

"*Faster!*" Eldrin shouted, his staff raised as if ready to blast the ceiling itself. "It's a puzzle. We have to get the mirrors aligned before we drown in sand!"

"Drown?" Elaria snapped, kicking at the rising mound. "We're going to suffocate before we drown!"

The sand climbed to our shins now, flowing like water, pulling at our legs as we stumbled through it. Alaric joined Marowen at her statue, trying to shift its angle. "These damned things are *cemented in place!*" His teeth were gritted, his scarred hands slick with sweat and sand.

"Marowen!" Eldrin barked, his voice tight with urgency. "See the beam—there! If we can catch the sunlight on the shield—"

"I'm trying!" she yelled, throwing her shoulder against the first statue. Sand flew up in choking waves as she struggled to turn it. The sunlight wavered, catching the edge of the second shield but missing it by inches.

The hiss of falling sand grew louder, a deafening constant. It was up to our knees now. Elaria's movements became frantic, clawing at the grit as she tried to clear the base of a statue. "We're running out of time! If this hits waist-high, we'll be pinned!"

"Then stop shouting and *push!*" Alaric barked. He slammed his weight into his statue, his boot braced against its plinth. It shifted with a loud *grind*—the beam slicing across the room to strike the third mirror.

The sudden flash of light burned across the sand, filling the room with golden glare. Eldrin shielded his face. "One more! Get the last one!"

The sand was at our thighs now, heavy and choking. I nearly lost my footing as I waded toward the final statue joining Elaria, the grit clawing at my legs like quicksand. "It's stuck!" she gasped, struggling to move it even an inch.

I didn't waste time answering. "Moving the statue!" I shouted. I threw all of my weight against it. My ribs were still sore from fighting in Briarhollow, and I felt that pain choose to resurface now. My hands slipped on sand as the mirror caught the beam and sent it shooting toward the last statue. The heat brushed my shoulder, but nothing beyond my clothing was singed.

"It's stuck, too!" I cried, pushing and pulling. "The base is wedged!"

Marowen swore, grabbed Elaria's dagger and used it like a lever, jamming the tip into the seam of the statue's base. I watched intensely as they forced it to turn. The last mirror caught the light just as the beam began to fade. Smugly, Marowen handed the dagger back to her friend.

With a deafening *clang*, the beam struck the sun motif on the door, igniting it with blinding golden fire. The door's carvings glowed as if molten, and the massive slab of stone rumbled open. The streams of sand ceased instantly, leaving the room in an eerie hush, broken only by our heavy breathing.

For a moment, none of us moved, still half-paralyzed by the panic of the last minute. Then Elaria let out a shaky laugh. "Next time," she gasped, "I vote we just... pick a different temple."

I wiped the sweat and sand from his brow with a shaking hand. "If there *is* a next time."

Eldrin's eyes lingered on the now-open doorway, his voice low and measured. "If this is what they built just to guard the door, I dread what lies beyond it."

Chapter Forty-Eight

"You have found us," the familiar voice echoed. It felt more solid. "Step into yourself."

The chamber beyond the massive sun door felt nothing like the first room. Heat pressed against my skin the instant I stepped through. It wasn't the dry warmth of the desert above, but something older, heavier, as if the stones themselves had been steeping in sunlight for centuries. The air shimmered faintly, distorting the edges of the high golden dome above.

My gaze followed the etched rays spiraling up the walls until they converged on the far side of the chamber — a towering relief of Eledrinna. Her amber eyes glowed faintly, catching on the gold dust in the air. That glow struck something deep in me, something that felt like recognition.

My breath caught. "This is... a sanctum," I whispered, though the word trembled between awe and dread.

Eldrin stepped past me, scanning the room with quick, precise movements. "No," he murmured. His fingers brushed the script carved into the dais at the center. *"The sun favors those who give of themselves, and burns those who deceive."*

A prickle ran up my spine. "What does that mean?"

Before he could answer, the floor shuddered and emitted a deep and grinding, like stone teeth chewing through the earth. Three black obelisks erupted around the dais, golden veins pulsing along their surfaces. Across the chamber, Eledrinna's eyes flared brighter.

Then the walls split. Thin seams ripped open around the chamber's edge, and searing shafts of sunlight knifed inward. The beams moved, sweeping across the floor in slow, deadly arcs. Where they touched, stone hissed and cracked, revealing a molten glow beneath.

Elaria jerked back from one that sliced past her leg. "What—what's happening?"

"It's a trap," Alaric barked, yanking his blade free as though steel could turn aside sunlight itself. "Those beams will cut us to ribbons."

"No," I said, the word coming out steady despite my pounding heart. A strange calm slid into me, like the weight of a hand on my shoulder. "It's not a trap. It's a test."

Eldrin turned sharply. "What kind of test kills you for a wrong answer?"

"The kind that wants faith," I replied, my gaze drawn to the blazing sun sigil beneath Eledrinna's image. "She's asking me to trust her."

The beams quickened their sweep, slicing the room into a shifting grid of light and shadow. Tiles within the sunlight began to sag, molten rock bleeding upward. The air reeked of scorched stone and singed metal.

Alaric shoved me aside just before a beam carved the floor where I'd been standing. His shield caught the edge and the steel sizzled, glowing red before he tore it back. "This will cook us alive!"

Eldrin's voice rang out, taut with urgency. "Look! The obelisks! There are handprints carved into them! They're part of the mechanism."

Elaria's eyes darted between them. "So we split up and hope the goddess doesn't fry us? Perfect."

"No," I said, louder this time. I swallowed hard. "Not we. Me. This is my trial."

Before they could argue, I ran. The heat hit me like a wall, air blistering in my lungs. A beam swept across my path. Alaric lunged, planting his shield into the light. The metal shrieked, heat blooming off it in waves, but it gave me a heartbeat's opening.

I slammed my palm to the first obelisk. Fire shot up my arm, raw and searing. I bit back a scream, clinging to the stone. Light roared from its surface, leaping toward the others like a chain of lightning.

"Two more!" Eldrin shouted.

Elaria and Alaric moved like a wall around me, deflecting and distracting, but the light was everywhere now, shifting, hunting. My boots slipped on scorched stone as I lunged for the second obelisk. I pressed my other hand to it. Agony tore through me, but I held on. Somewhere beneath the pain, I felt it — not destruction, but a question. *Do you trust me?*

The sun sigil blazed hotter, nearly blinding.

"Last one!" Eldrin called, voice breaking with strain. The floor began to splinter beneath him, molten cracks racing outward.

A beam cut across my final path. I froze and Elaria, reckless as ever, hurled herself through it. The smell of burning cloth and flesh hit my nose as she screamed, kicking the obelisk's base to tilt the light just enough for me to pass.

I dove, planting my burned palm against the last stone.

A shockwave of golden light exploded outward. The beams winked out. The molten floor hardened. The grinding ceased. Slowly, the obelisks sank back into the earth, and Eledrinna's statue split open, revealing a narrow passage lined with molten-gold carvings that pulsed like veins.

I fell to my knees, trembling. My palms blistered and raw, but in their centers burned two perfect sun-marks, light seeping from the skin.

Alaric hauled me up, his expression grim. Elaria, shoulder scorched black, managed a weak grin. "If she wants to test you again, tell her to try doing it herself."

But I could barely hear them. My gaze stayed on my hands. The marks pulsed in rhythm with my heartbeat.

"This wasn't just a trial," I whispered. "She's watching me now. Guiding me."

Eldrin glanced toward the glowing passage. His voice was low. "Then we'd better move quickly... before she decides to see how much more faith you have left to give."

Chapter Forty-Nine

A warm breeze crossed my skin and captured the wisps of hair around my face. The air was thick, hot, and suffocating, every breath tasting of iron and decay. I absently grabbed the disheveled braid over my shoulder as my eyes stared into the vast room before me.

The hall was a cathedral of ruin, its walls veined with cracks, its once-golden carvings drowned beneath a rust-dark patina of dried blood. At the heart of the chamber, where the broken tiles formed a circle of ritual markings carved deep into the stone, *it* writhed. I stared at what was less a creature and more a living abomination: a towering, half-formed shape of flesh and ichor that pulsed like an open wound. Its skin, if it could be called that, was a slick membrane stretched thin over a mass of writhing veins, each one pulsing and twisting as if alive on its own. Where its face should have been, there was only a gaping cavity, from which black-red ichor dripped in slow, viscous ropes. I felt the bile rise in my throat, and I had to swallow it down.

I stared at the long, serrated ropes of bloody tendrils that sprawled across the floor, some sinking into cracks, others twitching like the feelers of some insect. One thick tendril curled around a tall pillar, binding a human figure to the stone. I couldn't quite make out anything about them, but noted their head slumped forward, hair matted to their blood-smeared face. Another tendril pierced into the person's side, pulsing in rhythm with the demon's sickening heartbeat. It seemed to be siphoning her very life.

The creature's core was a mass of tangled arteries and glistening muscle that contracted and expanded with each breath, emitting a low, guttural moan that reverberated through the hall. Every contraction sent a spray of hot, steaming blood spattering across the cracked floor, as if the monster was birthing itself over and over from its own gore.

"This is a grotesque altar," Marowen said in a low voice beside me. I looked over at her to see the color had drained from her face.

I nodded and looked back at the blood that dripped from the creature, pooling in the shallow depressions across the floor.

I looked over at Eldrin, who stared in a horrified expression I had never seen before. "What is it?" I whispered.

He swallowed hard. "A Sanguimor. I had read about them, but I didn't know they still existed. They are ancient and horrible."

"You don't say," Elaria whispered, daggers in both her hands. We knew this fight would be ugly. Elaria glanced down at my side and cocked her head.

"What is going on with you?" She pointed at my leg, keeping her voice low.

I followed her finger to see a pool of soft, gold light was pouring from my leg and onto the ground. It formed a glittering path forward and disappeared into the blood pools. It was coming from Raewyn's dagger. My heart lurched as I feverishly examined the hall. Was she here? Was it a trick? My eyes suddenly caught on an altar across the room, beyond the Sanguimor. I gasped and pointed. "The Sun Stone!"

Suddenly, a low shuddering sound reverberated through the hall. The pool of blood beneath the monster began to churn, bubbles forming. Slowly, it lifted its head to look at us. And then the tendrils began to move.

Without warning, they lashed out with a thick, wet snap, striking the ground. One of them whipped around, taking out a crumbled pillar with it. Our group leapt in opposite ways, trying to dodge the aftermath. Tendrils lashed out and trapped each of them against the pillars. They struggled against their prisons, trying to be free.

The floor quaked as it moved closer, and I felt the familiar stir of magic in my veins—a heat that started at my heart and radiated outward, curling around my fingers like the warmth of a noonday sun. The air shimmered faintly around my hand as I summoned my power, my blade catching a faint golden hue as light magic ran along its edges.

"The Sanguimor is responding to your magic!" Eldrin shouted from the other side. "It hates it!"

I could somehow feel the revulsion coming from the Sanguimor. As much as I wanted the aid of my friends, I knew this had to be my fight. I couldn't free them. The Sanguimor had ancient power, and so did I.

It lunged first. A whip of gore lashed out, fast as a striking adder. I quickly rolled to the side, the tendril carving a long gouge in the stone where I had stood a breath ago. Another tendril lashed out. This time, I met it with a blast of sunlight from my hands, cutting cleanly through its length. The wound didn't bleed; instead, it was cauterized. Instead of immobilizing the monster, it grew two new tendrils from around the wound.

I gritted my teeth, planting my feet as the ground beneath me began to pulse. The Sanguimor's ichor seeped into the tiles, veins of red cracking across the floor and walls. I felt the bile rise in my throat. This was the most disgusting thing I had ever been involved in. I looked around to see the ruins were becoming an extension of the creature, every inch of the hall turning into its bloody hunting ground.

From its core came a voice, dripping into your thoughts like ink:

"Blood is life. You are mine. I will drain the sun from your heart after all this time."

Great. It had a vendetta against me longer than I had been alive.

I shoved the words away and raised my hand. Heat burst from my palm in a blinding wave, sunlight condensed into raw magic. It struck the closest tendril, searing through it. The Sanguimor recoiled, shrieking like a thousand screams overlapping at once. Its surface bubbled and split where my light touched it, its ichor burning to black cinders.

I barely had a chance to breathe before the Sanguimor lunged with all its tendrils at once. They whipped forward in a torrent of flesh and blood, a storm of barbed veins that left nowhere to run. I planted my palm on the ground and channeled my magic through it.

The hall exploded with light.

Golden fire, sharp and radiant, flared out in a dome around me. The tendrils struck it and burned away like paper against a flame, shriveling and curling back. The Sanguimor screamed again, but this time the sound was... *furious.*

My barrier flickered. Its hunger was relentless. It pressed closer, tendrils writhing and clawing against the barrier like the legs of some massive centipede. I was running out of energy. I was feeling weak, and I knew I couldn't go on much longer.

My gaze snapped to the woman. She twitched weakly against the pillar, her lips pale. The tendrils around her tightened, as if the Sanguimor meant to crush her before I could reach her. A flicker of movement behind her caught my eye. I recognized those wings. My heart lurched.

Raewyn. She was alive. But barely.

"Not her," I hissed.

I let the barrier collapse in my hands and through my arms. It burned like a white-hot star. With a shout, I sprinted forward. Tendrils slammed down, as though trying to cut me off, but every step I took, I blasted sunlight from my hands. Each strike burned through the gore, cutting paths through its living mass. The Sanguimor recoiled from the light, its body retreating even as its mass undulated across the ceiling, dripping crimson like rain. Now I really wanted to vomit.

As I raced towards the pillar, a massive tendril wrapped around my leg, yanking me off my feet. I hit the ground hard, both the Carnelian and Obsidian stones clanking on the ground. I had forgotten about them. Before I could grab them, another tendril coiled around my chest, pinning my arms. The thing hauled me into the air, pulling me closer to its gaping core. It absolutely reeked of the most vile smell to ever enter my nose.

The heart of the Sanguimor, if one could call it that, was a swollen mass of pulsing red tissue, translucent enough to see rivers of ichor flowing inside. It opened, a maw of writhing tendrils lined with serrated bone-like ridges. The voice filled my skull again, this time louder:

"I will hollow you. I will drain the sun."

My blood began to boil, and I was livid. I felt the tendrils around me tighten and another wave of exhaustion slammed into me. It was pulling my blood, trying to unravel me from the inside out.

Through the haze, I spotted Eldrin and my companions. I clenched my teeth and reached inward, summoning every drop of magic left in my veins. Heat surged, burning away the pull of the Sanguimor's feeding. My skin glowed faintly, golden veins of light racing across my arms and chest.

The tendril holding me smoked.

With a roar, I ignited. A burst of solar fire exploded from my body, searing through the creature's grip. Its tendrils burst apart, splattering gore and ichor across the floor. I stood tall, my entire form glowing like a living torch.

The Sanguimor *hesitated.*

I raised my hand and called down a sphere of sunfire. It burned like a newborn star above my palm, radiant enough to bleach the shadows out of the hall.

"Let. Her. Go."

The creature shrieked, lashing out with everything it had, but I threw the sphere into its core. The explosion was blinding. Flesh and ichor boiled and burst, spraying across the hall. The Sanguimor thrashed, every tendril flailing in agony as the light tore through it, burning it from the inside. It released Raewyn, whose unconscious body fell to the floor.

CHAPTER FIFTY

"Raewyn!"

Her name tore from my throat like it had been waiting there for months, raw and desperate. The sound seemed to echo in the ruined hall, swallowed by the damp air. My legs moved before I could think, carrying me forward in uneven bursts. The sticky black tendrils that were binding her loosened with every step, sagging like dying vines, but I barely registered them. Somewhere behind me, I felt the presence of my friends, shuffling boots, sharp intakes of breath, but they didn't matter. My entire world had narrowed to the figure slumped against the pillar ahead.

I had imagined this moment a thousand times in the dark hours of the night. In some dreams, she smiled and ran to me. In others, echoes of Thalassa's torment clouded my mind. I reached her too late. None of them prepared me for the reality.

Her head tilted weakly toward my voice. Eyes fluttered open, heavy with exhaustion, and then—there they were. That unmistakable, crystalline blue, bright even in the dim light. My knees nearly buckled.

She startled at the sight of me, a flash of panic passing over her face, but the moment I cupped her cheeks in both trembling hands, she stilled. The warmth of her skin, her real, living skin, sent a shock through me so strong my breath caught. My thumbs brushed over her cheekbones, memorizing the curves I thought I'd never touch again. Stray strands of hair clung to her temple, damp and tangled, and I smoothed them back.

Her wings sagged low, matted with grime from the Sanguimor, but they were whole. That alone made a sob rise in my chest. I searched her face for signs of harm, for bruises or breaks, but all I saw was exhaustion and that stubborn spark in her eyes.

My hands fumbled for my waterskin. I tilted it toward her lips, holding my breath until she took it, sipping slowly. Her throat bobbed with each swallow, and I didn't realize my own tears had started until they dripped onto my wrist.

"Idrial?" Her voice was paper-thin, fraying at the edges, but the sound of it was like sunlight breaking through a storm.

The year I had spent without her, between the sleepless nights and the gnawing dread, all collapsed in on me all at once. My composure shattered. A sob ripped free as I folded into her, pressing my face into the curve of her neck. She still smelled of saltwater and jasmine, faint but unmistakable. My arms locked around her, clutching as if letting go would make her vanish. My body shook violently, my breath hitching in uneven bursts.

Her embrace was weak but steady. Fingers pressed into my back, grounding me. My tears soaked into the tattered fabric of her sleeve, into her hair. Words tried to form, to explain everything, all of the nightmares, the hollow ache she'd left, but nothing came. All I could give her was the sound of my breathing and the weight of my relief.

Eventually, she shifted beneath me. A gentle pat on my back. I pulled away reluctantly, afraid the connection would break, but she was smiling faintly through her exhaustion.

"I knew you would find me," she said. Her voice was stronger this time, and she eased herself upright, bracing her back against the pillar. Her wings hung low, trembling with effort. Her gaze flicked past me.

"Eldrin." The way she said his name was soft, almost reverent. "I knew you would protect her."

I turned to him. My love stood frozen, his expression carved from shock and grief. His usually steady composure was gone. His lips parted, his eyes glistening.

"Raewyn," he breathed. "You live."

She gave him a faint, tired smile. "Barely."

Her eyes swept the hall then, landing briefly on Alaric. Whatever passed between them in that moment was quick, unreadable. She turned her head toward the far end of the room. "There's your stone, my Queen."

My breath caught. The Sun Stone.

I rose slowly, each movement deliberate, as though the wrong pace might break the fragile spell holding this moment together. The altar loomed ahead, carved from pale stone, flecked with centuries of wear. The Sun Stone rested in a wide bowl set into the altar's surface, its golden light spilling over the edges like warm honey.

I reached out, my fingers brushing the air above it first, feeling the heat radiating from its glow. When I lifted it, the warmth surged into my palms, and the light flared brighter at my touch.

But when I turned it over, my breath hitched.

Only half.

The missing curve where the other piece should be felt like a wound. I looked around, my gaze sweeping the floor as though it might have fallen nearby. My heart hammered in my ears.

I turned back toward Raewyn, holding the fractured stone so the light bathed her face. "It's only half. The rest is missing."

She braced herself against the pillar and began to rise, her movements slow and deliberate. Her wings flared slightly, feathers quivering with strain. And then her gaze locked on mine.

"Your mother," she said, the words cutting through the silence like steel. "She has the other half."

The hall seemed to still, as if even the air was holding its breath.

Trisha Otis is a writer, reader, and all-around creative spirit living in Missouri with her husband, son, two mischievous cats, and one very enthusiastic golden retriever. When she's not busy wrangling words, she's usually elbow-deep in the garden, upside down in a yoga pose, or chasing one of her many hobbies: think embroidery, watercolor painting, stained glass, bookbinding... and probably starting a new one soon.

She also spends her days as the Vice President of KC Book Beat, a buzzing non-profit that brings together local authors and creatives across Kansas City. Whether she's crafting a story or crafting with her hands, Trisha is always creating something!

Follow Trisha at:
@trishaotisauthor on Facebook and Instagram
@sunfoxbooks on TikTok
or at https://trishaotis.com/

9 781969 561016